DATE DUE

AUG 1 8 2004	
AUG 2 7 2004	
SEP 2 0 2004	
DEXT 9/17/04	
NOV 3 2004	
APR 1 9 2006	

DEMCO, INC. 38-2931

Desert Shadows

Also by the author

Desert Noir

Desert Wives

To receive a free catalog of Poisoned Pen Press titles, please contact us in one of the following ways:

Phone: 1-800-421-3976
Facsimile: 1-480-949-1707
Email: info@poisonedpenpress.com
Website: www.poisonedpenpress.com

Poisoned Pen Press
6962 E. First Ave. Ste. 103
Scottsdale, AZ 85251

Desert Shadows

Publishing Can Be Murder

Betty Webb

Poisoned Pen Press

First Edition 2004

10 9 8 7 6 5 4 3 2 1

Library of Congress Catalog Card Number: 2004106083

ISBN: 1-59058-113-X Hardcover

Poisoned Pen Press
6962 E. First Ave., Ste. 103
Scottsdale, AZ 85251
www.poisonedpenpress.com
info@poisonedpenpress.com

Printed in the United States of America

For Paul, as always

Acknowledgments

I am indebted to those who contributed in various ways to this novel. The usual suspects include the stalwart Sheridan Street Irregulars: Sharon Magee, Judy Starbuck, Eileen Brady, Dan Hagey, and Charles Pyeatte for his better-than-the-author's Spanish. Muchos gracias, mi compadres! More thanks to the ever-faithful Marge Purcell and Debra McCarthy for their tireless work. Kudos to the savvy librarians on DorothyL, whose comments on the First Amendment proved invaluable. Thanks to Dr. Deborah Mendelson for allowing me to use her name for a character, and especially for helping me describe the symptoms of water hemlock poisoning; any errors are my own. A heartfelt kiss to the rescue organization 4theLuvofDogz for Cody (who appears in these pages as Boz) and the unfailing joy my furry little friend has brought me.

But there would be no *Desert Shadows* without the incomparable Barbara Peters, Robert Rosenwald, Marilyn, Jen, Monty, Casey, and the rest of the gang down at Poisoned Pen Press who so kindly allowed me to watch a very busy publishing house in action.

Prologue

Gloriana Alden-Taylor wasn't exactly satisfied. The word rarely appeared in her personal lexicon, but with two new titles due out by Patriot's Blood Press by the end of the week, she felt, at a minimum, gratified. Both books had money written all over them, especially *A Man Stands Alone*, that odd little memoir penned by the Death Row inmate. She hoped the man wouldn't get the needle before she could coax a sequel from the recalcitrant creature. Say what you will about serial killers, some of them could really write.

Lips stretched into a rare smile, Gloriana let the waiter exchange her half-eaten Arizona agave salad for an even stranger chicken dish, then peered around the banquet hall. Was it her imagination, or had the number of publishers attending the Southwest Book Publishers Expo—SOBOP, to its friends—actually doubled since last year? Her smile faded. If the field became too crowded, her own market share might decline.

Gloriana was just wondering what strategy might work best if one of her competitors encroached upon her own hard-won territory when her heart began to race. The sensation wasn't unpleasant at first; it felt more like the bumpity-bump she'd experienced when she read the first-ever *New York Times* review of a Patriot's Blood title. Hardly a rave—*vilification* would be a more accurate term—but the national coverage put her little publishing house on the map. Almost immediately, orders from Idaho,

Utah, Montana, and even Vancouver flooded the sales department. Patriot's Blood had become international! Bad reviews be damned, sales was the name of the publishing game.

Someone laughed, high and screechy.

Frowning with disapproval, Gloriana looked for the laugher, only to find her table mates staring at her, mouths agog. When she shut her own mouth, the sound stopped.

"Oh, lord," she said, patting her lips with the overly starched napkin the waiter had foisted upon her. "I can't imagine what brought that on."

The brown man sitting next to her put his hand on her arm. What was his name? Something ridiculous, if she remembered correctly. Hernando O'Riley? Sean Gonzales? Just the thought of his name started another paroxysm.

"Mrs. Alden-Taylor, are you feeling all right?" The voice of the brown man with the ridiculous name sounded strange to her, thick and grumbly, like some fairytale ogre howling up from the bottom of a well. Surely she couldn't be losing her hearing. Then again, with her seventy-sixth birthday just around the corner....

Annoyed, she slapped his hand away. "Of course I'm feeling all right, you fool. Why wouldn't I?" Then, with a spasm-like motion, she stood up and stepped away from the table, all the while noticing her heart beating faster and faster, as if it were in a hurry to get someplace exciting. Perhaps the whole thing should have alarmed her, but it was fun, really, what the young people today called an adrenaline rush.

When she settled down, though, she'd have to talk to the resort manager about the banquet hall's lighting. What did he think he was doing, lighting a movie set? As she squinted her eyes against the glare, her hands and feet began to tingle. Maybe she should move around more, get her circulation going. Old age was such a bitch.

The people at the other tables gaped at her again. Not that she could blame them, because to her consternation she realized she was walking around in tiny circles, her legs lifting high in the air like a drum majorette's.

She wanted to ask the brown man if he knew why she was doing such a strange thing, but her throat, the same throat which had issued those bursts of laughter just moments before, had begun to narrow. Now she could only utter ungainly *uh-uh-uh* sounds.

How embarrassing! Almost as embarrassing as the nausea which threatened to make itself evident at any moment.

"Mrs. Alden-Taylor, I think we need to call...."

Before the brown man with the ridiculous name finished his sentence, Gloriana spewed her dinner. Then, horror upon horror, her knees buckled and she fell to the floor, landing face down in the middle of the puddle. But her legs continued to high-step, high-step, high-step on the way to some mysterious destination.

And what was this new mess?

If she hadn't known better, she'd swear that she, Gloriana Alden-Taylor, descendant of the Plymouth Brethren, kin to senators and presidents, was actually frothing at the mouth.

"I need to clear her airway!" A woman's voice. That dermatologist she'd been talking to earlier, the one who published the skin care books.

Skin care books in the desert, such a waste of time and money. Anyone with half a brain knew that no matter how much you pampered your skin in Arizona, by the time you were fifty you looked like a prune. Hadn't her husband constantly reminded her of that? "Old Prune Face," Michael had called her, pretending to joke. But she knew, oh, she knew. The slur was his way of excusing his behavior with all those sluts.

Yes, his words had hurt, but she had enjoyed her consolations. At least she was now a *rich* old prune, every sag, every crease bespeaking her Mayflower lineage. Why, she was American royalty!

Just before her throat closed for good, it relaxed long enough for her to rasp, *"Prune!"*

Then the pain began, Jesus, the pain. Had she broken her hip in the fall? No, everything hurt, quite possibly because her body was bending backward on itself, her head almost touching her heels. *Ahhhhh…*

A few minutes later, Gloriana Alden-Taylor's heart stopped. Despite the dermatologist's efforts, it never started again.

As he watched her die, the brown man with the ridiculous name murmured, *"Prune?"* Wonder what she meant by that?

Chapter 1

Indians never cry, so why were Jimmy's eyes red when he came through the door? He didn't have allergies and I knew he never drank.

Love trouble?

"Jimmy, what's wrong?" I didn't know whether to get up from my desk and throw my arms around him, or give him a chance to collect himself. Remembering that Pima Indians didn't approve of touchy-feely demonstrations, I chose the latter.

"Lena, I just need a minute here," he muttered, closing the door behind him.

My partner walked straight to his desk and fired up his computer. He even skipped his usual trip to the office refrigerator for his morning bottle of prickly pear cactus juice. Computers acted on Jimmy the same way booze acted upon others; they offered a soothing balm against life's ills. His addiction to cyberspace, coupled with his workaholism, kept Desert Investigations in the black no matter how many pro bono cases I accepted.

"Jimmy, please. Tell me."

Had something happened to his girlfriend? Or worse yet, to his girlfriend's thirteen-year-old daughter?

"Jimmy...."

"Lena, I said to wait." He stared at the computer monitor as the icons appeared, cocked his head as Bill Gates' cheesy chimes did their thing, and even managed a faint smile when his screen saver, a montage of ancient Pima pictographs, covered the generic blue. The chimes finally faded, replaced by a recording he had made of his cousin's Chicken Scratch band. As the raucous music rang out, he sighed in relief. "There."

Then he swiveled his chair around to face me. "Scottsdale PD arrested Owen last night."

Impossible. Jimmy's cousin Owen, a straight-up former Marine, had never received so much as a parking ticket. "Is this some kind of joke?"

Jimmy's red eyes gave me the answer.

"What did he do? Smart off to a traffic cop?" Owen would never do anything so stupid; he respected uniforms. But I wasn't yet ready to accept the evidence of Jimmy's ravaged face.

"The cops say he murdered Gloriana Alden-Taylor."

"What!?" The very idea that Owen Sisiwan, a Bronze Star-winning Afghan War hero, would murder an elderly woman was beyond ludicrous. Go gunsight-to-gunsight with a Taliban sniper, neutralize a land mine, enter a terrorist-filled cave, hey, no problem. But hurt an old woman? Not the Owen I knew.

"That's crazy, Jimmy. I'll straighten this out." I reached for the phone to call my old boss, Captain Kryzinski, head of the Violent Crimes Unit of the Scottsdale Police Department. Kryzinski admired Owen, too, and knew he'd never do anything violent. Outside of a war zone, anyway.

Jimmy leaned forward and placed his hand on mine, keeping me from picking up the receiver. "Listen to me before you make that call. The situation's worse than you think."

And it was.

His voice trembling, Jimmy told me that Gloriana Alden-Taylor, founder of Arizona's most controversial publishing house, had collapsed and died during a banquet the evening before at Desert Shadows, a Scottsdale resort.

"The medical examiner says she was poisoned by water hemlock, and the cops think Owen got the stuff when he took some people for a hike up near Oak Creek."

Oak Creek, about one hundred and twenty miles north of Scottsdale, was a popular recreation area thanks to its spectacular red cliffs and deep blue streams. "Some people, Jimmy? Who, exactly?"

He pushed a strand of long raven hair away from his dark face. "A bunch of publishers attending their yearly convention. Owen works...*worked* for Gloriana, and she wanted him to show them the sights. Supposedly, Owen brought the water hemlock back to the resort and sprinkled it on her salad. She died fast, I guess, but real ugly."

When is murder not ugly? "Where is Owen now?"

"He's already been transferred to the Fourth Avenue Jail."

I grunted. The Scottsdale City Jail serves mainly as a holding tank for drunks and batterers. Serious felons are ultimately moved to the new facility run by the Maricopa County Sheriff in downtown Phoenix.

I grabbed my carry-all and started toward the door.

"Lena! Where are you going?"

I stopped, hand on the doorknob. "To the cop shop to give Kryzinski a piece of my mind. Does Owen have an attorney yet?"

Jimmy shook his head. As usual, when upset, the curved tribal tattoo on his temple stood out in startling relief. "Janelle was talking to some lawyer on the phone when I got over to their house this morning. But the money situation, it's not real good, and it sounded to me like the guy wasn't eager to take the case."

The *money situation*, as Jimmy so delicately phrased it, was always the problem. Since the O.J. trial, it had passed no one's notice that money, not innocence, was the best defense. Owen's salary as Gloriana's chauffeur/bodyguard/handyman probably didn't amount to much, especially when you factored in a non-employed wife and three children, one of them barely a month old.

Jimmy stood, but I motioned him back down. "You stay here and take care of business, partner. I've got a feeling we're going to need the revenue."

He looked doubtful. "Owen's my cousin."

"Yeah, but now he's *my* client."

As I drove to the cop shop, I remembered my one run-in with Mrs. Alden-Taylor, or, as she preferred to be addressed, Gloriana. Jimmy and I had attended a Scottsdale Chamber of Commerce mixer to scout new clients when she walked up and introduced herself. She didn't bother to greet my partner. After all, he was just an Indian.

Gloriana was even taller than I, and her pale blue eyes had to look down to study the scar on my forehead. Unlike more polite people seeing the scar for the first time, she didn't disguise her interest.

"I've heard a lot about you, Ms. Jones," she said. "Judging from your stature and coloring, you have got good genes. Too bad about that scar."

From the articles I'd read about Gloriana in the *Scottsdale Journal,* I suspected why she approved of me. With my five-foot-nine-inch stature, natural blond hair and green eyes, I probably look like she thought an American was supposed to look. For a woman who claimed to trace her lineage all the way back to the Mayflower, she held oddly Germanic opinions about race.

"Oh, I don't know, Gloriana," I answered. "I think the scar gives me a certain panache."

I didn't bother responding to the remark about my genes. Anyone who followed my cases in the Arizona media knew I had no idea who my parents were, let alone the rest of my ancestral DNA donors. Raised in a series of foster homes, the name Lena Jones had been bestowed upon me by a particularly unimaginative social worker. For all I knew, I was descended from cannibals.

"The scar doesn't really matter, Ms. Jones. Your bone structure is quite marvelous."

As the old woman continued her head-to-toe inventory of my "bone structure," I wondered about her sexual preference.

Then I dismissed the thought. In my experience, lesbians tended to be more subtle.

Inventory finished, Gloriana said, "Good, very good. You can tell a lot about a person from the way they look."

Was she serious? "That's what the women who trusted Ted Bundy thought, too, Gloriana."

When she smiled, her desert-weathered skin creped around her thin mouth and eyes, making her look like an unwrapped mummy. "There might be an exception or two, but overall, breeding tells. That's why the Alden-Taylors have flourished. As you know, we are not only descended from the Plymouth Brethren, but we can count a president and several senators and generals among our number. The recent research I've commissioned even suggests a genetic connection to Thomas Jefferson himself."

"Through Sally Hemings?" I suspected the old bat might not be quite so thrilled if her genetic connection proved to be through Jefferson's reputed slave mistress.

A faint snicker at my side alerted me that Jimmy, at least, noticed the acid in my voice.

Gloriana missed the sarcasm. "Personally, Ms. Jones, I doubt the entire Hemings story. Jefferson was much too fastidious to get himself caught up in such a scandal."

For a moment, I considered another barb, but decided she wasn't worth the effort.

"Your, ah, genetic theories are certainly interesting." I turned to go.

She leaned forward and tapped my arm. "Oh, they're more than theories, Ms. Jones."

After I walked away, I brushed at my sleeve. It felt dirty.

The perfect March morning brought out the last of the snowbirds. Fat herds of Winnebagos, Airstreams, and Holiday Ramblers wallowed north up Hayden Road ten miles under the speed limit, tying up traffic and spewing diesel fumes into the crisp Arizona air. As much as Arizonans appreciate the money the snowbirds funnel into our economy, their turtle-paced driving makes commuters crazy. No wonder so many local vehicles sport bumper stickers that snarl, IF IT'S SNOWBIRD SEASON, WHY CAN'T WE SHOOT THEM?

I sounded the horn on my 1945 Jeep when a beige Wildwood with, ho ho, racing stripes, drifted toward my lane. At the very last second, its elderly driver remembered where he was (Driving. On a crowded city street. In a multi-ton vehicle.) and straightened his metal monster. Death once more averted, I unclenched my hands and continued north, Scottsdale's narrow green belt on my right, ass-to-ass condos on my left.

When Scottsdale North, the police department's main station, had been built a decade back, the city had pretty much ended at Bell Road. Now urban sprawl continued all the way to the foothills of the McDowell Mountains, more than twenty miles north of where the town first began. The pristine Sonoran Desert I loved was being replaced by tract homes and strip malls; the protests of various environmental groups had been unable to stop it. Not even the groups backed with Alden-Taylor money.

Gloriana had loved the desert, too, although this trait seldom endeared her to other environmentalists. She actually considered the wilderness her family's private legacy, not a resource to be enjoyed by everyone, rich or poor, Anglo or non. I suspected that if Gloriana had had her way, the entire Sonoran Desert would have been strung with barbed wire and patrolled by armed militia to keep out the riff raff.

Come to think of it, that kind of thing was already happening down by the Mexican border.

The more I reflected on Gloriana's self-involved life, the more I realized that her murder didn't surprise me. Given her ability to make enemies, it was odd that no one had killed her until now.

Chapter 2

The distressed look on my old boss' face resembled Jimmy's, so I didn't launch into the denunciations I had planned. Instead, I asked Captain Kryzinski why Owen Sisiwan had been the first person tagged for Gloriana's murder. As I listened to his reasons, I tried not to stare at his new gray suit. The current police chief, an Ivy League yuppy imported from the East Coast, had come down hard on Kryzinski, making him shed all his colorful Western wear. Now the captain looked just as dull as everyone else.

Maybe that had been the point.

"Let's see, why did we arrest Mr. Sisiwan? Well, kid, why do you think? Could it be because he had motive, means, and opportunity? Lena, our guys found water hemlock in his jacket pocket, more than enough to do the deed. You know what I think?" Kryzinski's tone softened and his face grew sorrowful. "I think the poor guy stayed in Afghanistan too long."

There it was, the standard excuse for any veteran's odd behavior, an excuse sometimes used to let a perpetrator off the legal hook, but more often to rachet up the charges. This time, our local hero was the vet du jour. Welcome back to the States, Corporal Sisiwan.

"Oh, please, Captain," I said, not bothering to hide my disgust. "Where's the murder book?"

Kryzinski tugged at his K-Mart tie until I thought he'd choke himself. "You know I can't let you see that, Lena. If the chief caught me, I'd get fired."

We'd danced this dance before. Kryzinski, still trying to lure me back into my old job at Scottsdale PD, had helped Desert Investigations *sub rosa* on various occasions. In return, Jimmy and I allowed his department to take credit for cracking cases that we had actually solved.

"You're not going to get fired and you know it," I said, confident that Kryzinski, a close friend of the mayor, knew too many secrets to be professionally vulnerable. His job was secure until the mayor, like so many other Arizona government officials, was indicted for corruption.

Kryzinski looked around and saw several other detectives watching us through his office's clear glass partition. When he scowled at them, they looked away. They probably knew why I was here, though, and wouldn't rat the captain out because they disliked the new police chief as much as I did. Besides, I knew most of them from the days I'd worked Scottsdale North, before a bullet acquired during a drug bust put an end to my police career.

With a theatrical sigh, Kryzinski slid a *Sports Illustrated* over his desk to me. "Check out the story on the Cardinals, page twenty-nine."

"Those losers." But I duly opened the magazine to the page, where, nestled next to the quarterback's mug shot (Drugs? Sexual assault? Insider trading?), Kryzinski had tucked some case notes and crime scene photos. There Gloriana Alden-Taylor lay, twisted like a pretzel on the carpeted floor of the Desert Shadows banquet hall, swollen tongue protruding from her mouth. A regurgitated leaf of something or other dangled from her ear.

I looked through the rest of the material while Kryzinski gave me a quick rundown. "The M.E. says that water hemlock, commonly known as cowbane, is some pretty serious shit. It used to be found only in elevations above six thousand feet, but lately has been popping up near San Antonio, San Diego, and now Oak Creek. Ain't we lucky? Apparently what we're getting is wicked potent, too. Affects the central nervous system, causes grand mal seizures, the mucous membranes swell, the throat constricts, then lights out, heart failure, el finito, sayonara. Toward the end there, the M.E. says that old Gloriana couldn't breathe at all. That's why the doc at her table was trying to give her CPR, not that it would have done the poor woman any good. In fact, it's damn lucky the doc didn't get any of that crap in her mouth or we'd be looking at more than one murder here."

I studied the close-ups of Gloriana's body a little longer, then moved to the photographs taken of her table. The centerpiece was some weird-looking purple vine twisted around an unidentifiable silvery object, the usual Southwest Modern decor nonsense. The place settings looked just as silly: white, gold-rimmed plates decorated with minuscule helpings of something that appeared to be a burnt chicken breast criss-crossed by strips of purple and green crepe paper. The whatever-it-was hadn't been touched.

"Raspberry Lemon Chicken à la Étienne," Kryzinski explained. "They got themselves a new chef up there, won all kinds of awards."

"Looks like the same old chicken shit to me," I muttered. "Give me a taco anytime." I continued to shuffle through the photos until I'd seen them all, then went through them again. "Let's see, Gloriana ate the salad, too bad for her, but didn't make it to the main course. How long after the waiter took her salad away did the chicken arrive?"

"The waiter took the salad away with one hand, served the chicken with the other. Here's the deal. People tell me that these big resorts try to hurry people through the meals so the staff can go do something else. By the time Gloriana exhibited symptoms, some folks had already started on the main course, the chicken shit, as you so delicately put it. All told, we're talking maybe ten, fifteen minutes. With water hemlock, ten minutes is apparently time enough to die."

I frowned. "Do you have any idea how Owen—if it was Owen, which I doubt—could have slipped the hemlock into the salad without being seen?"

"Easy as pie," Kryzinski assured me. "This was one of those damned big conventions, Lena. Bunch of publishers calling themselves SOBOP, short for Southwest Book Publishers Association. Most of the folks were in publishing seminars all afternoon. The last one, something about offshore printing, ran late and didn't end until about five minutes before the banquet was due to start. The salad plates were already on the table when everybody filed into the banquet hall."

"So how did the murderer know where Gloriana was going to sit?" Maybe it had been a random killing, some thrill-seeker playing a game of chance.

"Place cards," he answered. "Hand-inscribed by some fancy hired calligrapher. Apparently it was the same seating arrangement they'd had the evening before."

Not random, then. A thoroughly planned, cold-blooded killing. Owen was looking at a Murder One conviction, and in Arizona, we give the needle for that. I looked at the photograph of Gloriana's contorted body again, considered the anguish she must have felt.

Suddenly I couldn't look any more. A stab of pain crossed my eyes as I pushed away from Kryzinski's desk, stood up, and walked to the glass partition that separated his office from the rest of the Violent Crimes Unit. It was early in the day, so the detectives still hunted and pecked at their computers, typing up the previous days' notes. The giant mugs of strong coffee I remembered from my days on the force still covered their desks, but the overflowing ashtrays were gone. Times change, and even cops clean up their act. As I gazed at the too-clean room, I realized how much I missed the camaraderie, the jokes, even the spit balls. Back then, all the perps were strangers.

"Lena?" Kryzinski's voice.

"Yeah, yeah." I rubbed my forehead, hoping to make the pain go away. It didn't work. I returned to my chair and picked up Gloriana's death photo again.

"The M.E.'s sure it's water hemlock, then?"

"Oh, yeah. He's already writing a paper about it, gonna send it off to that dead people magazine he's always reading."

I put the photo back into the magazine and handed it back to Kryzinski. "*Coroner's Quarterly.*"

"Yeah, that one. He'll probably write a whole book on this case before he's finished. Says it's the first recorded water hemlock death in the state, give or take a few cows."

"How nice for him. Tell me, how did Gloriana's family take the news of her death?" Were Mayflower families like cops, did they stick together regardless of how offensive some blue-blooded cousin might be?

Kryzinski snorted. "Other than her grandson, who seems like a pretty decent guy, none of them batted an eye. But who knows? They say those old families believe in keeping a stiff upper lip."

Or maybe they just didn't care.

Thanks to the ongoing construction on the Pima Freeway, the trip from Scottsdale to the Fourth Avenue Jail in Phoenix took longer than it should have. The stop-and-go gave me more time than I needed to gaze out over the city's once-pristine flatlands and surrounding mountains. Dense smog already choked the azure sky, yet more cloverleafs were planned. How long before we turned into Los Angeles? How long before our ozone count rivaled that of Watts? How many cars could dance on the head of a pin?

By the time I maneuvered the Jeep into the crowded First Avenue garage, I felt more depressed than ever.

Oblivious to my mood, a whistling corrections officer led me back to the visitor's area, a long, fluorescent-lit rectangle with all the sickly charm of a morgue. Through the door's reinforced glass window I could see Owen waiting for me at a battered table, his back straight, eyes forward. Only a slight tic at the corner of his mouth betrayed his desperation. As the cheerful

C.O. opened the door and I entered the room, Owen stood up, manacles clanking. Ever the polite soldier.

"Ms. Jones, thank you for coming." His brown eyes looked slightly to the left of mine. Pimas believed it impolite to meet another's glance. This deference could have easily passed for a guilty conscience to someone unfamiliar with the tribe.

"Ms. Jones? C'mon, Owen. You've never called me anything but Lena before, and there's no point in changing that now, okay?"

"Yes, ma'am." Not much better, but at least he didn't snap his heels together and try to salute.

I sat down, hoping he'd do the same. He didn't. He just kept standing, feet slightly apart, manacled hands clasped in front of him. If he were a murderer, I'd eat my Jeep.

"Owen, I need you to tell me what happened. Don't leave anything out, no matter how inconsequential it seems. But, damn, guy, sit down first. It's lonely down here."

Back still straight, Owen lowered himself into his chair, but as he talked, he continued staring at the wall, not me. "There's not much to tell, nothing I haven't already told the detectives. The day before, just when I was getting ready to go home, Gloriana ordered me to take those people for a nature hike. I'd already put in sixty hours that week, the extra twenty without overtime pay, but she just said that if I wanted to keep my job I'd do as I was told."

For all the emotion Owen showed, he could have been reciting the alphabet. But the tic at his mouth had worsened.

Nothing about this sounded right. "You mean to tell me that Gloriana just up and volunteered your services for a nature hike to a bunch of strangers?"

He nodded.

I didn't buy it but decided to let it pass for now. "Had you two been on bad terms? Is that why she threatened to fire you?"

He turned his face even further away from me. So I couldn't see his mouth? "Gloriana liked people to do what she wanted, when she wanted. Anyway, you know I've got that new truck and

I'm still adding to my house on the Rez, so I needed the job. I called Janelle and told her I wouldn't be home that night."

I began to feel even more uneasy. "But Owen, that doesn't make sense. The Rez is, what, less than five miles from Gloriana's estate? Why couldn't you go home to your wife and then drive back in time to lead the hike the next day? Most people commute a lot farther than you do."

He finally looked me in the eye. The fluorescent light gleamed softly on his shoulder-length blue-black hair, and I noticed—not for the first time—what a handsome man he was. Had Gloriana thought so, too? I dismissed the thought as unworthy of everyone involved.

"Ms. Jo…Lena, You didn't know Gloriana. Once she got an idea in her head, it was the only thing that counted, not anybody else's plans. She said she wanted to fill me in on who was going on the hike, who was important and who wasn't. So I slept at her house that night. She calls…called it the Hacienda. There's a cot in the storage room. I've slept there before."

"Her house doesn't have servants' quarters?"

"Oh, sure. Over the garage. The thing is, her niece Sandra lives in it with her two kids. There's a small room at the back of the house, but that's Rosa's room. Rosa cleans and cooks, sometimes babysits for Sandra's kids, and I do everything else, which is a lot. The Hacienda is pretty old and something's always breaking down. When I complained about all the overtime, Gloriana always told me that work meant job security, and to just shut up."

I looked at him more carefully, noting his large, callused hands. They contrasted with his velvety skin and bulging biceps, the type that generally formed only after dedicated hours at the gym. Did he work out? And if so, where did he find the time? Nothing about his story rang true.

Ignorant of my growing suspicions, Owen continued. "Anyway, the next morning Gloriana sent me downtown to rent this big passenger van. Then I picked up the SOBOP folks, the publishers, at the resort at eight and drove them up to Oak

Creek Canyon. But we didn't hike in any of the usual places. I know of a tributary on state land, kind of hidden, where it's less crowded but just as pretty. So that's where I took them."

"How many of the SOBOP people went along?" I leaned over to take a pad and pencil out of my carry-all, ready to add the names to my suspect list. Then I remembered I'd left everything except my I.D. in the Jeep's bolted-down strongbox. No one, not even a licensed detective, can carry firearms into the jail. Purses were contraband, too, because purses—especially those as big as my carry-all—could contain large stashes of drugs. I'd have to work from memory.

"There were eight, plus me, on the hike," Owen said. "She knew most of them, I think. They'd all been talking at dinner the night before and somehow she came up with the idea that it would be nice for everyone to get away from the resort for a few hours. Take a break. So, yeah, she volunteered my services."

Without bothering to ask him first. "But she didn't go. Why not?"

"She was due to lead some morning seminar on niche publishing, whatever that is. I…I wish she'd come with us, then maybe…." His big hands clenched and unclenched. Then he forced them still. "The creek was running pretty heavy and flowers were blooming. We walked around for a couple of hours, and I gave everybody a rundown on desert wildlife, the bobcats, the javalina. You know, the usual. I identified the prickly pear blooms, Colorado four o'clock, blue eyes…."

Owen sounded like he was ready to reel off the entire Arizona botanical litany, so I hurried him along. "And the water hemlock, right?"

A pause. "Yeah. And the water hemlock." He looked down at the floor.

"Was the water hemlock blooming? Was that why you pointed it out?"

He looked back up at me through thick, dark lashes. I couldn't read his eyes. "No, Lena, hemlock doesn't bloom creekside until later in the season. The problem was, since all those books have come out on herbal medicines, everybody thinks they're experts. I caught a couple of people picking flowers, parsley, harmless stuff like that. The water hemlock looks an awful lot like the wild celery we've got around here, so I picked a handful of the hemlock and passed it around, pointing out the differences. I told them that just a few crushed leaves or root shavings could kill a thousand-pound horse in minutes, let alone a human being."

And by doing so, Owen had delivered a recipe for murder. "When everyone finished looking at the water hemlock, did they give it back to you?"

"Sure. I watched them every minute and I made sure none of them took any. I'm not dumb."

"I never said you were." I thought for a moment, then asked, "What did you do with the hemlock?"

"I put it in my jacket pocket." His brown eyes darkened to black, and his tic, back once more, jumped like a live thing. "I wanted to dispose of it where it wouldn't hurt any animals. Or people."

It all sounded strange to me, the impromptu hike, the flower-picking. But stranger things have happened here in the desert. "I have to ask you this. Other than your squabbles over working hours, how did you and Gloriana get along?"

He looked down at the floor, but not before I saw his tic increase big time. "She wasn't an easy woman, but I didn't get along with her worse than anyone else."

What a terrible liar. My excitement over the eight other suspects began to fade. "Had she threatened to fire you before?"

He gave me the first smile I'd seen since I entered the visitor's room. Damn, he was a good-looking man. "Only about once a week. Like I told you, Gloriana wasn't easy. But I needed that job. My house is running me double of what I thought it would. We've got the baby now...."

I still didn't understand why he hadn't left Gloriana long before. "Owen, with your background, you could have found another job."

"Gloriana told me that if I left her she'd give me a bad reference, say I stole from her."

I knew Owen well enough not to ask him if Gloriana's claim was true. At the same time, I could understand his concern. Not every prospective employer had my knowledge of his character. To most of them, he would be branded as just another thieving Indian.

I asked Owen a few questions about Gloriana and her relationships with her family, especially the niece who lived over the garage. He told me that Sandra worked for Gloriana's publishing company, as did Gloriana's grandson. Both sounded like they were pretty much under the old lady's thumb, but I guessed that wasn't unusual in those old families.

"Just a niece and grandson? No sons or daughters?"

"Her son was killed a while back in a car crash along with his wife. She has a daughter, but doesn't...didn't talk to her much. There's also a couple of older sisters over in the Arcadia District. Twins. When I took her over there just before the SOBOP thing started, she said she was calling her attorney, probably to sue them over something. I don't know what about because she always made me wait outside. Anyway, she was always talking about taking someone to court. Lawyers loved her."

So Gloriana was the litigious type. More fruitful territory for investigation. Perhaps an unknown party had decided to settle a lawsuit out of court via water hemlock.

But there was always the obvious motive: money. "Do you know who inherits Gloriana's estate?"

"Zach, probably. Her grandson. Once I heard her talking to him about, uh, what do you call it, primo genser? Primo...."

"Primogeniture?" Everything to the oldest male.

He nodded. "Gloriana was very old-fashioned, always going on about her ancestors, saying she was descended from that Mayflower gang. She said *primo* whatever kept estates intact."

I'd known Gloriana had money, but the way Owen told it, she sounded loaded. I said so.

He shrugged. "It's Scottsdale, and I've seen richer. But yeah, she sure had more money than I do. Almost everybody does." He managed another smile, and once more reminded me how handsome he was.

I was just beginning to muse about lonely old women and handsome young men when the corrections officer told me my time was up. Before I left, I had Owen give me the names of everyone who had accompanied Owen on the hike. I repeated them to myself twice, consigning them to memory.

Randall Ott, Emil Ramos, David Zhang, Zachary Alden-Taylor, Sandra Alden-Taylor, Myra Gordon, Arizona State Representative Lynn Tinsley, and…

The Reverend Melvin Giblin.

My foster father.

Chapter 3

When I was four years old, an undocumented Mexican national found me lying unconscious by the side of a Phoenix street, a bullet in my head. She carried me to the nearest emergency room, then dashed back out into the night.

I survived the coma, but the bullet left only an empty space where my childhood memories should have been. Mother, father—their names and my own—were as lost to me as the blood that had seeped into the Phoenix pavement. In dreams, sometimes, I could hear the singing of a dozen voices, understood that I was a passenger on a brightly lit bus hurtling through the night. The songs always ended in gunshots and pain.

Who am I? I don't know and possibly never will. My true name and the reason I was a passenger on that bus remain mysteries. But of the identity of the woman sitting next to me, the woman aiming the gun at me, there can be no mistake. She looked then as I do now.

My mother.

When I recovered from my coma, Child Protective Services sent me off to a series of foster homes that I endured until my eighteenth birthday and my entrance as a scholarship student into the criminal justice program at Arizona State University.

If you're a gambling person, you can lay odds that most foster homes are semi-adequate places to warehouse bereft children. Most of these people mean well, and they do everything possible to quell the fears of their tiny wards. Some, however, are lured into the program only to get the check that arrives every month. If their foster children are lucky, they are simply ignored. If they're not lucky....Well, things happen in foster care. Things that sometimes make the newspapers.

This much I can tell you about my own luck: I hadn't reached Reverend Melvin Giblin's foster home soon enough.

As soon as I exited the jail and climbed back into my Jeep, I fished a pad and pen out of my carry-all and jotted down the other names Owen had given me. That accomplished, I punched the Rev's number into my cell phone.

After three rings, the answering machine picked up and I heard the Rev's warm baritone. "Sorry you missed me, but I'm attending the Southwest Book Publishers Association Expo at Desert Shadows Resort. Starting Friday, I'll be manning SOBOP's sales booth at the Festival of the West, at WestWorld. If it's an emergency, you can call my cell phone at (602) 555-5550. And always remember, Jesus loves you."

After the beep, I didn't leave a message. I just started the Jeep and headed north.

WestWorld occupies what used to be empty desert and a few Arabian horse farms. Now the horse farms were gone, and so, almost, was the surrounding desert.

The massive equestrian complex hosted roping contests, rodeos, polo matches, Western trade shows, and once a year, the Festival of the West. The festival was attended by tens of thousands of folks, both locals and tourists, all eager to gawk at a few bored bison and perhaps even meet a real live tobacco-spitting cowboy or two. For added excitement, the Overland Stage, pulled by teams of wooly-footed Clydesdales, offered rides to the kiddies, and local actors reenacted the Gunfight at the OK Corral for the millionth time. Because of the money to be made with Western nostalgia, anyone who ran a remotely Western-themed business rented a booth at the festival, so it wasn't surprising that the Southwest Book Publishers Association had signed up, too.

Upon entering WestWorld's grounds, I aimed the Jeep toward an empty slot next to a similarly battered pickup truck, but I couldn't help noticing the rows and rows of yuppymobiles pretending to be work vehicles. As I rolled past a silver Hummer which had obviously never even seen a dirt road, much less a battlefield, I could almost feel the Jeep sneer.

Once parked, I followed a gaggle of tourists toward the festival entrance, situated midway between two large exhibit halls. A sign over the gate informed me that those who arrived in Western wear got in free, which explained the profusion of Yves St. Laurent cowboys surrounding me. I was clad in my usual black jeans and T-shirt, so the ticket-taker, an overly made-up woman dressed like a nineteenth-century hooker, made me fork over the entrance fee. After I'd given her five dollars, I asked for a receipt, at which point she whipped a Cross pen out of her SuperBra and scrawled one. She added a smiley face wearing a cowboy hat at the bottom.

"Have fun, cowgirl," she said.

I tipped an imaginary cowboy hat and entered the nearest hall. Facing me was a maze of stalls offering hand-tooled cowboy boots, Indian baskets, turquoise jewelry, and gaudy paintings of saguaro-sprinkled sunsets. I wandered among them until I found myself in front of a long, book-strewn table flanked by several tall bookcases. A banner draped over the booth declared, SOUTHWEST BOOK PUBLISHING ASSOCIATION—WE WRITE THE WEST.

"Lena!" Before I could step back, a big man detached himself from the other people manning the table and enveloped me in his arms. "What's it been, girl, three months, four?"

I tried not to pull back too quickly. It wasn't Reverend Giblin's fault that I hated to be touched. In my two years with him, he and his wife had been nothing but kind. But when Mrs. Giblin suffered a fatal stroke, Child Protective Services removed me and the other foster kids from his home. The next family CPS placed me with wasn't half as kind, although they took care never to let their "discipline" show on one of those rare occasions when a social worker dropped by. By the time CPS realized their mistake and moved me to the next home, I had developed malnutrition along with several hairline fractures.

Bearing up as well as I could at the unwelcome physical contact, I gave the Rev a quick peck on the cheek. "It's great to see you, too, but I need to warn you that I'm here on business."

The Rev let his arms fall and stepped back. Other than a few new wrinkles and a hardly perceptible softening of his jaw line, he looked pretty much like he had when I'd lived with him twenty-five years earlier. Silver now blended with the wild black hair he'd never been able to tame. The deep crow's feet framing his bright blue eyes merely added to their friendliness. His plaid polyester shirt and slacks looked like they'd been bought at a Salvation Army clearance sale—they probably had—and his rough-out cowboy boots could have used a good cleaning. He had packed on a few pounds, too. Judging from the big silver and turquoise belt buckle (a gift from me) which called attention to his newly plump belly, those pounds didn't embarrass him one bit. The Rev distrusted vanity, believing it to be one of Satan's many lures.

And yet he had always taken great care to compliment me on my own appearance, perhaps because as a child I'd been so self-conscious about my scar. My foster father may have held strong fundamentalist beliefs, but he never let them conflict with his fundamental kindness.

"Business, Lena? Don't tell me you're investigating Gloriana Alden-Taylor's death." His voice took on a note of caution.

"Owen's been arrested for her murder, Rev. That means I have to ask why you went along on that Oak Creek hike when I know you've been up there many times before. With me and your other foster kids, as a matter of fact."

He didn't answer right away, and during his silence, I became aware of the crowd surrounding us.

A woman with a well-bred Boston accent complained about the dearth of histories on women who'd helped settle the West. "Those miners and cowboys had to marry somebody, didn't they? Well, where are their wives? Where are *their* contributions? Why aren't women even *mentioned* in any of these books? Why is it always just men, men, men?"

Nearby, an elderly man grumped that he'd found eighteen typos in the first chapter of the book he'd bought from the SOBOP booth the day before. "Slipshod editing, young man. When I was your age, books came without mistakes like these."

But still the Rev said nothing, and his long silence began to worry me. After all, he had been on the hike and must have seen the water hemlock himself. Why was he so loathe to talk about it?

"Rev...."

"Yes, I remember taking you kids up to Oak Creek," he finally answered, his eyes no more eager to meet mine than Owen's had been. "It's beautiful up there, all that red rock. Even now, I grasp at any chance to go back again. And then there are the memories. You, Brian, Malik...."

Before he could finish recounting those few happy days of my childhood, an elderly woman wearing a purple Stetson and matching ostrich cowboy boots tapped him on the shoulder.

"I need God's magnificent love," she said.

So did I, but it wouldn't occur to me to go around asking for it.

The Rev merely smiled. "It's on special today for only $12.98." Then, when he saw my face, he began to laugh. *"God's Magnificent Love* was my first book and so far, it's been my best seller."

He dug into his pocket and made change for a twenty, then stepped back to the table and picked up a slim volume. "Want me to autograph it for you?" After the woman nodded, he scribbled something onto the title page, then handed it to her. "Enjoy. And remember, Jesus loves you," he said, as she trundled off, her feet obviously hurting.

The Rev motioned toward the bookshelves surrounding the table, and for the first time, I noticed his name on several books. *God's Magnificent Love. God's Magnificent Mercy. God's Magnificent Justice.*

"Why, Rev, you've been keeping secrets from me. You told me you'd gone into publishing, but I didn't know you were publishing your own books."

"Only a few of the books are mine at this point. That's the way a lot of small presses get started. You write a book but can't find a publisher, so you publish it yourself. Maybe it doesn't do very well, but that's neither here nor there because you've scratched an itch by only spending a couple of thousand dollars. Sometimes, though, you make a profit. Then a friend who's just finished his manuscript asks you to show him the publishing ropes, and you do. Then someone else asks. The next time it happens, you start thinking, 'Why don't I just publish these things myself?'

"There you are, the story of God's Love Press. We have twenty-four titles now, with three more due out next month. Most of the manuscripts come from other ministers around the country, but I'm still throwing a few of my own into the mix."

His smile dimmed for a moment. "Religious publishing houses are seeing a big increase in business these days. People need hope more now than ever before."

While I was no longer an atheist (a near-death experience in the desert had ended that)[1] the Rev's simple faith still made me uncomfortable. I hurried to change the subject. "Let's get back to Gloriana's murder, Rev. I need to interview everyone who sat near her at the banquet last night, and that includes you."

An unfathomable look. "I wasn't the only one there, you know." He glanced over at the SOBOP sales table. It was manned at one end by a yuppie-slick Asian, the counter card in front of him reading ARIZONA TRAILS PUBLISHING. In the middle of the table, behind a counter card that said VERDAD PRESS, sat a distinguished-looking Hispanic gentleman whose face seemed vaguely familiar.

---

[1] *Desert Noir*, Lena Jones' first recorded case.

Holding down the other end of the table, as far away from those two as was possible in the cramped area, sat another familiar face. A blond man in his forties, who—judging from his expression as he eyed his table mates—appeared unlikely to break out in a chorus of *Kumbayah.* The book displayed in front of him was titled *Losing America.*

The notorious Randall Ott.

With dismay, I saw the long line of people, all Anglos, waiting to have their books autographed by Ott. I also noted that his counter card proclaimed PATRIOT'S BLOOD PRESS. Considering everything I'd learned so far, I wasn't surprised to discover he was one of Gloriana's authors. His Whites-only views on immigration alone would have warmed her cold heart. He had gone on the fatal hike, too. Could he have been having—I hoped, I hoped—publisher troubles? I'd love to nail him for her murder.

The Rev ignored Ott's glower and waved. Ott didn't wave back. Was the Rev's hair too dark for Ott? Suspiciously curly? The Rev appeared not to notice the snub. "Tell you what, Lena. A few of us are breaking for lunch in a few minutes, so why don't you talk to us all at the same time?"

"Try to bring Ott along, too."

He lifted his eyebrows. "I'll try, but he's…well, let's just say he marches to his own drummer."

A big White drum with a military beat. Ott wouldn't be satisfied until Arizona and the rest of America were lily-white, and if it took a few armed encounters to bring that about, he proclaimed himself up for it. Word on the desert pipeline was that he had already begun amassing the arsenal.

While I much preferred talking to each of the SOBOP people separately, an immediate solo interview with each was not that critical. There was an up side to interviewing them together. Lulled by their associates' presence, they might be off guard, thus possibly more truthful. Satisfied, I arranged to meet the Rev and the others outside, at the picnic table closest to the Pima fry bread stand.

Before I left the exhibit hall, I browsed through some of SOBOP's books, finally choosing *Arizona Flora and Fauna* from Arizona Trails Publishing and *History of Arizona's Yaqui Indians* from Verdad Press. I purchased nothing from Patriot's Blood, but did take note of Gloriana's offerings. *Marriage or Miscegenation? Finding Your Patriot Ancestors through DNA Testing. Recreational Explosives and How to Build Them.*

Recreational explosives? God save our crazy state.

More curious than ever, I picked up a Patriot's Blood brochure, stepped to a less crowded area of the tent, and began reading.

> *Thank you for your interest in Patriot's Blood Press. We were founded as* Patriot's Blood Magazine *on the very day of America's Bicentennial—July 4, 1976—by Mayflower descendant Gloriana Alden-Taylor. At that time, we specialized in articles on the Revolutionary War. Eventually, our magazine branched out to include other conflicts: the War of 1812, the Mexican-American War, Panama, the World Wars, and of course, Viet Nam, Afghanistan, and Iraq. Anywhere a patriot's blood has been shed.*
>
> *Several years ago we expanded into book publishing. Our first title,* The American Triumph, *earned national attention when Strom Thurmond quoted its passages on the floor of the U.S. Senate. And now, yet another best-selling book adds to our ever-growing reputation.*
>
> Losing America, *by historian/journalist Randall Ott, rocketed to the number one spot on the* New York Times *best seller list and remained there for fifteen weeks straight. A full year since its printing, the book remains in the top ten.*
>
> *Ott's message is an important one. He believes that for America to regain its former stature in the world politic, we must stop all immigration into the U.S., especially that of Arabs, Africans, and Asians. Under certain strict guidelines, he recommends a program which will allow limited immigration of healthy, college-educated Northern Europeans.*

While Mr. Ott's views are not necessarily the views of the editors at Patriot's Blood, we do applaud his courage to speak out in a time when political correctness has all but silenced dissent.

Join us. Subscribe to Patriot's Blood Magazine *today, then begin building your own personal library of Patriot's Blood titles. By doing so, you will help restore America to her former glory.*

America needs her patriots now more than ever.

The signature below, in a spidery yet elegant script, was that of Gloriana Alden-Taylor.

I looked up from the brochure and stared across the exhibition hall at Ott, who was preening as a fan pointed excitedly to one of *Losing America*'s pages. An Anglo fan, of course; the book has always been less popular with readers of color. It was especially popular with the vigilante groups that had sprung up along the border Arizona shared with Mexico. An underlined copy had been found in the backpack of one "patriot" sharpshooter who had shot and killed a twelve-year-old Mexican girl trying to get into the U.S. with her mother.

Stuffing the brochure into my carry-all, I headed toward the exhibit hall's rear exit and soon found myself at the top of an artificial berm that sloped gently to the Old West Encampment.

Below me, in a manmade valley, sprawled a motley panorama of faux prairie schooners, faux tepees, faux wickiups, faux hogans, and faux log cabins. A few real Indians—mainly Pima, Navajo and Apache, wearing cynical smiles on their faces—strolled along in tribal dress. When I reached them, I saw they were handing out fliers inviting everyone to their next pow-wow. Cowboys, some of them actually real, did likewise. In the cowboys' case, however, the brochures hyped local dude ranches and city-slicker cattle drives. Near a deeply banked campfire stood a chaps-wearing cowboy poet I recognized as "Chaps" Peterson. His repertoire included poems about starlit nights, lonely trails, mean broncs, and unfaithful saloon gals. The freshening wind (rain tomorrow?) carried snatches of his current presentation.

Left my sweet lil' Sal back home,
Been ridin' the trail seven months and a day.
While I been gone, ol' Lonesome John
Done honeyed my Sal and took her away.

It was all phoney as hell, but who cared? The true West was no longer available except in old men's dreams, and the more the cities closed in, the more we needed the dream. While it might be pretty to imagine an Arizona unblemished by housing tracts and satellite dishes, that hope was no more realistic than imagining Manhattan without gridlock. Evolution happens, whether we like it or not.

An actor dressed like Wyatt Earp handed me a flier. "Shoot-out in fifteen minutes, be there or be square. We're gathering on the other side of the Pima fry bread stand."

"Where's that?" I asked Wyatt, remembering that the Rev planned to meet me there. I've always been a sucker for fry bread, especially the way the Pimas cook it: hot, puffy, and dripping with wild honey.

I followed Wyatt's directions to the stand, purchased a half-order, then found a seat at a vacant picnic table and began to eat. Pima honey was dripping down my chin when I heard a familiar voice behind me.

"Baby, I can explain everything."

Dusty.

Quickly assembling my thoughts, I turned to face a man I'd once thought I loved. "Well, well, look what the bobcat dragged in."

My insult was no exaggeration. Except for Dusty's always immaculate dude ranch attire, he did look like something coughed up by Arizona wildlife. His trail-weathered face had taken on a yellow tinge, and his lanky form seemed crumpled in on itself. Red veins streaked the whites around now-faded blue eyes, contrasting garishly with the purple circles beneath. His hands shook, and I suspected not from nerves.

"Lena, why won't you return my calls?" Even his voice sounded broken.

A few months earlier Dusty had discarded me for another woman, a tourist who'd made a successful play for him at the Happy Trails Dude Ranch where he worked. Still smarting from his betrayal, I wanted to hurt him as badly as he'd hurt me.

"You sure as hell didn't return my calls when you were off in Vegas with that…that…" I thought hard but couldn't come up with a better word, "…with that bitch."

Without invitation, he sat down on my right, his thigh pressed against mine. It was all I could do not to press back. Not that I still cared about him or anything.

"Baby, let me tell you what really happened. She and I…."

Thigh scalding, I shifted down the bench as far away from him as I could get. "As entertaining as your yarn might be, I'm not interested. Besides, I'm working."

He narrowed his bloodshot eyes at my fry bread. "It doesn't look like you're working."

I snorted. "There's a liar at this picnic table, and it sure isn't me."

"Please, Lena…."

To my great relief, I heard Reverend Giblin's baritone behind me. "Told you it wouldn't be long, didn't I, Lena? And great news. David and Emil here have agreed to tell you everything they know."

I looked past Dusty and saw the Rev flanked by two men I had seen earlier at the SOBOP booth. "That's wonderful. Let's get started."

The Rev, no dummy, raised his eyebrows. "Ah, will Dusty…?"

"The cowboy was just leaving."

Dusty clenched his jaw, and for a brief moment, I thought he might refuse. But then his dude ranch manners kicked in and he stood up. "I'll talk to you later, Lena."

"Not if I see you coming first," I muttered into the last piece of my fry bread. I wished my heart would quit hurting.

As Dusty stalked off, the Rev gave me a sad look. I knew what he was thinking, that I always managed to screw up my relationships. He was right, too. I didn't bother to tell him that this time, Dusty rejected me first.

After I was certain my voice wouldn't tremble, I patted the bench and said, "C'mon, Rev, take a load off."

Once the Rev introduced me to the Hispanic man, I realized where I'd seen him before. Emil Ramos, the owner of Verdad Press, made the local news broadcasts recently when he got into a spat at the Arizona Capitol with Representative Lynn Tinsley, the sponsor of the English-only bill. During the shouting match, Ramos screamed at Tinsley in five languages; besides the usual English and Spanish, Ramos was also fluent in German, Vietnamese, and Navajo. Responding in the fractured Spanglish she probably used with her maid, Tinsley called Ramos a "wetback." Ramos, whose family had lived in Arizona several generations longer than Tinsley's, reminded the congresswoman that if she wanted to return America to its native language, she'd have to learn approximately three hundred Native American dialects. Beside herself with rage, Tinsley then uttered the words that, although they were bleeped out on the local news, ran in their full glory on MTV. "Fuck you, beaner."

David Zhang, owner of Arizona Trails Publishing, kept a much lower profile. A fourth-generation Arizonan, he, like many other local Asians, descended from the Chinese laborers who built the railroad across the West in the nineteenth century. As Zhang proudly told me, he began his publishing house on the strength of one book, *The Iron Highway,* which contained selections from his track-laying ancestors' memoirs.

"My original publishing mission has expanded to include books on scenic areas all over the Southwest," Zhang finished. "Most of them are the big glossy, coffee-table extravaganzas you see in gift shops, but I also produce smaller, less expensive guides for campers and hikers."

I told Zhang that besides the book I'd bought a few minutes earlier, I also owned his beautifully photographed seasonal guide to the Grand Canyon. "My boyfriend bought it for me," I said. Then I remembered. "I mean my *ex*-boyfriend."

To forestall any questions, I quickly asked, "Randall Ott couldn't make it?"

Zhang grimaced. "Captain America's still signing books for his admirers. Besides, he only mixes with white people. But since you've got the prerequisite coloring, he might condescend to talk to you once we've left. Just don't be surprised if he forces you to buy that nasty screed of his in order to get an interview."

Losing America wasn't my kind of nightstand reading, but if that's what it took.... "As long as it's cheap."

"Doesn't get much cheaper," Zhang said. His tone made me suspect he didn't mean the book's price.

To my surprise, the stories the three told dovetailed with Owen Sisiwan's. The day before the murder, Gloriana had suddenly asked everyone at their dinner table if they'd like to go on a hike at Oak Creek, and—impressed by her good will—the group said yes. They had arrived at Oak Creek around ten in the morning and hiked for a couple of hours. At various points, several people had lagged behind to pick flowers and herbs, only to have Owen confiscate their haul.

"Owen had no patience with that kind of behavior," the Rev finished up. "He said that as long as they were on state land, they needed to keep their hands to themselves."

Ramos smiled. "As I remember, he told them if they wanted greenery, to buy it at the resort's flower shop."

"How well did you know the other people on the hike?"

He smoothed his silvered hair. "I know *of* Randall Ott, and his inamorata, Representative Lynn Tinsley. Perhaps the honorable Ms. Tinsley believed that the hemlock she picked would ward off those black helicopters she is so worried about."

I frowned, not certain that I'd heard right. "Black helicopters?"

Zhang winked at Ramos and grinned at me, flashing the kind of perfect orthodontia you only find in Scottsdale or Beverly Hills. That and his Armani sports coat hinted that Arizona Trails' books sold well. Or maybe he'd inherited money.

"You haven't heard about Tinsley's black helicopters?" Zhang asked. "The only things that worry her more than a child speaking Spanish are the black helicopters she believes are jamming the television signals at her house. Perhaps you haven't read her magnum opus, *The Area 51 Project the Government Doesn't Want You to Know About*. She had ten thousand copies published at her own expense and now she can't even give them away. So much for her dreams of matching her boyfriend's publishing success."

"Not enough hate in her book," Ramos murmured. "Just fear."

Frightened people frequently kill, though, so I filed the knowledge away for further consideration. "Who else spent their time picking plants?"

Ramos looked abashed. "I must admit that I was foolish enough to do so. My eye was captured by a purple aster, though, not hemlock. Owen made me give my treasure to him, which served me right for being so thoughtless. Another sinner was Gloriana's niece, Sandra Alden-Taylor. The woman is a lovely person, of that I am quite sure, but several times, Mr. Sisiwan had to caution her, also, to leave the plant life alone."

Zhang flashed his teeth again. "Yeah, Sandra seemed determined to shovel half the creek's flowers into her fanny pack."

That made several people who couldn't keep their hands off the plants, even those who should have known better. But I sympathized. The glories of Arizona's deserts, canyons, and forests could do strange things to people.

I noticed the Rev watching me closely, a worried expression on his face. Was it because of my questioning, or was it something else?

"What?"

"Lena, Owen made everyone hand over what they'd picked. Everyone. He did everything short of frisk us to make sure we didn't carry even a leaf away."

Going over everyone's stories, I began to run the numbers in my mind. "Ott, Tinsley, Gloriana's niece, you three...that's only six, plus Owen. Who have I missed?"

The Rev smiled. "Myra Gordon, an acquisitions librarian from Wyatt's Landing, down near Casa Grande. She was the only one on the hike who is actually staying at the resort. The rest of us here just drive up to the Expo every morning. Anyway, from what she told me, she's attending SOBOP to find locally published books for the Wyatt's Landing Public Library. And Zach, Gloriana's grandson, came along, too. But I can assure you that he didn't pick a thing. He was right in front of me, and I would have noticed."

I'd heard such assurances before. They seldom amounted to much. "Zach would have seen the water hemlock and heard Owen's warning, right?"

The Rev shrugged. "I guess. But he's a good man, Lena. One of the best."

Most of the men on Death Row had once been described by someone as "a good man." Especially by their mothers.

"One final question, Rev. Did any of you see exactly what Owen did after he confiscated the plants?"

"He replanted most of the herbs and flowers, and disposed of the too badly damaged plants in the brush. But he put the hemlock in his jacket pocket." The Rev's face looked glum.

Not good. Owen had probably collected enough lethal flora to wipe out the entire Arizona Diamondbacks team, and half the Cardinals to boot.

Then something else occurred to me, something that might help ease the pressure on Owen. "When you all got back to the resort, did you hear anyone talking about the water hemlock?"

Zhang nodded. "Yeah, Randall Ott was pretty ticked that some Indian had dared tell him what to do. I think most people ignored him, though."

Maybe, and maybe not. For the first time that day I began to feel optimistic about Owen's prospects. Not only did the hiking party know about the poisonous plant, but so did anyone else who had been on the receiving end of Ott's complaints. As for the others at SOBOP, I had already noticed that the book I bought from Zhang's display contained a full-color picture of the plant. The page even carried a bold type warning, in red, which detailed its poisonous parts: namely, all of them. I did a quick mental calculation. Anyone intent on killing Gloriana could drive back up to Oak Creek in under two hours, pick more hemlock, and return to the resort before the salad course was set out in the banquet hall. With the various seminars continuing throughout the day, one person's absence wouldn't be noticed. Unless....

"Did anyone not turn up where he was supposed to? Like on a panel?" I asked the Rev.

The Rev thought for a moment, then shook his head. "Not that I've heard."

Means and opportunity enough for everyone then, not just Owen. But what about motive? My early years with the police had taught me that barring the odd serial killer, gang banger action, or sloppier-than-usual robberies, the solution to a murder usually lay in the victim's own life. All I had to do was find out enough about Gloriana Alden-Taylor to determine who hated the woman enough to kill her.

"You gentlemen have been a great help," I told the three, reserving my warmest smile for the Rev. "One more question and then I'll let you get back to your display booth. I only met Gloriana once, so I don't know much about her. Tell me, what was she really like?"

From the frost that swept over the picnic table, you'd think a glacier had dropped from the skies. None of the men, including the Rev, seemed inclined to answer.

I waited until Emil Ramos, his eyes glittering with hatred, said, "Miss Jones, you want to know what she was like? Then I will tell you. Gloriana Alden-Taylor would disgust the Devil."

Chapter 4

Nearby, two "Indians" from indeterminate tribes told jokes in Brooklyn accents, while their three children, dressed as cowboys, play-shot each other with plastic guns. In front of the Old West Saloon, one stuntman punched another, who then rolled dramatically across the dirt, screaming old-time epithets while tourists' cameras snapped. Near the Overland Stage Stop, Wyatt Earp and his posse swaggered toward the Clantons, long-barreled firearms at the ready.

Glamorized killing, therefore not my problem. I specialized in the real deal.

As I looked into Zhang's and the Rev's eyes, I saw agreement with Ramos' shocking statement. Gloria Alden-Taylor had no admirers here.

"Perhaps you'd care to explain, Mr. Ramos."

"I would be happy to explain her evil if you have a free year or two in your schedule, Ms. Jones," Ramos answered, his words like razors. "But why do you not simply look at the Patriot's Blood catalog? The titles alone will tell you the kind of person Gloriana was." He closed his eyes and began to recite. "*Black and Brown: A History of the Degenerate Races.*" Or perhaps "*The Mexican Mud People.*" When he opened his eyes, the depths of hatred there frightened me.

The Rev cleared his throat. "I'm sure you realize by now that Gloriana's publishing house specializes in books that take an extreme political view. They are very, very troubling to large numbers of people, myself included."

Zhang's ire simmered only slightly less than Ramos'. "Randall Ott's book is disgusting, of course, but the idiot doesn't yet advocate killing immigrants at the border, or at least he didn't the last time I talked to him. Some of Gloriana's other authors actually do. As a publisher myself I have a strong commitment to the First Amendment, but as far as I'm concerned, in this political climate, Gloriana wasn't simply yelling 'Fire!' in a crowded theater. She was carrying gas cans toward the flames."

I agreed. In the light of recent events, what Gloriana had been doing was unconscionable. Two days after 9/11, a Scottsdale convenience store clerk had been shot dead by a gun-toting "patriot" too ignorant to know a Sikh from an Arab. Since then, many of the city's frightened Saudis, Pakistanis, and Egyptians had changed their phone numbers to unlisted ones and begun wearing Western dress to their mosques. Yet under the banner of patriotism, domestic terrorism continued to increase.

"Were Gloriana's books just money-makers, or did they reflect her personal beliefs?" I asked Zhang. Not that it made any difference. Gasoline is gasoline, whether you like the smell or not.

Zhang looked baffled. "I'm not certain. She didn't seem particularly bothered to be seated at our table. And don't forget, she arranged that hiking trip for us. Even after she'd seen the color of our skins."

"But she didn't go along."

"No, she didn't," he said. "Looking back on it, the whole thing was odd. But who's going to pass up a trip to Oak Creek, with somebody else paying for the gas? Certainly not me."

Something else seemed odd, too. "Who was in charge of the seating arrangements? Considering everything...." I didn't bother to state the obvious.

Ramos actually blushed. "I am sorry to tell you that my wife Beatrice was responsible for the seating. She knows few of the publishers personally, most are just names to her. After she sketched a preliminary seating chart, she did ask me to go over it, but I became so busy with other organizational details that I forgot. Later, when Beatrice realized what had happened, she blamed herself." He spread his hands in a gesture of helplessness, his thick gold wedding band glinting in the sun. "I am still trying to convince her that Gloriana's death was not her fault, that if it had not happened at SOBOP, it would probably have happened elsewhere."

Perhaps. But perhaps not. Someone with a grudge might simply have seized the day.

Ramos started to say something else, but just then a group of young men veered toward us. As they walked by, one of them—a buzz-cut bodybuilder—bumped him. Hard. Ramos, shock on his face, grabbed the edge of the picnic table to keep from being knocked to the ground. When he recovered his balance, he looked toward the young man, obviously expecting an apology.

Instead, Buzz Cut spit on the ground, too close to Ramos' feet for comfort, and sauntered back to his friends. He said loudly, "Too much mud around here."

With a laugh, the group turned on their heels and headed for the Wild West Saloon. As they walked away, I could see that the nape of each man's neck bore a double lighting bolt tattoo. National Alliance thugs. Just one of the many hate groups that had slithered out of Arizona's closet since the 9/11 attacks, soul brothers of the terrorists they claimed to despise.

For a moment I feared Ramos would charge after his assailant, but the Rev placed a warning hand on his arm. "Turn the other cheek," he said quietly.

"For the millionth time?" But Ramos' fists unclenched as his common sense overrode his Aztec warrior genes. He stared at the men's retreating backs. "Rats always travel in packs, don't they?"

Zhang's answer was less zoological, even less restrained. His own fists remained clenched.

This was no time to indulge the National Alliance's obvious desire for a dust-up, so I ripped a sheet of paper from my notebook and thrust it toward Ramos. "Do me a favor and show me where everyone was seated during the meal, plus all the entry and exit doors to the banquet hall. Write down the names of everyone at your table and the tables next to yours, anyone who had easy access to Gloriana's place setting." Although the salads had been waiting for the SOBOP people when they entered the banquet hall, there was a chance that the water hemlock had been added later.

Hands still shaking from suppressed rage, Ramos sketched a rough seating chart. Gloriana sat with her niece, Sandra, to her right. Next came Myra Gordon; Zhang; the Rev; Dr. Deborah Messinger, who had administered CPR; Randall Ott; and then, finishing up the table, Emil Ramos on Gloriana's left. At the next table sat Representative Tinsley; Zachary and Megan Alden-Taylor; John Alden Brookings, a free-lance writer whose byline I'd sometimes seen in the *Scottsdale Journal* (a relative of Gloriana's?); "Chaps" Peterson, the cowboy poet I'd heard earlier; and three men whose names I didn't recognize.

"Publishers from California," Ramos explained when I asked, his voice still tight. At least his hands had steadied. "They were attending the SOBOP Expo for the first time. I do not believe they knew Gloriana at all."

I looked at the seating chart again, still not finding the name I expected to see. "Where did Owen sit?"

The Rev's voice was almost as tight as Ramos' when he answered. I guessed that the confrontation with the neo-Nazis bothered him more than he cared to admit. "That evening, as with the evening before, Gloriana made Owen sit outside in the corridor on one of those fold-up chairs."

I took a moment to digest this information. "You mean he wasn't even in the room?"

The Rev shook his head.

No dinner for Owen, then, other than a heaping portion of humiliation. And Owen was a proud man. The more I studied the diagram, the more worried I became. Gloriana's table was located right next to the banquet hall's exit, with a probably furious Owen seated within poisoning distance. Even a Marine can only take so much. How easy it would have been to take the water hemlock he already had in his pocket and....

When I asked about the table's peculiar placement, Zhang gave me a sour smile. "You should have heard Gloriana carry on. Heck, I wasn't that crazy about sitting near the exit, myself. Half the people in the room strolled past us at one time or another, going in and out. Grand Central station, Arizona style." Then he flushed, probably remembering too late that Ramos' wife had drawn up the chart. "Oh, Emil, I'm sorry. I didn't...."

Ramos, after giving one last look toward the neo-Nazis, interrupted him. "The table placement was my fault, not Beatrice's. You see, I suffer from diabetes, and I have to get up and down a lot, so to make it easier for me, Beatrice sat me close to the corridor that led to the men's room."

A whole banquet hall full of suspects, then, walking to and fro past the victim's table on the way to the john. Getting the hemlock onto Gloriana's plate without being seen would have been relatively easy under any circumstances, whether before dinner or during. "Mr. Ramos, how many people attended the banquet?"

When he rubbed his forehead I noticed his hand was still shaking. "There were eight people at each table and there were fifteen tables. A few convention attendees may have missed the banquet, but I do not believe so. We publishers only meet once a year, and the time we spend together is quite valuable."

One hundred and twenty suspects, then. In actuality, though, the situation wasn't that bad. Merely a handful had opted for the hike and heard Owen's description of the fatal properties of water hemlock. Then I recalled Randall Ott's tirade upon his return to the resort. How many people who hated Gloriana or her publications heard him? I also remembered Zhang's guidebook on Arizona flora and fauna, with its big color illustration of the plant. The caption had read:

> *Once limited to high mountain wetlands, water hemlock can now be found along the banks of streams lower than*

3,000 feet in altitude. For the past few years, it has become profuse near Oak Creek Canyon. Its roots, stems, leaves and blossoms are extremely poisonous. Hikers beware.

"Mr. Zhang, that book of yours on Arizona plants. When was it published?"

In a tired voice, he answered, "Ah, yes, that damned book. It came out six months ago. What you're after, I guess, is how many people at SOBOP could have seen it, and the answer is—just about everyone. It's been on the SOBOP display table at the resort ever since the convention started." He heaved a sigh. "I have it sitting on a little stand, much as I do here, open to the page on water hemlock. I thought the artist did a great job on the illustration, and I wanted to show it off."

Even without Owen's creekside lecture, anyone with murder on his mind could probably have identified the plant from the book alone.

Then Zhang's face froze and I turned around, half-expecting to see the National Alliance thugs returning. But no, the man approaching us was merely Randall Ott, his nose raised so high in distaste at the brown skins around him that it was a wonder he didn't trip over Clydesdale crap.

Following closely was Lynn Tinsley, also looking up at the sky. I figured she was on the lookout for black helicopters. Tinsley's hairstyle echoed the Sixties, a blond bubble-do teased within an inch of its life, which made her tower over the minuscule Ott. Her pink shirtwaist dress sported enough ruffles to supply a Barbie Doll warehouse, while her dyed-to-match spike heels hinted at a bit of slut beneath the politico's cotton candy exterior.

"I think it's time for some lunch," the Rev said to Ramos and Zhang. "You two up for some Navajo tacos?"

They nodded, eager to get away from Ott and Tinsley. As a further inducement—one which I am certain the Rev had planned —the Navajo taco stand was in the opposite direction the neo-Nazis had taken.

I forced a smile as Tinsley and Ott neared the picnic table. Just for Owen, I'd attempt to get on their good side. "Representative Tinsley, Mr. Ott. Would you like some fry bread? I'd be happy to run over to the stand and bring some back." Truth be told, I was still hungry.

"I'm a vegetarian," Ott said, settling himself across from me, Tinsley by his side. "Those damned Indians use animal fat in everything. From uninspected pigs, too, probably." His voice was as thin as his hair.

Tinsley's heavily made-up face maintained that odd rigidity peculiar to Botox users. "Maybe I should look into that." Her gravelly voice hinted at decades of cigarettes and bourbon.

Ott shook his head. "No point. Their reservation, their rules. You can't change savages, anyway."

The corners of my mouth began to hurt, so I dropped the forced smile. "Representative Tinsley, I know you're a busy woman, so I'll come straight to the point. I'd like to know what, if anything, you observed on the day Gloriana Alden-Taylor died."

Ott cleared his throat. "Evening."

Tinsley rolled her eyes, but her eyebrows remained stationary. "Oh, please."

Ott's nose actually twitched. "You know I believe in being precise, Lynn. Gloriana died around 7:15 p.m., which makes it *evening.*"

Why did so many anal retentives turn out to be racists? But love is blind, and I caught a hint of affection in Tinsley's eyes as she gazed at him.

"Can we just go on and get this over with, Randall? Ms. Jones is right. I'm a busy woman and I don't have time to sit around here splitting hairs with you." Turning her attention to me, she said, "I didn't see anything until poor Gloriana started making those terrible noises. I'd been busy talking to Chaps Peterson." She motioned down the hill where the poet was still spinning his Wild West yarns. "Chaps shares many of my concerns about the federal government's secret projects."

I braced myself, expecting a harangue on black helicopters.

Fortunately, it didn't happen. Tinsley raised her nose again, as if smelling something unpleasant. "But Chaps said he didn't care about…to quote him exactly, 'that kind of bullshit.' He said he was attending SOBOP merely to find a publisher for his poetry, and he even had the gall to ask me if I'd introduce him to a few."

"Did you?"

"Chaps being a member of my constituency, yes, I did."

"And?"

Tinsley's mouth stretched as far as the Botox would allow. I think it was supposed to be a smile. "I talked to Gloriana first, but she just laughed at me. Called his work 'third-rate doggerel,' even worse than the poetry of Robert Service, who—before she heard Chaps—she'd believed was the worst poet in American history."

I wondered if Tinsley had conveyed Gloriana's literary criticism to Chaps. Given the politico's evident malice, the odds were that she had. "Was Gloriana the only publisher you approached for him?"

"Oh, I talked to David Zhang, what little good that did."

Somehow I couldn't see Arizona Trails printing odes to steers, but that was neither here nor there. "Ms. Tinsley, as a state lawmaker, surely you're familiar with the laws that protect plants on government lands. Why did you disobey Owen's orders on that hike? He told me you picked several plants."

Her shrug made the pink ruffles flutter up and down her suspiciously prominent bosom. "I'm not a botanist. I thought I was simply picking flowers, certainly nothing protected."

"Hell, as far as that goes, I picked a bunch of stuff, too," Ott piped up. "Not that I was allowed to keep it. That bossy Indian made me hand everything over. So if you're thinking that either Lynn or I sprinkled a little hemlock on Gloriana's salad, you can think again. Neither of us had any problems with the woman. She was my publisher, and I owe my considerable success to her.

Now, if you'll excuse us, we're going over to the kettle corn booth to get a decent lunch cooked by decent White people."

Judging from the look on Tinsley's face, I thought she might be more interested in the nearby Bar-B-Que Bison booth run by a couple of Sioux. Still, she followed Ott closely enough, her spike heels sinking deeper and deeper into the grass with each step. By the time they reached the kettle corn, she'd sunk almost to his level.

Ain't love grand?

Chapter 5

Even though Captain Kryzinski had asked the SOBOP attendees to remain in town for the next few days, I worried that some of them might defy his request and return home. I decided to drive up to Desert Shadows Resort and interview whomever I could find, starting with Myra Gordon, the librarian from Wyatt's Landing. Besides, after the confrontation with the National Alliance and my interview with Tinsley and Ott, the drive would calm my nerves.

But first things first. I pulled my cell phone out of my carry-all and called the office. Jimmy picked up immediately.

"I've got some names for you, all people who were on the hike with Owen," I told him. "Check them out."

I could hear his keyboard click as he copied them down. "Lena, do you think any of these guys might have done it?"

"Hard to say," I told him. "I've only interviewed a few people yet, but I'm on my way up to the resort now. I can tell you this, though. Zhang and Ramos both despised Gloriana. Tinsley and Ott are creepy enough to do just about anything."

"That's *Representative* Tinsley you're talking about?" His voice sounded doubtful, as if he had trouble believing a politician would do anything naughty.

I made a mental memo to urge him to get his nose out of those Internet magazines of his and start reading the newspaper. Especially the political section. "Yeah, that Tinsley. There's something about her that seems off, so I'd like you to dig around in her past, see if there are any gaps in her resumé." Whatever was going on with Tinsley, Jimmy would uncover it. No one could hack into sealed records and forbidden databases like my partner.

I'd just hung up and was heading toward the exit, when yet another despicable person crossed my path.

"Look, Lena, you can't ignore me." Was it my imagination, or were Dusty's eyes redder than earlier?

"Sorry, cowboy. I've got places to go, people to see."

He planted himself in front of me, digging the heels of his roping boots deep into the soil. The immovable object. I tried to go around him, but the crowd was so thick that I, the irresistible force, felt effectively cornered.

"You might as well talk to me. I won't leave you alone until you do."

I thought for a tantalizing moment of the .38 nestled snugly in my carry-all. If I popped him one, surely any reasonable judge would consider the deed justifiable homicide. Any reasonable female judge, that is. With my luck, the case would probably draw some crusty old buzzard who believed in equal killin' rights for everyone but females.

"Okay, Dusty. We'll talk. There's no point to it, though. You not only screwed around on me, but if my information is correct, you actually married the woman! You know me well enough to know that I don't fool around with married men, so it's over. I need someone with a little less baggage. If you think I'm carrying a torch for you, you are sadly mistaken."

I am so full of crap.

My eyes must have given me away, because he reached out and grasped my hand gently. "Honey, I'm sorry."

"You are one sorry son of a bitch, that's for sure," I muttered, as he led me into the shade of an acacia tree. It was all I could do to keep from bawling.

Dusty hadn't been my only man—I went through a brief period of promiscuity during my teens—but he'd been the only one I ever loved. But so what? If you can fall into love, surely you can fall out of it. And then maybe, if the gods are with you, fall into it again with someone more appropriate.

"She meant nothing to me, Lena."

It hurt too much to laugh. "Right. That's why you married her."

"The marriage wasn't legal." He rubbed his eyes as if they hurt. "It was just one of those Vegas things. Like Britney Spears and what's-his-name."

"With Elvis administering the vows? Last time I checked, cowboy, even Vegas marriages were legal."

"We didn't apply for a marriage license. And the guy wasn't really a minister, just an Elvis impersonator we met at one of the casinos."

"So why bother with Elvis? Why not just have your dirty little weekend, or whatever it was, and leave it at that?"

"Aw, Lena. I was drunk, that's why. I'd been drunk for a week, and you know what that can do to a person."

As a matter of fact, I didn't know. I don't drink. Never did. Not knowing my parentage, I feared my DNA might be loaded with any number of addictive genes, so I had long ago bypassed possible problems by drinking nothing stronger than Tab. In my personal habits, at least, I was as squeaky clean as a Temple-qualified Mormon.

"Dusty, what the hell were you doing drinking for an entire week?"

His bloodshot eyes met mine. "Lena, in some ways you are so naive. Haven't you figured out yet that I'm a recovering alcoholic?"

The Overland Stage came rumbling by again, making enough noise to render further speech pointless, but it gave me time to think. I cast my memory back over the four years I'd known Dusty. Since we lived at opposite ends of the county and had wildly conflicting schedules, we seldom got together as often as we would have liked. When we did, our dates usually consisted of Mexican dinners and action movies at the local cineplex. Then we would return to my apartment upstairs from Desert

Investigations for a little love-making, and in between bouts, sip on Tabs. I had never seen Dusty drunk.

I did remember one particularly stressful night when he showed up at my place with a shopping bag full of Pete's Wicked Ale. I hadn't thought too much of it at the time, not even when—after the night was over—he took the remainders back to the ranch with him.

In light of his confession, everything came together. Our off-again, on-again relationship. His frequent disappearances, his mysterious returns. Maybe the average woman would have challenged this behavior, but I'm not the average woman. I was used to strange behavior from men, and so I had accepted our oddly distant, if passionate, relationship. Oh, well, live and learn.

Once the Overland Stage rumbled away, I snapped, "You sure as hell don't look all that recovering to me, cowboy. Or did you pick up those red eyes on a trail ride? Surely you don't believe I'm stupid enough to excuse your behavior with that redhead just because you were drunk!"

"It's not about excusing, honey. It's about understanding."

"I'm not in the mood for understanding." With that, I pushed him aside and stalked up the hill, hoping I'd run into the National Alliance goons. I was spoiling for a fight.

The drive from WestWorld to Desert Shadows passed quickly, but not before I had time to lament the ruin of Scottsdale Road. Only a few years earlier, this had been one of the prettiest drives in Scottsdale, with unmarred desert reaching all the way to the McDowell Mountains. The Rev used to bring us kids here almost every weekend, pointing out bright clumps of Mexican gold poppy, upthrust stalks of burgundy lupine, the towering saguaro and ocotillo. At one point, a nature club had installed discreet signage along the road, giving each plant's Latin and common names, but those friendly little nature lessons were gone now. Everything disappeared when the developers moved in, dragging tract homes and shopping centers in their wake.

Like Joni Mitchell once complained, they paved paradise and put up a parking lot.

Desert Shadows Resort, however, had seen the bulldozers of progress headed their way, so the Japanese consortium which owned the place hurriedly bought up the surrounding acreage. Located several hundred yards from the highway, secluded in a shallow valley ringed with massive boulders, it could still project the illusion that it was miles from civilization.

The resort was internationally famous for its breathtaking golf course and rock-rimmed swimming pool complete with waterfall, as well as its luxurious suites and spas. Most of SOBOP's publishers must be doing well, I figured, to afford to stay here. Or maybe they'd wrangled one hell of a group discount.

After parking the Jeep next to a fleet of Mercedes and Beemers, I headed toward the lobby and its acres of glass, marble and palm fronds, where the concierge informed me that Mrs. Myra Gordon was not in her room. No problem, though, he said. Since she was one of the SOBOP people, she was probably attending some seminar or other. Would I like him to send a bellhop in search of her?

I declined the offer and, taking a map of the resort's various meeting rooms, set off to find her myself. After a brief stop at SOBOP's seminar sign-in table, I learned she was in Meeting Room 307, attending "The Bright Future of Minority Publishing." The seminar was due to finish any minute.

"She's wearing an emerald green silk shantung dress and carrying one of those cute little lunchbox handbags," said the blond woman at the table. Her own handbag resembled a mid-sized suitcase.

As I started toward the hallway that led to the meeting rooms, the blonde called after me, "Oh, and she's African-American. Gray hair."

I positioned myself outside Room 307 and waited until the double doors opened. Sure enough, here came Myra Gordon in an emerald dress and handbag emblazoned with a cartoon of a sly-looking poodle dressed in a pink poodle skirt. She started to walk by me.

"Mrs. Gordon?"

"Why, yes?" She stopped and offered me a smile. Approximately fifty, her skin, the color of gently creamed coffee, was sprinkled with freckles. Her eyes were a startling topaz. "What can I do for you?"

I showed her my I.D. and asked if we could go someplace quiet.

Her face closed down. "I've already talked to the police. And unless I am incorrect in my interpretation of Arizona law, Miss Jones, private detectives have no legal standing in murder cases."

Librarians. They know everything.

"I'm just trying to keep an innocent man out of prison," I said. "The accused is a friend of mine."

"Then I am very sorry for you and your friend." With that, she opened her poodle-purse and pulled out a lace-trimmed handkerchief. Dabbing her forehead, she added, "I've been so busy that I must admit I haven't kept track of things. I'd heard that someone was arrested last night, but...." She shrugged. "I didn't pay much attention."

"His name is Owen Sisiwan."

Her hand froze. "That sweet man who took us to Oak Creek Canyon?"

I know when to keep my mouth shut, to let someone's conscience do the work, so I just nodded.

She stood there for a moment, letting the stream of SOBOP folks pass us by. Then, tucking the handkerchief back into her handbag, she said, "Let's go to my room."

I followed her down the corridor, across the marble lobby, and into the residential wing of the resort, where we passed enough paintings and sculpture to furnish a small museum.

"Nice," I commented, as we walked along.

"A little pretentious, if you ask me," she said over her shoulder. "But who am I to criticize anyone's taste, me with my poodle-purse?"

"I like poodles in skirts."

She stopped in front of a door and inserted a card key into the lock. As the door opened, she said, "So do I."

The large room, which overlooked the resort's swimming pool, was furnished in Pima Modern, an ironic theme since the resort was built on land snatched from the tribe during the late 1800s. The sandstone-colored duvet on the king-size bed was decorated with replications of Pima pictographs, and the creamy, textured walls were covered with several signed lithographs of Kokopelli, the mythic Native American flute-player. The room must be costing Gordon a small fortune.

Seeing me check it out, she volunteered, "The SOBOP discount is the only way I can afford to stay here on my librarian's salary. Still, I'll probably be eating beans for a month when I get back to Wyatt's Landing."

"The library isn't picking up the cost?"

"No, I'm doing this on my own. Seeing a book described in a catalog isn't the same as leafing through its pages. And I do want to make certain our library carries a full selection of Southwestern books." She threw her handbag on the bed, so I followed suit with my carry-all. But I placed it carefully, so my .38 wouldn't clunk.

"Let's sit over here," she said, gesturing to a book-covered oak table surrounded by plush chairs. "Would you like a drink? The mini-bar's stocked with liquor, juice, and Evian."

Mini-bar water could cost up to eight dollars a bottle in Scottsdale, so I ignored my thirst and declined. I hoped she didn't hear my stomach rumble, because I doubted I'd be able to turn down twenty-dollar pretzels. That half-order of fry bread I'd eaten at WestWorld had only tweaked my appetite.

"Mrs. Gordon, I don't want to interfere with your schedule any more than necessary, so I'll be quick." I settled into the chair nearest the big picture window. "Did you see Owen pocket the water hemlock?"

She sat across from me and looked out toward the pool, where pale-skinned tourists splashed happily. Then she nodded, not taking their eyes off them. "Yes, I'm afraid I did. Some of the others on the hike were behaving foolishly, and Mr. Sisiwan did what he had to do. But I don't believe for a moment that he is responsible for Gloriana Alden-Taylor's death. He impressed me as a gentle man."

She knew nothing about the Taliban Owen had killed in Afghanistan, and there was no point in disillusioning her. "I had a look at the banquet seating chart. You sat right next to Gloriana, didn't you?"

"I wonder if they're wearing sun block," she said, still watching the pool action. "Those UV rays are dangerous. Are you aware of the number of melanoma cases in Arizona every year?"

I ask about banquet seating, I get a lecture on UV rays. Interesting. "Mrs. Gordon, could you answer my question?"

She finally looked at me. "Sorry, I wasn't paying attention. What was it you asked?"

"Weren't you sitting next to Gloriana at the banquet?"

She inclined her head. "Of course. Considering the types of books Patriot's Blood publishes, I thought the seating rather amusing. Or at least I did until the poor woman became ill."

"Before that, did she say anything that made you believe she might be afraid of someone?"

"Certainly not. We just chatted about the publishing business. At one point, she expressed a desire for me to look at some of her publications, saying that they would make a nice addition to Wyatt's Landing's collection."

I almost laughed. "Fat chance of that, right?"

"Ah, you are quite wrong," she said, patting one of the books on the table.

For the first time I noticed the title: *The South Was Right.* Patriot's Blood Press.

"A librarian is not a censor, Ms. Jones. We are enjoined to serve the public, and if the public wishes to read certain materials, materials that we ourselves may not care for nor even agree with, we still must make them available. Last year, for instance, I ordered several copies of *Losing America* because the demand was so great. Now it appears that I may order this, ah, historical work."

"Wyatt's Landing must be an interesting town," I said.

Another smile. "No more interesting than Scottsdale."

In other circumstances, I would have followed up this intriguing comparison, but this was not the time. "During the banquet, did you see anyone touch Gloriana's salad?"

Her initial hesitation to talk vanished, she cut to the chase. "No, I did not. And I did not touch it myself, either."

"Did you find her behavior offensive in any way?"

"If you're asking what I think you're asking, no. Gloriana made no racial remarks to me nor to any other person of color at our table. If anything, she was quite courteous. Generous, too. That trip to Oak Creek was her idea, taken at her expense."

But I thought Gloriana's generosity seemed unusual for such a self-involved old harridan, and I said so.

"In my case, perhaps she looked upon me and the library as customers, and was eager to curry favor. But I doubt it. She was no more polite to me than to Mr. Zhang and Mr. Ramos, although she did remark at one point upon Mr. Ramos' German first name. She said it didn't match his last. He didn't take offense. Remember, we were all invited on the Oak Creek trip."

It seemed important to Gordon for me to believe she had no motive for Gloriana's death. For now, I'd play along. "How about Owen? Did you hear any exchanges between him and Gloriana? Anything that sounded a bit heated?"

She didn't answer right away, just stretched her hands out on the table and pumped them, as if to exercise her fingers. I noticed a plain gold wedding ring, but saw only one suitcase sitting on the stand by the door. Hubby stayed home?

"The banquet hall was noisy," she finally answered. "I'm afraid any conversation that Gloriana and Owen might have had while she was in the hallway was lost to me."

"Gloriana went into the hall?"

"Several times. I took it for granted that she was visiting the ladies' room. Elderly bladders can be quite sensitive, I understand. And she was drinking quite a bit of tea."

After a few more questions, I realized that she would offer little more, so I thanked her for her time and let myself out. Once in the hall, though, I reflected that Mrs. Gordon had been more guarded than necessary.

And I didn't believe a word she said.

I spent a couple more hours interviewing other attendees at the SOBOP convention, but without success. Eerily similar to a banger drive-by in the ghetto, nobody seen nuthin', not the California woo woo publisher, the Washington state ecology pressman, nor the Vegas how-to-beat-the-odds publisher. When I pressed them, they made me feel about as welcome as an ex-wife at a wedding.

Finally giving up, I returned to the Jeep, but now that the distraction of questioning was behind me, I realized that I was starving. Instead of driving straight back to Scottsdale, I decided to detour through the nearby town of Cave Creek, eager for a big, fat hamburger at the Horny Toad Saloon. As soon as I turned west on Carefree Highway, though, the traffic thickened. To my surprise, I was soon bumper-to-bumper with a herd of Harley Davidsons and a long, snaky line of graffiti-covered vans, many of them bearing Idaho license plates. The motorcycles made sense. Cave Creek was the gathering spot for the Scottsdale Harley-Davidson Club, which despite its macho-sounding name consisted of a couple hundred business executives. But the vans....

Then I remembered what I should have at WestWorld.

Attracted by Arizona's rising tide of anti-immigrant feeling and Cave Creek's immigrant-friendly day labor program, the Aryan Nation and its brethren had selected the town as the site for their yearly picnic. Now the vans' graffiti made sense. The groups might have been too cowardly to display the swastika itself—they were too frightened of the Crips, Bloods, or even scarier, the Jewish Defense League—but they had found more subtle ways to trumpet their beliefs.

Four-foot-high blue letters on the rear of the white van in front of me blared, *14/88*. Every cop knew that the "14" stood for the "Fourteen Words" holy to White Supremacists everywhere: *"We must secure the existence of our people and a future for White children."* The "88" meant the eighth letter of the alphabet, H, as in "Heil Hitler."

Next to me idled a black van with the numbers "311" painted in red on the sides. "11" meant the eleventh letter of the alphabet, K; the "3" stood for K times three. KKK, Ku Klux Klan.

I checked out the driver. When I saw he sported a shaved head and the de rigeur lightning bolt tats on his neck, I lost my appetite. Swinging into an illegal U-turn, I headed back to Scottsdale.

By the time I made it back to Desert Investigations, the streetlights were on. The neighboring art galleries had closed, and Jimmy was locking up for the night.

"Don't take Esther and Rebecca to Cave Creek this weekend," I warned him. Jimmy had been dating Esther ever since we had helped her daughter Rebecca escape from a forced marriage to an elderly prophet in one of Arizona's notorious polygamy compounds.[2]

He was way ahead of me. "Fat chance, with those National Alliance jerks in town." Standing aside so that I could make it past him to the stairwell that led to my apartment, he added, "We're just going to kick back, have a little bar-b-que, and listen to some Chicken Scratch. But first, I'm going over to Wal-Mart to buy some toys for Owen's kids. Cheer them up. Speaking of Owen, did you find out anything that might help him?"

"I found out that Gloriana wasn't a very popular woman."

He turned the deadbolt behind him. "Yeah, Owen's told me stories. She wasn't in the running for the Humanitarian of the Year Award."

"Few people are." I made no move to go upstairs.

"I guess. Well...." Jimmy stood there, the tungsten light revealing a baffled expression on his face. "Is there something else? You know you're invited to join us, you always are."

---

[2] *Desert Wives: Polygamy Can Be Murder.*

I pictured him on the Rez, surrounded by his nieces and nephews, his girlfriend and her daughter, all the people he loved. Then I pictured my own empty apartment and decided to make the conversation last longer. "By the way, were you able to get started on those names I gave you?"

"It'll take a while. Right now they look clean, but we'll see what comes up when I go deeper." He frowned. "Lena, are you okay? Are you sure you don't want to follow me back to the Rez?"

"I'm fine, fine. Thanks anyway. I need to do some thinking, and it's easier when I'm by myself."

He tried not to look doubtful, but couldn't quite pull it off. "See you tomorrow, then."

"Yeah. Tomorrow."

After I watched his truck's taillights disappear down the street, I pulled my gun out of my carry-all and began the long walk up the stairs to my apartment. The long walk I took every night. The long walk I never ceased to dread.

The monster in the closet.

My childhood nightmares still haunted me, still crept into my waking hours. They had become so much a part of my existence that I could no longer imagine a world without them. But, oh, to not fear dark spaces, to welcome the night....

Such ease was not for me. Since living in my sixth foster home, I had never been able to enter a room alone without searching it thoroughly.

As usual, I had left the lights on, which I always do when there's a chance I will be out past sunset. Helped along by years of experience, the search went quickly. First the living room, a beige-on-beige box devoid of all personality other than the Two Gray Hills Navajo rug hanging over the sofa and the vivid George Haozous oil painting on the opposite wall. No monsters here, other than a few dust bunnies the size of alley cats lurking under the one window. Then an inspection of the hallway, the kitchen, the bathroom, and finally, the worst place of all—my bedroom.

Both hands trembling, I flipped on the lights, saw nothing. I looked under the bed. Nothing there, either.

Then I approached the long closet with its sliding double doors.

The monster in the closet.

My .38 cocked and ready, I slid back one door with my foot and parted the clothes with the gun. Nothing. I repeated the process on the other side. Another wonderful nothing. My apartment, my bedroom, my closet, all were empty of everything except the sound of my own heartbeats. I began to breathe again.

You'd think that I would hook up with someone if for no better reason than to forestall my fear of empty rooms. But as my relationship with Dusty illustrates, intimacy has never been my strong suit. Oh, I don't mean that easy physical intimacy which visits us all from time to randy time. I mean the real deal, *intimacy*, the deep emotional bond with another which is forged only after years of commitment.

I have never experienced that kind of intimacy and probably never will. Foster homes are not good training grounds for close encounters. Those of us who grew up in the wild round robin of CPS learned early on not to get attached to anyone because we understood that today's home was just that—today's and today's only. Tomorrow we might be someplace else. To us the word "home" itself was an abstraction, the description of a space where we temporarily stored our garbage bags filled with clothes. Why begin to love? Why ask for heartbreak? A child can only cry so much, and then the well—along with hope—runs dry.

Nightly apartment check finished and the remembered terrors of my nine-year-old self temporarily vanquished, I returned to the living room and laid the .38 on the coffee table. Then I leaned over my circa-1970 turntable and slipped on the John Lee Hooker vinyl masterpiece "Hooked on Blues" I'd found a few days earlier at a yard sale, but hadn't yet played. This simple joy would enrich the night. Bottleneck guitar licks on CD might be fine in the Jeep, but nothing could capture the nuances of an old bluesman like vinyl. While John Lee groaned his way through "Every Night, "I nuked a Michelina's macaroni and cheese dinner with jalapenos, a nod to us Southwestern gourmets. While eating, I listened calmly enough to "Boogie Chillen," "It Serves Me Right to Suffer," and "Drive Me Away." Then, halfway through "Will the Circle Be Unbroken," I found myself tearing up.

What the hell?

I am not a crier and the sudden tears spooked me, especially since I didn't know what prompted them. The stress of the day? My fears for Owen? Deciding that I had heard enough music for one night, I shut the turntable off and carefully slipped the old vinyl back into its paper sleeve. But I still needed some sound, something to light my own dark spaces, so after putting the empty Michelina's carton in the trash, I turned on FOX News. While Geraldo Rivera oozed ego, I busied myself around the apartment. I scrubbed the sinks, the tub, the toilet. I slaughtered the dust bunnies, I vacuumed. Exhausted, I finally settled myself at the kitchen table and wrote checks for the rent, the light bill, the water, my monthly Crisis Nursery donation.

No time to think, no time to remember.

My resolve faded around midnight, and I finally staggered off to bed. But as soon as I fell asleep, I entered Dreamland's time tunnel and found myself four years old again, back on that terrible bus hurtling through the Arizona night, while around me, voices rose in song. Above the song—still unidentifiable to my adult ears—I heard my mother scream that yes, she'd kill me, she'd kill me, just leave her alone to do it, for God's sake.

I saw her raise the gun, heard the explosion of gunfire, found myself curling over with pain. Then the hot desert air sucked away my breath as I fell through the bus door onto the broiling pavement. Over the sound of the bus speeding off, I heard a voice call to me in Spanish, felt tender arms pick me up....

Then mercifully, my nightmare, like my memories, was replaced by a comforting blackness.

But the respite was brief.

The dream started up again, and in the odd way of dreams, the bus morphed into to a barroom or restaurant, I couldn't tell which. I sat in someone's lap listening to John Lee Hooker singing "Will the Circle Be Unbroken." Not on vinyl this time, in the flesh. The spotlight on John Lee's face revealed a much younger man, not the ruined husk I had seen when I attended his Phoenix concert a mere month before his death. His dream face had not yet developed the crevices of age, nor his voice the quaver of time.

This younger John Lee sang and sang, his raspy voice rising to a gospel shout, promising the eventual reunion of mothers, fathers, sisters, brothers, all the loved ones who had crossed over the River Jordan. He sang of arms reaching out from Heaven to hold us tight, arms that would never let us go.

Then his voice changed. My dream-self looked over to discover that, no, not the voice, but the *singer* had changed. One of his band members, a young red-haired man playing a dobro, had stepped up to the mike. This man's voice, a high, clear tenor, briefly sailed above John Lee's, then swooped low, blending with the blues master in a haunting duet. "Will the circle be unbroken by and by, Lord, by and by?"

The person who held me, a woman I couldn't quite see, tightened her arms into a hug. Her perfume, a mixture of lily of the valley and lilac, softened the acrid stench of the cigarettes around us.

"Isn't he wonderful?" the woman whispered into my ear, and I knew she wasn't talking about John Lee.

As the spotlight caressed the young man's face, my heart clenched.

His eyes, a deep green, were the same color as mine.

Chapter 6

The next morning Jimmy updated me on his background searches into the Gloriana Alden-Taylor case.

"Zip on Myra Gordon. Emil Ramos looks fairly clean, considering that he's such a hot-tempered political gadfly. Nothing but a few parking tickets, all promptly paid. But David Zhang ran into some financial problems six years back, right before he started Desert Trails. He got real comfy again real fast, and I haven't found out why yet. Randall Ott looks promising, too. He's in hot water with the Anti-Defamation League, La Raza, the NAACP."

"Over *Losing America*?"

Jimmy shook his head. "That's the interesting thing. Sure, the Civil Rights crowd has been complaining loud and long to the media about Ott's faulty research and voodoo science, but I'm not talking about the book. The trouble is old trouble. When he was twelve, he got caught painting a swastika on a Scottsdale temple. Mommy and Daddy had to pay a big fine. At the ripe old age of fourteen, he and a few fellow travelers turned loose a grease-covered pig in a United Farm Workers' meeting—his parents paid for that, too. A year later, he was caught defacing a billboard advertising a Marvin Gaye concert. He actually did a stint in juvie for that."

I didn't know whether to laugh or cry.

"Granted, that's old history," Jimmy continued, "when he was your basic addle-brained delinquent. Apparently he cleaned up his act when he began writing. In a manner of speaking."

I tsk-tsked. "They're going to catch you some day, hacking into those files."

He responded with a sly grin. "I cover my tracks. But you haven't heard the best part yet. Lynn Tinsley? The honorable congresswoman?" He sat back in his chair, an expectant look on his face.

I played along. "I await your news with bated breath, oh Great Master of Cyberspace."

Gratified, he said, "Seven years ago, before she ran for the House, she was picked up for shoplifting a silk scarf from Neiman Marcus."

I flashed on Tinsley, with her too-teased hair, her frou-frou dress, her incongruous spike heels sinking into the dirt at WestWorld. So miss Girly Girl was a regular Miss Misdemeanor. "How'd it play out?"

"Charges dropped. Everything hushed up. Not even a fine."

"Hmm." Could Gloriana have found out this dirt and threatened Tinsley? And if so, why? What would Gloriana have to gain? The obvious answer was help with legislation of some sort, possibly exempting bulk book sales from state sales tax.

"Jimmy, keep checking on Tinsley, and keep an eye out for whatever legislation she's sponsored in the last couple of years."

"Gloriana-type legislation?"

"Exactly. And while you're at it, I want you to look at that librarian again. I've got a feeling about her."

"Will do."

As his fingers flew over the keyboard, I placed a call to Dr. Deborah Mendelson, the dermatologist who had tried to save Gloriana's life. The woman who answered the phone told me the doctor was having a busy morning and would have to call me back.

I left my number, as well as a brief explanation, and proceeded to burrow into the stacks of paperwork generated by various cases both past and present. Whoever forecasted that computers would create a paperless office had been sorely mistaken. Paper usage was up, not down. While I was on the phone to Office Max begging for new filing cabinets to be delivered to Desert Investigations as soon as possible, my second phone line lit up. Caller ID notified me that Dr. Mendelson was returning my call, so I picked up, leaving the Office Max clerk in the lurch.

"Dr. Mendelson, I'm a detective working the Gloriana Alden-Taylor murder case, and I'd like to ask you some questions."

A long silence, then, "Detective with whom, may I ask? Your prefix isn't right for Scottsdale PD."

No dummy, this doc. "I used to be with Scottsdale PD, but now I'm a private detective brought into the case by Owen Sisiwan's family. As you probably have heard, he's been charged with Gloriana's murder."

Another silence, shorter this time. "I remember Mr. Sisiwan. He seemed like a nice man. Ms. Alden-Taylor told him to sit in the hallway while she ate lunch, which I thought rather unkind. I asked her if I might take him something to eat, but she told me to mind my own business. Look, Ms. Jones, I only have a couple of minutes before my next patient comes in, so we'd better make this quick."

I'm no dummy, either, and I had my questions ready. "What made you think Gloriana's death wasn't natural? The captain in charge of the case said you alerted the EMTs immediately."

"Ms. Alden-Taylor's symptoms were clearly not those of a heart attack or stroke. At first I thought she might be choking on something she ate, but when I rendered aid, I found her air passages were swollen almost completely shut. After she expired, I remembered that the garnish on her salad didn't look quite the same as mine. That, coupled with her symptoms, ran up a red flag, so I shared my suspicions with the EMTs. They took it from there."

From her end of the phone, I heard a quick buzz.

"My patient's here, Ms. Jones. You'll need to call me at another time if you want anything else." With a soft click, Dr. Mendelson hung up.

I drummed my fingers on my desk until Jimmy turned away from his computer and asked, "Problems?"

"Just the usual nobody-knows-nothing. I'm really beginning to worry about Owen."

He didn't say anything for a second, then, "We're all worried about him, especially his wife." He told me about his visit with her the night before, of the dire straits Owen's family would endure without his paycheck. "The money he was getting from the G.I. Bill stopped when Owen's work schedule kept him from attending classes at Scottsdale Community College. Our family's doing what they can, but that's not much."

During my bill-paying frenzy the night before, I had also written out a check to help Owen's wife buy groceries, but that wouldn't help her long-term problem. Like most of the Pima Indians out on the Salt River-Maricopa Reservation, the Sisiwans had little money. Life had begun to look up since the Pima casinos had opened on the eastern edge of Scottsdale, but it would take time for the tribe to complete its climb out of poverty. War hero or not, Owen was as broke as everybody else on the Rez.

Thinking about Owen's real-life problems made my own nightmares fade. "You're visiting him tonight, right?"

"Yeah. Esther and I'll drive over to the jail after work."

"Tell him not to worry, that I'll have him out of there in no time."

I hoped my voice sounded more optimistic than I felt.

When I parked the Jeep in front of Zachary Alden-Taylor VI's house, I allowed myself a moment of surprise. I had imagined that Gloriana's grandson would live in grander digs, but I'd been wrong. Granted, South Scottsdale had never been known for its high-toned mansions—we left that sort of thing up to our posher kin to the north—but Scottsdale was still Scottsdale, right?

The street, while not exactly slummy, was lined with the kind of small, inexpensive tract homes you would find in any working class Arizona neighborhood. Bargain-basement stucco painted in ice cream colors attempted to relieve the monotony, but Zachary's house wouldn't have looked out of place in Appalachia. Its roof sagged, a sheet of crumpled aluminum foil patched a broken front window, and the indoor-outdoor carpeting covering the a-kilter porch had been ripped in several places, exposing the crumbling concrete pad beneath. The tiny lawn surrounding this wreck had long ago given up its fight for life and had let the desert take over. Someone had money troubles.

I stepped carefully up the short walk, dodging a couple of skittering scorpions, yet feeling my spirits rise. I could almost hear Owen's cell door open.

When I reached up to knock on the ripped screen door, though, a yellow flier fluttering from the knob temporarily drove Owen from my mind. Over the photograph of a blond-haired child, the headline on the flier read, MISSING: A FUTURE FOR WHITE CHILDREN. At the bottom was an invitation to join the National Alliance.

They were recruiting in Scottsdale now? I looked back along the street and saw yellow fliers on each door.

As I stood on the porch, wondering if I'd break any laws if I ripped the flier away (and if I cared), the screen door opened. A tall, dark-haired beauty with vivid blue eyes smiled down at me. "I told Boz you were coming for him and he's very excited."

Boz? "I don't think...."

She opened the screen door further, and I saw a small black and brown dog grinning up at me from between Beauty's ankles. Regardless of the fact that he was a mere Heinz 57 mutt, he had been groomed within an inch of his life and reeked of Giorgio.

"Cute dog," I said. "But I...."

"Get in here quick before somebody gets out." She grabbed me by the arm and pulled me into a tiny living room, which, after the bright sunlight outside, seemed barroom dark. As the screen door snapped shut behind me, the scent of Eau de Kitty Litter replaced the Giorgio. Even in the gloom I could make out a startling assortment of animals perched upon every conceivable piece of furniture. More dogs, cats, even several rabbits swarmed across a tatty, tweed-patterned carpet. The few areas not covered with shed hair and/or animals were heaped with books.

Beauty, whom I now saw was very pregnant, chattered on about Boz and paperwork. Surreptitiously, I stuffed the National Alliance flier into my carry-all.

"You'll need to fill out some papers swearing on the life of your first-born that you won't keep him on a chain in the backyard and other evil stuff like that, then you can take him home." She looked down at the grinning dog, who took that as a cue to chase his tail. "Would you like that, Boz? Would you like that?"

Boz paused in his tail-chasing to bark an affirmative.

Yes, a very cute dog, but not for me. This big dog hunted alone. "Look, ma'am, I think you've mistaken me for someone else," I said. "I'm not here about Boz."

Beauty scrunched her face, which didn't even begin to mar her astonishing looks. "Then you're not Mrs. Howell?"

"No, but it looks like Mrs. Howell is getting a great little dog."

Upon hearing the word *dog,* Boz made a beeline for my ankle, which he then proceeded to lick as if it had been slathered in liver. A ratty-looking white cat hissed at him from the corner.

"Bad dog, Boz. Bad cat, Andrew," Beauty said, obviously not meaning it. Then she leaned over—with difficulty, due to her prominent belly—and tugged the dog away from me by his collar. "Don't lick her, Boz."

I dug into my carry-all and handed her a card. "Lena Jones, Desert Investigations."

She released the dog's collar and her friendly face closed down. "I told you. It's being taken care of."

Interesting. Beauty had confused me with someone else yet again, even after I'd identified myself as a private detective.

Boz, sensing that something had upset his mistress, began to growl. A few other dogs joined the hostile chorus, making the room sound like the tuba section of the Scottsdale Symphony.

"Bad dogs!" This time she meant it. Boz and friends shut up, but Beauty's own voice turned to a growl when she said, "You'd better leave, Ms. Jones. And you can tell the people who hired you that this is getting ridiculous. Tell them to mind their own business and I'll mind mine."

People who hired me? "Look, Mrs. Alden-Taylor, if that's who you are, I don't know who you think I am, but I've been retained by Owen Sisiwan's family to investigate Gloriana Alden-Taylor's murder."

The frown left her face. "Oh. I thought...." She gave me a shame-faced smile. "The neighbors have been getting pretty irritated about my beasties, and....Never mind. That problem's about to disappear. As to Owen, the very idea that he would hurt a hair on Gloriana's head is ludicrous. Zach and I have such faith in his innocence that we're in the process of hiring an attorney for him right now. Here, take a seat. And yeah, I'm Mrs. Alden-Taylor, but call me Megan. Not even Gloriana used that pretentious double-barreled name."

I looked around at the various mounds of fur dozing on the sofa and chairs. "Er...."

"Just move somebody."

My eyes now accustomed to the dim light, I picked my way through the swarming mass of dogs and cats to the dingy La-Z-Boy recliner near a sofa which the cats had obviously been using for a claw-sharpening post. I leaned over the chair and picked up the fat black Persian whose hair, I hoped, wouldn't look too grungy against my black jeans and T-shirt. Then I sat down, lifting the "beastie" onto my lap. Through all this, the cat never moved, other than to increase the volume of his purrs.

Megan nestled herself on the ragged sofa between two stacks of books, whereupon two elderly cats, arthritic bones poking through beautifully groomed coats, immediately draped themselves over her thighs. She appeared not to notice the clumps of white and gray fur adhering to her denim maternity jeans. "All settled in now?" she asked them.

After they purred their assent, she addressed herself to my own lap-warmer. "Poor Black Bart, does Mama need to blow your nose?" Then, to me, "Pig-faced Persians frequently have breathing difficulties. Oh. My manners. Would you like some iced tea? I've got some made." She started to get up, whereupon her two cats yowled in protest.

I waved away the offer of tea, taking care not to dislodge Black Bart, whose purrs now revealed themselves to be catarrhal snorts. "Actually, I'm here to see Mr. Alden-Ta…, uh, Zachary, if that would be possible."

She shook her head, glossy brown hair rippling like a waterfall at midnight. With her deeply tanned face and vivid blue eyes, the effect was stunning, and I wondered if she had once been a model. If so, judging from the shambles around her, she'd certainly married down.

"Zach's at the office. He's the managing editor of Patriot's Blood Press, you know, and with Gloriana dead, there is a mountain of details for him to tackle. Canceling most of the summer catalog, for one. Not to speak ill of the dead or anything, but you wouldn't believe some of the garbage his grandmother was about to publish."

Neither Megan nor Zach sounded like National Alliance recruitment material, so I fished the flier out of my carry-all and thrust it at her. "This was stuck on your front door."

She looked at it and scowled. "Fucking Nazis." Then she wadded the flier up into a ball and rolled it across the floor, where several cats began to fight over shredding rights. "Jesus, to think that after all we've been through, Americans can still hate each other."

"Why do you think the National Alliance picked this neighborhood to recruit from?" Unlike North Scottsdale's mostly White enclaves, South Scottsdale was racially mixed, with a large Hispanic and Asian contingent.

"Probably because of the economy," Megan answered. "There've been a lot of layoffs around here, and these Aryan knuckleheads believe it's because minorities have taken all the jobs. The fact that corporate corruption might have something to do with it never enters their pointy heads. That's what Zach says, anyway, and I totally agree with him."

Given such a liberal mind-set, I wondered how her husband could bear to work for Patriot's Blood in the first place. This wasn't the time to ask.

Instead, I said, "It's nice to hear that your husband is making some changes at Patriot's Blood. So he inherits?"

"Of course. He's executive editor *and* publisher now, which is only right. Other than Sandra, Vicky, and the aunts, he's Gloriana's only surviving relative."

"Vicky?"

Megan brushed a cat hair off her cheek. "Victoria. Gloriana's daughter. But given her refusal to run Patriot's Blood, the chances of her inheriting anything sizeable have always been minimal. Same for Gloriana's older sisters, Leila and Lavelle. Identical twins. I heard through the family grapevine that Gloriana was thinking about taking over their affairs, but I don't know exactly why. They're not senile. Anyway, as I was saying, most of the estate comes to Zach."

She looked around at her wreck of a house. "Gloriana's death is sad, of course, and don't think I don't care, because I do. But with the baby coming and everything else going on around here, we really need a bigger place. Zach's moving us into the Hacienda, up by the Paradise Valley Country Club. I'll admit that I'm a little worried about how those folks will react to my menagerie, but maybe we can work it out. The Hacienda is isolated and the lot's certainly big enough. Twenty rooms on three acres."

Megan and her husband would need every inch of it, too. I had already counted seventeen cats and six dogs. I couldn't get a fix on the rabbits, because they stayed on the move. Or hop.

Animals weren't the only problem in the house, though. Several overflowing, mismatched bookcases lined the battered walls, with even more books stacked in tall columns on the fur-covered carpet. A glance at the pile nearest me revealed Wallace Stegner's *Angle of Repose*, Dean Koontz's *The Watchers*, Michael Cunningham's *The Hours*, and more than a dozen mysteries. Talk about eclectic taste.

"My animals need all the room they can get, so in one way, the Hacienda is the answer to a prayer," Megan continued. "On the downside, the place is pretty old and the upkeep is astronomical. If we sold it, along with the acreage up north, we'd have more options. Maybe we could even buy a little ranch out in the desert where there are no neighbors or zoning to worry about, and build a no-kill animal shelter. I am so sick of complaining neighbors."

I remembered Megan's reaction when she found out I wasn't here to adopt Boz. "How much do they complain?"

She frowned. "Last week they drew up a petition saying that if I don't get rid of my strays they'd take legal action. They don't care anything about the suffering that goes on out there, the dogs being dropped off in the desert, the cats being tortured, the poor 'Easter Bunnies' abandoned in the park to die a week after Easter...."

Having a soft spot for animals myself, I sympathized. "Did they give you a deadline?"

"Not yet, but it's only a matter of time." Her voice was as gloomy as the room.

I wished her well, but her pet problem wasn't mine. I was about to ask her about funeral arrangements when I heard squeals coming from the direction of the backyard.

"Megan, did I hear a pig?"

She nodded. "That's Emma. One of those shady pet shops sold her as a miniature Vietnamese pot-bellied pig, but of course she wasn't. When she grew too large, her owners dumped her at the pound. That's where our rescuers found her."

"Rescuers?" I wondered idly how the country club set would react to sharing their neighborhood with a pig.

"Oh. I thought you knew. I'm founder and president of Save Our Friends. Besides myself, about fifty volunteers take in strays and castoffs. We spay and neuter them, give them their shots, then foster them out to various homes until we find permanent adoptive parents. That's who I thought you were, Boz's new mom. She's due any minute now. Are you sure you don't want a dog? Or a cat? We have plenty up for adoption, and I can tell that you're good with animals. Black Bart certainly likes you."

Black Bart sneezed, depositing something nasty-looking on my jeans. "I'm allergic to cats. Dogs, too," I lied. "You mentioned something about Gloriana's daughter, that she refused to have anything to do with Patriot's Blood. Why?"

"Vicky has her own business to worry about. Maybe you've heard of her. She works under the name of Sappho."

The name rang a bell, a bell that wasn't tied to the classical Greek poet. "The film-maker?"

"That's her. She's won a couple of Sundance awards, and I think there's a pretty good chance she'll actually snag an Oscar nomination with her new film, a documentary about gay archetypes in the Old West. She hasn't released it yet, but Zach and I have seen the rough cut and it's brilliant."

During the past decade, Scottsdale had become a haven for creative types fleeing Hollywood's increasingly congested film colony, and I had met more than my share of actors, producers, and directors. Despite the public's perception, not all were wealthy. A big inheritance would buy a lot of expensive movie equipment.

"Did Vicky know her mother was leaving almost everything to Zach?" If not, she wouldn't have been the first person to murder someone while operating under the false belief of future riches.

"Of course she knew. Gloriana was up front about it, just like Gloriana was up front about me and my…ah, that she didn't like me."

I found this admission surprising. Although Megan's home was obviously a wreck and her bond with her strays a bit much, she seemed likeable enough to me. "What did she have against you?" I asked.

Megan scowled. "What *didn't* she have against me! For starters, she didn't like the fact that Zach married one of his students. That's where we met, in his creative writing class at ASU. For seconds, she didn't like animals, and I was already involved in Save Our Friends. But the real deal-breaker was that I didn't have the right bloodlines. I'm Italian, but it wasn't the Italian thing she minded so much. After all, Christopher Columbus was Italian. What she hated was that my family came over on the wrong boat." She laughed and tossed that glorious chestnut mane again. "As far as Gloriana was concerned, any boat but the Mayflower was the wrong boat. My grandparents arrived in steerage, on some leaky liner in the early 1900s, so you can see how many points that made with her."

I frowned. "She cared that much about heredity?"

The laughter died. "Sounds like you didn't know her."

I pretended ignorance. No point in telling her about my encounter with Gloriana at the Chamber of Commerce mixer. "Megan, at this point, I only know that Gloriana was wealthy, owned a publishing house, and got herself murdered." I'll probably go to Hell for all the lies I tell.

Megan didn't answer right away, simply stroked her lap cats, making them purr even louder. Then, as if coming to a difficult decision, she leaned forward as far as her belly would allow, and looked me straight in the eye. "I'm sorry, but I really disliked the woman. So that means you'll have to take everything I say about her with a grain of salt."

"Point taken." I tried not to let my amusement show. She was the first person I had ever met who apologized for disliking an in-law.

"Gloriana was aggressive about her snobbery. You could have won the Nobel Peace Prize or cured cancer, but as far as she was concerned, it didn't make any difference if you had the wrong ancestry. The only thing she cared about, and I'm not exaggerating here, was a person's last name. Especially her own. The damned Aldens. And the double-damned, slave-owning Taylors."

Considering Gloriana's remarks about my own DNA, I found Megan's statement odd. Or maybe there'd been a Jones on the Mayflower; I'd have to check. But Megan's comment did offer the chance to clear up a question that had intrigued me since I'd first heard of Gloriana. "Those double-barreled names are pretty rare outside England, aren't they?"

Megan smiled. "Feminists love them, too, don't forget. But I'll have to give the devil her due on that subject, at least. Gloriana didn't start that hyphen stuff. It happened back in the eighteen hundreds, when one of the lesser Alden women married a lesser grandson of Zachary Taylor. Two losers basking in the reflected glory of their ancestors. Today the damned name's nothing but trouble. With the hyphen, nobody knows how to file your name. Alden or Taylor? Taylor or Alden? Your insurance and mortgage records get screwed up...."

Suddenly her face changed, and she shoved the cats aside to pat her stomach. "He's dancing again," she said. "Want to feel?"

No, I didn't. Instead, I sat quietly for a moment, watching the wonder on her face. Had my mother ever looked like that when I was growing inside her?

Probably not. If she had, she wouldn't have shot me.

After a while, Megan settled back and let the cats climb back onto her lap. "I sound self-centered, don't I? Going on and on, as if I didn't care about the poor woman getting murdered."

Not really. Megan was merely a pregnant woman with more immediate worries than the death of an in-law who had disliked her. At least she was honest. I took the opportunity to steer her back to her original subject. "You were talking about Gloriana's ancestry. Actually, it surprises me that a woman with her background would run something like Patriot's Blood. Why didn't she use her money for more, um, tasteful projects. Charity work, for instance?"

"That's how little you know," Megan said.

Regardless of Gloriana's Plymouth Brethren connections, Megan explained, the Aldens never did as well in trade as the other Mayflower families. Then, as the Pilgrim blood thinned through the centuries, Gloriana's branch had degenerated into near penury. But Gloriana, who had apparently been quite the looker in her youth, married a fairly well-heeled stockbroker. When he keeled over from a coronary at the Phoenix Open Golf Tournament, she inherited his seven-figure estate, and the Alden-Taylors were relatively flush again.

"Zach tells me that she blew a lot of it fixing up the Hacienda," Megan said. "By then, she'd started Patriot's Blood magazine, and the profits helped stem the flow. Then something happened that changed everything."

She told me that in the Eighties and Nineties, the large New York publishing houses had merged into conglomerates. "The country wound up with, what, six major houses? And some of those houses had offshore owners, typically the Europeans. They brought in MBAs who fired editors wholesale, released writers from their contracts.... It was a literary bloodbath."

I looked at the books piled beside her, around the room. "Looks to me like there are still plenty of books to go around."

"Take a look at the spines," she said. "Most of these come from publishing houses you've never heard of. Niche houses."

Before I could ask what that meant, she explained.

"Niche houses are small, specialist presses like Patriot's Blood, companies who had the foresight to sign the writers the big houses released, even some new writers. Companies who were willing to take a chance on people *not* named Stephen King or John Grisham."

Her eyes took on a dreamy look. "You know, for a while I wanted to be a writer myself. That's why I was in Zach's creative writing class."

The revelation didn't surprise me. I could easily see Megan writing sensitive stories from an animal's point of view, possibly creating something like a modern version of *Black Beauty.* Or maybe even one of those cat detective books.

She patted her stomach. "As it turned out, I didn't want it enough. There were other things I wanted more. Like Zach. And all the little live things." She leaned over and nuzzled the cats. "That's a Wallace Stegner title, *All the Little Live Things.* I'd planned to be like Stegner, to write the story of the Southwest. Instead, I got Zach and all my own little live things. And now my baby. I guess love isn't a bad trade-off for a writing career, is it?"

Given my own background, I had no idea. But I did know that if Megan loved her baby only half as much as she obviously did her strays, the baby would have a wonderful life. A wave of jealousy swept over me for a moment, and only with difficulty did I manage to quash it. What had Jim Morrison sung in that Doors song? *"Some are born to sweet delight, some are born to endless night."*

I remembered my mother firing her gun in my face. My own endless night.

"Lena? Are you all right?"

I forced a smile. Never let them see you bleed. "Probably a touch of indigestion. You were talking about Patriot's Blood. Was it successful right away?"

"To a certain extent," Megan continued, stroking a tiny white kitten which had climbed up her leg to join the elderly nappers. "But it became more so when she began publishing books. Everyone knew Gloriana's background, so even in the beginning she had an in with researchers who were working on books about the Founding Fathers. She signed them, and the reviews were good, but the income wasn't great. And Gloriana liked money, so she decided to, as she put it, 'broaden the company's publishing guidelines.' Zach had no idea how far she'd go. God, you should see the stuff in her latest catalog."

"I've seen a brochure." The titles alone should be good for a few more nightmares.

Megan gave a little shudder, making one of the old cats grumble in complaint. "The full catalog's even worse. Gloriana didn't originally plan to publish that type of material, but...." Her shudder turned to a shrug. "Well, once she got started with books like Randall Ott's, most of her original authors deserted her. She didn't care. Why should she, when she was making money like she'd never dreamed of? That's what Gloriana was all about, money. At the expense of everything decent."

"Was she aware of how you and Zach felt about the new editorial direction?"

The anger in her face hardly marred her beauty. "Of course she was. Zach fought her tooth and nail, but Gloriana didn't care." Her former glow returned. "Everything will change now, though. Zach will return Patriot's Blood to its original mission, maybe even start publishing some literary fiction. I'd like to see him do a nice mystery line, to tell you the truth. These days, it seems like mystery novels are the only places where good triumphs over evil. But that's beside the point, isn't it? People like Gloriana....Well, she suckered Zach into coming to work for her by telling him he could head up a new fiction imprint. Then as soon as he resigned from ASU and came on board as her managing editor, she changed her mind. Or maybe she'd simply been leading him on in the first place. Whatever the truth, by then I was pregnant."

I asked the expected question. "When are you due?"

"In forty-five days. It's a boy. We promised Gloriana we'd name him Zachary Alden-Taylor VII, but now maybe we can just call him Joe. Or name him after my father. Marcello. Now there's a beautiful name."

I was getting ready to ask her another question when the doorbell rang. Dogs, cats, and rabbits scattered in all directions.

Megan lumbered to her feet, but not before gently placing her lap cats on the floor. "That must be Mrs. Howell to collect Boz." Did I detect a note of relief in her voice?

Boz, hearing his name, chased his tail again, and woofed.

I knew a good exit line when I heard one, so as Megan opened the door to a short, middle-aged woman bearing a leash and a big smile, I waved goodby. I stepped outside just in time to see the door open at the house across the street. A rumpled-looking man in stained overalls lifted the National Alliance flier from his doorknob. He stood there reading it for a moment, but instead of crumpling it into a ball, he nodded.

Then he went back inside, taking the flier with him.

Chapter 7

Like most women with a penchant for black jeans, I keep a lint remover in my Jeep, so when I parked in the lot behind Patriot's Blood Press, I took a few minutes to de-hair myself, then walked around to the front entrance.

The office was located in a strip mall on Goldwater Boulevard at the end of Scottsdale's famous Art Gallery Row. I had expected the place to be painted in red, white, and blue, but in accordance with the city's stringent zoning restrictions, the front of the office sported only a discreet gilt sign that whispered *Patriot's Blood Press*. No rabble-rousing books filled the picture window, only an assortment of hanging plants that looked as if they could use some watering. When I opened the door, a dog barked and I looked down to see a gray, wire-haired fox terrier. She began licking the same ankle that had so fascinated Boz.

"Don't worry, Casey doesn't bite," said a heavy blond woman at the front desk. So many manuscripts were stacked around her that if they ever fell over, I feared they would kill her. The blonde's face, a bit on the pasty side, appeared bloated, and the bags under her dark eyes testified to either too much carousing or a serious sleep disorder. Her flowered dress didn't look quite clean.

The other office workers didn't lift their heads from their computers; they kept typing away.

"Seems to be my day for dogs," I muttered, nudging the animal away with my foot. "Uh, is Mr. Alden-Taylor here?"

"Zach?" The blonde frowned. Maybe she thought I was a desperate author in search of a publisher. "Do you have an appointment?"

I fished a business card out of my carry-all. "I'm a private detective, and I'd like to speak to Mr. Al...Zach for a few minutes."

The hand she reached toward my card trembled. A hangover, or anxiety? Could have been either. Her fingernails had been bitten to the quick.

"A detective? Wha...what do you need to see Zach about?"

"I've been hired by Owen Sisiwan to look into Gloriana's death."

She relaxed. "Owen wouldn't hurt a fly."

"You know him well, then?"

She nodded, revealing dark roots at the base of her blond hair. "Oh, yes. Gloriana worked him half to death. Tell you what. I'll ask if Zach can see you now. Anything I can do to help Owen, I will."

When she rose from her desk and walked toward the back, I saw that the hem of her dress had ripped away. It flapped around her stout legs like a ragged banner. Did she not know, or did she not care?

Soon she returned, trailed by a tall man in his mid-thirties. With his tanned skin, sun-streaked brown hair, and a Kirk Douglas chin, he bordered on handsome, but his eyes were red and his too-flat nose skewed to the side, as if he'd once taken a blow to the face and decided not to have it fixed. He looked more like a boxer than a publisher.

"Hi, Ms. Jones, I'm Zach," he said, holding out his hand for me to shake. "Great work you did up at that polygamy commune, getting that little girl out of there. Too bad the attorney general didn't follow up and arrest those perverts."

My relief that Zachary Alden-Taylor knew who I was almost wiped out the memory of my fury at Arizona's cowardly AG. Almost, but not quite. "He said something about polygamy being a matter of religious freedom."

Zach snorted. "Since when is the rape of underage girls a matter of religious freedom? No, you can bet that money's involved in it somehow. It usually is when serious crimes aren't prosecuted."

"I couldn't agree with you more," I said, trying to stay calm. Every time I thought about my last case, my stomach churned. "But right now, I need to talk to you about your grandmother's murder."

Like his receptionist, Zach sounded more than willing to help. "Follow me back to my office so we can leave poor Sandra here to her many miseries."

Poor Sandra threw him a grateful look and settled her wide bottom back on the chair. Zach nudged me along a narrow hallway made even narrower by the dozens of cartons lining its walls. Stacks of loose books and manuscripts were piled on top of the cartons.

He ushered me past a closed door and into a tiny office lit by a flickering tungsten lamp where even more manuscripts moldered upon the battered desk, the floor, and the ripped Naugahyde visitor's chair. A computer hummed on a chipped, faux wood credenza behind the desk. I decided that Zach's office was little neater than his home. Just with less hair.

He cleared the chair for me. "I kept intending to do something about this, but....Now I'll be moving into my grandmother's office soon, so there's no need to clean."

As I sat down, a cloud of dust puffed upward from the chair. "I guess not," I said, once I was through sneezing. "As I told your receptionist...."

He gave me a bleak smile as he sat down in his own chair, which appeared to be held together by duct tape. "Receptionist? Sandra's my cousin and she's a senior editor, in charge of the other people you saw out there."

"Sorry. I thought...." I stopped myself from saying that she looked like an accident that had already happened.

As if oblivious to Sandra's appearance, Zach chattered on. "Most small publishers like us don't enjoy the luxury of a receptionist. Everyone here does several jobs, including Sandra, who coordinates the reading of all new submissions."

He then launched into such a detailed description of Sandra's duties that I grew restless. "Zach, do I need to know all this?"

"Probably not. It's only my long-winded way of saying please don't call my poor overworked cousin a receptionist. Now, what can I do for you?"

I explained the situation, told him about my earlier interview with Megan, and watched his face for any sign of alarm. After all, with Owen in jail, the police had stopped looking for other suspects. If I proved Owen innocent, Zach might wind up as the next candidate.

But Zach's face displayed only approval. "Great! The more people who work on this, the better. When the police told me they'd arrested Owen we were all shocked. Just yesterday Megan begged me to get him an attorney. After I made a few calls, I realized we could. Since I already sign the checks around here, the estate's executor—Gloriana's attorney—gave me the go-ahead for the bail money a little while ago. In fact, I was getting ready to drive down to the bail bondsman's office when you arrived. I'm hoping to get Owen back to his family by the end of the day."

I wanted to cheer in relief, but the celebration would have to wait. Making bail was one thing, being cleared of murder charges another. "Your wife told me you're Gloriana's primary heir."

He smiled. "Which makes me the primary suspect, too. Right?"

Right, but I wasn't about to admit it. His forthrightness, like Megan's, intrigued me. By admitting to his obvious motive, Zach Alden-Taylor VI was either the dumbest murderer I'd ever met, or an innocent man. I didn't know enough about him yet to figure out which. Then again, not everyone killed for money. Passion and revenge made dandy motives, too.

"I imagine the estate is sizeable?"

The figures he rolled out weren't quite as high as I'd expected, but impressive nonetheless. In addition to her house, the publishing company, and a tidy stock portfolio, Gloriana also owned that forty acres of undeveloped desert land near Pinnacle Peak, an upscale enclave near Scottsdale's northeast border. Once the will cleared probate, Zach and his wife would enjoy a more comfortable life. I said as much.

Zach's smile broadened, and a tendril of brown hair fell fetchingly across his forehead. "The Hacienda is five times the size of our current house, and since you've seen Megan's menagerie, you can appreciate how much we need the space. As far as Patriot's Blood goes, well, I'm changing the company's entire publishing philosophy. Later today I'll draft a letter to some of our authors canceling their contracts. I imagine there might be a few lawsuits coming our way after that, but the desert acreage will give us a nice financial cushion."

"You can do that, cancel book contracts?"

He nodded. "The librarians we've been selling to sure won't weep bitter tears. The bookstores, they've been through this kind of thing before and we'll straighten it out. As for everyone else...." He laughed. "I don't give a damn about the disappointment of the National Alliance and its fellow travelers."

His comment gave me the chance to clear up the confusion I had experienced since speaking to Megan. "It's nice to know they'll have to go elsewhere for their reading material, but I'm curious. Given your own obvious feelings about these books, how could you stand working here?"

He shifted in his seat, and one strip of duct tape on the chair peeled away. I noticed that he had stopped meeting my eyes.

"When my grandmother lured me away from my job at ASU, Patriot's Blood was an entirely different kind of house. The magazine was a product any publisher could be proud of, and the books were reputable. But after 9/11—which was *after* I'd come on board, you have to understand—everything changed. Gloriana saw a way to cash in on tragedy, and so she did."

"Why you didn't leave?"

The flush deepened. "You've heard that story about the frog in the saucepan, haven't you? At first the water is cool, so he's comfortable and doesn't try to hop out. Then it warms up a little, he's still comfortable. By the time the water gets hot, it's too late to move. Well, I'm that frog. The first few, ah, *worrisome* titles Gloriana purchased weren't that bad, merely distasteful. I figured she was trying something out, so I didn't say anything. The next few titles we had words over, but it was like spitting in the wind. The new line was bringing in so much money she ignored everything I said."

He still hadn't answered my question. "Couldn't you have gone back to ASU? Resumed your academic career?"

After a bitter laugh, he answered, "Au contraire, Miss Jones. The head of the creative writing school had a long waiting list for my position. And now that my resumé includes *Losing America* and its nasty brethren, no university will touch me. In case you didn't notice when you were out at the house, Megan and I aren't rolling in dough."

He sighed. "By the time I realized my grandmother had no intention of listening to my complaints about her progressively scarier author list, it was too late. Megan was pregnant, and Patriot's Blood was our insurance carrier."

The frog, trapped in boiling water; sounded like a great murder motive to me. "I saw some of your titles when I stopped by the SOBOP booth at WestWorld, so I know how hard it must have been for you."

"Then you only saw the books, which account for a mere fraction of our income. Most of the company's profits come from our computer games and music CDs. I halted production on those first thing this morning."

"Computer games?"

Zach got up and walked over to a gray steel bookcase, which, I now realized, held as many software boxes and CDs as it did books. "Let me show you," he said, turning his back to me and inserting a disc into his computer.

After the prerequisite hums, the screen filled with red letters on a black background, proclaiming we were about to play BORDER RUN. Zach double-clicked something on the menu at the lower left of the screen, and as I watched over his shoulder, the letters were replaced by a crudely animated version of a rifle-toting skinhead wearing a T-shirt decorated with the American flag and the numbers 311.

The National Anthem began playing from the computer's speakers, and a deep voice filled the room. "SOLDIER OF FREEDOM, IT IS YOUR JOB TO KEEP AMERICA PURE. SHOULDER YOUR RIFLE AND GET READY TO DEFEND YOUR COUNTRY."

The black background morphed into a cactus-strewn landscape reminiscent of the arid borderland between southern Arizona and Sonora, Mexico. A few chunky rabbits jerked across the bottom of the screen, but the skinhead ignored them. I had the feeling he was waiting for bigger game. I was right. The National Anthem died, replaced by "La Cucaracha," as several Hispanic-looking people—men, women, and even children—began running back and forth between the saguaros. When Zach exchanged the mouse for a joystick, the skinhead began firing. Blood spatters appeared on the foreheads of the "border runners" as his shots found their mark.

Zach released the joystick. "That's the Hispanic version of the game. Click on a different icon and you get your choice of Asians, Native Americans, African-Americans, Jews, Arabs. Anyone who's not flagrantly Anglo-Saxon. The purpose of the game, as I'm sure you've figured out, is to keep America, ah, racially pure. Under my grandmother's leadership, Patriot's Blood manufactured more than a dozen games like that, each one worst than the last. But that's not all. Would you like to hear some of our music CDs? We've recorded groups like American Nation, Manifest Destiny, Power Police, and Aryan Arms. Gorgeous stuff." His bitter voice belied his words.

"Holy crap!" I finally managed, as Zach grabbed the joystick again and the last standing Hispanic's head exploded in a blossom of red.

"That holy crap brought my grandmother a couple million dollars in gross revenue last year," he said, shutting the program down. "Hate is big business in America these days, and domestic terrorism has become downright chic in some quarters. If al-Qaeda doesn't destroy us, our own fanatics will."

I cleared my throat. "You plan to replace this, ah, lucrative sideline with…?"

"With nothing, unless I can figure out how to design a video game starring Shakespeare and Kit Marlowe competing in a poetry slam at the Old Globe. My wife wants us to concentrate on books, to sign some of those midlist authors who lost their contracts when the big publishers began their merging frenzy, but I…."

Midlist authors? I guess my puzzled look showed on my face, because he immediately stopped his rush of words.

"You have no idea what I'm talking about, do you?"

I shook my head.

He took a deep breath and began to explain. "Do you know about the mergers?"

I repeated what Megan had told me.

"Good. Here's what she left out. Up until the mergers, books were seen as an art form, or at the very least, a craft. But the MBAs the publishing consortiums brought in saw books merely as commercial products, no different than dish detergent or cars. Products that didn't sell were dropped from the production line. Authors who didn't increase their sales volume more than fifteen percent each year lost their contracts, regardless of their standing in the literary community. This happened to…." He rolled out the names of several authors I recognized.

"The good news for Patriot's Blood is that all this writing talent is still out there hunting for new publishers," Zach continued. "Megan's been pressuring me to sign some of them, especially the mystery authors. Business-wise, she's probably right. She does seem to have a good head on her shoulders where money's concerned."

I heard the hesitation in his voice. "But?"

"But that's not where my heart is. I'm more interested in literary non-fiction and non-linear transformative works."

Non-linear transformative works? "Is there money in, uh, non-linear…?"

"Who knows? Not enough material's been printed to find out. But Patriot's Blood will start publishing real literature again, not racist rants. I've never believed that the word 'patriot' should be a synonym for hate."

My sympathies were with him there, but I had a job to do, and bemoaning the current state of American publishing wasn't it. "As you said earlier, it sure sounds like you have an excellent motive for murder." I watched his face carefully.

"People have killed for less," he agreed, snapping the "Border Run" CD into its plastic case and tossing it into a waste basket. "Not that my denial will mean anything to you, but rest assured I didn't murder my grandmother. Someone else did, and I don't have the foggiest idea who, except that it wasn't Owen."

"You were on the hike, and you were sitting near Gloriana at the banquet."

"Yes to both. Before you ask, no, I didn't pick any plants. And at the banquet, everyone at my table was so deep in conversation that we didn't notice anything wrong until my grandmother collapsed."

"You didn't see anyone fooling around with Gloriana's salad?"

"How could I? I'd been next door attending a seminar on offshore printing, and by the time I made it into the banquet hall, the salads were already on the tables. Anyway, haven't you ever been to one of these things? They're zoos. People are always walking back and forth between the tables, going over to say hello to friends, keeping an eye on competitors, that sort of thing. A kangaroo wearing a tutu could have hopped by singing 'Waltzing Matilda' and I wouldn't have noticed."

It sounded reasonable, but most lies did. I switched tactics. "You don't seem too broken up over your grandmother's death."

He frowned. "Then you're not a very good observer, Ms. Jones. Despite her faults, and they were legion, I was very fond of my grandmother."

Was he referring to his red eyes? Well, Dusty had frequently sported red eyes, too, and I had just learned that they had more to do with a drinking problem than grief. No point in alienating Zach, though. "I'm sure you were. By the way, was that Gloriana's office we passed on the way in here?"

"Want access?"

"I'd appreciate it."

His frown turned to a smile. "No problem. I have nothing to hide, do I?"

I spread my hands and smiled back, but said nothing.

He chuckled. "You're a hard woman, Ms. Jones. Tell you what. I'll unlock everything for you, but then you're on your own. I've got a date with a bail bondsman. Owen's been in jail too long."

Startled, I said, "You're going to leave me alone in Gloriana's office?"

"Why not? As I told you, I have nothing to hide, other than some pretty embarrassing books and games, but since those were all Gloriana's projects, not mine...."

He let the sentence trail off as he ushered me down the hall to Gloriana's office, calling to his cousin to give me any kind of help I needed after he had left for the bail bondsman's. Most people would have interpreted such openness and cooperation as signs of innocence, but past experience had taught me better. Any sensitive information in Gloriana's office would have already been erased.

But I was wrong.

Chapter 8

Gloriana's office was the opposite of her grandson's. Large. Light-filled. Luxurious. Obsessively neat.

Sun streamed in from a pair of tall French windows, creating creamy rectangles on the hand-tied carpet covering the saltillo-tiled floor. Against gold brocaded walls, glass-fronted floor-to-ceiling mahogany bookshelves groaned with Patriot's Blood's products, almost but not quite overpowering her massive, hand-carved desk. Several leather-covered chairs anchored the rug, the largest of which sat behind the desk. I imagined Gloriana sitting in it, dreaming up new vehicles of hate. The only incongruous element in the room was the battered old Underwood typewriter that squatted in the center of the desk.

"My grandmother didn't trust computers for her own writing," Zach explained, as he unlocked the drawers to the desk, then did the same for the closed bookcases and the bank of steel file cabinets underneath a large oil painting of Gloriana herself. I'd seen posed photographs of her on the society pages of the *Scottsdale Journal,* of course, but society shots seldom reveal their subject's personality. This portrait did. The artist had portrayed her seated in her mahogany-on-mahogany office, dressed in a gray suit, holding a gold pen in her hand. In the only apparent concession to aesthetics, the bulky Underwood had been replaced by a vase of red, white, and blue peonies.

At first, the portrait seemed little different from any which could be found in a thousand boardrooms across the country.

A closer study showed that the artist had a unique talent for revealing more about his subject than his subject probably realized. He had captured arrogance in the uplifted chin, greed in the narrowed eyes, and—incongruously—a hint of sensitivity in the thin-lipped mouth. I peered at the artist's signature: Pearl Tuc Nguyen.

I turned away from the portrait and gestured toward the typewriter. "Zach, you mentioned something about your grandmother's writing. Did you mean business correspondence?"

"No, she dictated that. I'm talking about her memoir-cum-family history," he answered, unlocking the last file cabinet. "The Alden ancestry was her true obsession. To hear her talk, you'd think we Aldens rowed the Mayflower across the Atlantic all by ourselves. Her opinions should have made intriguing reading, but from the few pages she showed me, she didn't have much writing talent. It's my guess our ancestors were a lot more interesting, not to mention less saintly, than the flag-waving stereotypes she created.

"As for dramatic tension, well, even memoirs need focus and an arc of action, but she was weak there, too. If she'd been in one of my writing classes at ASU, I'd have flunked her. But that's all water under the bridge. Since she's dead, I doubt if her scribblings will ever see the light of day. They would have been nothing but a vanity project anyway, printed by her own publishing house because no one else would want to publish them. Now you'll have to excuse me." He pocketed the keys, then started for the door.

"Zach, wait!" I had to scratch an itch, whether it helped solve Gloriana's murder or not.

He turned back around, his ugly/handsome face a study in impatience. "Make it quick."

"I'm appreciative that you're giving me free rein in her office, but I've always felt that seeing where someone lives, how they live, can tell even more about them than their working environment." Certainly about the secrets they kept. "Do you think I could take a look at the Hacienda?"

He didn't say anything at first, and I feared I had lost his good will. But then he said, "Why not? I consider Owen a friend, and if it'll help him...." He picked up the phone on Gloriana's desk. After punching in a number and waiting mere seconds for an answer, he began speaking in fluent Spanish to the party on the other end of the line.

Even with my rudimentary Spanish I could follow that he was telling Gloriana's maid to let me in the house, to stay with me and make certain I removed nothing, but to give me total access.

"What time can you get up there?" he said, holding the phone away from my ear. "Rosa has tomorrow off, so if you're going, it has to be today."

I figured that it would take me a couple of hours to go through Gloriana's office, probably less at the house. Then I remembered that I had another appointment, one I didn't dare break.

I looked at my watch. "Is five o'clock too late?"

He checked with Rosa again. "Five is fine. Rosa's been with my grandmother for going on thirty years, so she can give you the grand tour and tell you anything you need to know. She liked Owen, too." Scribbling the address down, he said, "Honk three times at the gate," then turned and left me standing alone in the office.

Did he trust me that much? Or was his apparent openness a ploy to make me believe he had nothing to hide? If so, it backfired. His apparent lack of concern, an attitude I had seen in many convicted murderers, put me on my guard.

I dropped the keys into my carry-all, gave Gloriana's portrait one final look, and then proceeded to burrow my way through her papers. Most, I discovered, related strictly to the business. Invoices for printing (I'd never realized it cost so much), gargantuan shipping invoices (per cubic inch, books were apparently heavier than pianos), and all the usual odds and ends relating to any business. Electric bills, plumbing bills (three in the last year for the office toilet alone), and bills from a cleaning service.

I found her memoir filed under M, what else? A quick look at the last page—page 203, in which Gloriana reflected on the family's role in the American Revolution—warned that my original time estimate was way off. A cursory read-through of a few pages proved that Zach's literary critique had been dead-on. Gloriana's writing might have been serviceable enough for business correspondence, but even to my own unliterary ear, the style seemed weak. So weak that even the Mayflower's voyage—which I'd been taught in school had been fraught with thrills and chills—sounded dull. I decided to get back to the memoirs later so I set them aside and scanned through other material.

The R for "Rejections" file was more entertaining. A few authors had taken rejection hard, firing back letters of protest. One such letter, dated several months back, said, "Ms. Alden-Taylor, you wouldn't recognize talent if a B-52 dropped it on your head in a sack. I hope you choke, bitch. Sincerely yours, Sanford Leavitt."

I looked at the envelope stapled to the letter and saw a Hartford, Connecticut, postmark. Would a rejectee travel more than two thousand miles to bump off his rejector? Doubtful.

A few more letters from rejected authors echoed Leavitt's opinion of Gloriana, but their postmarks bore addresses also too far away to worry about, at least for now. Still, I took note of the names. Regardless of current security measures and rising fuel prices, air travel remained relatively fast and cheap. Of more interest was a series of letters written on Arizona Department of Corrections stationery which revealed an ongoing correspondence between Gloriana and Barry Fetzner, one of Patriot's Blood's authors. The first letter, dated a year earlier, expressed gushing delight that Patriot's Blood had found *A Man Stands Alone* deserving of publication.

At last a publisher of INTEGRITY, a publisher who has found the advancement of TRUTH superior to the mindless pursuit of MAMMON, wrote Fetzner, A.K.A. Inmate No. 947303-37. Fetzner (the name sounded familiar but I couldn't quite place it) continued purring with gratified ego for a month or so, then eventually began to express irritation at Gloriana's request for manuscript changes.

What I said in the third paragraph on page 42 is perfectly clear to ANYONE with even MINIMAL I.Q. But if you INSIST I will comply. After all, my warning to the AMERICAN people is more important than your CONSTANT QUIBBLING over STYLE.

Maybe Gloriana had told him to knock off the upper case.

Last month, the tone of Fetzner's correspondence changed dramatically. In a letter wild with caps and underlinings, he informed Gloriana that he had decided against publication, and demanded that she return his manuscript. Gloriana wrote back that she was holding him to the terms of the SIGNED contract (caps hers). His book was already at the binder's. Fetzner fired back another letter threatening a lawsuit.

Gloriana didn't answer, or at least I didn't find a copy of her answer. But I did find one last letter from Fetzner, postmarked the week before Gloriana's death.

I repeat, HAG, you must STOP, CEASE, DESIST publication of A MAN STANDS ALONE immediately. This is an ORDER from GOD'S AVENGER HIMSELF, and you WILL OBEY or be subject to the DIREST of CONSEQUENCES! YOU KNOW WHAT THEY ARE! What I have learned about you, MRS. LIAR, proves that you and your FELLOW TRAVELERS AT PATRIOT'S BLOOD are UNFIT to carry my HOLY MESSAGE to the FAITHFUL. You hid your true nature well, but I NOW know you are the ENEMY, you are a TRAITOR to your BLOOD, you are herewith sentenced to HELL AND DAMNATION. And you can FORGET the sequel.

"God's Avenger!" I whispered. Now I remembered. Fetzner had been sentenced to death for killing seven Hispanic prostitutes working Phoenix's red light district on Van Buren Boulevard. Or at least he'd been convicted of seven killings. We suspected Fetzner had been responsible for nineteen. He would pose as a customer and lure the working girls into his car. Then, after knocking them out with the wrench he kept on his front seat, he would drive them into the desert where he disemboweled their still-living bodies. Real Jack the Ripper stuff.

In the notes he left at the scenes—the man was proud of his work—he accused the women of breaking "GOD'S HOLY LAW" and contributing to the weakening of "GOD'S HOLY SPIRIT IN MAN."

He signed them, "GOD'S AVENGER."

I had encountered Fetzner once. Lucky Lil, as prostitute Lilly Salazar had been dubbed by the press, had been staked out in the desert a few miles east of Scottsdale and was actually watching Fetzner's knife descend when two Pima men rode their horses onto the scene and broke up the party. God's Avenger managed to run back to his car and speed away. He'd taken the trouble to rub mud onto his license plate, but both Pimas had seen his face. As, of course, had Lucky Lil. The subsequent IdentiKit rendering resembled a man who had recently spent a night in our drunk tank. My partner and I were among the hordes of uniforms dispatched to his Scottsdale apartment as backup for the detectives.

Fetzner hadn't put up a fight. He had been so certain that the legal system would reward him for ridding the world of sin that he cheerfully confessed. The surprise on his face when he was sentenced to death had been highly gratifying to the prosecutor.

Fetzner was nuts, of course, but the court ruled that since he could tell the difference between right and wrong, he was legally sane. The Arizona Supreme Court and then the Ninth Circuit Court of Appeals had both upheld his conviction. As far as I knew, he was still slated for execution within the month unless the U.S. Supreme Court found constitutional problems in his trial.

I had heard that while awaiting the needle, Fetzner had become involved with the Aryan Brotherhood, as did so much of the prison's rough trade, which might explain how his memoirs eventually wound up at Patriot's Blood. With Fetzner's hatred of women in general and of Gloriana in particular, he made a tempting suspect. Yes, it would probably be difficult to sprinkle water hemlock on someone's salad when you were locked behind several feet of reinforced concrete, steel, and razor wire, but the Aryan Brotherhood's arms were long. Easily long enough to reach all the way from Florence to the Desert Shadows resort.

As I mulled over this new element, Poor Sandra stuck her head in the office.

"I'm going to lunch, so I'd appreciate it if you would, uh...."

"Leave?" I offered.

She gave me an embarrassed smile of agreement, which turned to horror when she saw Gloriana's memoirs spread across the desk.

"Do you think you could copy all this before you go?" I asked her. "I've checked out most of the other stuff, but I wasn't able to get to these."

Poor Sandra's face crumpled, but she nodded. "I'd be happy to."

As I followed her to the copier, I wondered if being kicked down a flight of stairs also made her happy. "How long have you worked here?" I asked, merely to make conversation as she fed sheets to the machine, which began to spew smudgy-looking copies.

"Since my husband left me," Poor Sandra replied. "That's two years ago."

"Do you like your job?"

"Not much."

"Can't you get a job anywhere else?"

"Probably. But Gloriana not only gave me a decent paycheck, she let me live in the servant's quarters for about half the rent I'd have to pay elsewhere."

"That was nice of her."

"First time I've ever heard that word in connection with Gloriana." As Poor Sandra was about to continue, the copier made a rattling sound, followed by a heavy clank. Then, with an almost human grunt of spite, it shut down.

"Broke again," she moaned. "Just like the toilet. Everything in this office is falling apart. God, it's like the Hacienda. Maybe you could come back next week? We should have it fixed by then, and I'll have someone run off those copies for you."

I hated to leave the unread memoirs in the office and told her so. "Why don't you let me take them with me? My office is right down the street. I can copy them myself, then bring them back tomorrow morning good as new."

She shook her head. "Regardless of my feelings about Gloriana, this manuscript represents almost four hundred years of Alden-Taylor family history. I can't simply let it walk out the door."

Disappointed, I fished a business card out of my carry-all. "Could you give me a call as soon as the copier is fixed?"

She threw a disgusted look at the copier. "If I remember. I have so much to do. I have to get the plumber over here before we all float away, there's seven manuscripts on my desk waiting to be read, the fall catalog needs to go to the printer....Oops. Not that. Not anymore." Her smile was malicious.

"Then why don't you give me your card and I'll call you." Daily. Starting tomorrow.

"I'll try to find one." She turned on her heel and began walking down the hall. I grabbed the few pages the copier had spit out before it broke down and followed her. Back at her desk, Poor Sandra rummaged through a drawer and finally came up with a card that looked as if mice had been chewing on it.

I looked at it. SANDRA DESIREE ALDEN-TAYLOR. "You took your maiden name back when you got divorced?"

She shook her head. "I never changed it. Gloriana didn't change hers, either, when she got married. When there aren't enough boys around to carry on the family name, the husbands of Alden-Taylor women are expected to change theirs instead so that their children will be Alden-Taylors. *Tradition*, you know." Showing the first sign of spirit, she spat out the word as if it were an Anglo-Saxon expletive.

I'd heard that aristocratic English families sometimes required that men take their wives' names, but this was the first time I'd seen an American version of the custom. Not my business, but I asked, "How did your husband feel about that?"

A wry smile twisted her face, making her look even more unattractive. "Bob was fine with it as long as he believed I'd inherit."

"But Zach was the actual heir. Did you know that then?"

A dark laugh. "Of course I did. Excluding Vicky, Zach is Gloriana's only direct descendant. If I'd told Bob that, though, he never would have married me. And I was pregnant, so what was I supposed to do? Have an illegitimate Alden-Taylor? As it is, he eventually found out the truth and left. Now the laugh's on him. I do inherit something, enough to buy a house for cash. Frankly, a little independence looks good to me. Now that Zach's got a kid of his own on the way, I can foresee all kinds of problems if I stay where I'm at."

She knelt down to pat Casey, who had emerged from wherever she'd been hiding. "It's not easy being a single mother."

"I'm sure it's not."

When I got back in my Jeep I sat there for a moment, wondering how hard Poor Sandra's life really was. Would she kill to change it?

Chapter 9

I have a memory…

A memory of a soft hand against my cheek, a quiet laugh. My mother's laugh. The woman who would later shoot me.

"You see?" she says, the wind whipping her blond hair across her face. "We'll finally be free."

She is not talking to me, her eyes are on the man next to her. A tall, red-haired man.

We are standing by the door of a white bus. It is open, calling us in. The wind increases, chilling me. I begin to cry. I don't want to leave this place. It is my home.

"None of this feels right," the man says.

The woman caresses me again. "Life's too hard here. Do it for her. For me. Things will get better."

The man again, quietly. "Only because I love you."

He follows us onto the bus.

Chapter 10

It should have taken less than five minutes to get back to my office from Patriot's Blood, but throngs of tourists swarmed on foot back and forth across the streets in pursuit of postcards and bolo ties. So intent were they upon finding these treasures that they paid little attention to traffic lights. More than once as I edged the Jeep down Main Street, I almost hit some sunburned fool.

"Light, light!" I shouted to one wingtips-and-shorts-clad man who'd stopped in the middle of the street to goggle at my ride. Yes, my sandstone-colored vehicle, with its custom paint job of Pima symbols (courtesy of Jimmy's uncle) and hood-mounted steer horns, was somewhat unusual, but he could have admired it safely from the sidewalk.

"You interested in selling that thing?" Mr. Tourist asked, refusing to budge. I noticed that his big, red nose had begun to peel.

"It's not for sale," I snapped. "Now move before you get gored." I revved the Jeep's engine. He moved.

I beeped and nudged the rest of the way back to my office, and with relief parked in the side lot. I couldn't wait for summer, when most of the tourists, shocked by the city's 120-plus-degree heat, would return home. We natives didn't like summer either, but at least it thinned the herd.

Jimmy was in the process of shutting down his computer when I walked through the door.

"Good news, partner," I announced. "Zachary Alden-Taylor is on his way to bail Owen out."

Jimmy threw me a brilliant smile, his facial tattoo softening into smokey curves. "Zach called Janelle and told her. She's busy with the kids, so I volunteered to pick Owen up. The paperwork will probably take a few hours, but I don't want him to wait a second more than necessary."

I waved him goodbye as he headed out the door, then sat down at my desk and flipped through Gloriana's memoirs. Seventy-seven pages had made it through the copier before it broke. The smudgy copies promised a challenge, but plowing through them would be worthwhile if they held the answer to her murder.

I began to read.

> *How does one begin to tell the history of such an illustrious family as the Alden-Taylors? With great humility, I, Gloriana Alden-Taylor, will attempt to do so for the benefit of not only my descendants, but for the world.*

I had a bad feeling about this.

> *What magic, what divine touch of the Godhead brought the Alden-Taylors from the cold villages of England, first to the unfriendly, narrow streets of Holland, then finally to the warm, welcoming arms of Plymouth Rock?*

Rocks had arms?

> *No Mayflower family, not even the Astors, has made as many contributions to American history as the Alden-Taylors. We count among ourselves presidents, senators, governors, judges, and if I may be so bold—publishers. Yes, publishers! Those upholders of America's first and most important Freedom, the Freedom of Speech! Truly, God has infused our Alden-Taylor blood with a rare and precious gift. We are....*

I hurried through the rest of the pages and found them filled with more of the same purple-prosed swoonings. Sadly, I saw nothing that would provide clues to her murder. Except on the last toner-challenged page.

> *...but that person down in Florence, not being of Alden-Taylor blood, he is incapable of grasping the concept. How could he? Superiority is not found in the color of our skins—it is found in the DNA passed down to us from our sainted forefathers and foremothers. Oh, foolish man! But thus is it ever so for men of his ilk to believe....*

Here the copier's ink failed completely and Gloriana's stilted words faded from the page.

I stared at the manuscript. Could the passage be alluding to Barry Fetzner, aka God's Avenger? I leafed back a few pages, then a few more, and I didn't see his name anywhere. But who else could Gloriana have meant by "that person down in Florence"? Outside of a few ranches and cotton farms, Florence was best known for the Arizona State Prison complex.

Then I recalled the letters Fetzner had sent to Gloriana, their increasing ferocity. And the long reach of the Aryan Brotherhood.

After calling the State Attorney's office and securing access to Death Row, I locked up Desert Investigations and went back to the Jeep. One more appointment to keep before I headed up to Gloriana's house.

An appointment I dreaded.

Heart thumping with anxiety, I drove to the new office complex on the edge of the Salt River Pima-Maricopa Indian Reservation and parked in back where no one would see my all-too-recognizable Jeep. This created an additional problem for me, for it meant I would have to use the building's deserted rear entrance.

I did not start up the stairs until I thoroughly checked the stairwell's shadowed corners. Then, .38 in hand, I hurried to the second floor, listening carefully for footsteps other than my own. Once I arrived at my destination, I opened the door and looked into the small waiting room to make certain no one lurked within. Satisfied, I put my .38 back into my carry-all and headed for a chair. Before I could sit down, the door to the inner office opened and Dr. Dolores Gomez smiled her practiced smile at me.

"Hello, Lena. How have you been?"

"Fine." Never tell a psychologist the truth.

Gomez' smile never wavered as she ushered me into her large corner office. When I had settled on the leather couch (sitting upright, of course, I was damned if I would lie down), she started in on me.

"This is what, Lena, our fourth session together?"

I didn't answer. We both knew which session it was.

Gomez pretended not to notice my silence. "Right. Our fourth session. Our fourth *court-ordered* session. And we're making absolutely no progress, are we?"

My turn to smile. "No, we're not." Only six more sessions to go. I could do that standing on my head. I looked out the window. The view revealed the graceful palms of Scottsdale to the west, the barren flats of the Rez to the northeast. Overhead, hawks rode the thermals, while a V-shaped formation of Scottsdale geese flapped their way from one manmade lake to another. How I wished I flew with them.

"Defendant admits to spontaneous bursts of anger that sometimes result in physical violence." As Gomez always did at the beginning of a session, she flipped through the court documents, stopping every now and then to read aloud.

And as I always did, I laughed out loud at this legalese version of my righteous actions. "Spontaneous! Oh, come on, Gomez. When I saw the creep beating that child, I did what any decent human being would do. I stopped it."

"You are saying that any decent human being would knock the woman down?"

This was such a waste of time. "I didn't really hurt her. If I had, I'd be in jail with my PI license under review, wouldn't I? Not sitting here talking to you."

"You bloodied the woman's nose, Lena."

"But I didn't break it. Besides, she asked for it."

Gomez sighed. "When the police arrived, you were sitting on her chest, threatening to....Let's see." She looked down at the court papers again. "Threatening to, it says here, 'Rip off your head, bitch, and shit on the stump.'"

I shifted in my seat. The sofa seemed lumpier than usual. "Something to that effect."

A month earlier, I'd been shopping for ramen noodles at my neighborhood Safeway. On my way back to the Jeep, I saw a woman built like a Sumo wrestler standing beside an elephant-sized SUV, pounding away with closed fists on a sobbing child. As I explained to the judge, I'd simply brought an end to it. Why the judge saw fit to sentence me to a series of anger management sessions remained a mystery. After all, I wasn't the problem; the child-beater was.

"Lena, just before you arrived, I read the witnesses' account again and noticed something interesting. The victim of the initial assault was a little girl four years of age."

I shifted around again but couldn't seem to get comfortable. In my opinion, leather is much too hot a fabric for the desert. Backsides tend to stick to it. "So?"

"Weren't you four years old when you were, ah, found unconscious by the side of the road?"

"Hardly a news bulletin, Gomez. The story made all the papers at the time, and every now and then, some sensation-mongering reporter resurrects it."

"That's right. Someone shot you."

"Call it like it was, doc. My mother shot me."

I saw my mother's face every night in my nightmares. It was the same face that stared from the mirror at me every morning. You would think that a woman who looked so much like her daughter would cherish her child, not shoot her.

"When you regained consciousness, you couldn't remember your name or who your parents were, and they never stepped forward. You were raised in foster homes."

I yawned. "You're sharp, Gomez, no doubt about it."

She stretched a brown hand toward me. "Tell me why you were never adopted, Lena. Blond-haired, green-eyed Caucasian children are always at a premium in America."

I looked out the window again. Something big was gaining on the geese. An eagle? They drifted down from the mountains every now and then, when pickings were lean. But when I squinted, Big Bird revealed itself to be a blue heron. He caught up to the geese and stationed himself near the rear of the formation. I chuckled. Herons in the desert. What next? Two-headed dragons?

"Lena, you didn't answer me. Why weren't you adopted?"

"Maybe because little girls with behavior problems aren't at a premium anywhere, regardless of their coloring."

Her voice softened, which I had learned to recognize as a danger signal. "What kind of behavior problems are we talking about, Lena?"

The flock turned sharply west, the heron still bringing up the rear. They were headed for the manmade lake at Eldorado Park. Good fishing there, I've heard. At least for birds.

"Lena?"

Gomez really should replace the sofa. It wasn't fit for the Salvation Army, let alone a shrink's office.

"Lena?"

Exasperated, I finally gave her what she wanted. Nothing else. The rest was my business, not hers. "I kept getting in fights, that's why. And stealing. Now are you satisfied?"

She frowned. "Didn't you receive therapy as a child?"

"In Arizona? You must be kidding. The state legislature slashed funding for children's mental health services years ago, so therapy wasn't an option." I took a deep breath. "Not that I needed it."

"I'm familiar with the state's budgetary problems," she said, as she continued flipping through the court papers. "So. Unable to find permanent placement with an adoptive family, you were warehoused in the state's foster care system. Hmm. Am I right in surmising that some of those foster homes were less than satisfactory?"

The monster in the closet. I shut that particular nightmare out. "Give or take a few beatings, they weren't so bad."

With a "gotcha" smile, she leaned toward me. "After all you've been through, Lena, you must be very angry with your mother for not only shooting you, but leaving you to be raised by...." She stopped, obviously searching for the right words. "Ah, raised by *uncaring* people."

Uncaring? I stood up and walked to the window, still wishing I could follow the heron. "Gomez, your insight amazes me."

She didn't answer right away, and when I looked back, I saw her staring at me with no visible emotion other than narrowed ebony eyes. After a few moments of mutual silence, she spoke again.

"You realize, Lena, that you can't go on like this. Creeping into rooms as if something horrible were waiting for you...."

I hadn't realized she'd noticed. "Don't be silly."

Gomez ignored me. "...taking the law into your own hands whenever you see a child being threatened...."

I returned to my seat on the lumpy sofa. "Look, Gomez, the child wasn't being threatened, she was being beaten. There's a difference. And what's with this *whenever* business? I've only done it a couple of times before." That I could remember, anyway.

She nodded. "Perhaps you could get these outbursts of violence under control if you quit running away from your fears and began to face them."

What an idiot. "Run away from my fears? If anyone is crazy in here, Gomez, it's you. I've never run away from anything in my life."

As a cop, I had been shot, stabbed, beaten, and even spit upon by HIV-positive perps. As a private detective, I have faced down murderers in both city and wilderness, yet I had never once backed down. So where was the running away?

"I never said you were crazy, Lena."

I was shaking now, but not with rage. Gomez' precious hide was safe from me. "You implied it."

"No, I didn't. All I did was point out the obvious fact that it's time you quit running away from your memories. You need to heal your broken life."

After I could speak again, I said, "You sound like some cheap pop psychology book. I thought shrinks were supposed to sit there and take notes, not give advice."

She smiled faintly. "I'm a cognitive therapist, not a Freudian. But I'd be glad to jot down a few notes if that would make you feel more comfortable."

I glared at her.

When the session ended thirty minutes later, I was still glaring.

Chapter 11

Leaving Gomez and her prying behind me, I steered the Jeep toward Gloriana's Paradise Valley estate.

Most out-of-staters don't realize it, but for all Scottsdale's tony reputation, the real high-rollers live in PV, the hilly little burg which separates Scottsdale from Phoenix. There are probably more millionaires living in the shadow of Mummy Mountain than rats in Manhattan. Not that I'm drawing any comparisons.

I turned east off Tatum Boulevard, PV's main drag, onto Hogan Drive, then wound my way through a frou-frou series of imitation Territorials and Frank Lloyd Wright rip-offs until the street forked at Warpaint and Teepee. I followed Teepee halfway around the mountain until I ran out of asphalt. Glad of the Jeep's four-wheel drive, I crawled forward on gravel along the top of a steep-sided canyon teeming with chirping, hissing wildlife until I came to a massive iron gate. Behind it rose a Spanish hacienda that took my breath away.

Built of true stucco, rock, and wood—much of it in disrepair—the Hacienda appeared to be centuries old. Knowing the history of the area as I did, I guessed it had been built in the early 1900s as some business magnate's desert retreat. Gloriana's grandfather?

Although the Hacienda was partially hidden by lacy jacaranda trees and purple bougainvillea, not to mention the six-foot-high adobe wall that fronted the three-acre estate, the rambling wreck was gorgeous. Tall arched windows welcomed the light, while the balcony that wrapped all the way around the house offered spectacular views of Mummy Canyon. Through the gate, I spied a burbling fountain, its surround studded with handpainted ceramic tiles.

"Must be nice," I muttered. Then I remembered that its owner had died a hideous death. No, not so nice after all.

I honked three times.

The gate rolled slowly back, and I pulled forward, circling around the saltillo courtyard and onto a fine gravel parking area in front of what appeared to be stables. But I could smell no horses. Then I remembered that they'd been altered to provide servants' quarters, and that Poor Sandra and her children now lived there.

As the Jeep clanked to a stop, a middle-aged Hispanic woman dressed in black opened the Hacienda's massive double doors and motioned me inside.

"Good lord," I exclaimed, gawking at the house's interior.

The woman ignored my shock. "I am Rosa. Little Mr. Zach, he said to show the pretty blond lady everything she wants." Her stiff face displaying no emotion, she led me along the two-story-high foyer, but not before I took a moment to study the exquisite stained-glass skylight that cast jewel-colored light onto the tiled floor.

"It is pretty, yes?"

I nodded, holding out my arms so that reds and blues danced along the tanned skin. "Not pretty. Beautiful."

Rosa's face relaxed into a smile. My admiration of the house had won her approval. "Miss Gloriana, she drew the picture for that skylight, then my father built it."

That such delicate beauty could emerge from Gloriana Alden-Taylor's hands surprised me. But I was here to learn more about her, wasn't I?

"I take you through the first floor now," Rosa said, leading me past a double staircase that swooped gracefully up to a gallery lined with oil paintings. More portraits. I recognized the twelfth President of the United States, Zachary Taylor, but the other faces, many of them in military uniforms, one Confederate, escaped me. The man next to Old Rough and Ready, though, looked enough like him to be his son.

Rosa followed my stare. "Miss Gloriana's grandfather. He built the Hacienda when he come here from Louisiana. He was rich, but not so much as his father or his father's father, the President. After the war, the family did not do so well."

"Which war?"

"The one between the states."

I wondered what it must have been like, growing up in the shadow of those fierce-visaged men, having them stare disapprovingly down from the wall at you, as if assessing your life and finding it wanting.

Lucky orphans, who had no one to live up to.

Lucky me?

A child's voice broke through my thoughts. "Rosa, we've finished our homework. Can we play now?"

A somber blond girl of around eight stood in the doorway, holding a younger boy's hand. Although there appeared to be at least two years between them, with their Nordic features, they looked enough alike to be twins.

Poor Sandra's children.

"Yes, you may go to the playroom, but you must stay in there until your mother comes home," Rosa said, her voice tender. "I will bring you some pop later."

The little girl led her brother away, still holding his hand.

"Caroline and John," Rosa explained. "They miss their great-grandmother."

I wondered if little John was called John-John. Curious, I asked, "Was Gloriana close to the children?" It was hard to envision that stiff-spined martinet unbending for anyone, even a child.

"I believe that Miss Gloriana loves...loved children," Rosa answered. "But she was not a demonstrative woman. She showed her love by giving them a beautiful home."

Gloriana had certainly done that. While I had seen my share of gorgeous houses before, none came close to touching the perfect lines of the Hacienda. But as Rosa led me through the house's main floor, I began to see the skull beneath the skin. The place was falling down, the plastered walls crumbling, the wooden window lintels shot through with dry rot. The saltillo tile flooring cracked in a thousand places, and the ancient carpets were dangerously thin. Most of the furniture looked ready for the dump.

As we exited one particularly decrepit room—the library, with its myriad shelves of spine-split volumes—Rosa said, "Miss Gloriana, she put everything she had into the Hacienda. It is not so bad as it was."

This was the *after* of the before?

The maid pointed toward the vaulted ceiling, with its massive dark beams. "Those are new. They are not for decoration, they hold up the roof. The old beams, they were no good, so Miss Gloriana had them replaced. You would not believe how much it cost."

"So she was renovating."

She nodded. "Oh, yes, always. Because of the cost, Mr. Michael, Miss Gloriana's husband, he did not like living here. He resented the money she spent on the Hacienda, and I heard him say many times that for what she spent, they could own three new houses. I think he was right, but Miss Gloriana did not want three new houses, she wanted only her Hacienda."

Scarlet O'Hara and her Tara, I thought, trying to picture old Gloriana dithering in crinolines. Nope. Didn't work. Gloriana had probably never dithered in her life.

Rosa continued. "When Mr. Michael died, Miss Gloriana continued to fix up. When her business began to make money, she fixed up even more." Here, she motioned to the beams. "A place like this, you must always be fixing. Old houses, they are like people. They get sick."

And go on life support.

I wondered briefly about Mr. Michael's death, but pushed the thought aside. From what I'd heard, he had keeled over in public at the Phoenix Open. Little chance for murder there. Then I remembered how Gloriana herself had died. In public. By poison. What goes around comes around?

With uncanny perception, Rosa said, "Miss Gloriana loved Mr. Michael. She would not harm him, not even for her Hacienda. When he died, she did not speak for days. But it was even worse when Big Mr. Zach was killed."

"Big Mr. Zach?"

"Little Mr. Zach's father. He died with his wife in a terrible wreck, right down the road from here. A tire blew, and their car rolled into the canyon and burned. The doors, they were smashed in and Big Mr. Zach and Mrs. Zach, the poor things, they could not get out. We heard the noise and we ran to them, but…." She shrugged her shoulders. "Miss Gloriana grieved so hard I thought she would die, too. She walk around like a zombie for months, not caring about nothing."

I remembered Gloriana's stern face. A buttress against pain?

Rosa continued. "When she start that magazine, I was so glad. It gave her something to think about, something else to love. Then it went wrong, like so much of what she do. But she could not see because she in the grip of the Fever."

"The Fever?"

"That is what I called it, the Fever. It is when Miss Gloriana begin to do things that start off good, but keeps doing and doing until they turn bad. When Miss Gloriana in the grip of the Fever, she doesn't notice nothing. She was like that with this house, always the Fever for her Hacienda."

Fever was as good a word to describe obsessive-compulsive behavior as any other I'd heard.

"I'd like to see the storeroom where Owen slept, if I may."

Rosa waved a hand. "Little Mr. Zach said show you whatever you want."

Little Mr. Zach. I smiled, wondering if she called him that to his face, then decided that she probably did. Old habits die hard.

The storeroom was just that. A room to store things, mainly broken lamps, odd pieces of china, and boxes. A cot had been shoved into one corner, a set of barbells in the other, which might explain Owen's buff bod. Considering his complaints about overwork, I thought it odd that Gloriana would allow him the opportunity to work out.

I poked around in the room for a few minutes, finding nothing more of interest, then had Rosa lead me to the second floor.

The upstairs rooms proved in little better shape than those on the first. Stucco crumbled, windows rotted, carpets frayed. Several of the bedrooms had been turned into display rooms for Gloriana's various collections of Revolutionary pewter, film noir posters, miniature tea sets, and Route 66 memorabilia. One room, not yet filled, held sketches and paintings of Thomas Jefferson and his home at Monticello, as well as several objects I couldn't put a name to. I did admire, though, the large soup tureen which stood in lonely glory on a gilt-edged table.

Farther down the hall were two more rooms housing an extraordinary collection of Barbie dolls, most of them still in their shiny cardboard and cellophane boxes. What a pack rat. Everything from the sublime to the absurd.

Turning away from the dolls, I said to Rosa, "Had she always collected like this?"

"Not so much before Mr. Michael died. This Fever came after."

A reaction to grief, then. Apparently even monsters could feel sadness. "I'm ready to see Gloriana's personal rooms now." The lair of the dragon was preferable to this.

Gloriana's bedroom would have suited Queen Elizabeth, if the Queen had been down on her luck. The canopied poster bed in the middle of the huge room looked like it was about to collapse, and a tall oak wardrobe canted sharply to one side.

But the view was a killer. Standing at one of the three matching floor-to-ceiling windows, I could see acacia, creosote, and saguaro rolling all the way to the sage-stippled rise of Mummy Mountain. A veritable Eden. Gloriana must have enjoyed the view, too, because to the side of one of the windows stood a tripod with a Pentax Spotmatic fitted with a long lens perched atop it. As I looked around the bedroom, though, I saw only one photograph, that of a handsome, silver-haired man with lines of humor bracketing his mouth. The picture stood on the nightstand in an antique silver frame, angled so that anyone lying in the bed could see it.

"Mr. Michael," Rosa said. "She never forget him."

Studying the photograph more closely, though, I thought I saw a trace of cruelty in the man's eyes. What had been the true relationship between Gloriana and her husband? But since he was long dead, it hardly mattered.

I turned back to the window. Directly below, someone had been in the process of constructing a patio, the centerpiece of which was a conical adobe fireplace. It seemed odd to me that Gloriana would begin a new project when there was so much work to be done to keep the old house from collapsing around her ears.

I pointed to the camera. "Was Gloriana into photography?"

Rosa didn't answer right away, choosing instead to smooth the ancient velvet spread on the canopy bed. But the spread couldn't possibly have been made any smoother, not even if she whipped out a steam iron. Obviously, my question made her uncomfortable.

"Tell me about the camera, Rosa."

She straightened up and gave me a nervous smile. "Miss Gloriana used it to take pictures."

Well, duh. "Pictures of what?"

"Things."

"Such as?"

"Deer. Coyotes. You know, animals. They come out of the canyon, right up to the house." She began smoothing the bedspread again.

Then where were the photographs? I hated to bully the woman, but I needed to find out what she was hiding. "Don't you remember what Mr. Zach said, Rosa? Show me Miss Gloriana's photography. All of it."

The hands smoothing the bedspread began to tremble. "Little Mr. Zach, he don't know about this. If he did, he not let you look."

What was the problem? A collection of photographs so poorly done that they made Rosa cringe in embarrassment for her employer? I left the window and strode toward the double doors on the other side of the room. I had taken it for granted they led to a master sitting room, but perhaps I'd been wrong.

Rosa followed closely behind. "Miss Gloriana no let me clean in there, she do it herself. She say it her private place!" She sounded breathless, frightened.

"Calm down, Rosa. I won't damage anything."

I opened the well-oiled doors to find not a sitting room, but a photography studio mounted with surprisingly expert black-and-white prints. No embarrassment for Rosa here. On one wall were landscapes: large, sun-splashed images of giant saguaros, roiling storms above the Grand Canyon, eagles caught in mid-flight.

The prints on the facing wall at first didn't appear to have any theme at all, until I remembered Gloriana's interest in genealogy: a large stone with the numbers 1620 carved into it—Plymouth Rock, probably; the houses and outbuildings of Monticello; and a host of graves, graves, and more graves, most of them situated in cemeteries framed by huge oaks dripping with Spanish moss.

"Did she travel to all these places just to take pictures of the graveyards of her ancestors?"

"Yes," Rosa replied. "When Miss Gloriana have the Fever, she do anything."

Yet another wall had been devoted to portraits, most of them posed by the tall window I recognized from downstairs: more photographs of Gloriana's husband; one of a furious-looking teenage girl in a headband and tie-dyed shirt; several of a handsome young couple dappled in morning light; then one of a little boy with haunted eyes wearing a funereal black suit. Zach.

"That her family," Rosa said. "She take the pictures herself. So. You seen it all. We go back downstairs now." She walked hopefully toward the double doors, motioning for me to follow.

"Wait." I wasn't through looking. The photographs that interested me most were the three self-portraits on the family wall. One showed Gloriana as a young woman, smiling into a mirror, pointing a camera. Pale eyes, pale hair, the glacial beauty of a young Grace Kelly. Then, Gloriana at around forty, smiling into a different mirror, holding a different camera. Fine lines outlined her eyes and mouth, but her beauty remained essentially intact. The last picture, unflatteringly lit, showed Gloriana as an aged ruin. She no longer smiled into the mirror. Instead, her expression was empty of any emotion at all. The desert had done its work on her face, sucking the moisture out of her skin, turning it into crackled parchment.

I had to marvel at Gloriana's blunt honesty. It had taken courage to turn such an unforgiving lens on herself, to accept and document the ever-deepening lines and sagging flesh. Had her husband shared her courage? But he had died before his own beautiful face had begun to disintegrate.

"I said we go back downstairs now," Rosa called from the doorway.

"Not yet," I told her. I'd once taken a photography class at ASU, only to find that I had neither the talent nor the dedication for the craft, but my studies had given me the knowledge to understand what this room told me. The photography equipment in the studio was anachronistic. A large collection of cameras sat in glass-fronted cabinets: a couple of Leicas, a Rolleiflex, a Kodak Retina, some Nikons, and several brands I had not run across. Probably more than a hundred cameras in all, but not one digital unit among the lot.

"Is that the darkroom?" I pointed to a closed door on the far side of the room.

Rosa glared at me from the doorway. "What you mean, darkroom?"

I waved my hand at the cameras. "Gloriana was a wet room photographer, and I'm betting she developed her own prints."

"It nothing but trays and machines and chemicals in that place. Smells real bad."

I bet it did. "Show me."

With a disapproving grumble, Rosa came back into the studio, fished a key out of her pocket, and unlocked the door.

"You should be ashamed," she said over my shoulder as I shoved my way past her. "Nosing into Miss Gloriana's private life."

I had worse things to be ashamed of, so I didn't apologize. Besides, after I'd pushed my way into the matt black room, past the long table crowned by a Litz enlarger, I was struck dumb by the dozens and dozens of prints clipped to several clotheslines to dry. Prints that explained the tripod at her bedroom window.

Photograph after photograph of Owen.

Owen picking up litter, his long dark hair shading his face. Owen, stripped to the waist, skin gleaming with sweat as he hoed weeds. Owen troweling cement onto the new patio outside. Owen hauling tiles in a wheelbarrow, bulked-up muscles stretching his skin taut. Owen sitting on a boulder in the back of the house, staring up at the face of Mummy Mountain. Owen urinating into the canyon, a pale tip of penis protruding from his dark jeans.

Owen. Gloriana's latest Fever.

Chapter 12

More interviews at Desert Shadows Resort turned up no new information, so I shed no tears when Captain Kryzinski finally let the SOBOP attendees return home.

My investigation proceeded anyway.

Two days after the last Californian climbed aboard Southwest Airlines, I headed for the Arizona State Prison complex in Florence. There are two ways to get there from Scottsdale, the quick way and the scenic way. Since the wildflowers were in bloom and the morning air so crisp you could almost touch it, I opted for the scenic route. Highway 60 to Florence Junction, then south on 79 to the old town itself.

Out-of-staters who visit Arizona in spring usually go away believing it to be Paradise. On 60 alone, they view purple mountains' majesty along with a riot of primary color, courtesy of the three-foot stalks of crimson monkey flower erupting from a carpet of yellow bottle primrose. These were accented by orange desert mariposa and the purple redmaids creeping near the tall green saguaros. Myself, I was partial to the more subtle oxeye daisy, with its creamy center peeping out from its surrounding white petals. A common flower, but unlike Gloriana, I was a common gal, and proud of it.

Then why my fixation on the past? Easy. Denials to Dr. Gomez notwithstanding, most past-obliterated adoptees and orphans want to know more about themselves. Even if you discovered you sprang from a long line of horse thieves, drunkards, and whores, you'd at least have the certainty of knowing the worst.

Knowledge is freedom.

Look at the Alden-Taylors. They obviously knew everything they needed to know about themselves. And it showed. When I had talked to Zach, he had exuded that casual self-confidence knowledge always brings. He knew where he'd come from, and didn't doubt where he was going.

However, self-confidence isn't everything, is it? The photographs in Gloriana's darkroom proved that even knowing your ancestors' names couldn't keep you from making a mess of your life. Neither could extraordinary beauty. Beauty fades, and always betrays you in the end. But does desire?

At the end of her life, as the final remnants of her beauty fell away, Gloriana desired Owen, a married man who probably saw her only as his employer, not as a woman with soft, giving flesh. What shared emotion could ever pass between them, what meaningful conversation? Her words to him could have been little more than—Owen, move that rock; Owen, fix that fence; Owen, build the patio....

So I can take pictures of your naked back.

I wondered if Owen had known the depths of Gloriana's obsession.

And if so, had he done anything about it?

After little more than an hour's drive, the cotton farms on the outskirts of Florence began sprinkling the landscape, and soon after that, I approached the town itself. Looming above it were the heart-numbing towers of Arizona State Prison. I could almost sense the hate and despair seeping through the reinforced concrete walls. It did no good to remember that some inmates were here because of me.

I parked in the visitor's lot and began the long clearance process to the sub-complex known as Death Row. My calls to my friends in the State Attorney's office had gained me access, but it still took more than an hour—and one uncomfortable, too-intimate pat-down—before I was allowed to clear the holding area and enter the Death Row visitor's room.

Barry Fetzner looked nothing like I remembered. When I had worked his arrest, he had been clean-cut enough to pass for normal, but those days had vanished. The sides of Fetzner's shaved head revealed a wealth of new tattoos. Intertwined snakes wrapped around his skull from ear to ear, and a blood-colored swastika the size of a saucer blanketed his bare dome. Running up his thick neck were the double lightning bolts I'd seen on the goons up at WestWorld and in Cave Creek. His new look left no doubt that Fetzner was a full member of the Aryan Brotherhood.

His sleeved-out arms were variations on the same theme. Tattooed all the way down to his wrists, the illustrations included more snakes, several naked women, Germanic-looking eagles, and a horrifyingly accurate lynching scene. I had to look back up at Fetzner's nightmare face simply to gain relief. But his eyes hadn't changed. Jittery, never resting for long on any person or object, always skittering around the room as if on alert for some unseen enemy.

Not too different from my own eyes, actually.

"It's been a long time, Officer Jones," God's Avenger said with a broad smile.

I smiled back. "I left the force some time ago, Mr. Fetzner. I'm on my own now."

"So I hear." Still the smile. "You must still have friends in the D.A.'s office, or you wouldn't be here. They screen my visitors pretty good these days."

All the smiles were beginning to creep me out, so I erased mine. "I've kept my contacts up. I came down because I was hoping you can help me. I'm working a case...."

"Why should I help you?"

I gave him the only answer that would stand the remotest chance with this mad creature. "Just for the hell of it."

His white-toothed maw opened and I heard a sound like two garbage trucks colliding. Fetzner was laughing. "Oh, I like you, I do, Officer Jones!" His laugh was so flagrant with madness that I marveled he had been judged sane enough to stand trial.

His laughter stopped so suddenly that I had to catch my breath. But his smile remained. "Yes," he said. "I'll help you. Just for the hell of it. After all, Hell and I are intimate friends, aren't we?"

Fetzner leaned across the table, and I had to force myself not to lean away from him.

"What do you want to know, Officer Jones?"

There was no point beating around the bush. "Why did you write Gloriana Alden-Taylor and tell her to cancel publication of your book?"

Fetzner didn't reply right away. He kept staring at me with that horrible smile. Then, in an almost-whisper, he said, "Even serial killers have a code of ethics." The garbage truck laugh again. "I discovered that Gloriana Whore Alden-Taylor was not a Believer."

"Not a believer? What do you mean?"

He looked at the ceiling and for the first time I noticed the tattoo under his chin: a cockroach crawling out of a bleeding wound. "You heard what I said. Gloriana Whore Alden-Taylor was not a Believer. Gloriana Whore Alden-Taylor was not a soldier in the Army of Righteousness."

I knew better than to laugh. "I grant you that Gloriana didn't wear fatigues and combat boots, but judging from Patriot's Blood's publications, I think you could at least call her a camp follower."

"A witty but unperceptive comment, Officer Jones. You are so wrong. Gloriana Whore Alden-Taylor did not believe in the superiority of the true Aryan. Like a true agent of Satan, her belief was in the almighty dollar."

"I don't think…." I stopped, noticing for the first time how pointed his white teeth were. Somehow I kept from visibly shuddering.

"No, you don't think," he continued. "But I do. Because I have so much time to think, I finally figured out the truth. That Gloriana Whore Alden-Taylor would publish any lie as long as it made money for her."

I remembered Patriot's Blood's book titles, the games, the CDs. "I'm not sure you're right there, Mr. Fetzner. Her publications all seem to have a certain, ah, slant."

"American stain, American pain!" he howled. He slapped his manacled hand on the table. The two corrections officers guarding him moved forward a few inches.

With an effort, I kept my voice steady. "I don't understand. What pain? Yours?"

His voice returned to normal. "It's a book title, you idiot."

"I still don't understand."

"Then let me make it easy for you, Officer Idiot Jones. *American Stain, American Pain.* I saw it in the Patriot's Blood summer catalog they mailed me, the same catalog my book is in. To think that my book, which is so filled with light and truth, will share the same bookshelves as that...as that...." Even Fetzner's evil mouth couldn't complete the sentence.

If Zach was to be believed, Fetzner's book would never make it to market. But I wasn't about to let him know that.

"Why does that bother you, Mr. Fetzner?"

He made a sound of disgust. "Have you never seen a publisher's catalog, Officer Jones?"

I shook my head. "I picked up a brochure at WestWorld which listed some of Patriot's Blood's past titles."

"Ah, the past." He closed his eyes for a second, and somehow I knew that he was remembering the scent of blood, the feel of knife against flesh. I tried not to shiver.

Fun time finished, he opened his eyes again. "Then let me enlighten you, Officer Idiot Jones. The Patriot's Blood summer catalog carries pictures of the books, pictures of the authors." He paused for a moment, and smiled at some memory. "To do my part, I sent Gloriana Whore Alden-Taylor several pictures with close-ups of my body art. But that was before I decided not to let her publish *A Man Stands Alone.* Or its sequel."

"I'm still not clear on that, Mr. Fetzner. Help me out here."

Garbage truck noises again. "You cunts are all so stupid."

"Mr. Fetzner, I'm warning you." A corrections officer.

Fetzner flicked his eyes toward him. "I'm finished with this non-believer. Take me back to my cell."

I rose from my chair. "Wait...."

But the corrections officers were already hustling Fetzner out the door. As they headed down the hallway, Fetzner called over his shoulder, "Look at the pictures, Officer Idiot Jones. Remove the blinders from thine eyes."

Then he raised his fist and shouted, "RaHoWa!"

Racial holy war.

Chapter 13

I took the fast route back to Scottsdale and instead of going straight to my office, headed for Patriot's Blood. My timing couldn't have been better. I arrived just as Zach Alden-Taylor, both hands clutching several bags from Baja Fresh, was struggling with the front door.

"Let me help you with that," I said, pulling the door open for him.

He gave me a grateful smile and didn't protest when I followed him from room to room as he portioned out tacos and fajitas to a surprisingly full office. He'd even brought a taco for Casey, who snapped it up with an ecstatic moan and disappeared under a desk.

"I called in all of our free-lance editors to tell them about Patriot's Blood's new direction," he explained, handing over a sack to Poor Sandra, who looked even more disheveled than she had yesterday. "Most are pretty happy about it, and some have even put forth a few authors' names. I'm thinking about adding a few poets."

Poor Sandra managed a smile, revealing lipstick smears on her teeth. She looked at Zach adoringly and said, "Poets are too often relegated to small presses, but with Patriot's Blood's current clout, we can get them into the public eye." The other editors nodded enthusiastically.

As happy as I felt about the change in editorial direction from hate to flowers, or whatever poets were writing about these days,

I hadn't come here for a literature lesson. "Has the copier been fixed yet?" I asked Poor Sandra.

Her smile disappeared. "The repairman said maybe tomorrow, that we're getting near the top of the list. I'll call you when it's fixed."

And the check's in the mail. "I'd appreciate that."

Out of the corner of my eye, I saw Zach heading back down the hall to his office, so I left Poor Sandra to her fajita and hurried after him. He didn't appear to mind as I followed him into his tiny office and collapsed into the ripped Naugahyde chair across from his desk. It took me a moment to realize that I had been able to sit down without removing piles of manuscripts. Then I noticed the cartons stacked against the walls.

"Moving?" I said, waving at the boxes.

"Yep. Into Gloriana's office, one carton at a time." He held a paper-wrapped taco toward me. "Want one? I've enough to share."

Not really. After giving the others to his staff, he only had four left, and he was a big man. "I'm not hungry. But you go ahead and eat."

"You sure?"

I could hear his stomach growl. I hoped mine wouldn't attempt a duet. "I'm sure."

He took a big bite of a taco, and a stream of salsa spilled out onto the manuscript he'd obviously been reading. He didn't bother to wipe it away. "I wanted to move everything all at once, but it's not working out that way. There's too much to do. The coroner will be releasing my grandmother's body in a couple of days, so I have to get the funeral on track. And informing her pet authors that we're changing editorial direction has been a nightmare. They're not taking it well."

I briefly wondered how many other publishers in the United States would take a nibble at their manuscripts. None, I hoped.

"Listen, Zach, I just had an interesting experience with one of your authors." I filled him in on my visit to the Arizona State Prison.

"The really weird thing is that we have more pre-orders for Fetzner's anti-female screed than any other book in the catalog," he said, when I had finished. "Frankly, that scares me to death. But I can tell you why Fetzner was disillusioned with Gloriana. No, on second thought, let me show you."

He put his taco down on the manuscript and scrabbled around in one of the cartons. When he didn't find what he wanted, he stuck his head out of the office door and yelled, "Sandra, could you bring Ms. Jones a copy of the summer catalog?"

In a minute, Poor Sandra, a trace of red sauce hovering around her mouth, thrust a catalog into my hands.

"Anything else?" she asked Zach.

"Enjoy your lunch."

"Sure." With a bleak smile, she returned to the reception area, trailing a scent of garlic and cheese.

"Page eighteen," Zach told me between bites of his taco.

When I turned to the page, I understood why God's Avenger wanted to change publishers. *American Stain, American Pain* was a scholarly treatise on slavery, and the caption under the author's photo explained why he was uniquely qualified to write it. George Willard Harris, Ph.D., professor emeritus of the Black Studies Department at Alabama State University, was the African-American descendant of two Alabama slaves. The short bio beside his picture said that he now owned the plantation where his great-great-great-grandparents had lived in bondage. He was in the process of turning the former slave quarters into a slavery museum.

I looked up from the catalog at Zach, who was now blotting his mouth with a page from the manuscript. "I don't understand. Given her usual material, why would Gloriana publish a book like this?"

"Why not? She had a talent for picking books that sell, and this one certainly will. Dr. Harris' work is not only scholarly, it's actually readable, which is more than you can say for most Ph.D.s. In fact, he is one of the only Patriot's Blood authors I plan to retain. I still want to continue with a certain amount of Americana."

"But, Gloriana....He...he's *African-American!"*

Zach seemed amused. "Your point being?"

"My point being the obvious. Why would a woman with Gloriana's views on race publish the work of a black man, however scholarly? And why would a black man pick her as his publisher?"

"You're making the same mistake everyone does about my grandmother. You've seen our titles and have jumped to the conclusion that Gloriana was a racist. And that would be incorrect. Color was irrelevant to her. She chose her authors according to how much money she estimated they could add to the coffers. And that was strictly so she could pump money into that decrepit Hacienda."

Maybe Zach was right, but Gloriana had taken the racism of others and funneled it into her cynical business. Which was worse? Honest hatred? Or cold greed?

Zach threw the remnants of his lunch into a waste basket, along with a soiled page from the manuscript. Then, evidently realizing what he'd done, he pulled the page back out and attempted to wipe it down. The salsa stains remained.

Poor author.

Oblivious, he continued. "As for Dr. Harris, I've talked to him. He knew his writing style wasn't convoluted enough for the standard university press, so he tried the big publishers in New York. He was offered a contract at one house, but the deal fell through during a merger. His book went homeless.

"Then his agent brought it to Gloriana, and she called him up and made him an offer he couldn't refuse. Look, Dr. Harris is a man of the world. He told her he figured publication with Patriot's Blood was better than no publication at all, and at least the work would get read, which was all he really wanted."

I don't know which shocked me the most: Gloriana turning out to be a mere money-grubber, or a black scholar allowing his work to be included in Patriot's Blood's catalog. I said as much to Zach.

He spread his salsa-stained hands. "Ah, well. Publishing makes for strange bedfellows. Another point in Dr. Harris' favor came when she discovered that his family had entered the country not long after the Plymouth Brethren—albeit in very different transport. They got here so early that she considered them also to be Founding Fathers, although lamentably unrecognized. Remember, it was *heritage* Gloriana cared about, not race. You wouldn't believe the number of lectures on genealogy I had to endure as a child. My poor father probably went through the same thing, too, which helps explain why he married my mother. It was an act of rebellion."

I raised my eyebrows. "Because…."

"Mom's grandparents immigrated from Lithuania right after the second world war. Just a bunch of Johnny-Come-Latelys, Gloriana called them."

Johnny-Come-Latelys. I wondered if that was what my parents were, too. "If she disapproved of your mother, why didn't she stop the marriage?"

He chuckled. "Dad was as headstrong as she was, that's why. Oh, she tried. She threatened to disinherit him, the whole works. But in the end he always did exactly what he wanted. That's what Alden-Taylors do. These days, anyway. Somewhere along the way we acquired a little more backbone than our famous ancestor."

Ah, yes. The "Speak for thyself, John" guy. "So did she disinherit him?"

"Of course not. He was an Alden-Taylor, and a male. What really upset her, though, wasn't the Lithuanian business, but the fact that her son married a maid. I think she'd been hoping to link up the Alden-Taylors with another old family. Maybe the Astors, although they've snubbed the Aldens for centuries. Some old quarrel over a goat."

"Wait a minute. Your father married a *maid?* Whose? Your grandmother's?"

He shook his head. "No, my Aunt Lavelle's. Mother was working for her, which is how she met my father. They fell in love. Gloriana was furious about the whole thing, but in the end she must have decided that the grand Alden-Taylor heritage was strong enough to override those servant-class genes. Besides, after my parents were killed, she no longer had anyone else to leave Patriot's Blood to except Aunt Sappho and Poor Sandra. Sappho's refusal to have anything to do with the company worked against her, and Poor Sandra, well....She's just a niece."

"How about your aunts? Lavelle and...."

"Lavelle and Leila," he said.

"Don't they get anything?" I remembered what Owen had told me about Gloriana threatening them with some sort of legal action.

He didn't answer, merely wrote an address on a sheet of paper and handed it to me. "Why don't you ask them yourself?"

I looked down. An address in Phoenix's Arcadia district. "Could I have their phone number? I'd prefer to call first."

A wry smile. "Don't bother. They won't answer the phone, but they'll be there. They never go anywhere."

After stopping off at Baja Fresh for some tacos of my own, I drove to Arcadia, a small neighborhood tucked between Scottsdale and Phoenix proper. Although the area was a former orange orchard, developers had long since uprooted most of the trees. Now long ranch houses rambled over spacious lawns that soaked up the Valley's precious store of water. Attractive enough, perhaps, if you overlooked the fact that Arcadia seemed to be trying to pretend it was the lush Midwest or East, anywhere other than Arizona.

Gloriana's sisters lived in a multi-gabled monstrosity that reminded me of Hawthorne's sinister House of Seven Gables. On closer inspection, I realized the house's apparent size was merely an illusion. For all its dormers and meandering shingled roof, it was little larger than the typical Arcadia spread.

Unlike the other houses in the neighborhood, it appeared ill cared for. Several shingles had disappeared from the roof, and fading blue paint blistered the trim and door. Old-fashioned paper blinds, ragged at the edges, shuttered every window, hinting at gloom within. The garage leaned at a slight angle away from the house, making me worry about the safety of whatever it sheltered. Locusts hopped through the lawn, while two dying orange trees—remnants of the old orchard—drooped their branches in depression.

I parked my Jeep at the curb and walked up the weed-strewn cobblestone path to the house. A paper note taped to the screen door greeted me. Scrawled in wobbly script were the words: NO SOLICITORS—THIS MEANS YOU!

Underneath this dangled yet another piece of paper, a yellow flier uncomfortably reminiscent of one I'd recently seen. When I looked more carefully along the street, I could see the same yellow sheets fluttering from other doors. The National Alliance strikes again.

I peeled the flier away and found a slightly different message from that left at Zach's and Megan's house. My, the Nazi scriveners had been busy.

In big Gothic letters the flier proclaimed: MILLIONS OF NON-WHITE ILLEGAL ALIENS ARE POURING INTO THE COUNTRY RAPIDLY CHANGING THE PURE COMPLEXION OF OUR POPULATION AND THE QUALITY OF THE CIVILIZATION OUR ANCESTORS BUILT.

Complexion? I wondered how ineffectual a person's life could be when his only claim to fame was his complexion—something he'd been born with, not accomplished. Talk about your basic underachiever.

As I had done at Zach's house, I stuffed the flier into my carry-all. No point in troubling Gloriana's bereaved sisters with the thing.

I pressed the doorbell, but heard no sound. Out of order? I opened the unlocked screen and rapped on the edge of the heavy door with my knuckles. Nothing. I waited for a few seconds, then rapped again, louder. When no one answered, I counted to fifteen, then repeated the process with both hands.

In response to my thundering, the door finally opened and two elderly women peeped out. They stared at me through oyster-colored eyes.

The twins were identical, with a much stronger resemblance to Sandra than to Gloriana. Their dazzling white hair sat piled on their heads in identical top-knots, and faded twin house dresses hung loosely from their bony frames. But they were easy to tell apart thanks to the bruise one sister sported on her cheek.

"Leila and Lavelle Alden-Taylor?" I asked. "Your nephew sent me."

They looked at each other briefly, then began to close the door.

I hurriedly stuck my foot in the opening and flashed my private detective's I.D. "I'm Lena Jones, a private investigator, and I want to ask you some questions about Gloriana."

"Who?" The twin with the bruise.

I frowned. "Your older sister. Gloriana Alden-Taylor."

"Sorry, she passed away." The other twin, with no glimmer of sadness.

Had she purposefully misunderstood me? "Look, can I come in? The sooner we get this over with, the sooner I'll go away."

They looked at each other again, nodded in unison, then stepped back from the door.

I hurried inside before they changed their minds. As soon as I was through the door, a fug of stale air enveloped me, and I wondered how long it had been since the windows had been opened. Looking around, I saw that unlike most Arizona homes—which tended to be filled with sunshine and soft, Southwestern colors—the interior of the twin's house aped its exterior depression. Fusty gold-flocked wallpaper darkened the large living room, a darkness only intensified by the deep avocado carpeting. While the carpet's color might have been decades out of date, it looked almost new due to the plastic runners that crisscrossed it. The same care had been taken to protect the furniture. Plastic slipcovers glimmered on matching settees and armchairs.

I had seen homes like this before. Such hyper-protection usually meant one of two things: extreme frugality, or encroaching poverty. Which was true in their case?

For all its careful preservation, the house wasn't quite clean. Dust covered every object in the room.

My assessment of the twins' housekeeping skills hadn't gone unnoticed. "Maid's day off," No Bruise cackled, as the two settled together onto the sofa. Uninvited, I lowered myself into a matching chair nearby. Plastic crackled around me.

"Don't you mean maid's *year* off?" Bruise. "Perhaps if you were less demanding...." When No Bruise threw her a dirty look, she fell silent.

I didn't care about their help problems. "As I said, I'm investigating Gloriana's murder, and I hoped you'd be able help me fill in some blanks, Mrs. uh...."

"I'm Lavelle," Bruise said, plucking a piece of lint from her frayed collar.

"Sandra's mother?"

Lavelle flicked the lint onto a plastic runner. "Yes, I am, not that you'd know it from how seldom the girl visits." The whine in her voice hinted at long practice.

No Bruise sounded more assertive. "I'm Leila, and I have no children to break my heart, thank god. But Miss Jones, we really don't see the need for your visit. According to our information, that handyman of hers has already been arrested."

We. Our. The usual speech pattern of twins.

"There's some doubt about Owen's, uh, the handyman's, guilt."

Leila, obviously the more dominant twin, ignored my statement. "Gloriana should have had more sense than to hire him. Having strangers around the house never comes to any good." A meaningful glance at Sandra's mother.

Lavelle heaved a tremulous sigh. "It's so sad. Last night I was remembering what Gloriana used to be like as a young girl. Did you know, Miss Jones, that she was once almost as pretty as you? And so popular...."

"*Used to be* being the operative term," Leila interrupted, her voice acid. "That so-called charm of hers vanished a long time ago, and you know it. No one could stand her. If you ask me, Sissy, even her precious Zach was only interested in her money, and the same goes for your darling daughter."

Instead of defending Sandra, Lavelle merely looked down at the plastic-covered carpet and said nothing. It was easy to see where Sandra had inherited her hangdog personality.

"When did you find out Gloriana had been murdered?"

Leila flashed her dentures at me. They looked due for a cleaning. "Both Zach and Sandra called us right afterward. Then the next day two detectives came by and asked us all sorts of personal questions. They even dared ask if we'd profit financially from our sister's death. I told him we did, but the amount was hardly enough to murder for."

Knowing that people had killed for pocket change, I paid no attention to Leila's disclaimer. Their house obviously needed some work. Still, the twins looked too old to be running along an Oak Creek river bank searching for water hemlock. "Was the bequest merely a token, then, or…?" Might as well be as rude as the police.

A snort from Leila. "Depends on what you'd call a token, doesn't it, Miss Nosy? Our baby sister might have had her problems, but lack of family loyalty was never one of them."

"You were close, then?"

Lavelle looked up from her perusal of the carpet and struggled to smile. "We used to be. When Gloriana was younger, she was fun to be around, but after she married Michael, well…."

"That husband of hers, a regular tom cat," Leila interrupted. "But that's most men for you, isn't it?"

Considering recent events in my own life, I was tempted to agree. "You didn't like Michael?"

A harsh laugh from Leila. "That's one way of putting it. But no matter what we told her about him, Gloriana thought the sun rose and set in that man. Such a fool."

"Sissy, do we need to…?"

"You're right." Leila's face appeared to soften for such a brief moment that I wondered if I'd imagined it. "She never had any sense about men, and now she's dead. Let's leave it at that." Then to me, "You see, Miss Jones, we can't help you, so you might as well leave."

I dug in my heels. "I've heard that you and Gloriana had some sort of disagreement recently. Is that true?"

She lifted her lip in disdain. "We were always having disagreements with her. They never amounted to much."

An obvious lie. I tried again. "Did she ever say that anything or anyone was bothering her? Maybe one of her authors?"

Lavelle opened her mouth to answer, but Leila cut her off. "Gloriana never told us about what was going on at that ridiculous publishing house of hers. Why should she? She had her life, we had ours."

Lavelle looked back down at the carpet. I wondered if she was musing about her lack of a life.

Merely out of curiosity, I asked, "Do either of you know what water hemlock looks like?"

"Socrates died from it, didn't he?" Leila poked Lavelle in the arm with a spindly finger. "Speak up, Sissy. You used to be a school teacher. Enlighten us."

Lavelle brightened slightly at this chance to display her knowledge. "You are correct, Sissy. Socrates died a few minutes after he said he owed a cock to Asclepius."

"Nice to know Socrates paid his bills." Leila, with a smirk. "He did better than us."

A nervous laugh from Lavelle. "No, Sissy. Asclepius was a god. Socrates was bribing him for a painless death."

My suspicion that the two were trying to distract me deepened, and I decided to end their excursion into Greek history. "What else could you tell me about your sister that might be relevant to her death?"

Twin frowns, timid Lavelle's the larger of the two this time. "Well, if you ask me, I don't see why Zach should get the bulk of the inheritance. It's unfair. Considering everything Poor Sandra had to put up with...."

"That's your own fault," Leila snapped, her temporary good humor vanished. "If you'd kept quiet, everything would have been all right, but no, you had to go ahead and shoot your mouth off." She gave her twin a punch on the arm that looked more painful than playful.

Lavelle scooted to the other end of the sofa. "But I had to tell her, didn't I? Otherwise...."

I rose from my armchair and sat down between the two. "Tell Gloriana what?"

Leila, thus blocked from punching her sister again, sulked. "You're one of those modern women who works out, aren't you?" She poked my own arm with that sharp finger. It hurt.

"Every day. Tell Gloriana what?"

"Who, not what," Sandra's mother mumbled, from her safe distance.

"Shut your mouth!" Leila snapped. "Our family affairs are none of this woman's business."

Lavelle hung her head, too dispirited to meet my eyes.

I made a mental note to call Zach as soon as I left. Perhaps with his newfound wealth, he could afford to hire a nurse or social worker to check up on his aunts. Especially on Lavelle, who obviously endured much.

I tried one last time. "Tell Gloriana about who?"

But I might as well have been talking to the plastic slipcovers. Leila just glared at me, and Lavelle continued looking at the floor.

I let myself out, wondering if what I had just seen constituted elder abuse. Then again, would it still be termed elder abuse when abuser and abusee were the exact same age?

Chapter 14

While the Jeep idled at a red light on Indian School Road, I called Zach from my cell phone. When I voiced my concerns about Lavelle, he pointed out that Sandra stopped in to see her mother a couple of times a month.

"She's never mentioned seeing anything out of the way, Lena, certainly not bruising. You must have caught them on a bad day. Besides, when two people are as close as they are, you have to expect a squabble or two."

"They didn't seem all that close to me." I remembered the punch and Lavelle's attempt to evade it. Then I wondered if Gloriana had noticed any bruises during her last visit.

Zach's laugh hissed through the line. "They're probably too close. That's why their marriages didn't work out. Lavelle's, a late marriage, lasted long enough for her to have Sandra, but Leila's, same late type of deal, was all over with in a matter of months. They moved in together then and haven't been apart since."

The light changed to green and I shifted the Jeep into gear. The traffic heading back to Scottsdale was heavier than usual. Not for the first time I wished the city would install some mass transit other than buses, but no, that made too much sense.

"Lena, is there anything else?" Zach's voice startled me out of my revery.

"Uh, yeah. While I was at the house, they mentioned warning Gloriana about someone, but I couldn't get the specifics. Do you know what they were talking about?"

After a moment's silence, he responded, "I haven't the slightest idea. Unless maybe they were angry with me. On my last visit, about a month ago, they both seemed to have lost some weight, so I suggested they start thinking about a move to an assisted living facility. When I got to the office the next day, I mentioned my worries to Gloriana, and she said she'd look into it. Maybe she did, maybe she didn't. We'll never know. Now, I have some phone calls to make, authors to disappoint, so...."

No one can say that Lena Jones can't take a hint. "Thanks for your time, Zach."

Feeling dissatisfied with the conversation, I disconnected.

Later in the day, Owen Sisiwan stopped by to thank me for the work I was doing on his behalf. Recalling Gloriana's intimate photographs of him made me uneasy, but I don't think he noticed.

"I haven't helped much yet, Owen." I tried not to blush. "Wish I could give you better news."

"Jimmy says you've solved worse cases than mine," Owen said, his face serene.

Past successes weren't always indicators of future triumphs, but I kept my concern—and my suspicions—to myself. "Owen, how close were you to Gloriana?"

"Close?" The dark eyes were unreadable. "I worked for her, that's all. Gloriana wasn't the type to confide in the help."

I noticed that Owen didn't use Rosa's more respectful "Miss Gloriana," just "Gloriana." Did it mean anything? "She never attempted to engage you in a personal conversation?"

His face remained blank. "What kind of personal conversation would she have with a handyman?"

"I'm only fishing around for ideas. By the way, how much do you know about Gloriana's sisters?"

He gave me a gorgeous smile. "Those two? Not much. Well, except for last time she visited them. She seemed real upset on the way back home."

Something had gone on between Gloriana and her sisters, something important enough to shatter her frosty reserve. "What exactly did she say?"

"She told me to drive fast, that she had some phone calls to make." Then he added, "She didn't carry a cell phone. She hated them. Just like she hated computers."

"She didn't say who she needed to call?"

His face revealed a hint of impatience. "I told you, Gloriana didn't discuss her private business with the help. But it was probably something about lawyers, the usual. I didn't really pay that much attention."

More questioning elicited no further new information, so I gave up and turned the conversation to another subject. "Owen, what are you doing now that, uh, your job...." I trailed off. What I really wanted to know was, Owen, do you have enough money to take care of your family while your case drags though the courts?

But I didn't have to ask. Owen's bronze face creased into a big, teeth-glittering smile. "I'm working for Zach. Some deliveries, a little gardening, some fetching and hauling for Megan's rescue organization. Apparently Gloriana's attorney told them they could go ahead and move into the Hacienda, so things haven't changed for me that much. Except that life is more peaceful now."

A slip, perhaps. He had so much as admitted there had been strain between him and Gloriana. I remembered that Gloriana had forced him to sit in the hallway during the banquet. Not for the first time, I wondered why. Could she have been punishing him for something?

"Say, Owen. I've heard that at the SOBOP banquet she made you sit out in the hall, rather than at the table. What was that all about?"

He looked away from me for a few seconds, out Desert Investigations' big picture window. When I followed his eyes, I didn't see anything interesting out there, nothing but tourists in rental cars driving slowly up and down the street.

When he finally looked back, he said, "Gloriana said it wouldn't be appropriate for the help to eat at the same table as her business associates."

I remembered the cameras, the photographs. "And that didn't bother you?"

"Why would it?" As if it hadn't fazed him.

But I knew better.

Then I chased my suspicions out of my mind. Owen had enough troubles without his own private investigator investigating him.

The rest of the day went by quickly. Using various computer search engines, one of them even legal, Jimmy discovered two felons among the applicants for a high-security job at a local computer chip manufacturer. While he reported his findings to the company's personnel office, I busied myself making phone calls, lining up appointments with various people connected to Gloriana or Patriot's Blood.

In March, the days are still fairly short, and by six the light began to fade. Jimmy left early in order to visit Owen, so when I was through with my paperwork, I locked up. Then I climbed the stairs to my apartment.

The monster in the closet.

As I searched through the rooms with my gun drawn, Gomez' words mocked me. *"You realize, Lena, that you can't go on like this. Creeping into rooms as if something horrible were waiting for you...."*

"Shut up!" I snapped to empty air. But I made quick work of the search this time. Progress?

I had just settled down on the sofa to watch the evening news when someone knocked on the door. Snatching the .38 from the coffee table, I walked to the double-bolted door and stared out the peephole.

Dusty.

"Go away!" I yelled.

"Not until we talk." He voice was muffled through the steel-reinforced wood, but clear enough.

"Then you'll sit out there all night!"

"Fine with me."

I watched through the peephole as Dusty settled himself into a corner. Then I went into the kitchen, nuked some ramen, and came back to the sofa where I watched the top of the news, which had become little more than a laundry list of the day's terrorist attacks. Recitation of the list completed, fatalities intoned, the anchors began talking about the latest celebrity accused of murder. I turned the TV off and headed for the bathroom.

I do some of my best thinking in the shower, but every time I tried to make sense out of Gloriana's death, old voices kept intruding.

"Lena, honey, you've got to let someone love you sometime." Madeline, the foster mother who had to relinquish me back to CPS when she developed breast cancer.

"Perfect love wipeth out all fear." Reverend Giblin, trying in his own way to help.

They'd both seen through me, understood that my rage was no more than a cover-up for my terror.

Gomez had probably figured it out, too.

I leaned my head against the shower stall and whispered, "Why can't you all shut up?" That's when I realized that not all of the water on my face came from the shower.

What seemed like hours later, soggy and still miserable, I stepped out of the shower and wrapped myself in my terrycloth robe. I strode to the door and looked out the peephole again.

Dusty was still sitting on the landing.

I opened the door.

"Come in, you son of a bitch."

Chapter 15

Dusty opened his arms and started for me.

I grabbed the .38 from the coffee table. "Touch me and you're a dead man." He had no way of knowing that I'd sooner shoot myself than him.

But he stopped anyway. "Please....Talk to me."

I pointed the gun toward the corner chair. "Sit."

Dusty sat. So did I. On the sofa. About eight feet away.

"You can put the gun down now, baby."

"Stop calling me 'baby.'" But I returned the gun to the coffee table. "Is that something you picked up from your cheap redhead?"

He smiled. "She wasn't all that cheap."

"Good. I hope she took you for everything you've got." Which wouldn't have been much. Dude ranch cowboys like Dusty seldom owned more than a horse and saddle.

"Just my pride. And my girl."

"You better not mean me, cowboy. I'm nobody's *baby* and I'm nobody's *girl.*"

"You're so tough." Still that heartbreaking smile.

"Tough enough for me not to put up with crap from you."

"You won't have to, ba...Lena. I've learned my lesson."

Isn't that what they all say? Still, there were so many things I needed to know, so I took a deep breath and sat back. "All right, Dusty. Start talking."

He talked well into the night. He told me about the Vegas trip, the redhead—an advertising agency account executive from Manhattan—then the rehab center he checked himself into when he returned to Arizona.

"Working on a dude ranch may not pay much, but the group insurance is solid," he finished up. "I stayed in rehab for six weeks, and after the first few days, it wasn't too bad. Considering."

"Considering?"

He looked down at the floor. Shuffled his boots. Then looked back up, his eyes sadder than I'd ever seen them. "There's no point in boring you with the details, other than to say that I've been going on these benders since I was a teenager. But this is the first time I ever let one interfere with our relationship."

"Are you telling me that all those times you neglected to call me for weeks didn't interfere with our relationship?" The moment the words left my mouth I regretted them. Dusty's disappearances had served my purposes, too. They kept us from getting too close.

He must have read my mind. "You never seemed to care all that much. Every time I came back you'd pretend nothing had happened."

"Yeah. I guess I did." Was this the time for me to say I would change? Want more? Give more?

Silence filled the room, filled only by a dripping tap in the kitchen and the sound of an idling car. Probably one of Main Street's fussbudget art dealers had returned to straighten a painting.

"Ain't neither of us perfect, ba...honey."

I was wondering why "honey" didn't bother me when the redhead came through the door I'd forgotten to lock behind Dusty. Her gun was a lot bigger than mine.

Before I could compliment her on her gold-toned, .50 caliber Desert Eagle, I heard a sound like an artillery explosion and the drywall over my sofa exploded into white mist. Dusty and

I dove for the floor, overturning the coffee table in the process. Unfortunately, my .38 went tumbling across the carpet, out of reach.

Dusty threw his body across mine, not that it would do any good. I'd counted five shots already, but I knew the Desert Eagle was good for seven. Each round packed enough fire power to cut through both of us and into my office below, if she ever managed to bring the gun under control.

Time to pray.

The redhead was screaming something, but the ringing in my head distorted her words. So I kept mumbling one of the only two prayers I knew, something about sheep. Then, as I reached the "He leadeth me" part, I decided I'd rather die fighting, not praying.

Shoving Dusty off me, I scrambled to my feet and charged across the room. Before the redhead could react, I grabbed her wrist, then wrapped my leg around her knees. We fell together in a tangle of arms, legs, and hair. As soon as I chomped my teeth down on her wrist, she released her hold on the heavy Desert Eagle and it fell to the floor with a clank that I, even in my sound-blasted condition, could still hear.

"Stupid bitch!" I yelled at the woman over the ringing in my ears. "Next time, get a gun you can handle!"

"He's mine! He's mine!" she screamed, snot and tears running down her face.

"Dusty, get the gun!" I yelled. I was too busy holding her down to do much of anything else.

Dusty scrambled forward, picked up the Desert Eagle with a look of loathing, and clicked on the safety. He then slid the thing under the sofa. Unlike most Arizonans, he didn't like guns.

But now he came into his own. The killing machine out of sight, he ripped the television set's extension cord from the wall, and, within seconds, had the redhead roped and tied like a recalcitrant calf.

I fished the Desert Eagle back out from under the sofa—the damn thing must have weighed twenty pounds—and took it to my bedroom, where I stashed it under a pile of dirty laundry. I returned to the living room in time to see Dusty picking up the phone.

"Put that down," I said. It was late, so late that all the art galleries on Main Street had long since closed, and the tourists were tucked safely back into their overpriced hotel rooms. With luck, no one had heard anything.

Dusty didn't get it. "We have to call the police, Lena. Joanne's nuts, and she might pull something like this again."

Joanne. So the Devil had a name. I didn't doubt that she might "pull something like this" again, but Dusty knew nothing about my own recent legal problems and court-ordered therapy. The last thing I needed was for my old buddies at the cop shop to show up at my apartment and put my name on yet another police report. Because of the glare of increased media coverage, the days when cops could cover each other's butts were long gone.

I placed my hand on Dusty's and guided the receiver back down. "No."

"You women." But he walked away from the phone.

A quick look at the wall above my sofa demonstrated why a woman should always choose the right gun for the job. The bullet tracks started about three feet above where our heads had been, climbed up sharply to the ceiling (I now could see dark sky) then trailed downward again at the corner. The redhead, who had probably seen too many Dirty Harry movies, had hardly been able to lift the Desert Eagle, let alone aim it.

I went back to the redhead and showed her my own .38, a comparatively delicate little thing that was easy to hold, aim, and even shoot to kill at close quarters.

"You have some interesting choices to make now, Joanne. Choice Number One, you can lie there for the rest of the night and listen to me tell you what a jackass you are. Or Choice Number Two, you can get the hell out of my apartment."

She ignored me and addressed Dusty instead. "You said you loved me."

I wanted to kick her. Then Dusty.

"Joanne?" I pressed the barrel of the .38 against her temple hard enough to hurt. But I didn't pull the hammer back.

She began to cry.

Dusty paced back and forth, muttering "Jesus, Jesus, Jesus."

How like a man. They went through life raising hell, lying to this woman and that, humping anything that would lie still long enough, then disappearing into the sunset when they got bored. But let a woman cry and they fell to pieces.

"Oh, shut up, Dusty, and let the woman think!" I snapped.

"Jesus. Jesus, Jesus." But at least he stopped wearing out my carpet.

I let Joanne cry off the adrenalin for a few more minutes, then fetched some tissue out of the bathroom. I even wiped her nose for her.

"Now, if it were me, Joanne, I'd get the hell out of here," I told her. "Then I'd drive down to Sky Harbor Airport and hop the next plane back to Manhattan where they don't have two-timing cowboys and big guns aren't so easy to buy."

Her face sagged in resignation. "All right. Let me up and I'll leave."

"Good. Then I won't have to shoot you." I backed up but kept my .38 at the ready. "Dusty. You do the honors."

"Lena, I think...."

"That's a refreshing change. Go ahead and untie her, okay? Then usher her out the door. You can leave, too."

"But, Lena...."

I swung the .38 toward him. "I'm not feeling romantic right now."

"Jesus, Jesus, Jesus."

He did as he was told and shortly thereafter, I was left alone staring glumly at my ruined wall and cursing my therapist. I wanted my paranoia back. At least paranoids kept their doors locked, even while their no-good boyfriends were visiting.

Chapter 16

"Jimmy, you know anyone who works with drywall?"

He turned away from his beloved computer with a surprised expression. "That's an odd question coming from you."

"I had a little trouble with my walls last night. Ceiling, too."

"What sort of trouble?"

"They fell down."

"They fell down?" He stared at me, which was unusual because Pima Indians are some of the most polite people you'll ever meet.

"Yes. Now I need someone to put them back up. Do you know anyone or not? I'd prefer not to let Gus know about this, ah, situation." I could imagine my landlord's face if he saw the walls. And the ceiling. He might even be irritated enough to break my lease.

"Drywall." Jimmy looked like he wanted to ask another question. Instead he gave me the name of someone from the Rez. "Remember that Owen does a little carpentry here and there, too."

"Owen's too busy these days so I'll go with the other guy."

"That's it, then?"

"Sure is." Unless the redhead came back with a new gun.

As soon as I'd placed a call to Jimmy's buddy I started to make some notes on the case, but Jimmy interrupted me.

"Before you get too deep into that, I've got some news. That librarian, Myra Gordon?"

I put my pen down. "What about her?"

"When I first ran her through the system, I came up with nothing, but then I discovered that Gordon uses her maiden name. Her married name was Mbisi. Does that ring a bell?"

I thought for a moment, waiting for it to come to me. When it did, I exhaled in shock. "You don't mean *George* Mbisi?"

"The same. She's his widow."

"Oh, hell." Feeling sick, I put my head in my hands.

Two years back, while I was still with the Scottsdale PD, George Mbisi, an executive for one of the local airlines, had been carjacked by three skinheads. They drove him out into the desert and, after torturing him with lit cigarettes until it got old, beat him to death with a tire iron. They then burned his body and buried it in a shallow grave. To celebrate, they dropped by a local bar where their boasts had been overheard by the bartender, who just happened to be the daughter of a Phoenix police sergeant. She called daddy, and within hours, Mbisi's murderers were behind bars, where they remained to this day, awaiting execution. As details of the case came back to me, I remembered the furor that had erupted when the search of the skinheads' apartments revealed a bevy of hate literature. Much of it bore the imprint of Patriot's Blood.

"Oh, man, Jimmy. What a motive." I remembered Myra Gordon's face, her carefully guarded conversation.

"That doesn't mean she did it."

No. But even without taking the hike, a librarian would know where to find water hemlock. Figuring out a way of getting the hemlock onto the right salad would be easy, too, especially with those place cards. Was that the real reason Gordon/Mbisi had attended the SOBOP Expo? And was the fact that she had been seated near Gloriana at the banquet table no coincidence?

I picked up the phone and called Emil Ramos, who told me he'd have his wife call me right away. Fortunately, she did.

"Mrs. Ramos, did anyone at the conference make a special request about seating?"

"Certainly," she said. "Married couples wanted to be seated together, friends did, too. There was a space on the registration application for those requests."

"How about at Gloriana's table?"

"David Zhang wanted to sit with my husband—they're friends—and that nice librarian wanted to sit near Gloriana."

"Did she give a reason?"

Mrs. Ramos was silent for a moment, then said, "You understand that there were more than one hundred people there, Ms. Jones. But if I remember correctly, she wrote down on the form that she wanted to talk to Gloriana about the Patriot's Blood line."

I closed my eyes.

"Ms. Jones? Is there anything else?"

I opened them again to find Jimmy watching me intently. "How far in advance did she register. Do you know?"

"Registration closed thirty days before the conference. The resort needed to know which banquet hall to use, the big one or the small one."

One month. More than enough time to read up on water hemlock, and to take the necessary drive to harvest the deadly stuff. She couldn't have known that Gloriana would make procuring it so easy, not that it made any difference in the end.

"Thank you, Mrs. Ramos," I said softly. After I wrangled Myra Gordon's Wyatt's Landing telephone number from her, we said our goodbyes and I hung up.

Every now and then private detectives question their commitment to truth, and this was one of those times. If Myra Gordon/Mbisi had murdered Gloriana, I didn't want to know. Yet I had to know because a friend's life was at stake.

"Bad news, huh?" Jimmy asked.

"You got it, partner." I picked up the phone again and dialed Gordon's number. All I got was her message machine, telling me to leave my number. I did.

To calm myself, I went back to my case notes and jotted down this new information. Once I'd returned to normal, or what passed for normal for me, I remembered there were other people who might have wanted Gloriana dead. So I poured myself some coffee (standard black brew, no pretentious Seattle crap) and wandered across the street to the Damon and Pythias Art Gallery where my friend Cliffie Barbianzi knew about all things art and all things gay. I found him hunched over his Louis Quatorze desk, sipping at what smelled like a double shot of hazelnut cappuccino from a Royal Doulton cup. As I approached, he rose politely. His immaculate linen suit, the same pale gray as his hair, hadn't yet wrinkled.

"To what do I owe this pleasure?"

I waved my coffee mug at him. "Thought I'd join you for a cuppa."

"Really? Just a nice morning visit between friends?" He smiled. "Who's dead?"

"Can't put anything over on you, can I, Cliffie? This time around, it's Gloriana Alden-Taylor, the publisher. Jimmy's cousin has been charged with the murder."

Cliffie took another sip of his brew, then frowned in distaste. I doubted it was the coffee. "Can't say I'm sorry she's dead. You should see some of the irresponsible bilge that press of hers has published. I swear, it's enough to make you make you think twice about the First Amendment."

"No laws are perfect," I murmured. I gave him a brief rundown on the case, then asked the question that had brought me here. "Do you know anything about a film-maker named Sappho?"

"Everyone knows Sappho. But what does that delightful woman have to do with the unpleasant Gloriana Alden-Taylor?"

"Sappho is Gloriana's daughter."

Cliffie's cultured veneer slipped as his mouth dropped open. "You shittin' me?"

"I shit you not. Now, what can you tell me about her?"

Cliffie stared into his fancy coffee cup for a moment, then looked back up at me, the façade back in place. "Well, my dear, I can tell you that Sappho has been out of town for the last month, so she certainly couldn't have done anything to Gloriana even if she'd wanted to. And she most definitely doesn't have a reputation for violence."

I took the character reference with a grain of salt. Cliffie trusted everyone, even me. "You say she's been out of town for the last month. Where?"

"She's shooting a film in Superior. A gay Western."

I raised my eyebrows. "I didn't know there was such a thing."

He took another sip of his coffee. "You think gays were invented this century? We've always been around. In fact, I'm betting that a lot of those 'old marm' schoolteachers were gay. Same for those 'buddy' cowpokes. As for myself, I've always had grave suspicions about Pancho and Cisco. Not to mention Red Ryder and Little Beaver."

I tried to look shocked but failed.

Superior was an old mining town approximately sixty miles east of Scottsdale. It had seen better days. Now the silver mine and most of the huge open pit copper mine were closed, and the miners' homes had weathered far beyond picturesque. Only a few residents had remained to work the pit, a huge maw which gaped at the edge of town. Their grown children had long ago left to find jobs in Phoenix and Tucson.

Lately, though, Superior had begun to enjoy new life. The Arizona Film Commission had touted the town's rough-hewn attractions to Hollywood, and Hollywood had responded with one film crew after another. As I followed Highway 60 through Superior, I spotted veritable forests of lighting equipment and dozens of heavily made-up men and women sitting around in directors' chairs, fanning themselves under patio umbrellas. I stopped by one such gathering and asked a rumpled-looking man sipping designer water if he knew where Sappho was shooting.

He directed me back the way I'd come. It was only as I drove away that I realized I'd been talking to Nick Nolte.

Sappho had set up her encampment on the outskirts of town in rugged terrain that in many finished films had doubled as Old California, New Mexico, or Montana. Rough hills encircled a flat basin of sand and sage, while above, a few buzzards flapped their wings in annoyance at the ruckus below.

I parked the Jeep behind an empty horse trailer and got out. The film crew was small compared to some of the others I'd seen in town, probably only around thirty people total. Some wandered back and forth across the dirt road muttering imprecations about the glaring light and the drifting sand. A few yards away, three bored-looking women dressed in Stetsons and chaps sat astride well-groomed horses.

"Can you tell me where I could find Sappho?" I asked a large person of indeterminate sex.

"Over by the catering truck." The sweet, high voice of a woman. She gestured toward an even taller woman who, in the midst of taking a Coke from the caterer, had her back to me. Then the woman turned around and I gasped. She looked like Gloriana must have looked thirty years earlier. Talk about strong genes.

Sappho's exact age was hard to determine because she was one of those long, lean women who seasoned rather than aged. Her beautiful face, deeply browned by the sun, made her blue eyes seem startling in contrast.

But they were the saddest eyes I had ever seen.

Not certain of the welcome I'd receive, I showed her my I.D. and explained the reason for my visit.

"I imagine a lot of people wanted to kill my mother," she said in a deep, almost masculine voice. "I used to fantasize doing it myself when I was a child. But I got over it."

"She was up here filming when it happened, with at least thirty witnesses," said a petite brunette standing nearby. The heavy pancake makeup on her face revealed her to be one of the film's actresses.

Sappho turned to her and smiled. Her voice was gentle when she said, "Thanks, Lainie, but I can take care of this myself." She turned back to me. "A couple of detectives have already been up here asking questions, and they seem satisfied with my answers. I don't know what else I can tell you, but I can assure you that I'm even more anxious to find my mother's murderer than you are. And by the way, I never for one moment believed that Owen killed her. He's not the type."

"What type is that?"

"Poisoning is cowardly, and Owen is no coward. He confronts his enemies." She motioned toward a picnic table which had been set up in the shade of an ancient mesquite. "Grab yourself a Coke or something from the catering truck and let's sit and talk."

A half-hour later, I'd learned little more about the murder itself, but gained insight into the Alden-Taylor family dynamics. I'd also learned that, surprisingly, Sappho's preference for film work had angered Gloriana more than her sexual preference.

"So many people misunderstood my mother on race, and especially on lifestyle." Sappho started on her third Coke. "She once told me she didn't care who I slept with as long as I got pregnant somewhere along the way and perpetuated the glorious Alden-Taylor genes. When she finally figured out that the idea of sleeping with a man disgusted me, she suggested I find a sperm donor and a friendly turkey baster. But I couldn't see myself as a mother, especially once I got started in the film business. I've never believed that nonsense about women being able to have it all, family and a high-powered career. Someone always winds up suffering in those situations, and the sufferer is usually the kid. I should know."

Sappho's tone was bitter, making me wonder again about Gloriana's mothering skills. For all her obsessions, none of them had seemed to be children, not even her own.

"She disinherited you?"

"Not entirely. I still get something. When I told her that I refused to carry on the press if something happened to her, she pretty much gave up on me and turned to Zach."

"How long ago was that?"

"Three years, five? I've been too busy to keep count."

"How do you feel about Zach inheriting the bulk of the estate?"

Sappho shrugged. "Good for him and Megan. They can use it. I talked to her yesterday, when she called about the funeral arrangements. God, I'm glad Zach found that woman. He needs all the love he can get. Did you know that his parents were killed when he was only nine?"

I nodded my head and she continued. "Zach's mother's parents were both dead, so Mother decided to raise him herself. If there's anything I feel guilty about, it's him. At the time of the accident, I was old enough to take care of him, and probably should have, but I was about to premiere my first film at Sundance. So...."

Her voice faded and the sadness returned to her eyes.

"He seems to have turned out well," I said.

"You think so? Interesting. I should have done more to help him, but I was busy leading my own life. After the accident that killed my brother and his wife, Mother....Well, let's just say other people didn't exist for her for a long, long time. Mother doesn't...*didn't* do grief very well. She retreated emotionally, just like she did when my father died.

"It was rough on Zach, not having someone to lean on. I think that's why he and Megan are so into the rescue work with those abandoned animals. They both can relate to the poor things. But Mother. I've not done her justice, I'm afraid. Maybe she wasn't maternal, but she was no monster. She made certain Zach's needs were taken care of, but other than that....She wasn't too negligent unless she was caught up in one of her obsessions. Then she'd forget the poor little guy was even alive. When she was on the trail of whatever she'd fixated on, nothing else in the world mattered, not even her own grandchild. At least Zach had Rosa."

Gloriana's Fevers, shoving away the pain, but creating misery for everyone else in an ongoing cycle. "When you say obsessions, are you talking about the Barbie dolls or the Hacienda?"

"Either. Both. It wasn't only things, though. Sure, she'd take off on month-long buying trips without warning, leaving me, and then Zach in his time, to whatever maid was around. One year she became fixated on baseball. Baseball! Can you believe it? She decided that, given our Plymouth Brethren origins, she should root for the Red Sox, so she'd fly all over the country to watch them play."

"She never took you along?"

"No, and I hate baseball to this day because it took her away from me." She sounded fragile, and I could see her as a lonely child with only maids to talk to.

I remembered the handsome man in the photographs, Sappho's father, and decided to double-check something. "I heard your father died at the Phoenix Open."

Her answer was odd. "Technically, yes."

My radar blipped. "What do you mean, technically?"

"He'd been feeling pretty ill earlier in the day and thought about staying home, but Mother told him to go ahead." Sappho's voice held that note of caution every detective learns to recognize.

"Why, if he was sick?"

She flicked a look at the set and saw the camera people still fussing with the equipment. Then she sighed. "She and my father had been arguing for a week, and I think she simply wanted to get him out of the house."

"What were they arguing about?" A private detective is nothing if not nosy.

"A woman. Satisfied? He'd been having yet another affair."

"You knew this for sure?" I had a vision of a little child cringing against her bedroom door, hearing her parents brawl over sex. Then she straightened me out.

"Oh, everyone knew. The woman, like a couple of his others, was one of the cocktail waitresses at the country club."

"You hung out at a country club?" It was hard to envision Sappho with the Ladies Who Lunch.

A strange smile. "We had a family membership, of course. But that's not how I found out. The woman told me herself. She was my lover, too."

I took a slug of my Diet Coke. It didn't help.

"Daddy died in happy ignorance, sipping on his fifth bourbon with Arnie Palmer. Mother began collecting the dolls right after that. Lord, Mother owned at least three of each Barbie ever manufactured, literally thousands of the creepy things."

She gave a theatrical shudder. "All those beady eyes blinking and blinking at you. Like female versions of Chuckie, the Killer Doll. They gave me nightmares when I was a kid. But those Barbies are probably worth a small fortune today, so who am I to criticize Mother? Anyway, after the Barbie era, she started on pewter, then antique books. She has…had…a library full of first editions, many of them signed. Zach got those. And somewhere along the line came her film noir posters, which she left to me because she knew I loved them, too. And lately, of course, there was all the Jeffersoniana. Lord, Mother was into anything and everything to do with Thomas Jefferson. She bought paintings of him, books about him, she even bought a chamber pot he supposedly used. You know, 'Thomas Jefferson shat here.'"

I remembered the pretty object I'd mistakenly identified as a soup tureen. Well, live and learn. "Zach told me Gloriana believed you Alden-Taylors are related to him."

Her smile seemed forced. "That was Mother all over for you. Before an obsession could run its course, she would always take it to the most ridiculous level. Something she heard along the way, heaven knows what, made her decide that Jefferson was one of our ancestors, so a couple of months ago she sent one of her lackeys up here to swab out my mouth. I don't know why testing her own DNA wasn't enough."

But I did. The compulsive Gloriana wanted everyone in the family tested as a matter of course. I was about to say so when the brunette actress I'd noticed earlier approached Sappho and laid her petite hand on the film-maker's arm.

"Darling, I hate to spoil your little trip down Memory Lane with this lovely blonde, but we need to get my scene in the can before we lose the light."

Sappho covered the tiny hand with her own and looked up at her. This time the smile was genuine. "Thanks, Lainie." Then to me she said, "Here I am telling horror stories about my obsessive Mommie Dearest, and I'm such an obsessive talker that I damn near blew the shoot! Now, if you'll excuse me I have to get back to work."

We both stood up and said our goodbyes. As I walked toward my Jeep, Sappho called out, "Have you talked to my aunts yet?"

I nodded.

Her laugh was harsh. "Then I'm sure you noticed that they have their own obsession. Plastic."

"Yeah, I noticed."

She was still laughing when I drove away. But underneath the laughter I detected a well of sadness. For all her Hollywood sophistication, Sappho remained a lonely little girl who needed her mother.

Chapter 17

I have a memory…

A memory of green.

I am walking across green with a woman, her filmy blue skirt rippling in the breeze. She is laughing. Now and then she stoops to toss a ball to a small yellow dog, its fur almost the same color as the woman's hair. We are in a pasture. There are cows in the distance, some horses. Framing them, tall glossy-leafed trees with big white blossoms.

A male voice calls. "Helen! It's time!"

My mother turns, calls back something I don't understand. Then she calls to the dog, picks me up, and we all return the way we came, the grass still bent under our footsteps.

The dog barks, begs her to throw the ball again.

My father waits for us, smiling, his eyes almost the same color as the grass.

Chapter 18

I pulled into the parking lot at Desert Investigations in time to lead the drywall guy up the stairs to my apartment. He turned out to be another of Jimmy's cousins, and like Jimmy, he was almost unflappable. He expressed no curiosity about the bullet holes, simply set to work.

"It'll take a couple of days to fix this," he said. "And it's going to be noisy, so at least while I'm working, you might want to be somewhere else."

A good idea. I decided to pay a visit to Emil Ramos, and then David Zhang, whose Scottsdale Air Park offices weren't far from each other. First I stopped by Patriot's Blood to see if the copier had been fixed. I still needed to read the remaining pages of Gloriana's memoirs. The door to the office was locked, but when I tapped on it, Poor Sandra peeped out.

"We're closed until Monday, Ms. Jones." She looked more harassed than usual. "The toilet's not functioning and the copier's still down, so Zach gave everyone the day off. I'm not even supposed to be here, but I figured I'd sneak in and get some extra work done in all the peace and quiet."

She turned down my request to read Gloriana's memoirs on site.

"Sorry. I really can't let you in. Like I said, I'm not supposed to be here myself. Even Casey stayed at the Hacienda with Zach."

It took me a moment to remember that Casey was the office dog. I told her I'd be back Monday.

After stopping by Phylos & Phalafels for a late lunch, I drove to Scottsdale Air Park, where a small publishing center had grown up around Spanish tile showrooms, real estate offices, and cryogenics labs. Somewhere in one of these warehouses, Walt Disney reportedly dangled upside down in a liquid nitrogen solution and Ted Williams' frozen head stared blindly at a blank wall.

David Zhang was half-buried behind a stack of paper when I walked through the door of Arizona Trails Publishing. He gave me a blank look which only slowly slid into one of recognition. His act was good, but not good enough.

"Ms. Jones, what a delight to see you again," he said, pushing the manuscripts aside. "I've been so inundated with mule's ear, yarrow, and bladder campion that I hardly recognize myself anymore, let alone anyone else."

"Bladder campion?"

He gave me a slick smile and pointed to one of the manuscripts. "Native Arizona plants. I'm thinking about buying this manuscript. It's the diary of a Viet Nam vet who lived alone in a one-room cabin in the mountains for twenty years. Trapped and shot everything he needed, didn't talk to one human soul for all that time."

I settled myself into a chair. I felt almost at home in his office because it had no more personality than my own. Everything was beige and fake. Whatever Zhang was spending his money on, it wasn't office furniture. "What happened to the guy?" I asked. "He finally started pining for civilization?"

"Not exactly. Some hikers found his body when they broke into the cabin to take refuge from a sudden snowstorm. He was mummified by that time. They were trapped up there for almost a week, and after hauling his corpse to the woodshed, they read his chicken scratchings to keep themselves from going crazy. When the weather cleared, they hiked back out with the manuscript and reported the death to the authorities. Turns out the guy had a wife and a grown daughter he hadn't seen in years, so after probate cleared, the manuscript reverted to his widow. One of the hikers was familiar with Arizona Trails' books—he happened to be carrying *Guide to Arizona's High Country* in his backpack at the time. Anyway, he suggested she send it to us. The manuscript is pretty good, considering."

"Considering?"

"The poor guy thought he could communicate with bears. He'd talk to them, they'd talk back, that sort of thing. I have an appointment with the widow tomorrow so we can figure out what to do. Leave the bear conversations in or edit them out? I need to determine the direction I want the book to take. It could be either an Arizona version of Dr. Doolittle or the standard how-to-survive-in-the-wilderness book."

That didn't make sense to me. "Why can't it be both?"

He shook his head. "Every book needs a focus. No book can be all things to all people."

Myself, I'd like to read what the bears had to say, but publishing was Zhang's business, not mine. After a little more chat about mountain men and bears, I brought the subject back to Gloriana. "Where were you immediately before dinner that evening?"

"At a seminar. That's where we all were, even Gloriana."

"Hmm." I looked at his hands. They were playing the piano on the bare desk. "You know, Mr. Zhang, we ran a background check on you."

The piano playing intensified. "My record's clean."

"I know. What I don't know is where you got all your money after you went broke."

The temper I'd noticed at WestWorld flared. "That's none of your damned business!" With a great effort, he brought himself under control. Even his hands stopped moving. "Sorry about that. My financial problems and their eventual solution had nothing to do with Gloriana Alden-Taylor. I'd tell you if they did."

Somehow I doubted that, but I let it slide.

"I made some good investments," he finally offered. "And then got out before the market tanked."

I was about to ask him something else, when he snapped his fingers. "Hey, I remember something. The only thing is, I don't know if it's relevant. And besides, it probably didn't have anything to do with the murder."

I told him everything was relevant in a murder investigation.

"If you say so." He took a deep breath, and began. "There was this guy Brookings, he was an editor for Patriot's Blood. A pretty good writer himself, I hear, but she hired him to make major repairs on maybe half the books on the list. The guy's full name was John Alden Brookings, and he told Gloriana he was a direct descendant of *the* John Alden, you know, the Mayflower wimp. Only it turned out Brookings made up the Mayflower stuff simply to get the job. His ancestors didn't come over on the Mayflower any more than mine flew here on the Space Shuttle. So Gloriana fired him."

The information sounded promising. "How long ago did it happen?"

"Couple of years, I think."

Less promising. If Brookings had wanted to kill Gloriana, he'd probably have done so long before now. I said as much to Zhang.

Zhang didn't want to let it go. "Gloriana didn't only fire him. I'm sure you've heard what an obsessive bi...woman she was, so firing him wasn't enough for her. She wanted to completely destroy the man. She faxed his corrected resumé—there were some other exaggerations and misrepresentations on it, I believe—to every publishing house, magazine, and newspaper in the state. I received a copy myself. After that, Brookings' career was trash."

Gloriana was lucky such behavior didn't get her sued, and I said so.

"He threatened to sue, all right, but since the information she faxed was true, nothing came of it."

"You know where Brookings is now?"

Zhang nodded. Much too enthusiastically, I thought. "Yeah, he finally got a job, although it's only part-time. You'll find him two buildings down from here, at Verdad Press."

"Isn't that…?"

"Yep, Emil Ramos' publishing house."

"*Brookings* doesn't sound Spanish," I pointed out.

"The guy's fluent. So am I, as a matter of fact. After all, this is Arizona. If you don't already know Spanish, you'd better learn." He then rattled off a long passage which I, with my embarrassingly rudimentary Spanish, had difficulty following.

"Sostenemos como evidentes estas verdades: que todos los hombres son creados iguales; que son dotados por su Creator de ciertos derechos inalienables…."

The Spanish translation of the Declaration of Independence.

"Beautiful," I said, meaning it. "Look, before I leave, maybe you can clear something up for me."

Zhang tensed. "If I can."

"I'm a little confused about something. Before I started working on this case, I didn't know much about publishing. Still don't, actually. But there appears to be more money in it than I'd realized. Am I wrong there?"

He relaxed. "Publishing is a multibillion-dollar business, Miss Jones. When you say 'publishing,' people tend to think in terms of the big New York houses. But believe me when I tell you, those guys are merely the tip of a very, very big iceberg. We little guys make up a full two-thirds of the publishing industry. There are around 75,000 independent presses like mine, and last year we had sales upward of thirty billion dollars."

My surprise must have been apparent, because Zhang grinned. "Not all of us are rich as Gloriana. Some of us prefer to bring quality material to the table, as opposed to her racist swill." He paused, then added, "As you can see, I don't mind speaking ill of the dead."

When I reached the parking lot, my mind was swirling. Above the airport runway, private aircraft floated down from the sky, their noisy little engines churning up the polluted air. Below, a roadrunner high-tailed it across the parking lot toward the brush, a squirming gecko in its beak. Casually dressed workers strolled back and forth between upscale sedans, chatting about blended funds, trunk modifiers, and human popsicles.

I finally figured out what was bothering me. The minute I'd begun pressing Zhang for his own movements the evening of Gloriana's murder, he'd drawn my attention away from himself by offering up Brookings. Coincidence? Or cleverness?

Before heading over to Verdad Press, I pulled my cell phone out of my carry-all and dialed Myra Gordon's number again. Still no answer. This time I didn't bother leaving a message.

I followed Zhang's directions and, after winding my way through the business complex, found Verdad situated in a stucco-sided building designed to look like a pueblo from the front, a generic warehouse at the rear. When I opened the door, an old-fashioned bell dinged my arrival, followed quickly by the tippy-tap of high heels.

"May I help you?" asked a pretty Hispanic woman who bore a faint resemblance to Emil Ramos. His daughter?

I asked to see Ramos and handed her my card. She frowned at it, then disappeared into the back, leaving me to study the hand-carved Mexican credenzas and bookcases. Just as I started to pluck a book from a shelf, Ramos emerged from the hallway, his hand stretched toward mine. "Miss Jones, how nice to see you again."

I shook his hand, wondering where all this pleasantry came from, private detectives not usually being known for bringing joy into peoples' lives.

"I'm fine, Mr. Ramos, but I need to ask you some more questions."

"Come, we will be more comfortable in the conference room."

After a final hand squeeze, he led me into a long, narrow room where the Mexican design motif continued. Yaqui masks, from the humorous to the horrifying, hung on the walls, which were lined with even more glass-fronted bookcases filled with Verdad publications.

"How many books have you printed?" I asked, as we sank into two deeply cushioned chairs on opposite sides of a long refectory table.

"You probably mean *titles*, not actual copies of books. We're up to almost two hundred titles now. Adult books, young readers, even a few graphic novels, which are the new big thing. There remain few areas of publication these days that do not interest us if they appear appropriate for the lucrative bilingual market. The rewards there, as we have discovered, have been quite satisfying. So has the respect our titles have been accorded. Verdad publications have been placed in schools and libraries nationwide. Native Spanish readers enjoy them because of the content, but increasingly they have become popular with Anglos who are learning Spanish as a second language. We've even begun our own book club, the Adult Easy Readers."

"Adult? You mean…?"

"No, Miss Jones, I do not mean 'adult' as in *Hustler* magazine. I mean 'adult' as in grown-up, which few *Hustler* readers are, in my opinion. Our Adult Easy Reader Club provides books of mature content for adults whose Spanish reading skills are still in the rudimentary stage. Before we came along, these people had to read children's stories, which both bored and humiliated them. With our publications, they can read creative fiction and non-fiction with sophisticated content. Yet the language usage is uncomplicated enough for readers relatively unskilled in the language. Here, let me demonstrate."

He opened one of the bookcases, took out a brightly colored book, and slid it across the table to me. *Las Mysteria de las Madonna Muerta: The Mystery of the Dead Madonna.* The novel was set in the Guadalupe section of Phoenix and featured a Hispanic police detective named Consuela Lopez. The first half of the book was in Spanish, the back half, English.

"The author was born and raised in Guadalupe," Ramos said. "She still lives there and teaches English as a second language at the community center. We've already printed four books in that series. Our readers can't get enough."

The cover photograph showed a woman who looked suspiciously like Ramos' daughter, crouched behind an ancient statue of the Madonna. She held a cocked .38 in her hand, so I immediately identified with her. I opened the book to the title page. *Many thanks to my friends at Verdad! Maria Elena Rodriguez. Muchas gracias mis compadres.*

Handing the book back, I said, "It must be gratifying for you to be doing so well in this market."

"Yes, Verdad is respected, and that is gratifying. But our marketing share is small and distribution is the key to profits, so we endeavor to keep expenses low. My wife does the accounting, my eldest son takes care of the shipping. And my beautiful daughter, who will soon have her MFA from Arizona State, is one of our copy editors and a sometimes model for our covers. The rest of our employees work part-time only."

My cue. "I believe you have a John Alden Brookings working for you?"

He pursed his lips. "Mr. Brookings is one of our part-time employees, yes."

"Is Mr. Brookings here now?"

"He only works two days a week. Today is not one of them."

Acceeding to my request, Ramos wrote down Brookings' phone number and address, which wasn't too far from Megan and Zach's former home. As I tucked the piece of paper into my carry-all, I asked, "I've heard that Gloriana made it difficult for Mr. Brookings to find work. Did she fax his 'corrected' job history to you?"

A faint smile. "She most certainly did. You have heard the story about the 'Alden' part being inaccurate? Well, I do not care if Mr. Brookings' ancestors rode that particular leaky boat or not. The only thing that concerned me when he applied here was his editing skills, and they were—and continue to be—excellent. He can take a hopelessly garbled manuscript, find the nugget of interest, and build a solid book around it."

I thought back to my conversation with Zhang. "I'm sure most publishers in town didn't care about the Mayflower business, either. But I've also heard the resumé contained other, ah, inaccurate information."

"Perhaps you should ask him that yourself. Now, if you'll excuse me, I was in the middle of a good book." The smile was brilliant.

"One more thing, Mr. Ramos. When we spoke at the Festival of the West, you seemed quite emotional about Gloriana and Patriot's Blood. Did Gloriana ever do anything to damage you or your publishing house?"

He shook his head. "I am not certain she realized Verdad even existed. After all, none of us came over on the Mayflower. Our own ancestors arrived with Cortez a century earlier. But if Gloriana had ever turned her viper gaze toward Verdad.... Well, let me assure you that coming under Gloriana Alden-Taylor's scrutiny would be an uncomfortable experience for anyone. It is well known in the publishing community that there was no moderation to be found in her. Once she became enraptured by a thing, she stayed focused on it to the exclusion of all else, even family."

"What do you mean, 'even family'? I thought that was one of her major obsessions—family."

"Her family's bloodlines, yes, but not *la familia*. There is a difference. People were not human beings to Gloriana, merely symbols of some abstract idea. For proof of this, you only need to see how she treated her *familia*. She was a neglectful mother, a hostile sister. Her niece...well, her treatment of that poor girl was unconscionable. A young mother, made to work all those hours, it is a scandal. But even her grandson was little more than an employee to Gloriana. She only cared what he could do for her."

"But she left almost everything to Zach. House, Patriot's Blood, the whole deal."

He shrugged. "Who else was there to leave it to? She disapproved of her daughter's lifestyle and she cared little for her sisters. At least Zachary is of her blood and understands the world of publishing. Not that he will put that knowledge to use. He dreams of something called *literature*." A soft chuckle.

I'd been wondering about Zach's plans, myself. "Tell me, Mr. Ramos, do you think he has any chance to make a go of it publishing the kinds of books he's talking about, all that experimental stuff?"

"While I very much admire Zachary Alden-Taylor as a decent human being, I have little faith in his publishing acumen. Few people wish to read 'literature' anymore. We are all too busy working two or three jobs to peruse long descriptive passages about the memories that a madeline may invoke."

"Who's she?"

He corrected me. "Not who. What. The name of a French butter cookie Proust wrote about with such great effect in his *Remembrance of Things Past.* But that was another place, another time. Whether we decry the fact or not, this is the twenty-first century and people's lives and reading preferences have changed. So much so that it is my belief that if Zachary continues on his unwise path, Patriot's Blood will be bankrupt by the end of the year."

While I didn't know anything about publishing, it sounded to me like Ramos' prediction made sense. Poor Zach. Poor Megan. Poor strays.

Before I left Verdad, I purchased all four books in the Detective Consuela Lopez series. Thanks to a trigger-happy redhead, my evenings remained free. Sublimating my murderous impulses toward a certain cowboy with a well-written mystery seemed like a fine idea.

It sure beat sitting in jail.

Chapter 19

John Alden Brookings lived in Wigwam Court, one of the few remaining trailer parks in southern Scottsdale, but it was no luxury RV park for vacationing or retired seniors. The Wigwam was a place populated by down-and-outs who had little money and even less hope. I steered the Jeep through the trailer park's narrow lanes and took note of the rusting single-wides and unkempt grounds.

I pulled up to Space 34 with a sense of foreboding. The weeds in Brookings' tiny front yard grew knee-high, and the old red Monte Carlo up on blocks in the driveway looked like restoration efforts had long since been abandoned. The grill was crushed, the front window shattered and its once-red paint sun-bleached to the same color as Brookings' pale pink trailer. Brookings hadn't just fallen upon hard times—he'd been buried by them.

When I stepped out of the Jeep, I noticed a wheelchair ramp leading up to the trailer's door. And on that door, yet another National Alliance flier. The boys sure got around. I was about to remove it when the screen door opened and a gaunt face peered up at me from a wheelchair.

"You're late."

Before I could tell Brookings he must have mistaken me for someone else, he wheeled away from the door, calling over his shoulder, "Well, don't just stand there, come on in and let's get this over with. I don't have all day, ha ha."

I entered the trailer, my eyes straining against the darkness. "Mr. Brookings, I think...."

"What a nice change, someone from a government agency actually thinking. Will wonders never cease."

The trailer smelled like old beer and even older cigarettes. A few flies buzzed around a bowl filled with wrinkled apples.

Magazines and books lay scattered on every available surface, even slopping over from the tiny kitchen's countertop into a sink which appeared not to have been scoured in years. If the trailer had ever held a sofa, it was long gone, replaced by a crude desk constructed by placing a cheap, hollow-core door across two battered file cabinets. I glanced down the hallway toward the tiny bedroom, where I could see no bed, merely shelves of books, books, and more books. Where did the man sleep? Stretched out across the Encyclopedia Britannica?

"So why are you denying my claim this time? As you can see, I'm as crippled up as ever." He plucked a cigarette from a crumpled pack but didn't offer me one.

"I'm not denying you anything, Mr. Brookings, because I'm obviously not who you think I am." I handed him my card.

He favored me with a dry chuckle, which quickly turned into a vicious cough. He lit the cigarette anyway. "So not only does the State usually show up late, sometimes it doesn't show up at all. What can I do for you, my pretty? No, let me guess. Private detective. Hmmm. Since my ex-wives have long since figured out they won't be bleeding any money from this miserable old stone, you must be here about something else. Hmmm again."

Then he raised his hands in manufactured surprise. "Could it....Oh, could it be that your visit has something to do with a certain late-but-unlamented publisher?"

I tossed his bitter tone back at him. "You're quick, Mr. Brookings, no doubt about it."

His grin revealed surprisingly white teeth, and I realized that he wasn't as old as I'd first thought, probably only somewhere in his forties. Although his clothing was rumpled, it was clean, and his fingernails had recently been manicured.

He took another drag on his cigarette. "Have a seat, detective, and let's talk."

I looked around, but the only "seat" I saw in the trailer was a step stool parked next to a walker, so I headed toward that.

"I don't get many visitors," Brookings explained, after I'd propped myself against the stool's hard surface. "Those I do get, I generally don't want to stay long. I might make an exception for you, though. You're hot, but then I doubt if I'm the first man to tell you that."

His eyes settled on my scar. "A run-in with a bullet, lovely Lena?"

Most people took it for granted that I received my forehead scar during a traffic accident. "Yeah, you're quick."

With a grunt, he rolled up his right sleeve. Snaking toward his shoulder was a red scar almost the mirror image of mine. "A parting gift from my third wife. No, no, don't waste your sympathy. I had it coming. Hell, I didn't even bother pressing charges against the woman. Considering everything I pulled on her, I figure she still owes me a couple more of these punctuation marks."

I motioned toward his wheelchair. "Another wife's editorial comment?"

He threw back his head in laughter. "Naw, just a four-day bender topped off by a car wreck. At least I didn't hurt anyone else, only some scraggly mesquite out on the Rez. The tree's still there, I hear, and flourishing. Wish I could say the same for myself. I'm here, but flourishing doesn't exactly describe my state. Thanks to Gloriana."

"Speaking of Gloriana, Mr. Brookings...."

"Oh, please. John. Yes, let's speak of her. I love getting in my licks. The hag ruined me."

It looked to me like he'd done a pretty good job of ruining himself. "I hear Gloriana took exception to your job application, is that right?"

After a long, luxurious drag on his cigarette, he answered me. "You show me a person who doesn't pad his curriculum vitae and I'll show you a fry cook at McDonald's. Yeah, I padded the damned thing. I added some editing jobs I didn't really hold, for Doubleday and the like. I'd free-lanced for them back in the Dark Ages, but I was never actually on staff. I'll tell you this, though. I didn't pad my skills. I could do everything I said I could do. Gloriana herself said I was the best editor she'd ever worked with. What set her off was when she found out that while my middle name might be Alden, it's not the Alden she cares...cared about."

I tried to wave the cigarette smoke away, but it was hopeless. There was no ventilation in the trailer, just stagnant dreams. "Did you lie about the Alden thing, too?"

A solitary fly floated up from the fruit bowl and lit on Brookings' head. He didn't notice. "Not really. As I said, Alden is my middle name, my paternal grandfather's *first* name. But when Gloriana saw it on my paperwork, she got excited. Since I'm no dummy and really needed that job, I let her believe what she wanted to believe. If I'd known she ran deep checks on her employees, I wouldn't have done it."

I frowned. "Deep checks? What do you mean?"

"Such as hiring private detectives like you. Why she felt it was necessary to go to all that trouble with employees who didn't even handle money remains beyond my comprehension. But she did. God knows the woman was thorough. Anyway, I'd already been at Patriot's Blood six months, edited well nigh a dozen deranged books and helped rewrite a pile of garbage that should never have been accepted in the first place. Then suddenly I was called into her Chamber of Horrors, whereupon she fired my ass. She enjoyed doing it, too. Relished it, one might even say."

"I hear that she faxed your 'corrected' resumé all over town."

"Yup. If you ask me, which I am certain you will get around to sooner or later, the answer is no, I didn't kill Gloriana. I'm too much of a cripple. But believe me when I say that the woman was a murder victim waiting to happen."

I looked at the walker, suspecting that Brookings might be more mobile than he wanted me to believe. But was he mobile enough to drive up to Oak Creek, climb down into the creek bed, and harvest water hemlock? Also, no one had mentioned seeing someone tooling around the banquet either on a walker or in a wheelchair. However, I'd noticed that most people averted their eyes when confronted with the physically challenged. As for Brookings' obvious transportation problems, yes, that car of his probably hadn't taken him anywhere, but there were other ways for the wheelchair-bound to get around: Dial-A-Ride, Hertz, cabs.

I guess he could tell what I was thinking, because he said, "I haven't used that walker in a year."

Then why wasn't it covered in dust? Everything else was. "Is there anyone who can vouch for your whereabouts the day Gloriana was killed?"

"Probably not. But I was here doing my usual, drinking and editing, editing and drinking." The fly finally annoyed him enough that he brushed it away, lifting up a few strands of silver hair in the process.

"But you're working again."

He flicked an ash on the floor. "A couple of days a week at Verdad, a few private jobs under the table. I get along."

"What kind of private jobs?"

Brookings explained that he helped people who couldn't find publishers bring their own books to market.

"I edit their manuscripts, then find vendors such as typesetters, printers, and binders who won't take advantage of their ignorance," he said. "Most of the books I help with are memoirs and family histories, lots of family photos, letters, that kind of thing. We're only talking about a hundred copies per title. But there are always a few people out there, novelists, usually, who think large and put up good money, hoping that they can crack the bestseller list. Ha. For them, I do publicity, marketing, work the phones, set up signings....Pointless, really, but it pays the rent."

In other words, Brookings sold his editorial expertise to self-publishers. "Do any of these folks ever recoup their investments?"

"It's possible that in the centuries-long history of publishing such an event may have occurred once or twice." He vented that cough-laugh again. "But I don't lie to them about their chances and I get my money up front. I also take care that none of those benighted souls knows where I live. We have our editorial meetings at Verdad, one of the little perks Ramos allows me. I have an office there. And Ramos' daughter is a sympathetic soul. When my little self-publishers come in, she calls me Mr. Brookings and pretends to be my secretary. Verdad's a pretty classy setup, and it impresses the hell out of my clientele."

For the first time, his eyes looked wistful, as if reflecting on the life he could have lived.

We continued chatting about the publishing business for a while until I eventually steered the subject back to Gloriana's murder. "Let's say I take you at your word that you didn't kill Gloriana. And let's say the man accused of the murder didn't kill her, either. Do you have any other likely suspects?"

He pretended to think for a moment before saying, "Likely suspects? Hmmmm. If I were a betting man, I'd probably put my money on David Zhang or Sandra Alden-Taylor."

I tried not to look surprised. "Why would either of them want to kill Gloriana? Especially Poor Sandra."

His face, never kind, took on a new malice. "So Sandra sucked you in? The bitch. Well, lovely Lena, I'm not the only person who got called into the Chamber of Horrors and had the riot act read to. Wait a minute. Is that a dangling participle? Oh, who the hell cares. Listen, the only difference between me and Sandra was that I got fired, while Sandra, being family, was given another chance."

"What was Sandra's crime, Mr. Brookings?"

"Helping herself to the petty cash, a habit of hers."

This information didn't surprise me as much as it should have. I'd sensed an odd current of desperation in the woman. But for all her sticky-fingered behavior with the petty cash, Sandra had not been written out of Gloriana's will. I wondered if the amount had been enough to alleviate all her money troubles.

"I can see your point about Sandra," I told him. "But why would David Zhang want to kill Gloriana?"

Brookings flicked some more ash on the floor. "No particular reason, other than the fact that he has the worst temper I've ever seen on a Chinaman."

I was as tired of Brookings' cynicism as I was his trailer's squalor, so after saying goodbye, I let myself out. I tore away the National Alliance's flier as I left, wishing that I could ram it down Brookings' throat.

I must have been in Brookings' trailer longer than I realized, because it was full dark as I settled myself into my Jeep. With lights off, I drove a few spaces away, stopped in front of a double-wide, and picked up my cell phone. I didn't want Brookings to hear me tell Jimmy to run one of those infamous deep checks on him. As well as on Sandra.

"Already a done deal on both," Jimmy's voice crackled over the poor connection. "Brookings has a rap sheet. Back in ninety-two, he got drunk and almost killed some five-year-old kid walking home from school. Sentenced to two years, released in eighteen months. Then a few more DUIs, a few more wrecks, a few stints in rehab. Suspended license, of course."

Somehow Brookings had neglected to tell me about the child and the prison sentence. Maybe he forgot. "Jimmy, he seemed to be expecting a visit from some kind of state representative. In fact, that's who he thought I was at first. Do you know what that's all about?"

The cell phone hissed some more (I really had to buy a better one some day), then Jimmy's voice emerged again. "He's collecting SSDI, Social Security Disability Insurance. They're probably checking on him to make sure he's still disabled."

I frowned. "There are doubts?"

"If they're making home visits, yeah. Looks like they suspect he's leeching off the system. Lots of that going around, these days."

I remembered Brookings' walker, obviously used. And then the trail by Oak Creek. How steep was it? With a little care, could any reasonably adept person clunk along the trail with a walker, pick a few plants, then clunk back to their car? I'd have to ask Owen. One of the residents at the Wigwam Trailer Park might not have minded renting out their car for a few bucks. And kept quiet about it for a few more.

"What did you get on Sandra Alden-Taylor? Brookings said she was pilfering petty cash from Gloriana. If that's true, I want to know why, and if she's stolen from anyone else." I didn't add that Brookings appeared to have a personal hate on for Sandra. Perhaps she had helped get him fired?

More hissing on the line. I rolled the Jeep forward a few feet, and the hissing stopped. I repeated my question.

"Sandra Alden-Taylor. That's...ah, I'd rather not talk about her over the cell. Come on back to the office and we'll discuss it."

I looked at the darkness around me. Time for Jimmy to go home. I pointed this out.

"I'll wait until you get here. This is stuff you need to know."

I ended the call, curious about Sandra's other sins. Before turning the key in the ignition, I placed yet another call to Myra Gordon/Mbisi. No answer. I would have to drive to Wyatt's Landing and hunt her down, either at home or at the library. I no longer cared which.

Then I switched on the Jeep's lights, and headed toward my office, yellow National Alliance fliers glowing in my rearview mirror.

When I arrived back at Desert Investigations, Jimmy looked the picture of misery. "Sandra Alden-Taylor is in the red at all the local casinos, and she's carrying some pretty heavy online debt, too. Her credit cards are maxed out, she's behind on the consolidation loan she took out a year ago, and her car's been repossessed. She's been using one of Gloriana's cars to get back and forth from work."

Gambling debts. Apparently, like many put-upon people, Sandra had found an escape. And like most obsessive-compulsives, she had turned her escape into an even worse trap.

"Um, there's more." Jimmy's eyes flicked away from mine.

"Such as?"

"I called one of my cousins at the casino, and he told me he'd heard some rumors about her."

"Rumors?" What was wrong with the man? Such coyness was unlike him. "Come on, Jimmy, spit it out."

He ducked his head in embarrassment. When he spoke, he addressed the floor. "The rumors are that she likes a little action."

"Which means?"

"Geez, Lena. Do I have to say it?" When he looked back up at me, Jimmy's mahogany-colored face had flushed bright red, making the tribal tattoo on his forehead stand out in startling contrast. Suddenly I realized what he meant by "action."

Amused, I said, "So Sandra's promiscuous, eh? Hardly a big deal these days."

"It's more than a little messing around, Lena. My cousin told me that Sandra got herself hooked up with a casino crowd that likes to party hearty, sexually speaking. He also said that during one of those parties somebody got busy with a camcorder and posted the whole deal on the Net."

Good thing for Sandra that Gloriana didn't like computers. If she had known about the orgy, the scandal would probably have been the final straw. Bye-bye new house.

"Good work, partner," I told him. "Listen, you go ahead and lock up. We'll talk about this more tomorrow."

On my way back to Desert Investigations, I had noticed that the lights were still on at Patriot's Blood. On the off-chance that Sandra was burning some midnight oil, or stealing more petty cash, I decided to pay a visit.

She looked surprised to see me, and her face, smudged with dirt from moving cartons, paled when I confronted her with what I had learned.

"I never stole from the office," she said, her voice quavering. "Whoever told you that is lying." Then she chewed on her already well-gnawed fingernails.

"Okay, Sandra. Let's say you're telling me the truth about the petty cash. What about the videotape?"

Her mouth gaped in guilty horror. "Videotape? What videotape?"

"*Sandra Does Scottsdale.* Did Gloriana see it? Someone could have downloaded it, shown it to her."

Sandra refused to meet my eyes. "I don't know what you're talking about. Now please go away. I've got a lot of work to do, that's why I'm still here." She made a big show out of shuffling papers. Some of them were blank.

I refused to let up. "Sandra, it's going to come out when...."

I never finished the sentence because the air around me suddenly changed, as if someone had sucked all the oxygen out of the building. Then a wall of heat rushed toward me at the same time a roar slammed against my eardrums.

Before I could react, I felt myself lifted into the air.

So this is what death is like, I thought, as the bomb's shockwave hurled me through the plate glass window.

Chapter 20

For an instant I lay stunned on the pavement, able only to stare at the flames licking the remains of Patriot's Blood. The bomb's concussion had deafened me, so even while glass continued to shatter and beams fell, the horrific scene appeared no more dimensional than a silent movie.

Then I remembered Sandra.

Was she dead? Or was she trapped inside, screaming for help to a woman who could no longer hear?

Mercifully numb, though I knew the pain would come, I scrambled to my feet and looked desperately along the pavement. My carry-all lay a couple of feet from me, but the cell phone peeking out of it had cracked down the middle. So much for calling 911. Still, someone nearby must have heard the blast and would send help. But probably not soon enough for Sandra. If she had any chance for survival at all, it would have to come from me.

I took a deep breath and ran back into the building.

The reception area was a shambles, with overturned file cabinets and desks partially covered by smoldering heaps of crumbling drywall. Thankfully, the worst of the fire was still confined to the back of the building, but it was only a matter of minutes, possibly seconds, before all of Patriot's Blood's paper-rich offices blossomed into a funeral pyre.

"Sandra!" I shouted, ignoring the fact that I couldn't hear her even if she answered. If she still lived, I wanted to give her hope.

The heat was intense, bearable only because the blast had punctured the roof so that the flames at the back of the office vented upward. My immediate problem was the acrid black smoke rolling slowly toward me, lit at the edges by sulfurous yellow and orange. Remembering that more people die of smoke inhalation than burns, I ripped off my blouse and tied it, bandana-like, over the lower part of my face. A weak protection against the approaching smoke's deadly chemicals, but better than none.

I screamed Sandra's name again.

"Sandra! Where are you?"

As I staggered barefoot through the rubble, keeping my head as low as possible, my ankle slammed against something hard. Looking down, I saw Gloriana's old Underwood typewriter. The blast had thrown it through the wall and into the reception area, where it now rested on its side against a metal filing cabinet. Nearby, a tongue of flame licked through the yard-wide hole the typewriter had left behind.

"Sandra! I can't hear! You'll have to move, show me where you are!"

Nothing.

The flames from the back marched silently toward the reception area, consuming stacked manuscripts and books. All of Gloriana Alden-Taylor's ugly dreams. And me, eventually, if I didn't get out of here.

But not without Sandra. Refusing to give in to my fear, I forced myself to look away from the flames' steady progress.

"Sandra! Please! Show me where you are!" My throat was so raw with inhaled dust and smoke I wondered if I had made any noise at all. I continued calling her name, turning over large pieces of drywall that could hide a human body.

"Sandra! Move! Do something!"

Then, from underneath a toppled file cabinet, a movement. A small hand inching its way out, fingers fluttering.

Sandra was still alive, the cabinet that crushed her also protecting her.

I stumbled sore-footed across fallen beams to reach her, screaming that I was coming, that I would save her, to hold on. Ignoring the splintered beam that raked its teeth across my leg, I knelt down and grasped her hand. "Don't worry, I'm getting you out of here."

Could she breathe? The air around us was beginning to thicken, sucking away what little oxygen remained in the ruined room. I probably had only seconds before, blouse bandana or not, noxious fumes overcame me.

I let go of her hand, grabbed the corner of the file cabinet, and heaved. Nothing. The file cabinet was too heavy, probably loaded down with manuscripts.

"Sandra, try and help me! Push against the cabinet!"

A feeble twitch, then nothing. She was too weak. God only knew what injuries she had sustained.

I pulled at the cabinet again, but even with my years of weight-training at the gym, I didn't have the strength to do more than shift it slightly. Was I injuring her further? Was she screaming?

Greenish-black smoke belched toward us, and right behind it, a wall of flame. Now the heat was almost unbearable. If I stayed here, I was as doomed as Sandra.

Who was I kidding? The whole situation was hopeless.

I turned away from her, hoping that the way remained clear to the door. It did. Hardening my heart, I started toward it.

Then out of the corner of my eye, I saw Sandra's hand again. Reaching up, palm out. Begging for her life.

I turned back.

"I won't leave you!" I screamed at her, struggling once more with the file cabinet.

After one more heave, the file cabinet shifted, but not enough to free her. I needed something to give me leverage.

And then I saw it.

Like Gloriana's typewriter, the toilet plunger had been thrown through the reception room wall all the way from the bathroom. It lay on top of an overturned desk, rubber suction cup half burned away, but with the wooden handle miraculously intact.

In one fluid movement, I grabbed the plunger, shoved it under the edge of the filing cabinet and heaved. The cabinet shifted. I slipped the handle even further under the cabinet and heaved again.

The plunger snapped in two.

But not before I saw Sandra, lying on her stomach, one hand over her head, the other stretched toward me.

Still alive.

The smoke rolled closer, followed by the hungry flames. Desperate, adrenalin spiking, I looked around for another tool.

There. A two-by-four, fallen from the ceiling.

I took it in my hands and shoved it under the cabinet. Then, with one final heave, the cabinet slid away from Sandra. Her mouth opened in a scream I couldn't hear. "There, there," I said, leaning down, trying to lift her into my arms.

Sandra was too big. She was every bit as tall as I, but much heavier. A safe carry wasn't possible, so I'd have to do the best I could.

Realizing I was probably aggravating her injuries, I slipped my arms under hers, wrapped them around her chest, then locked my fingers together. I could feel her uneven breaths. Was she still screaming? No matter. Gritting my teeth against the heat, I began to drag her limp form over the rubble-strewn floor. Behind us, the flames consumed the wall and started across the floor. The file cabinet I'd found Sandra under was already scorching.

"It's okay," I lied. "We'll be fine."

Once, her shoe—miraculously still on—snagged on a splintered piece of wood, and I had to stop to free her once again. In my haste to rip her shoe away, I tore her skin and she began to bleed from yet another wound.

But pain was better than death. I should know.

"Hold on. We're almost there," I grunted, wishing that I could hear her, if only to know that she was still alive.

The smoke was blinding me now, an almost solid mass churning around us, as if purposely keeping us from escape. The blouse I'd wrapped so hopefully around my face no longer kept out the fumes, and I could feel them enter my nostrils, my throat.

Would I be able to make it to the blown-out door before the smoke won and I lost consciousness?

Better not think about that. Think about the jasmine-scented night air, and beneath it, the cool pavement. All I wanted was to reach the street, lie down, and sleep. Then again, why wait? I closed my eyes against the smoke, thinking that all I had to do was drop my burden, buckle my knees, and go to sleep right here. Why continue this ridiculous struggle?

Then Sandra's hands grasped mine. I opened my watering eyes, squinted through the seductive tendrils of black smoke, and saw her lips move.

I think she was saying "My babies, my babies...."

No, I couldn't give up and die right now. Not with a clean conscience, I couldn't.

Refusing to look at the flames, to breath in the acrid smoke, I hitched her up again and hauled her forward.

Toward the soft night.

Chapter 21

I hate hospitals.

I hate doctors, nurses, and all those vampires who draw your blood.

Yet none of them are half as bad as the visitors.

During my first full day at Scottsdale General Hospital, it seemed like half the people in my life—with the noted exception of Dusty—trooped into my room, shoving flowers in my face, waving their arms, and moving their mouths at me, totally ignoring the fact that I couldn't hear a word they said. Every cop I'd ever worked with dropped by, and they were the worst of all. They flapped their mouths like ventriloquists' dummies, while all I could do was grin and nod, hoping that I wasn't agreeing to marry one of them.

At least Jimmy understood that the blast had pretty much deafened me. Besides keeping the press at bay (I'd made headlines again), he kept me informed via notepad on Sandra's condition: smoke inhalation, first and second degree burns, a broken collarbone, three broken ribs, a punctured eardrum and various cuts and scrapes. But she would live.

The paramedics who had scraped us off the pavement after a flurry of 911 calls from a gaggle of tourists had rendered expert care to us both on the way to the hospital. Not that I could remember any of it.

My own injuries were confined to flash burns, minor smoke inhalation, miscellaneous cuts, and a plate-sized bruise on my ass where I'd landed on the sidewalk. The most painful wounds of all were those on my feet, which were covered with burns and gashes, one of them almost to the bone. The blast had blown me out of my shoes, and I had run back into the building barefoot, stepping on a burning beam here, a little broken glass there. I couldn't remember feeling much pain at the time, but I felt it now. So much so that the doctors insisted I remain in the hospital for one more day.

This made me a captive audience for too many garrulous visitors.

Megan Alden-Taylor, my eighth drop-in of the day—it wasn't yet noon—stood with Zach by my bed, shedding dog and cat hairs all over the hospital's clean white linens.

She said something, but I couldn't quite make it out. Figuring that she'd asked me how I felt (that seemed to be the standard question for everyone), I said, "I'm fine. I've been to rougher parties." I lied in as chipper a tone as I could manage without being able to hear myself. I wished she and Zach would go back to the ICU's waiting room where they had been hanging out all night, waiting for word of Sandra's condition.

But Zach had a few things to say, too. From what little lip-reading I could manage, he blamed himself for the situation. If he hadn't taken such advantage of Sandra's need to be abused, she would not have been at the office when the bomb went off.

"Don't be silly," I told him. "You didn't hold a gun to her head. You...." Then I shut up in shame, remembering that only recently, I'd done exactly that to a woman.

The *Scottsdale Journal*, which Jimmy handed me, revealed that Patriot's Blood Press, as well as the insurance office next to it, had burned to the ground. A spokesman from the Bureau of Alcohol, Tobacco, and Firearms divulged that the bomb in Gloriana's office was basically an incendiary device. Unlike the more common pipe bombs which were set off in the Phoenix area from time to time, this bomb resembled those arsonists used, designed to destroy real estate, not lives. The ATF spokesman also pointed out that the bomb's timer had been set for 7:00, when by rights the office would have been closed and all employees long gone. The bomb-maker could hardly have known that Sandra would return to finish up some work.

Nice theory, but I wasn't sure I bought it. The Aryan Brotherhood, whom I suspected had planted the bomb, was hardly known for its compassion. In my own opinion, the time had probably been picked to give its maker time to get far, far away. Like to some whack-brained militia compound in Idaho. Gaining access to the office wouldn't have been a problem. Most of the Brotherhood knew how to pick locks.

Jimmy interrupted my thoughts by handing me a note. *When you are released, you are coming home with me.*

I shook my head, then regretted it. The movement made my ears ring.

Jimmy scribbled some more, then stuck the notepad back in my face. *Don't argue. You will do this.*

Blinking in surprise, I looked up at him. Jimmy was the mildest of men. For him to order someone around was almost unheard of.

I opened my mouth to protest, but he raised a warning finger and shoved the pad in my face again. He hadn't erased the message.

I shrugged as best I could, considering the soreness in my shoulders. "Okay." Maybe my ears were getting better, because I could swear I heard him sigh with relief.

Eventually I dozed off, only to awake later to find Jimmy and the Alden-Taylors gone and Reverend Giblin sitting in a chair next to my bed, Bible in hand. His lips were moving, so I figured he was praying for me. What the hell. It couldn't hurt.

I went back to sleep.

The next morning, in response to my pleas, a nurse handed me a mirror. One look assured me I wouldn't be entering beauty contests any time soon. My eyelashes and eyebrows had been singed, my eyes blackened, my swollen face resembled a ripe tomato, and half my hair was missing, burned off as I was dragging Sandra out of Patriot's Blood.

"Aw, hell," I moaned. Then gasped. I'd actually heard myself! Not perfectly, but the words were audible, rumbling through my ears like a poor tape recording played at a too-slow speed.

"How now brown cow. The rain in Spain falls mainly on the plain." I heard every word.

"We're feeling better, are we?" the nurse asked.

"Oh, yes, we are." In fact, I felt so good that I didn't even protest when the nurse gave me our bath.

Clean once more (but how dirty can you really get lying in bed all day?), I slipped on the robe Jimmy had brought me, and with the nurse's help slid into the wheelchair the hospital provided. Then I rolled myself down the hall toward the ICU waiting room, where Zach and Megan sat.

"Sandra's doing as well as can be expected," Zach said. "Thanks to you, she's going to live. In fact, she should be able to go home in a couple of weeks. The scarring on her arms won't be too bad. Plastic surgery can perform miracles these days, even with burns."

Zach and I chatted for a while. He told me that Gloriana's funeral had taken place that morning and that it had been gratifyingly well-attended. I didn't volunteer my opinion that the woman's enemies probably wanted to make sure she was dead.

After a little more desultory conversation, I rolled back to my room, struggled from the wheelchair into my bed, and promptly fell asleep.

When I woke again, Reverend Giblin had returned.

"How's my little girl?" He spoke loudly enough that I could hear him without too much trouble. He looked ten years older than he had the day I'd seen him at WestWorld.

"Your little girl's doing fine."

He smiled, but it was a sad smile. "That's what you always said when I'd ask what was wrong."

I didn't like the way this conversation was going. Trips down Memory Lane weren't my style. Too many nightmares had built their houses there.

The monster in the closet.

I forced that particular nightmare away.

"No, really. I'm fine. The doctors said they'll release me tomorrow, and then I'm going to stay with Jimmy."

"Didn't the court order you into therapy after that last incident?"

Oh, here we go. "Anger management, that's all. I'm fine."

"Word is that Shakespeare helped write the King James version of the Bible."

I was about to ask him what that had to do with anything, when he continued.

"Shakespeare knew a lot about human nature, such as women who protest too much. When you first came to stay with us, we'd been foster parenting for fifteen years, but in all that time, I'd never seen such a frightened little girl. And the saddest thing was, you were even more terrified of showing that fear. Did you think we'd do something terrible to you, more terrible than had already been done? You'd wake up in the middle of the night screaming. By the time Mary Kay and I made it to your room, you'd have this forced smile on your face. You'd tell us you were fine, just fine, and order us back to bed."

I coughed up some more smoke. "Look, Reverend, I'm fine. I was fine then, and I'm fine now."

"Lena, you are one of the bravest human beings I've ever known. But for all that, you keep running away from your memories as if they'd kill you if they ever caught you. Don't you think it's about time you faced them?"

I didn't answer. Instead, I stared at the ceiling and tried not to remember.

Then, since the Rev showed no signs of leaving, I rolled over and feigned sleep.

After a few more minutes of silence, the Rev gave up. But before he left, he placed a book on my bedside table. After the door shut behind him, I squinted at the title.

The Only Demons Are Those We Create for Ourselves.

Chapter 22

A week later, I was anxious to leave Jimmy's trailer and return home, but every time I mentioned it, he pointed out the long flight of stairs that led to my apartment. "You're not good with crutches. You'd fall and wind up back in the hospital."

"No, I wouldn't."

"Yes, you would."

"Wouldn't."

"Would."

Jimmy had become a little bossy in the week since I had moved in with him, and I wasn't sure I liked it. I resented anyone telling me what to do, even my partner, and was about to tell him so when he added, "Your apartment's not finished, anyway."

Good point. In the way of workmen everywhere, the drywall guy who had been repairing my ceiling and walls had accepted another job. Once he battened down the hatches against rain—which Arizona tended to experience in March—he pointed out that his work for me was below scale. He'd received a more lucrative offer up at the Biltmore Resort, and wanted to take it.

"It'd be for a couple of days." He raised his voice so I could hear him above the roaring in my ears.

"Be my guest," I muttered, consigning myself to more time in Jimmy's trailer.

I hadn't realized Jimmy was such a party animal, but his trailer seemed to serve as Party Central for his many Pima cousins and friends. To add to the throngs of visitors, Jimmy's girlfriend

Esther frequently dropped by with her daughter. Watching Jimmy interact so naturally with them made me feel more alone, more isolated, even made me miss Dusty.

Dusty, who had not shown up at the hospital after the explosion.

Dusty, who had not even sent me a get-well card, let alone flowers.

Fine with me. Who needed the faithless son of a bitch?

"Jimmy, weren't we supposed to have dinner over at Owen's?" I asked one day, as I tested my feet for odd spots of tenderness. The wheelchair and ear noises long gone, I sat on the sofa, watching Jimmy fuss around the trailer's galley kitchen. As with many other areas in the trailer, the kitchen was lively with Pima designs, which turned its former blandness into a running pictograph history of his people. The cabinets over the sink showed Elder Brother wrestling power away from Earth Doctor, the creator of First World. On the double doors under the sink Jimmy had painted the Maze, the underground labyrinth where the humiliated Earth Doctor took refuge after his defeat, and where—the Pimas say—he still lives. Coyote, Spider Woman, and Snake danced along the hallway walls leading to the back bedroom where Jimmy had moved my things.

Above the sofa, which had been slip-covered in bright colors to match the Navajo rugs flanking the trailer door, hung elaborately framed photographs of Jimmy's parents. All four of them. His Mormon parents, who still lived in Salt Lake City, and his biological parents. Etched into the wooden frame beneath them were the Pima words which Jimmy had translated for me: *Soul reunited with Soul.*

Two orphans. Two completely different lives. Jimmy had found a place in the world. I never had.

"Dinner at Owen's? Good thing you reminded me." Jimmy put away the package of hamburger meat he'd been getting ready to fry. Compared to me, he was a gourmet chef. "I don't know where my mind's been these days."

But I did. Obsessing over Owen's looming murder trial.

Earlier that morning at Desert Investigations he had downloaded the video in which Sandra played a starring role. The quality had not been good, and at first all I could see were squirming bodies, none of them recognizable. But then the cameraman—or camera*woman*, let's not be sexist about this—hit his/her stride. The camera steadied, the focus tightened, and there was Sandra, dirty blond hair spilling across her face, arms and legs splayed out, a motley assortment of men and women poking at her various orifices. The whole scene looked as appetizing as a bunch of intertwined worms in a bait can.

Jimmy turned away with a grimace. "That's nasty." He had always been a prude.

I'm not. I leaned closer to the screen, studying it carefully. "Freeze the picture here, Jimmy."

"I'll freeze it, but don't expect me to look at it."

Tapping the screen, I said, "Right there. Look."

Although he didn't want to, he looked. "Now you're going to tell me that's Kama Sutra position number eighty-two, right?"

"I wouldn't have the faintest idea. But I'll tell you one thing I do know. The guy there? That's John Alden Brookings."

John Alden Brookings, who had been so quick to tell me about Sandra's sins. Why? Because he shared them?

When I called Brookings, all I got was his answering machine. Maybe he was at an editorial meeting.

Or filming another X-rated movie.

Even in the early twilight, I could tell that Owen Sisiwan's house was coming along nicely. Smack dab in the middle of the Rez, it reflected the extra money Owen had made from his job as Gloriana's handyman. At least that's how I hoped he had earned all that extra money.

Unlike so many Anglo homes in design-muddled Arizona, Owen's house didn't ape those in Seville, the Mediterranean, or New Mexico. The design appeared to have been ad-libbed as construction continued, yet somehow it all worked. The gently curved walls rose discreetly, their soft, sand-colored stucco barely interrupting the surrounding desert. A half-built loggia at the rear held out promise of a large patio; the untouched palo verde tree rising safely through its open beam work testified to Owen's reverence for nature.

A large brown dog, pedigree indeterminate, ran barking to me as I climbed out of Jimmy's Toyota, trying not to trip over my own crutches.

"Don't let Rebel scare you," Janelle Sisiwan called from the door. "He's a big phoney."

Threats duly delivered, Rebel proved Janelle's words by capering along with us to the door. "You can't come in," she said to him. "You'd make an even worse mess."

After a brief whine, the dog trotted over to Owen's truck and lay down.

"Try not to trip," Janelle warned, as we entered. "We're still trying to get things together."

Like the outside, the interior of the house proved to be a work-in-progress. The walls were rough, the seams which held the drywall together still obvious. Other than the furniture, the only items of decoration in the not-quite-finished living room were several Pima baskets hanging over the sofa. Janelle ushered us to the completed family room, where the Sisiwans apparently did most of their living. But over the delicious aroma of baking chicken, I could still smell the fresh drywall.

The walls in the family room were also relatively bare, except for a large, dark blue flag displaying the insignia of the U.S. Marine Corps, and an even larger American flag. The flag wasn't the standard Stars-and-Stripes issue, however. A portrait of a war-painted Plains Indian had been superimposed upon the red stripes. Sitting Bull, the guy who'd whipped Custer's ass at the Little Big Horn.

Beneath the flags, Owen and his children laughed together as they played with an assortment of Hot Wheels on the carpeted floor. The baby burbled at us from his basinet. From the CD player in the corner wafted the sounds of Carlos Nakai's wooden flute, his tune a modern riff on an old Navajo song.

A pang of envy struck me. Even in its unfinished state, this house was a home already.

I heard a car pull up outside, Rebel barking. "Excuse me," Janelle said, rushing past us toward the door. "More guests."

A minute later, she ushered Esther and Rebecca into the family room.

Jimmy's eyes lit up in delight as Rebecca threw her arms around him. Her mother, mature enough to have picked up on the Pimas' less demonstrative ways, just smiled. But her smile held as much affection as did Rebecca's hug.

At first, dinner at the Sisiwans' seemed to be as pleasant as ever, but after a while I thought I detected strain in Owen's voice. And he didn't seem to want to meet my eyes.

Cultural differences, I told myself. The Pima Way.

Part of me knew better. Owen was open enough with Esther and Rebecca, even teasing Rebecca about her newly pierced ears. And he was his usual jovial self with his wife and children. It was conversation with me that he was trying to avoid.

For a while, I played along, eating more than my share of Janelle's delicious baked chicken and spicy bean casserole, an old Pima recipe. I even coaxed Owen into conversation about his flags, treading delicately—I thought—around Native American sensitivities.

"Cool flag," I said, pointing toward it.

"Which one?"

I smiled. "Both, I guess. But where'd you get the flag with the Indian? I haven't seen any like that before."

"They sell them all over the Rez. Flags are very popular out here, even the standard Red, White, and Blue."

I had noticed. It was unusual, in these post-9/11 days, to see a Pima home that didn't have an American flag flying somewhere on the property, or to find a recruitment center that didn't have a steady stream of Indians filing into it. Considering the government's shabby treatment of Native Americans, their never-failing patriotism surprised me. Cautiously, I said as much to Owen.

His eyes flickered, and for a moment I thought he wouldn't answer. Then he did. "We're warriors, Lena. It's part of our heritage. Remember Ira Hayes?"

Hayes, a Pima, had helped raise the flag on Iwo Jima, and had been immortalized in both the famous photograph and the statue. But back in the States, he died alone in a ditch, forgotten by the country he had served.

"Ira Hayes is exactly my point," I said. "Look what he did, and look what was done to him. That was wrong."

Owen's eyes were dark and thoughtful. "Lots of wrongs out there in the world, plenty to go around for everyone." Then he looked back over at the flags. "But before you get too carried away with Anglo guilt, think about this. Regardless of what happened to my grandfathers, America is my country. And sometimes we Americans have to choose what kind of country we want: a strong one or a fair one. I'm not sure the two always go together."

If there had been a fly in the family room, it would probably have flown into my open mouth.

As if to purposefully increase my shock, Owen snapped off a quick salute. "*Semper fi,* Lena."

Sometimes I think I'll never understand people.

After dinner, the children—including Rebecca—went outside to play with the dog, leaving the grown-ups to clear the dishes.

But I'm not the dish-clearing type. I seized the moment and said to Owen, "Say, guy, let's you and me step outside and get some fresh air, shall we?"

Jimmy frowned at me from the sink, knowing that I was about to mix business with pleasure. Janelle didn't look happy about it either, but I didn't care. When Owen began to mumble his excuses, I said under my breath, "I don't think you're going to want Janelle to hear what I'm going to ask you. And I will ask, either in here or outside."

He glanced at her briefly, saw that she and Esther were preoccupied with the dishes, then headed out the door, motioning me to follow.

The children were grouped under the back porch light, thirteen-year-old Rebecca towering over them, playing what appeared to be Ring-aound-the-Rosie with Rebel. Owen and I walked away from them, toward the palo verde at the edge of the darkness, and settled ourselves into the two plastic patio chairs there. I waited for him to talk, but he didn't. He lit a cigarette and stared off into the night.

"That'll cause cancer," I said.

He shrugged. "Cancer or diabetes, same difference. They both kill you."

There was no answer in the face of such fatalism, so I canceled the rest of the lecture. "I've got a couple of questions I need to ask you. First, could a man using a walker get down into the section of Oak Creek where you took those hikers?"

He took a drag of his cigarette. "If he has enough strength in his arms, it's possible."

I remembered Brookings showing me his scar. That biceps had looked pretty powerful.

Easy info collected, I now entered difficult territory. "Owen, tell me about you and Gloriana."

"She was my boss." The light was poor so I couldn't see the expression on his dark face. Too bad.

"I found the darkroom. And the prints."

"Don't know what you're talking about."

Impatiently, I shifted on the hard chair. The night was cool, yet mosquitoes had already begun to swarm near the glow of Owen's cigarette. If this kept up, I'd either freeze or contract West Nile before I learned what I needed. "C'mon, Owen, don't tell me you didn't know. Gloriana was in love with you."

"In lust, maybe."

"She didn't arrange that hike to be nice to the SOBOP attendees, did she, Owen? She did it so you'd have to spend the night at the Hacienda."

"So you say."

"But the night didn't go the way she wanted, and that's why she was so nasty to you during the banquet. Made you sit in the hallway while everyone was eating."

The end of his cigarette glowed brighter. "You've got a reason for everything, don't you?"

Not everything, but I was getting there. "Tell me what happened that night, Owen. The night before the hike."

"That's between Gloriana and me."

"She's dead."

He shrugged. "It's still private. Show the poor woman some respect."

Poor woman? Slapping away a particularly determined mosquito, I said, "She treated you like dirt."

"Women in pain sometimes do angry things." He flicked his eyes toward the house.

"What other angry things did Gloriana do to you?"

"Not as many things as you believe." He sighed, relaxed. "Yes, she was a hard woman, and yes, she was not easy to work for. But much had been done to her. One time, when we were measuring out the area for the new patio, she told me that her husband's nickname for her was 'Old Prune Face.' She had tears in her eyes when she said that. If I comforted her then, it was only from kindness."

What kind of "comfort," I wondered? "Jesus, Owen! She was in love with you, and you knew it. You should have found another job."

A dark laugh. "You've seen my house and how much there's still left to do. Besides, if Gloriana wanted to love me, to take photographs of me, why should I care? It's a free country." The next laugh sounded even darker, and no wonder. He had learned well the fallacy of his statement. America wasn't free; it was very, very expensive. Especially its legal help.

"But she was seventy-six!"

Another shrug. "She was still a woman who needed love. And she enjoyed giving it as much as receiving it."

I was speechless. Most American Anglos, worshipers at the Altar of Youth, have been conditioned to think of passion as something that dies with the appearance of gray hair. Other nationalities knew better.

A noise from behind me made me turn around. Janelle. I hoped she had merely been in the process of drying the big butcher knife she held in her hands.

"Gloriana was crazy, and so are you if you think my husband had anything to do with her," she said, approaching me, knife raised.

I guess my backward scurry tipped her off to my alarm, for she immediately lowered the knife and gave it a couple of flicks with the drying towel. Then she put the knife down on a wheelbarrow.

"Janelle, I didn't say he had anything to *do* with...."

"She wanted him to." Her voice was as fierce as I'd ever heard any woman's. "But I told her he was mine!"

Did I hear what I thought I heard? "Janelle, are you telling me you actually spoke to Gloriana about Owen?"

Owen's voice was sharp, a Marine barking orders. "That's enough, Janelle! Go back into the house!"

"Don't tell me that's enough," she shot back. "Nothing's enough when that woman had the nerve to drive out here in that big car of hers, looking down her nose at me and the children, saying she'd make it *worth my while* if I'd give you up!"

I wouldn't need an eye lift for decades. "Do you mean to tell me that Gloriana came out here and asked you to give her your husband?"

Janelle's laugh was ugly. "Give? Oh, no. Not Mrs. High-and-Mighty Gloriana Alden-Taylor. Before I sicced Rebel on her, the bitch offered me ten thousand dollars for him. She said considering what he had to offer, it was a fair price."

On the drive back to Jimmy's trailer I tried to make light of the situation. "Well, partner, nobody's ever going to say it's dull out here on the Rez."

"I'd really rather not talk about it now." His voice held an edge that could cut stone.

So much for my ability to charm. I had entered a warm, loving home and left behind an igloo.

More trouble waited for us at the trailer.

Dusty sat on the front steps, twirling his cowboy hat on his finger.

"The fun never stops," Jimmy muttered, pulling the pickup into the drive.

Chapter 23

Dusty, uninvited, followed us into the trailer. "Lena, why the hell didn't you call me?" His eyes were red again, something I now recognized was a danger sign. He was probably back on the sauce already.

I collapsed onto the sofa to take the weight off my throbbing feet. "Maybe I just wanted you and your redhead to leave me alone. God knows my life is complicated enough."

Behind us, Jimmy banged around in the trailer's kitchen area trying to make a pot of coffee, but succeeding in doing little more than spilling coffee grounds all over the counter. "Folks, could we have a little less noise, please," he begged.

Dusty sat down next to me, so I edged as far away as the small sofa would allow. "Bab…Lena, I was out on one of those city slicker cattle drives. I didn't know about the explosion until I got back and saw it on the news."

A likely story. "No cell phones or transistor radios out there in God's country?"

He looked hurt. "We were in the Little Grand Canyon, Lena. You know you can't get a signal there."

Maybe the likely story was true, but so what? Dusty and his redheaded "wife" had caused me nothing but trouble, not to mention major drywall expenses. I decided to stop things before they got any worse. "Dusty, every relationship eventually burns out, and it seems to me that we're wading around in a pile of ashes here. Let's cut our losses, okay?"

A crash from the kitchen made us both look up. Jimmy had dropped the Mr. Coffee, whether by accident or design, I couldn't tell. His face wasn't pretty, and for a brief moment, I remembered Owen's words about Native Americans' warrior heritage. A frisson of fear crawled up my spine.

"Look, you two," he growled. "I may have been raised Anglo, but I'm still Pima, and I can't take this White silliness anymore. You two are in love, so for God's sake, stop ragging on each other and do something about it. I'm leaving for Esther's. Try not to get blood on the walls."

With that, he stomped out. Seconds later, I heard his truck start up, then gravel hitting the sides of the trailer. He'd left us alone to make either love or war.

Neither of us said anything for a while. Then, with a tired sigh, Dusty walked into the kitchen area, knelt down, and began picking up the mess on the floor. "Looks like you'll have to hit McDonald's for your morning poison."

"That's better than the kind of poison you've been hitting."

As much as I like to see a man on his knees, the look he gave me from that position made me uncomfortable. "I told you, Lena. I stopped drinking."

"Let's hope."

The rattle of plastic, the clink of broken glass. Then the cabinet door opening, shutting. Footsteps coming toward me. The sofa sagging under his weight. Gentle fingers on my cheek.

"I got back to the ranch this afternoon, and as soon as the dudes were all squared away, I drove over to your apartment. When you weren't there, I went across the street to Cliffie's to find out where you were. He told me about the explosion, about you getting hurt. Then he said I'd find you at Jimmy's."

Maybe he was telling the truth. Today was Thursday, which was always Art Walk night in Scottsdale, when the art galleries stayed open until nine. And heaven knows that Cliffie—an unreconstructed romantic—would be more than delighted to rat me out to my no-good, two-timing boyfriend.

Gentle lips replaced gentle fingers. "Oh, Lena, I love you so much."

I turned my face to meet his kiss.

Screams in the distance. Explosions. Angry voices.

I am running through a forest, a tall blond woman running alongside me. I am small. Only a child.

"The ranger station isn't far. I think we can make it." A man's voice.

I look ahead to see a big man with red hair. His face looms white against the night but a stripe of moonglow reveals green eyes.

Running with us are more children, white, black, Hispanic, Asian. Most of them are older than me, except for one, a dark-haired little girl of around four. My age. The blond woman who holds her hand is almost dragging her through the woods.

I am fleet, like the blond woman. I don't need to be dragged.

More noises behind us, now. Closer.

My legs hurt. I have a stitch in my side. I want the red-headed man to pick me up and carry me along, but he can't. In each arm he holds a baby. There is no room for me up there. Thoroughly miserable, I begin to whimper.

"Quiet, Tina! No tears!" The blond woman. As we leave the shadow of the trees and enter a moonlit clearing, I can see that she looks like me.

Obediently, I shut up, earning from her, "My brave little girl."

But then the dark-haired girl, not so brave, begins to wail.

"No, no!" the man cautions her. "You can't."

The girl, now as frightened by the red-headed man as by our pursuers, wails even louder. The babies in his arms, startled, join in. Their screams blend with hers.

Angry voices now. Right behind us. "I hear them!" someone calls. A man. Then a woman, her voice shrill in the night, answers him. "Don't let them get away!"

All emotion leaves the red-headed man's face. There is no longer anything there I can recognize, no love, no fear. It is as if he has already died, yet remains standing.

"We have to split up," he says to the blond woman. "You take Christina and the other two, and double back. If they catch you, pretend you were never with me, that you plan to do as they demand. Maybe you can find a way...."

"No!" The blond woman doesn't want to go. Neither do I.

But his will overrides her love, and eventually she obeys. He hands over the silent children to her and tells the noisy ones they need to follow him.

We can hear our pursuers' footsteps.

Before we leave the red-haired man, the blond woman tells him she loves him. He tells her she owns his heart.

Then he looks down at me and says, "Christina, remember me."

And with the crying children trailing after him, my father strikes out across the clearing.

I awoke screaming.

"Lena, baby, it's all right. You're safe now, safe with me." Dusty's arms tightened around me.

Like those long-ago children, I wailed into the night.

I knew I'd never be safe again.

Chapter 24

I was still shivering, and not from the crisp March morning, when I arrived at the hospital to interview Sandra Alden-Taylor. She had been moved from intensive care to a private room, and was now allowed visitors. Dusty, who had the day off, told me he'd wait for me in the hospital cafeteria. Having been kept awake all night, he needed coffee.

Me, I was still wired on adrenalin.

But the minute he disappeared down the corridor, I pushed the night terrors from my mind.

I was good at that.

Swinging along on my crutches, I headed toward Sandra's room. The door was open, and a man's voice drifted out. Unless I was mistaken, John Alden Brookings was paying a social call on his orgy mate.

Not wanting to walk in on an embarrassingly intimate conversation, I stomped my crutches down hard on the tile floor, then cleared my throat and coughed a couple of times for good measure. Having thus announced my arrival even to the dead, I crutched into the room.

"Mr. Brookings, how nice to see you again."

Brookings, wearing an only slightly out-of-style gray suit, stood over the bed, caressing the unblistered side of Sandra's face. His own face had softened in that way a man's does when he loves a woman. Or is pretending to. "Thank you for saving her," he said, his voice hardly audible. Maybe my ears were going out again.

"You can stand, I observe," I said to him. "You must be getting better."

His eyes narrowed; for a moment I thought he was going to tell me what I could do with my observations, but he didn't. "Look behind you, Miss Jones."

I did, and saw his wheelchair parked near the door.

"I can hobble a few feet. Not enough to amount to much."

"Not enough to go for hikes, right?"

The narrow look again. "Right. Especially to the place you're thinking of."

"Such as?"

"Oak Creek Canyon. I couldn't even make it across the parking lot. My legs would give out first."

I wondered if it were true, but decided to let it go. I'd come to see Sandra, not give him the third degree.

"Mr. Brookings, if you don't mind, I'd like a few minutes alone with Miss Alden-Taylor."

He shook his head. "I'm not leaving her. Not ever again."

Great. I'd interrupted them in the middle of some sort of reconciliation scene. A lot of that seemed to be going around these days.

Sandra finally spoke up, her smoke-damaged voice raw. "I don't mind what John hears." She reached toward him with a bandaged hand. He took it, kissed the bandages. "You can say anything to me you want, that I'm a whore, that I'm a bad mother, a bad niece, I don't care. You saved my life and I…I owe…you." Her voice became even rawer at the end, and I wondered whether it would hold out.

Her gratitude could work to my advantage. "Did you know your little romp is plastered all over the Internet?"

She made an odd sound, which I finally realized was laughter. "The…whole world…knows. I'm a fucking star. Li…Literally."

"I don't care about the whole world, just Gloriana. Did she know?"

Sandra started to answer, but Brookings placed his hand softly across her mouth. "That's enough about the tape." Then, to me, "Sandra has a hard time talking, in case you haven't noticed. Ask me your questions and I'll answer for her."

I didn't like it when men presumed to answer for their women; as a detective, I liked it even less. I repeated my question. "Sandra, did Gloriana know about the tape? And if she did, what did she do about it?"

Sandra flicked her eyes at Brookings. "I don't know," she rasped.

She was lying. Gloriana knew.

As it now stood, Sandra would inherit enough money to purchase a home of her own. I studied Brookings carefully, remembering his trailer, the possibility that he was about to lose his disability payments. When the will cleared probate, Sandra would not be rich, but she wouldn't be living in a run-down trailer, either. How much money did it take for Brookings to forgive old grudges?

No point in asking the question, so I tried another. "Sandra, will you go back to work at Patriot's Blood when you're able?"

She waved Brookings' cautionary hand away. "If I watch… watch my money, I won't have…have to work for awhile. But Zach's offered John his old job back."

Well, well. A new home. A new job. Life was certainly looking up for John Alden Brookings.

Women and their men. Dusty was able to do what Jimmy hadn't, convince me to rent a car with an automatic transmission. My feet were still too sore to depress the Jeep's clutch, but the teal-colored Dodge Neon I drove away from Budget Car Rentals had no such old-fangled equipment. As much as I hated the sleek little thing, I had to admit that the car would at least get me from Point A to Point B until my feet healed.

I dropped by the office to assure Jimmy that Dusty and I hadn't killed each other during the night, and stayed long enough to read the *Scottsdale Journal.* In addition to the usual murder, mayhem, and low-fat recipes, I saw that Representative Lynn Tinsley's English-only bill had cleared the Arizona House and had been sent off to the Senate.

"It's time we reclaimed the King's English for Americans," Tinsley was quoted as saying. Which confused me. I thought by now it would be called the Queen's English. Then again, what did I know? Enough to remind myself to drop the *Journal* a line about Tinsley's shoplifting adventures. They were long overdue for an investigative journalism piece.

Tossing the paper aside, I took off again, this time to Zach and Megan's house. However, when I banged on the door, there was no answer. The house appeared deserted. No barks, meows, or oinks. What had happened?

As I hobbled back to the car, one of Zach's neighbors—perhaps moved to pity by my cheap car and crutches—opened his screen door and yelled, "They're gone!"

"I noticed that!" I yelled back. "Know where to?"

"They moved up to his grandmother's place. The pig and everybody, thank God. If you see them, tell them not to come back!"

I could see the neighborhood was going to miss them.

I took two wrong turns before I found myself pulling up to the big iron gate. I honked the horn, and a pack of dogs, cats, and Emma-the-not-Vietnamese-pot-belly trotted through a jumble of cars, vans, and pickup trucks to confront me.

Megan, looking like she was ready to pop, waddled forward to open the gate, little Casey at her heels. I wondered if the people down by the golf course could hear the racket.

"Back!" Megan yelled, shooing Casey and the other animals away. "Everybody get back!" She hauled the gate open by hand, calling for me to move the car through quickly, before any of her animals escaped.

"Half of them might run off to find their former owners, the very shits who abused them," she grumbled, as she helped me and my crutches out of the car. Since I'd last seen her, her eyes had become shockingly dark, as if she hadn't been sleeping. I also noticed that the front of her maternity jeans was wet. Had her water broken? Was she going to ignore this signal of imminent birth, simply squat down somewhere and have her baby, with Rosa doing midwife honors?

As I braced the crutches in the loose gravel, she gave me a pitying look. I feared for a moment that she might pat my haunch and ruffle my ears, but she simply asked, "Is there anything I can do for you, Lena? Anything at all?"

"I'm fine, Megan." I wished people would stop asking, because I was getting tired of my answer.

I had made my way halfway to the house when Casey, who had obviously found something interesting on the bottom of one of my shoes, knocked a crutch away. Off-balance, I fell to the gravel. I landed on my butt, but my carry-all fell upside down, spilling its contents.

Megan bent to help me, then jumped back, her face white. "My god, that's a gun."

"Of course it is, Megan," I said, attempting to put everything back in pretty much the same order it had been without adding any gravel to the mix. "I'm licensed to carry."

"I don't like guns. They're dangerous." The gun now safely out of sight, she pulled me to my feet, then handed my crutches back to me.

"Guns being dangerous, I believe, is the whole point." At least my handcuffs hadn't fallen out. Then she would have really freaked.

Her beautiful face turned grim. "No, you don't understand. My rescue organization gets too many gun-shot dogs and cats. It's a slaughter out there, and not just during hunting season. Some people actually pick up strays to use for target practice."

I'd heard rumors to that effect. It was fortunate that the evil in the world was balanced by the goodness of people like Megan. I hoped she would continue to care so much about her animals when the baby arrived. I would hate to see Casey, Black Bart, Emma, and the rest of the four-footed crew packed off to the pound.

After helping me brush the gravel off my clothes, she escorted me to the house. "I'm surprised you moved up here so quickly," I told her. "Aren't you supposed to clear probate first?"

"Technically, yes, but Gloriana's executor said that since the office had been destroyed, we could continue Patriot's Blood business up here. Since we were moving the business, he said we might as well move ourselves, too. I really like it, because everyone in Save Our Friends can meet here at the same time. No more A to M on Saturdays, N to Z on Sundays."

She opened the big double doors for me, allowed me to hop through quickly, then closed it, almost hitting Emma on the rump as she did so. The pig, which was almost the size of a Shetland pony, trotted ahead of us, her cloven feet tap-tap-tapping across the saltillo tiles, leaving little wet "V"s in her wake.

I head a noise from the direction of the living room, and looked back to see Rosa running toward us, a mewling kitten in each hand. "Miss Megan, I told you so many times, you should let me do those things." Animal hair covered Rosa's black dress, her eyes were wild. "You take care of the pets, I take care of the house."

Megan shrugged. "I was already outside with Emma."

"The pig." Rosa sounded like she thought Emma belonged on a bun.

"It's the day for her bath."

"Dios mio," Rosa muttered. "Which bathroom you use?"

Megan looked at her like Rosa had gone off her head. "Don't be silly, Rosa. I'm not using a bathroom. I'm using the fountain."

With that, she set off after the pig, leaving me with Rosa and two squalling kittens.

"You need a maid, Miss Jones?" she said, displaying the first sign of humor I'd seen in her. "Have feather duster, will travel."

I returned her smile. "Sorry, Rosa, it'd take you all of five minutes to clean my apartment. I'm here to see Mr. Zach. He around?"

"Sure. They are all in the library, working."

"All?"

She shrugged, making one of the kittens complain even more loudly. "Shush, you," she murmured, caressing it with her wrinkled cheek. "If you not good, I not take you to play with Caroline and John-John." Then, to me, "Oh, yes, everybody here, the whole office. They in there figuring out what to do, but you can go in. I take these cats to the children. Miss Caroline, she like to feed the littlest babies."

With that, she walked off, leaving me to make my way unannounced into the new Patriot's Blood offices.

The library had been transformed from a museum for books to an office that produced them. While the valued first editions remained secured in their glass-fronted cabinets, every other square inch of space had been usurped. Dozens of people sat around chatting on the leather sofas and chairs, on table tops, even the floor. Some clutched manuscripts, others held floppy discs. A large easel stood against one wall. On it, a chart illustrated which level in the publishing process each manuscript or game had attained. I counted eighteen projects frozen in various places between ACCEPTANCE LETTER and SHIPPING. A few books, not yet arrived at BINDING, had thick red lines slashed through their titles. To my delight, Barry Fetzner's *A Man Stands Alone* was among them. My joy was lessened only by knowing that the book's cancellation would please Fetzner, too. All the video games and CDs had been canceled. No more *Border Run* and its hateful cousins. What would the National Alliance do for fun now?

A silence fell across the room when I crutched in. "Is that her?" someone asked.

"Yes, Ms. Jones is the detective who saved Sandra," Zach said, smiling toward me. "Everyone take a break. She probably needs to ask me some questions."

The questions had to wait until I suffered through a series of handshakes and hugs. Eventually, Zach led me out of the library and into a neighboring den where I perched myself on the edge of a high-backed sofa, taking care not to sit too far back. It was strange how even the smallest habits must change when you are on crutches.

"Miss Jones, we're holding a pretty important meeting here, so please make it short." Zach watched me position my crutches against the end of the sofa. His dark hair was combed neatly and he even wore a good suit, although a few stray bits of fur clung to it. The expression on his face, though, was that of a busy man tolerating an interruption.

This new Zach made me curious. "Now that you're living in the Hacienda, what are you going to do with the other house?"

"I turned it over to a real estate broker this morning," he said, his foot tapping impatiently. "As I'm sure you know, this place is falling down, and it'll take a fortune to make it truly liveable. I could sell that acreage up north and put some of the proceeds into the house like Megan wants to do, but the question is—is the Hacienda really worth it? Wouldn't my money be better spent on, say, a less spectacular place but one in better shape? Megan also forgets that I need to find new offices for Patriot's Blood. We can't keep operating out of here."

"Megan mentioned something about building an animal shelter," I said, made curious by Zach's choice of words: I, my, mine. Not we, ours. Where did Megan's dreams fit in with his plans?

Zach's mouth twisted. "Look, Megan's hobby is fine in its place, but she needs to get it under control. I'm not going to live the rest of my life with all these animals under foot. She needs to get rid of them."

I didn't like what I heard. "Have you discussed this with Megan?"

"Of course I did. Needless to say, it didn't go well. But that's her problem. I'm running things, now."

His callousness made me wince, but after all, I wasn't here to talk about the fate of homeless animals. "Zach, how did the authors take it when you called, the ones whose contracts you dropped?"

"With varying degrees of outrage. At the high end, some were philosophical. At the low end, I got a few death threats. The game designers were the worst, probably because they tend to have trouble discerning fantasy violence from the real thing. But a couple of authors were pretty vituperative, too."

"Such as?"

"Randall Ott, for one. How my grandmother was able to deal with that hothead is beyond me."

"I thought Ott's book was your biggest money-maker. You're just going to let it go?"

He sniffed. "It certainly was, accent on *was.* Since Patriot's Blood will not be associated with his type of material any more, I suggested that he take his sequel to another publisher. Perhaps that National Alliance publishing house in West Virginia. He refused, saying their distribution is too narrow, which is probably true. They've never been able to crack the New York Times best-seller list like we have."

He looked at his watch. "Ott's due up here any minute to sign some papers. We're reverting his rights back to him. So if you don't mind...."

I can take a hint, but I don't have to abide by it. "Zach, since you've scratched Gloriana's entire publishing philosophy, what are you going to put in its place?" Cowboy poetry? Odes to pintos?

"Real literature," he said, pride neutralizing the impatience on his face. "I'm going to start out with a strong non-fiction line, then as novels arrive, I'll look at those. Right now, I'm drawing up contracts for some very exciting titles. *Essentialism and Modernism. The Violence of Rhetoric.* And my own personal favorite, *Pedagogy, Gender and Equity Examined through Poststructural Dialectics.* It's a brave new day for Patriot's Blood."

At first I thought he was joking, but the fervor—*Fever*—in his eyes proved him serious. "And you think you can make money with books like that?"

His earlier impatience reemerged. "I'm aware that any new venture takes time. Readers have been so inundated with chick lit and other pap passing for literature that they need to relearn how to read. That's why I'll debut my non-fiction line first, as a teaching tool. Then, after I've reeducated the public, I'll roll out my experimental fiction line. Given the proper groundwork, all I have to do is print quality and the book-buying public will be lining up at the bookstores."

If I print it, they will read.

I remembered Megan's hopes about the new direction Patriot's Blood might take. "I thought there was talk about publishing some mysteries."

Zach's nose twitched as if he smelled something bad. "That was Megan's idea, not mine. I'm trying to legitimize Patriot's Blood, and I don't see how that can be accomplished by moving from one type of trash to another."

On the way out, I passed a furious-looking Randall Ott walking up the gravel drive. Megan was too busy washing Emma in the fountain to say hello to him, but I gave him a wave for old time's sake. He didn't wave back.

Chapter 25

As soon as I left the property, I pulled to the side of the road, took my cell phone out of my carry-all, and punched in Myra Gordon's number. The librarian still wasn't picking up. Enough being enough, I flipped open my Arizona map and looked for Wyatt's Landing. I found it a few miles off I-10, almost halfway between Phoenix and Tucson. An hour's drive, if the traffic gods were with me.

They were. Snowbirds were nowhere in sight, and the only vehicles left on the road were eighteen-wheelers and SUVs hauling ass to get to wherever. For safety's sake, I positioned the tiny Neon halfway between two semis, and watched the landscape fly by. This area of the state resembled the pictures taken by the Mars Rover, without the pretty pink coloring. Miles and miles of flat beige desert and gray rocks, relieved every now and then by the bright red of fresh roadkill.

With relief, I swung off the freeway at the Wyatt's Landing exit and entered the outskirts of the tiny farming community, with alfalfa fields on my left, a few cheap motels on my right. The town itself was so small you could spit across it, little more than a collection of gas stations, fast food outlets, and elderly stucco homes.

The Wyatt's Landing Public Library—due to the town's infinitesimal size, there was only one branch—nestled between a Taco Bell and a Burger King. At first I suspected that the cars in its parking lot represented overflow from the fast food joints, but when I walked through the library's glass doors, I discovered I was wrong. Men wearing bib overalls trundled back and forth from the SCIENCE to AGRICULTURE stacks, while over in the corner, a group of women huddled together, avid looks on their faces. They all had copies of the same book on their laps: *The Life of Pi.* Then I remembered it was OneBookAZ month, the time every year when we were supposed to all be reading the same damn book.

I walked up to the information desk and asked for Myra Gordon.

"This is her day off," a middle-aged woman wearing Harlequin-style reading glasses studded with rhinestones told me. Her hair was the color of merlot, the same color as her glasses. She was so Retro she was chic.

"Think she's at home?"

She pushed the reading glasses up and parked them on her head. "I wouldn't know. Are you a friend?"

"Oh, yes," I lied.

As I left, I saw her reflection in the glass doors. She was already punching a number into the phone.

Myra Gordon lived a mere two blocks away, in an old stucco house that was probably an original Territorial. When I pulled behind her blue Honda, she was rushing out the door. Her face fell when she saw me.

"Mrs. Mbisi, if I didn't know better, I'd think you were avoiding me," I said.

She stared at me for a moment, her eyes snapping with fury. Then she forced herself to calm and put her car keys back into her poodle purse. "I see there's no getting rid of you, so you might as well come in."

Nothing like a warm welcome to make a detective feel at home. But I swung my crutches out of the Neon and hobbled to the porch.

Her eyes softened. "Oh. I'm sorry. I forgot about the bomb. And what you did to help that poor woman." She unlocked the door, ushered me in, and asked me if I'd like something to drink.

Not knowing how long my visit would be, I accepted a Diet Coke. Even in March, Arizona air is desert dry. While she was in the kitchen clanking around with ice trays, I studied the African print throws on the sofa, the African masks above it. The coffee table and each end table held African carvings, some of animals, some of women. The only non-African decorations in the room were two studio photographs: one of a handsome, dark-skinned man with short-cropped gray hair, and the other of a lighter-skinned young man in an Army uniform.

When Gordon/Mbisi returned with my Diet Coke, she noticed me checking out the room. "My husband was from Ghana," she explained. "He brought most of the art with him. I added a few pieces later."

"Is that your son?" I asked, gesturing to the younger man's picture.

When she nodded, the anger returned to her eyes. "He was killed in Baghdad on the day of the first assault."

"I'm sorry."

This time the anger didn't leave. "And my husband was murdered, which makes two loved ones dead because of White men. But you know that, don't you? That's why you're here."

Sometimes detective work is dirty work; I had little choice. Owen was looking at the needle if I didn't clear him. "That's right, Mrs. Gordon. Or do you prefer Mrs. Mbisi now that your secret's out?"

"Gordon. When I testified at the trial, my husband's murderers told me their friends in the Aryan Brotherhood would 'take care of me,' so I'm doing what I can to make that difficult. That's why I took my maiden name back and moved here."

No wonder she had been so hard to contact. I hoped for her sake that the Aryan Brotherhood wasn't as Internet-savvy as my partner. Then I comforted myself with the realization that they probably weren't. I doubted if their collective I.Q. would add up to room temperature.

"Mrs. Gordon, my partner ran a search on you and found out everything about the trial, including the interesting fact that the men who murdered your husband had some Patriot's Blood books in their apartment. Also, the woman who drew up the seating chart for the SOBOP banquet told me that you'd asked to be placed at Gloriana's table. Did you want to make sure you could watch her die?"

Gordon didn't bat an eye. "I wanted to look into the face of the woman who had murdered my husband."

I didn't know what to say to that. "Mrs. Gordon...."

She waved my words away. "I know, I know. You're going to tell me that she didn't murder him, that all she did was publish books. I'm no fool, Ms. Jones. I don't necessarily believe my husband would still be alive if Gloriana Alden-Taylor had printed only harmless children's stories or Regency romances. But everyone who contributes to hate, whether by speech or by printed word, is morally culpable for the pain their words cause others."

"Not legally, though." I hated myself for even pointing this out.

She inclined her head. "No, but think of this. If her products were illegal, Gloriana would be alive in prison, not dead in the ground."

There was a picture, Gloriana Alden-Taylor sharing a cell with the female version of God's Avenger. Too bad it would remain only a fantasy. "Did you kill Gloriana, Mrs. Gordon?"

By now the anger had burnt away from her eyes and only sorrow remained. "No, Ms. Jones, I did not kill her. I have too much intimate acquaintance with violence ever to contribute to it myself. And with all the First Amendment's faults, I'm still a believer. If we relinquish free speech, we diminish our souls."

"Admirable sentiments, Mrs. Gordon, but I didn't drive all the way down here to God's country for a lecture on the Bill of Rights. Convince me you didn't kill Gloriana."

She looked at the photograph of her dead husband, her dead son. Then back at me. When she finally spoke, there was no expression on her face at all. "All I have for you is the truth, Ms. Jones. I arranged to be seated next to Gloriana so I could look into the face of evil. But when I met her, I didn't see evil. All I saw was the face of a lonely old woman. A woman just like me."

When I got back to Scottsdale, the drywall guy was just pulling into the office parking slot, having obviously completed his job at the Biltmore Resort. I inched my way carefully up the stairs and let him into my apartment. After taking another look around, he told me the place would be good to go by the end of the day.

Pleased, I hobbled back down the stairs to the office and reported the conversation to Jimmy, who tried to hide his relief. "One more week at my place and those feet should be healed enough for you to navigate your stairs." His face froze. "Wait a minute. Didn't you just say *you let the guy into your apartment?* Lena, how'd you get up there?"

I waved a crutch at him. "I've been practicing."

"You're going to do what you're going to do, but I think you should give it a little more time." There was resignation in his voice.

If I stayed at Jimmy's trailer any longer I might destroy a beautiful partnership, not to mention friendship. But I didn't tell him that. Instead, I said I was homesick. Not that I knew what "homesick" really meant. When you've grown up in as many "homes" as I had, you can't grasp the concept.

"Can you help me move back tonight?" I asked.

"It'll have to be tomorrow. Tonight Esther and I are taking Rebecca to the movies. I've finally found a film we can all see together without one of us losing his mind."

I thought for a moment about calling Dusty, but then decided against it. Relying on my partner for help was one thing; relying on my boyfriend yet another. "Tomorrow it is, then."

Satisfied with the way things were going, I returned to the business at hand, making a list of the people I needed to interview again. Sandra, most definitely, without Brookings standing guard. Yes, she had almost died in the fire, but Gloriana's murderer hadn't necessarily set it. The Aryan Brotherhood remained likely suspects.

I wrote down SANDRA ALDEN-TAYLOR and JOHN ALDEN BROOKINGS.

Both their lives had taken an upward turn after Gloriana's death, and I wasn't foolish enough to believe that blood was always thicker than water. Nieces had killed aunts before. Daughters, mothers.

And grandsons, grandmothers.

Of all people whose lives had been most enriched by Gloriana's death, Zach topped the list. Not only was he now able to re-create Patriot's Blood in his own image, but he had inherited a spectacular house in the bargain. And that undeveloped desert acreage I kept hearing about. At the beginning of this case, I had liked Zach, but since he inherited full control of Patriot's Press, I found myself liking him less. Had arrogance always lurked under that veil of harassed humility? Or had it been born with his new power?

I drew a double line under ZACHARY ALDEN-TAYLOR.

Who else? I wrote down OWEN SISIWAN, and after some thought, added JANELLE SISIWAN. Owen gave every appearance of being a committed family man, but appearances frequently meant little. It was entirely possible that after a life of hardship on the reservation, he had decided to partake of the Good Life via Gloriana's lust for him. Unless I was wrong, Janelle was perfectly capable of committing murder to keep her man. As for procuring the water hemlock, many Native Americans were adept at identifying poisonous plants. That no one had mentioned seeing Owen's wife at the Desert Shadows Resort meant little. Few if any of the SOBOP folks knew her, but even if they had, she could have thrown a white apron over a black dress and blended into the background. Even Gloriana wouldn't have recognized her. No one pays attention to the help.

Then I corrected myself. No one pays attention to the help unless they look like Owen.

I drew a double line under JANELLE.

Who else? After careful thought, I discounted the dermatologist who had sat at Gloriana's table at the SOBOP banquet. The doctor had no motive and had actually tried to save Gloriana. But that wasn't true for the other people who had sat at the table.

After writing down MYRA MBISI/GORDON, I added DAVID ZHANG. Then EMIL RAMOS and REPRESENTATIVE LYNN TINSLEY. And how about RANDALL OTT? Gloriana was ruthless; Ott, crazy. A nasty combination. Anything could have happened between those two.

I wrote down LAVELLE and LEILA ALDEN-TAYLOR. While I couldn't see the twins actually doing the deed, they were obviously hiding something.

BARRY FETZNER made my list. Considering the far-reaching loyalty of prison gangs, it would have been relatively easy for a member of the Aryan Brotherhood to come to some sort of arrangement with an outside killer.

I added CHAPS PETERSON, too. A long shot, but even cowboy poets do not like to hear their talent denigrated. Then, after thinking about it for a while, I wrote down REVEREND MELVIN GIBLIN. The fact that he had been good to me did not cancel out the possibility that he could be a killer. The Rev, who certainly knew his Arizona fauna and flora, might have killed Gloriana merely to keep her from spreading her press' awful brand of hate any further. A long shot, but so were some of the other names on my list.

I sat there staring at the Rev's name for a while, remembering the happy times I had spent with him and the other foster kids out on the desert. Remembered the songs around the campfire, remembered my sorrow when he—still half mad with grief over his wife's death—told us we couldn't live with him any longer. Remembered his tears when the CPS van came to pick us up.

I looked at the name some more.

Then I erased it.

Jimmy was still running names through the system when I pushed myself away from the desk and grappled with my crutches.

"Going upstairs to check on the progress," I told him. "And after that, I'm driving up to Scottsdale Air Park to talk to David Zhang and Emil Ramos again. I have some follow-up questions."

"Please be careful."

I didn't bother asking who or what I was supposed to be careful of. It would elicit another lecture. Instead, I bumped up the stairs, only to find the drywall guy packing up his things.

"Finished." He handed me an invoice.

When I saw the amount, I regretted not telling my landlord about my little hole-in-the-wall problem. But then I saw the now-sleek ceiling and walls and realized that he'd done a better job than my landlord would ever have paid for. The guy had even smoothed out a few extra spots, holes not put there by a big Desert Eagle. Which, I reminded myself, I had yet to get rid of. Maybe I should drop it down a sewer somewhere.

And Dusty's pistol-packing redhead with it.

"You'll need to paint," the drywall guy said, interrupting my murderous thoughts. "I think that's Navajo White up there, but I'm no expert. Maybe you want to throw a little color in here, too."

Maybe. Those white walls sure didn't do much for the beige carpet, beige sofa, and beige coffee table.

But who cared? The apartment was a place to eat and sleep. Nothing else. It wasn't a home. There was no kidding myself. I'd never had a home and probably never would.

When I maneuvered my crutches into Verdad Press an hour later, Emil Ramos was adding another book to a shelf in the reception area. The bell tingled and he looked around, his expression forming into dismay. He hurriedly masked it with his usual smile.

"Ah, Miss Jones, it is so nice to see you alive."

His words startled me until I realized that I had not seen Ramos since the Patriot's Blood bombing. "I think it's nice to see me alive, too, Mr. Ramos. How goes the book business?"

He patted the book into place, then stepped away from the bookcase. "We are still waiting for the Hispanic Michael Crichton to appear on our doorstep. Other than that, business is fine. But I am certain you did not drive up here to discuss the ins and outs of the publishing business. What may I help you with this time?"

As he led me to the conference room, I told him what I'd discovered about Gloriana, that her perceived racism appeared to be more financial than heart-felt. Ramos didn't appear as surprised as I'd thought he would.

"That makes her behavior even worse," he said, helping me into my seat.

My thoughts, too. But I asked him why.

He settled back into his chair, his face troubled. "To do what you believe in, that is the course of action all honest men and women should follow, even to the death. But to spread such lies only for money, that is unforgivable. The poor, yes, they frequently commit terrible acts to feed themselves or their children, or even out of some other desperate need. Gloriana Alden-Taylor had none of these excuses. She was born into wealth. How can her greed ever be understood?"

"She wasn't born into as much wealth as you think." I explained Gloriana's financial situation, the condition of the family home.

The troubled look cleared. "Then I understand."

I heard a noise behind me, and turned to see John Alden Brookings, ensconced again in his wheelchair, leading an elderly lady down the hall. He gave me a curt nod, then rolled into a small office with her and closed the door.

"One of Mr. Brookings' private clients," Ramos explained. "But he will be leaving soon to return to Patriot's Blood. I suppose I should be happy for him, but now I must find another bilingual editor. The hiring process always depresses me. There are so many good people out of work these days, and I cannot help them all."

I sympathized, but steered him away from what looked to be the beginnings of a long monologue by asking my next question. "Mr. Ramos, you said you understand Gloriana's behavior. What did you mean by that?"

"Ah, Ms. Jones. People will kill, or even die, to protect their homes, so if Gloriana loved her Hacienda as much as you say, then I am not surprised by anything she did. We had such a case in my own family, an elderly relative who refused to leave her adobe even as the bulldozers pushed down the walls."

Could the world really be that small? "Mr. Ramos, are you talking about the adobes that were razed for the new art museum?"

I'd worked that case, a very messy one which had almost gotten me killed. As it had turned out, a member of that old woman's family—the woman who had preferred to die with her house—saved my life. This put me in a difficult ethical position. Yet, for all Ramos' Old World courtesy, he could still be a murderer.

"Why, yes," Ramos said, surprised. "The woman involved, Magdalena Espinoza, was my great-aunt."

It was true, then. Pushing aside my moral qualms, I decided that the past is the past, and that whatever Ramos' kin had done for me, he himself had played no part in it. But even if he had, I was still a detective.

There was no point in letting Ramos know about my ties to his family, so I barged ahead. "I think I remember reading about her. It was a very sad situation."

He nodded. "You see what I am saying, then. For people who are no longer young, a home can be a sacred thing, especially for a proud woman like Gloriana Alden-Taylor. But I understand something else about the woman now, too."

Then he was doing better than me. I just couldn't seem to get a fix on Gloriana. "What do you understand about her?"

"Great love, great desire—they often go hand in hand with great blindness."

I frowned. "What do you mean, great blindness?"

He looked around at the bookcases in the room, the proof of his own great desires. "You Anglos have the saying, 'Love is blind,' which is, of course, true. We all know that no one is more blind to ugly truths than a lover. But when passions cool, vision clears; the floodlight of truth reveals all. If that revealed truth is unacceptable, a great hatred will grow in its place, a hatred as great as the passions that came before. Did such a thing happen to Gloriana Alden-Taylor? Did the thing she once loved become her great hate? And is that why she had to die?"

"Did the thing she once loved become her great hate?"

Ramos' words stayed with me as I hobbled across the parking lot to Arizona Trails Publishing and the offices of David Zhang.

What did Gloriana love? Her exalted lineage. Her crumbling Hacienda. And, possibly, Owen.

Who or what had she turned against? And why?

Zhang was in, but the young woman who stuck her head around the corner told me he was finishing up an editorial conference and asked me to wait. She then disappeared again.

I settled myself and my crutches on a sleek chair designed more for looks than comfort and flipped through a stack of magazines on the side table: *Road and Track, American Baby, Cosmopolitan.* Not being all that interested in cars, and even less in babies, I picked up the *Cosmopolitan.* I'd begun reading an article titled "Jealousy: The Most Destructive of the Seven Deadly Sins," when I heard approaching voices.

David Zhang, and a mellifluous baritone it was hard to forget. Chaps Peterson, the cowboy poet. What was he doing here?

Intrigued, I watched as Zhang, who hadn't yet spotted me, shook hands with Chaps at the door. "I'm looking forward to a long and profitable relationship," Zhang said, his salesman's smile wide, bright, and phoney.

"Right, pardner, we'll be riding a lot of fence together in the next few years," Chaps agreed. His too-overt "cowhand" accent sounded off today, but maybe it was just me.

With a tip of his weatherbeaten hat, Chaps finally exited, leaving Zhang in the doorway.

"Ahem." I gave him a wave.

Zhang's brilliant smile dimmed for a nanosecond and I caught a flash of temper in his eyes. Then the smile flared again. "Why, Miss Jones! How nice to see you again!" His professed joy sounded every bit as phoney as Chaps' accent.

Before I could say anything, Zhang made a show of checking his watch. "Look at the time! We're about to close up. Perhaps you can come back tomorrow?"

There's a reason detectives like to drop in on people unannounced. Why give suspects time to perfect their lies?

"I have a couple more questions," I said, delivering a whopper of my own. "I'll be out of your hair in no time."

"Make it quick then." Unlike Ramos, Zhang didn't invite me into the conference room. Instead, he perched himself on the chair across from me as if to punctuate the lateness of the hour.

"Wasn't that Chaps Peterson I saw leaving?" I asked.

Zhang looked relieved. "Yes, it was. We signed him to a three-book contract."

So much for Arizona flora and fauna. "I didn't know Arizona Trails published Chaps' kind of work."

"I've been thinking of branching out into other areas of Southwestern interest, and since Mr. Peterson is one of the most popular poets around, why not?"

I noticed that he said *most popular*, not best. But when I mentioned his lapse, he laughed.

"Whoever said publishing is about quality hasn't studied the bestseller list lately. It's a freak show, Miss Jones, top heavy with wrestlers, teenage pop stars, and political has-beens confessing their sexual peccadillos. Mediocre books produced by mediocre ghostwriters. Perhaps publishing used to be about developing talent and producing the best books possible, but today it's all showmanship and sales. And when it comes to showmanship, Chaps is one of the best salesmen around. In fact, I am so confident of that I am sending him on a ten-state book tour when his first collection rolls off the press. As I am sure you noticed at the Festival of the West, people from the East Coast lap up the cowboy business."

And the cowboys themselves. Look at Joanne's passion for Dusty. But I didn't have time to worry about her now. "Speaking of the East Coast, don't I detect a wee bit of Brooklyn in Chaps' accent?"

Zhang's face closed down again. "Chaps assured me that not only was he was born and raised in Arizona, but also that his father and both grandfathers were cowboys."

Well, yippee-ki-yo-ki-yay, youse guys. There seemed to be no point in raining on Chaps' parade when I had other issues to pursue. "Better have him watch those Brooklyn 'R's then. But back to what I came here for. As you must surely know, someone bombed Patriot's Blood last week. Do you have any idea who might have done that?" Not that he would tell me if he did.

Zhang looked relieved at the change of subject. "If the bombing had happened before Gloriana died, I could have said anyone. The NAACP. The Jewish Defense League. PETA, even, because some of that racist propaganda she published has been urging the Aryan types to eat more meat. You know the kind of thing, 'Real racists don't eat quiche.' But everyone knew that Zach was going to change editorial policy as soon as he took over, so fire-bombing the place just as he'd started to do so makes no sense to me."

It didn't make any sense to me, either. Something else bothered me, too. "Are you aware of the material Zach wants to publish now?"

Zhang laughed so hard he almost fell down. "Oh, God, yes!" he finally managed, wiping his eyes. "Look, Zach's a great guy and all that, a heart of gold under all that literary pretentiousness, but the man has no financial sense. I'm betting he'll run through Gloriana's money in a year, two at the outside. Nobody's going to buy that…" here he drew out the word "…LIT-ER-AH-TURE. He's his grandmother all over again, blind to everything except his own obsession. At least old Gloriana understood money."

His praise for Gloriana surprised me, and I told him so.

"Oh, well," he said, shrugging. "At Harvard, where I received my MBA, they teach you great respect for money. And the people who make it."

Chapter 26

On my way back to the office, I stopped by the site where Patriot's Blood once stood.

The area was surrounded by a hastily erected fence, built without even sight holes for the customary sidewalk superintendents. As a further deterrent to gawkers, Day-Glo CRIME SCENE stickers plastered all over the barrier warned people to keep their distance. I prowled back and forth along the fence in the dimming light, looking for entry but finding none. It probably didn't make any difference, since I doubted if the ATF had left behind anything worthwhile. After I had circled the perimeter several times, a cool rain began to fall. When it hit the ash on the other side of the fence, the acrid smell of burned wood expanded for a moment, then dissipated.

As I hurried back to the Neon, I wondered if Gloriana's memoirs had perished, too. The file cabinet storing them had looked fireproof, but I doubted if it was blast proof.

For some reason, I was reluctant to leave. While the rain fell, I sat in the Neon, staring at the remains of Gloriana's dreams.

I was stepping out of the shower, getting ready to towel off, when someone knocked on my door.

Not Dusty's knock. Not Jimmy's.

Throwing on a robe, I grabbed my .38 and limped to the door. On the other side of the peephole stood Joanne, her wet red hair plastered to her head, a forlorn expression on her face.

"Put down your purse and show you hands!" I called through the door.

She did.

"Now take off your coat, lift up your blouse, and turn around!"

She did that, too, revealing that she didn't need a bra to keep her implants pointed north.

Satisfied, I delivered the required warning. "Joanne, I'm letting you in, but be warned that I've got a gun, and unlike you, I know how to use it. Your handbag stays outside."

She nodded wetly, and I opened the door, grateful that I had left my crutches in the bedroom. I did not want her to know how vulnerable I felt.

"Close the door behind you," I ordered, as she stepped through. "But don't lock it. You may be leaving real fast."

Still obedient, Joanne did exactly as I said. "May I sit down?"

I waved the revolver toward the beige corner chair that faced the door. "Sit. Speak. Then get the hell out."

She shuffled over to the chair and sat down. "I brought my checkbook. I want to pay for the damage I caused before I fly out in the morning."

On her broom, no doubt. "Stay where I can see you." I kept the gun on her as I eased myself out the door and recovered the handbag she'd obediently left on the landing. Still covering her with my gun, I rifled through the thing (Hermes, real leather, what appeared to be solid silver clasps) and found the checkbook in a side flap next to an expensive-looking pen. I tossed both to her.

"How much?" she asked.

I told her.

"May I see the invoice?"

"Only if you promise to shove it where the sun don't shine."

She blinked. "There's no need to be rude."

Did tourists leave their brains at the airport? "Joanne, you couldn't get a Manhattan pedicure for the amount I quoted."

She shook her head, and a few wet strands fell across her forehead. "I need to give it to my accountant."

"Just write, 'For drywall damage incurred during attempted double homicide' on the subject line."

She opened her mouth, then closed it again and wrote out the check.

"Drop it on the floor."

The check fluttered to the beige carpet.

"Bye." I motioned the gun toward the door.

"No, wait."

What now?

"I want my gun back."

I began to laugh. "Are you completely out of your mind? Give you back the gun you tried to kill me with? As far as I'm concerned, it's finders keepers."

Joanne frowned. "That was a very expensive gun." The amount she quoted me made me raise my eyebrows.

"A Desert Eagle only runs about half of that. Next time you want to shoot someone, do a little comparison shopping first." But I suspected why the gun cost her so much. Not being an Arizona resident, Joanne would have trouble purchasing legal firearms on the spur of the moment here. She'd gone off-market.

"You're going to keep my gun? Well, maybe I should tear up my check!" She made as if to pick the check up off the floor, but froze when I cocked the hammer on the .38.

"Time to leave now, Joanne."

She burst into tears.

Normally, women's tears do not affect me. I know how easily they can be manufactured, but Joanne's held real heartache. Her haggling had been mere camouflage.

I eased the hammer home and let her cry until her sobs settled into mere gulps. "You're not getting the Desert Eagle back and from the looks of you, you're not getting Dusty, either. It's time to cut your losses and go back to where you know how to play the game."

"It wasn't a game," she said miserably. "I love him. When I was with him, it was like having a different life, a better life than product pitches and idea meetings. Dusty was from another world. Handsome. Tough. And yet so, so tender. I'd never met anyone like him before."

Poor bitch. Softening my voice, I said, "The point is, he doesn't love you, regardless of what he said while he was drunk."

"He lied?"

"Men do lie to women, Joanne." I wondered how often Dusty had lied to me. Not recently, I hoped. Then I remembered some of the things I'd told him. "And sometimes women lie back."

"He won't talk to me. And they won't even let me on the ranch property now."

"Then it's time to go back to New York. I'm sure if you look hard enough, you can find a handsome, tough, and tender man there, too. It's a big city."

She gave a heavy, trembling sigh. "This has all been such a mess."

I agreed with her. "It sure has, Joanne. Good-bye." I stepped away from the door.

She got up, leaving the check lying on the floor. "Tell Dusty… well, tell him I'm sorry for all the trouble I caused."

"Will do."

She started to leave, then stopped.

I raised the .38 again. "What is it now?"

Her eyes were bleak. "He told me…he told me you didn't love him. That you couldn't love anyone. Is it true?"

I did not answer, because I did not know the truth. "Good-bye, Joanne."

As soon as she walked through the door, I bolted it behind her.

Chapter 27

First thing the next morning, I called Kryzinski.

"I found a gun in the alley last night," I told him. "Want me to bring it in?"

His voice was cautious, probably because he knew me so well. "Since when do you hang around in alleys, Lena?"

"Oh, I thought I heard something back there, so I went out to check. That's when I found it. Big .50 caliber Desert Eagle."

Kryzinski whistled. "Serial number intact?"

"Filed off." Not that it made any difference. A good ballistics expert could probably raise the number and trace the gun's point of origin. Which would result in good news for some lucky gun collector out there, because most black market guns, especially the higher-priced models like the Desert Eagle, came from burglaries.

"Yeah, bring it in," Kryzinski said. "I'm anxious to take a look, not that I'll ever be able to afford one of them babies. Not on my salary."

"Be there in a few minutes."

The gun was a ruse. When I arrived at Scottsdale North, I turned the Desert Eagle over, and after Kryzinski had fondled it for a while, I got down to business.

"You still think Owen looks good for the Alden-Taylor killing?" We sat in his glass-walled office with the door closed. A couple of detectives looked up from their paperwork and waved at me. One blew a kiss. I reciprocated. Satisfied, he went back to work.

"Owen's the DA's problem now, not mine." His eyes had trouble meeting mine.

I refused to let him off the hook. "How carefully did you question the other people at the banquet, the people who actually saw Gloriana die?"

"We talked to everyone, Lena. Other than those people on the hike, most didn't know her personally. And since we didn't have enough leads to keep them in town, we let them all go back home."

I knew that the witnesses were now scattered all the way from Dallas to Lodi, but in the end, it would make little difference. "How hard did you run at Gloriana's grandson?"

Kryzinski gave me a cagey look. "Considering that he's the primary heir, we looked at him pretty carefully, regardless of what you might think."

"And?"

"And nothing. Zachary Alden-Taylor went on the hike, but during the day's last seminar and during the banquet itself, he was always within sight of someone. And I'm not even counting his wife, because wives do tend to lie for their husbands. Lena, he *didn't* do it."

I remembered the ashes at Patriot's Blood Press, the rise of Zach's dreams. "Zach really hated his grandmother's products, Captain."

Kryzinski snorted. "I hate working for a living, too, but I do it anyway."

Talking to Kryzinski was like talking to a stone. He didn't hear what he didn't want to hear, so I left him there, still fondling Joanne's Desert Eagle.

I didn't look forward to my next stop, but there was no choice. The rain had stopped and I would have made good time over to the Arcadia District, except for the usual out-of-state RVs dogging the speed limit. Frustrated by the traffic tie-up, I found myself sympathizing with the bumper sticker I saw on a passing delivery van: SO MANY SNOWBIRDS, SO LITTLE FREEZER SPACE.

The twins let me in without a word. A quick look at Lavelle revealed that although the bruise on her face had faded, new bruises the size of fingertips darkened her arms. Time to call Adult Protective Services.

Leila's cranky voice interrupted my thoughts. "The detective returns, all crippled up." She didn't offer me a seat.

Bracing myself on my crutches, I tried to keep the distaste out of my voice. "Yes, all crippled up and back again with more questions. When I was here before, you led me to believe that Sandra inherited little under the terms of Gloriana's will. Since then, I've discovered she received enough to buy a house."

Lavelle frowned and rubbed her sore arms. "Compared to Gloriana's fortune, it's nothing. She should have inherited everything."

"Why?" After all I had seen and learned the past couple of weeks, I suspected the answer, but needed confirmation.

Leila pushed her aside, none too gently. "Don't pay any attention to my sister. She doesn't know what she's talking about."

But for once, Lavelle showed some spirit. "Oh, yes, I do."

This brought a snarl from Leila. "Keep your mouth shut about your slutty daughter and don't cause any more trouble."

I stepped between them before Leila could add more bruises to Lavelle's collection. *Any more trouble?* During my previous visit, they had mentioned warning Gloriana about something.

I directed my next question to Leila. "Gloriana came by a few days before she was murdered, right?"

Leila nodded. "Yes, Miss Rich Pants honored us with one of her once-in-a-blue-moons. So what?"

Lavelle gave me a pleading look. "It's not relevant, Miss Jones. Just a family matter."

But Alden-Taylor family matters were looming larger and larger in my mind these days. "Zach told me there was some talk about moving you two into an assisted living facility, that he'd discussed it with Gloriana."

Alarm flashed in Lavelle's eyes. "Sandra would never have allowed that!"

But maybe Sandra also suspected what was going on in this house. Assisted living would provide her mother some protection.

"Shut up, Sissy," Leila hissed. "This detective already knows too much of our business. Why complicate things?"

The timing of Gloriana's last visit intrigued me. She'd shown up, possibly to urge the sisters to move, and soon afterward had been poisoned. Yet there was no way the sisters could have committed a murder. I doubted if they had enough money to contract a hired killer even if they'd been able to find one.

"Were there any harsh words between you and Gloriana when she came by?" Harsh words, such as "I'm calling my attorney."

Leila offered a mean smile. "Gloriana was sorry she came out and bothered us, I'll tell you that. We fixed her."

"Sissy, don't," Lavelle begged.

Fixed? In what way, *fixed?*

Lavelle's plea meant nothing to Leila, who had already worked up a full load of venom. "We took her down a few notches, we did. Her and that so-called grandson of hers."

"Oh, no," Lavelle muttered.

So-called grandson? Leaving Lavelle looking more distressed than ever, I said to Leila, "Zach wasn't really Gloriana's grandson, was he? That's why she came by, not to talk about moving you into assisted living."

She crossed her arms in front of her sagging breasts. "You're a regular Perry Mason, aren't you?"

"Sissy, please!" Lavelle reached out a hand to her sister, but Leila slapped it away.

I began to put it together. "Gloriana had been trying to prove a connection to Thomas Jefferson, so she had all the family members swabbed. The DNA testing proved that Zach wasn't related to any of you, didn't it?"

"Sissy and I suspected it all along," Leila said. "Zach didn't really look like any of us. His mother was my maid's daughter, for God's sake! Nothing but a tart! The girl was pregnant when she married Big Zach, but sly minx that she was, she told him the baby was his. That's what happens when you let the help get too friendly. They take advantage."

Lavelle bit her lip. "We were always afraid that if Gloriana found out, she'd blame us. And cut us out of the will. Then what would we do?"

Leila punched her arm before I could intervene. "Nonsense! Gloriana would never disinherit her own flesh and blood. It was a joke for us, that's all, watching Miss Rich Pants make a fool of herself over the little bastard. We'd…Well, *I'd* always planned to tell her the truth, and I was getting close to doing it, too, when she started that silly Thomas Jefferson business. So I decided not to spoil the fun, to let her find out the truth on her own. But, Lord, was it ever rich when Sissy let it slip who Zach's daddy really was! That's just what Gloriana deserved, chasing after old Jefferson as if we Alden-Taylors weren't quality people on our own. We didn't need *him!*"

Overwhelmed by her combination of arrogance and malice, I hurried the next few questions. "What did Gloriana say she was going to do about the situation? Did she plan to change her will? Cut Zach out?"

Lavelle, whose forearm was beginning to redden from Leila's punch, finally spoke up. "Of course she was! Why let Zach inherit everything when my daughter was her true blood relative?"

And the real carrier of those oh-so-magnificent Alden-Taylor genes. Only one question left. Not that it mattered, anymore, but I was curious. "By the way, the supposed Thomas Jefferson connection. How did that turn out?"

Leila smirked. "Inconclusive."

Once I settled myself back into the Neon, I dug the cell phone out of my carry-all and placed a call to Adult Protective Services. The harassed-sounding social worker who answered took my info and told me she'd send someone out, but I doubted it would happen anytime soon. I thanked her anyway, then called Kryzinski. As I waited to be put through, fat black clouds scuttled across the sky, threatening more rain. The few people strolling along the tree-lined Arcadia street wore no raincoats nor carried umbrellas. Arizonans didn't believe in rain, not even when they were standing in it, which is why every winter so many of the damn fools drove their cars into streets-turned-rivers and had to be lifted out by helicopter.

Kryzinski finally came on the line. "What now, Lena? I only have a minute." I could hear the police chief in the background, telling everyone to take their seats. Another damned meeting. One more reason I was glad not to be a cop anymore.

"Then I'll be quick. Did you talk to Gloriana's attorney about her will?" The police chief was now telling everyone to turn their cell phones and beepers off.

"Hiram Johns? Sure. He told us that almost everything goes to Gloriana's grandson, except for a couple hundred thou to her niece, and half that to her sisters. But none of them did it, Lena. It was Owen. Now I've gotta go." He disconnected before I could ask another question.

I decided to get the answer straight from the horse's mouth. I punched in the number for Information and got Hiram Johns office address, which turned out to be in Old Town Scottsdale, not far from my office. The rain began to fall in torrents as soon as I pulled into the office building parking lot. By the time I'd crutched my way from the Neon to the entrance, I was a sopping mess—not necessarily a bad thing. There was always the chance, albeit a slim one, that a rain-washed blonde on crutches might stir even an attorney's hard heart to pity.

But not, as it turned out, the attorney's receptionist.

The dour crone sitting at the front desk as I hobbled in informed me that no one saw Hiram Johns without an appointment, and sorry, he was full up today and tomorrow. Full up next week, too. "This is a busy office, Miss Jones," she said, her voice firm. "You can't just drop in here and expect to see someone. Especially Mr. Johns. By the way, you're dripping on the Persian."

I moved off the Persian—a carpet, not a cat—and shifted strategies. "I completely understand, Miss...Miss...."

"Maxwell. And it's *Mrs.* Maxwell."

Belatedly I noticed the wedding ring. "Of course, of course, and I'm sure you're both very happy. But I have a question only Mr. Johns can answer, about Gloriana Alden-Taylor's will."

She sniffed, but appeared mollified. "Mr. Johns won't tell you anything about a client, especially about the contents of a will. Surely you know that."

"I already know what's in the will. I just need to know if Mrs. Alden-Taylor made an appointment with Mr. Johns sometime in the last two weeks."

Another sniff. Then her face scrunched into an even bigger frown. "Wait a minute. Aren't you that woman who pulled poor Sandra Alden-Taylor out of that fire?"

Hot diggedy dog. "Yes, ma'am, I am." I shifted my weight from foot to foot and grimaced, as if they both hurt. Which they did.

"How brave of you!"

Looking good. I ducked my head and tried to look modest. "It was nothing. The doctor says I might be able to walk without crutches some day." Next week, actually.

She spun around and tapped a few keystrokes into her computer. "Mrs. Alden-Taylor made an appointment to see Mr. Johns nine days ago."

Gotcha, Zach. "Thank you, Mrs. Maxwell. Thank you so much."

I clunked around and headed for the door, only to stop when she added, "But the day before Mrs. Alden-Taylor died, she called back and canceled."

"Canceled?"

Mrs. Maxwell nodded. "She sounded strange." Then she lowered her voice. "If I hadn't known her better, I'd swear she was crying."

Chapter 28

The rain stopped as soon as I reached the Neon, yet I drove up the road to the Hacienda slowly, dreading the misery I would soon cause there. But a murderer was a murderer, regardless of how pleasant he might be. Not that Zach had been all that pleasant during my last visit. Even though he was apparently no Alden-Taylor, he had begun to exhibit signs of that family's obsessiveness. Maybe there was something to be said for nurture versus nature, after all.

The more I learned about the Alden-Taylors the more they baffled me. For all their passions—their Fevers—they were essentially a cold family. Even Zach. Although married to a warm woman who needed him, he cared only for his vision of a new Patriot's Blood Press. The twins had their dysfunctional relationship; Sappho, her cameras; Sandra, her gambling and promiscuity.

And Gloriana?

Gloriana remained an enigma to me. Her lust for Owen appeared to be simply that—mere lust, with no real affection or human concern. She just wanted what she wanted when she wanted it. The only thing she seemed truly to care for—besides her raging hormones and bloodline—was the Hacienda. Even Patriot's Blood Press existed merely to service that crumbling house. And as long as the money rolled in for repairs, why should she care how much misery her books and games caused the world?

A house.

Dead ancestors.

Bound pages.

Surely there had to be something more to the woman.

Why had Gloriana canceled her appointment at the attorney's office? What had made such a glacial woman cry?

There was something missing.

This time when I arrived at the Hacienda, there were no animals in the stable yard, and only two battered pickup trucks. Where was everyone? Curious, I tapped the Neon's horn twice, and after a minute, the gate opened. When Rosa met me at the door, Casey at her heels, the meows and barks behind her proved that Megan's menagerie was still in residence. At least Zach hadn't packed them off to the pound. Yet.

"Hey, Rosa. Any other humans around?"

She gave me a pained smile as a kitten tried to climb up her stockinged leg. It looked like one of the pair she had been bottle-feeding the other day. "The children are here, and Miss Megan, but Mr. Zach is away."

I did not know whether to be disappointed or relieved. I still needed to ask him a few questions before I took my theory to Captain Kryzinski. For instance, why had Zach burned down Patriot's Blood? With Gloriana already dead and the company willed to him, what would be the point? I wouldn't ask him directly, of course; I'd make a few vague inquiries about insurance and see what happened.

As Rosa bent down—to swat the kitten away, I thought—I asked, "Could I see Miss Megan, then?"

Rosa didn't swat the kitten. She picked it up, a fond look on her face. Maybe this rescue business was catching.

"Miss Megan out in the back, fixing someone." Still holding the kitten, Rosa led me through a furry tide until we reached the large French doors that opened onto the property's rear acreage. I could see that one of the outbuildings had recently been painted white. Milling around outside the building were Emma and the rest of Megan's herd, which now included a limping llama.

When I gestured questioningly toward the building, Rosa said, "Her new animal hospital. She pick up a couple of dogs yesterday, some cats. And Juan."

"Juan?"

"That thing." She pointed to the llama. "She say the owner beat him."

Suddenly I did not feel so triumphant. What would happen to the animals when Kryzinski arrested Zach? To Megan and the baby? But Owen had a family, too. What would happen to them if I did not prove him innocent? Leaving Rosa behind with her kitten, I hobbled across the rugged ground to the outbuilding.

"Hi, Lena," Megan said, as I walked through the door. "Give me a moment here." She looked terrible. Since I had last seen her, the skin around her eyes had purpled, and her cheeks looked sunken.

Next to her, an elderly woman bent over a table, studying a thin black dog which had only three legs.

A wave of nausea hit me. Clutching my stomach, I stepped outside again. After gulping air for a few seconds, I managed to close my mind to everything but the investigation. Then I went back inside.

"We'll never find a home for this guy," Megan was saying.

"Want me to put him down?" The woman's voice held the brisk, vaguely compassionate tone common to the medical profession. Probably a vet.

Megan sighed and the dog's tail thumped against her in answer. "Dr. Weitz, I don't need any more animals."

"Then I'll prepare a syringe."

Megan, obviously undergoing a change of heart, stayed her with a hand. "No. Other than the leg, he appears to be healthy. All he needs are a few meals and a bath. I'll keep him."

"You sure?"

Megan sighed again. "Yeah, I'm sure. Oh, lord, Zach's going to kill me."

I winced at her turn of phrase, even though I doubted if Megan was in danger from her husband. He would gain nothing from killing his wife and baby.

Or would he?

Dr. Weitz gave Megan a wintry smile. "Want me to fit Stumpy here with a prosthesis, then?"

For a moment Megan appeared to take the question at face value and even seemed to be considering it. "How much…?"

"It was a joke, dear, a joke." Dr. Weitz patted her on the back, then reached down to the table and did the same for the dog. "Plenty of three-legged dogs around."

The vet lifted the dog off the examining table and put him down carefully on the ground, where he sat and gazed at Megan with adoration. Ignoring him, Dr. Weitz threw a few items into a big leather bag and snapped it shut.

"How much do I owe you?" Megan asked.

"I'll send you a bill." With a wave, Dr. Weitz shouldered her bag and left.

Megan finished tidying up the room, which was—truth be told—now neater than the Hacienda. "She never does, you know."

"Never does what?"

"Send a bill. Dr. Weitz has worked pro bono ever since I started all this. She's more or less retired, but still…I think I'm her only non-paying customer."

As we left the building, Stumpy hopped along with us, never once taking his eyes off Megan. The sky had cleared and the sun beamed through. The scent of damp earth and sage drifted toward us from Mummy Mountain. "Another foundling?"

"What? Oh, the dog. One of our volunteers picked him up in the desert. He'd been dumped."

I wondered what kind of person would dump an animal in Arizona's desert and leave it to fend for itself. In our harsh landscape, mountain lions and even coyotes could die of hunger. Domesticated dogs had no chance at all. Especially three-legged dogs.

My stomach heaved again and I gulped more air. When we entered the Hacienda with Stumpy at our heels, the other animals ran to greet us, Casey in front. A little Yorkie I hadn't noticed before knocked into my crutch and almost sent me sprawling.

"Bad Peppy," Megan said. "Sit. Sit."

Bad Peppy sat. So did Stumpy, Casey and several other members of the fur herd. Someone had once loved them enough to train them.

"Megan, how many dogs do you have now?" I asked.

She thought for a moment. "Twelve. And fourteen cats. Three rabbits. A pig. A llama. But like I told Zach, it's not as bad as it sounds. We've already found homes for six of the dogs and a few of the cats. I might be stuck with Emma, though."

"How about the llama?"

"Juan? Already promised to a farm near Buckeye. So you see? I'm not totally irresponsible."

Her quick use of the word intrigued me. Someone had obviously called her that, and recently. Zach, probably. Whatever he thought of his wife, though, didn't make any difference now. When I'd done what I needed to do, putting up with Megan's animals would be the least of his problems.

"Listen, Megan, I came up here to talk to Zach, but since he's not here, maybe I could ask you a few questions."

"Of course. Let's go…oh!" A strange look crossed her face. "He's moving!"

"Moving?"

She grabbed my hand and pressed it to her stomach. To my astonishment, I could feel a large lump sliding horizontally across her large belly. Every now and then it slowed, poked outward briefly, then continued on its path.

"That's his foot," she said, her face rapturous, her hand still on mine.

Zach's baby. Oh, Jesus, what was I going to do? Half sick with guilt, I pulled my hand away. "Wonderful, Megan. You must be excited."

Her glow came back, almost erasing the shadows underneath her eyes. "I'm living a miracle."

I didn't know how to respond to that, so I just smiled my Judas smile.

When the baby finally stopped playing kickball or whatever it was doing, she led me into the den, where I settled with relief onto a catless chair. There was something to be said for big houses and lots of furniture; they provided room for everyone, even humans. Megan sat across from me, Stumpy at her feet. With his broad, squared-off snout and three gangly legs, he looked like an unholy cross between a St. Bernard and a Great Dane. I had to agree with her earlier statement. She would never find a home for the ugly thing.

"You sure made a friend there," I said, pointing out the obvious.

She nodded. "He took to me so fast he must have belonged to a woman."

I couldn't imagine a woman dumping a three-legged dog to die in the desert. Maybe something had happened to her. Maybe her body was still out there, waiting to be found.

As if reading my mind, Megan said, "The off-roaders who found him looked all over the place for his owner, but they couldn't find anyone. They said they didn't see any buzzards."

I shuddered. Arizona's Sonoran desert had long been the repository for the bodies of lost hikers, not to mention a favorite dumping ground for murder victims. And dogs who had outgrown their welcome.

No time to worry about that now, though. "Megan, when will your husband be back?"

She gave me a wry smile. "Tomorrow. He flew to Iowa to talk to a couple of students attending the writers' workshop. Their instructor thinks they've written publishable manuscripts."

"Literary stuff, right?"

The shadows underneath her eyes returned, and she shrugged. "Yes. But there's always the chance that he'll get lucky and one of the students will turn out to be the new Michael Cunningham.

You know, the man who wrote *The Hours*, won the Pulitzer Prize, and made all that money on the movie."

I'd seen the movie, but hadn't finished the book. "That would be nice."

She winced. "Nice. And maybe someday Stumpy will grow his leg back." It was the first time I'd ever heard an edge in her voice, but it disappeared almost as soon as it emerged. She gave a little laugh, then leaned over with great difficulty and petted Stumpy on the head. He rewarded her with a gaze of unconditional love.

Whoever had dumped that dog was a fool.

Before Megan could say anything else, Sandra's two children came running into the room. "Aunt Megan, can we go see Mommy at the hospital tonight?" John-John asked.

Megan shook her head. "I'm sorry, but with everything that's going on, I can't manage it. Uncle Zach will be back tomorrow, we'll go then. For now, why don't you take our new dog and give him a bath?"

The disappointment on the children's faces vanished. "Can we wash him in the fountain?" Caroline.

"Sure." Megan nudged the big dog toward the children, and after an initial hesitation, he hobbled after them.

Megan sat back and sighed. "The doctors say Sandra might be able to come home next week. With all these animals and her kids...." She didn't finish the sentence, but added, "Thank God for Rosa."

Megan looked like she was about to collapse from stress. I wondered if she was worried about the possible loss of her dreamed-of animal shelter, or if she was beginning to suspect that her husband had killed Gloriana.

In an odd way, I found myself more disgusted with Zach for abandoning Megan in her frail condition than for murdering his grandmother. How could some miserable manuscript mean more to a man than his pregnant wife? But that was the Alden-Taylors for you. Once an obsession took hold....

I reminded myself that Zach was no Alden-Taylor, merely a cuckoo in the nest. Still, he had been raised by Gloriana, and apparently her predisposition to Fevers had infected him, too. One had driven him to murder.

"Megan, have you tried, I mean *really* tried to talk to him about Patriot's Blood and the new editorial direction?"

She nodded glumly. "Oh, yes. We've had several long talks, well, arguments really. He won't budge. He keeps saying that he left his job at ASU believing that he'd be developing an experimental literature imprint, and now that Gloriana's dead, he can finally do what he set out to do. He wouldn't listen to my suggestion that it might be a good idea to have at least one Patriot's Blood imprint operating in the black, that the income generated from mysteries or thrillers could help support his, uh, more experimental stuff."

She sounded every bit as enthralled with his dreams as Zach did with hers. The difference was, he had the wherewithal to fulfill his. All she had were pleas. Once again I congratulated myself on staying single. "What exactly did Zach say?"

The shadows around her eyes grew darker. "He made fun of everything I suggested. He even said that it was time I grew up." Then those beautiful eyes welled up. "Oh, Lena, I don't know what's happened to him!"

Money's what happened to him, Megan. But I didn't say it.

She sighed. "Zach used to be such a reasonable man. All you ever had to do was present a good case for something, and he'd listen. Like Save Our Friends. When I first came up with the idea of starting a rescue organization, I told him what I thought it would entail, jotted down a cost estimate, and he said to go ahead, that somehow we'd find the money. Now you can't tell him anything. He's...he's *driven.*"

The perfect opening. Now was the time to see if Zach had told Megan about the results of the DNA test. "It's interesting that you say that, Megan. I've interviewed all the Alden-Taylors, and I've never seen such a driven group of people in my life. The twins, well, hopefully that problem gets taken care of soon. As for Sappho, she's so obsessed with her films she walked away from a fortune. Frankly, I'm surprised you expected Zach to be any different."

Megan flicked a sharp glance at me, then quickly looked away. But not before I saw the knowledge in her face. As if to cover her lapse, she rubbed her still-damp eyes against the back of her wrist. "Not everyone in a family is alike, Lena. I'm not much like either of my parents. How about you? Are you like yours?"

Now there was a question. "Megan, I don't have the faintest idea if I'm like my parents or not." Then I told her about my life, the shooting, the foster homes. I didn't tell her everything, though. There would be no point.

During the telling, her eyes grew so dark they looked bruised. Then, to my great discomfort, she struggled out of her chair, stepped over to me, and gave me such a tight hug that I could feel the baby moving again. "Oh, God, Lena, I'm so sorry."

I peeled her away from me as gently as I could. What kind of person could ever hurt this compassionate woman?

The detective kind, that's who.

Chapter 29

For the perfect end to the perfect day, I needed to make yet another trip to Dr. Gomez. Due to my injuries from the explosion, I had missed my last appointment and I didn't dare miss this one. Appearing uncooperative—well, at least more uncooperative than ususal—could get my license pulled.

No license, no Desert Investigations.

Gomez had the grace to look concerned as I limped through the door. "I read about the explosion," she said, watching me fuss with my crutches. "Your actions were extraordinary."

Her praise made me uncomfortable. "Well, I couldn't exactly let the woman burn to death, could I?" All I need is another nightmare to add to my collection. Balancing the crutches against the sofa, I lowered my backside, only to find the cushion lumpier than usual.

Or maybe my ass was scrawnier than usual.

Gomez tapped her pencil on her desk, a sign she was impatient with her patient. "Many people would have let the woman die, Lena. You were already injured, yourself."

"So?" I didn't understand what she was getting at. Although I was no longer on the force, I had been trained as a police officer. Serve and *protect.* That's what cops did.

But when I reminded her of this, the pencil-tapping intensified. "Lena, you haven't been a police officer in two years. Why is it still so important for you to save other people, even at the risk of your own life?"

I frowned. "It's instinct, that's all."

She stared at me for a moment, saying nothing. Then she put the pencil down and leaned back in her chair. "Tell me about the foster homes."

I looked over at the window, but saw no flying geese today, no herons. Nothing but the cloudless Arizona sky.

"Lena?"

I reached down and rubbed my feet, although they hardly hurt at all anymore. Anything to escape Gomez' stare.

"Lena, you need to cooperate."

What a pointless remark. "I'm here, aren't I? That's cooperation."

Gomez cleared her throat and leaned forward, the same expression on her face that I had frequently seen on Captain Kryzinski's when I'd done something to annoy him.

"Lena, stop fooling around. It's obvious to me that you don't understand anything about yourself, that you're a troubled, angry woman who acts without thinking, sometimes violently. Yes, you're brave, and yes, you saved Ms. Alden-Taylor's life. But you've done damage, too. You're licensed to carry a concealed weapon, and that worries me. How long will it be before you do even more damage to someone than you did to the woman you saw beating her child? You are simply going to have to get your anger under control, and you can't do that unless you start opening up. Beginning now."

This was what it had come down to, then. Me spilling my guts under court order. After one last, hopeful look out the window, I asked, "What do you want to know?"

"For starters, how many foster homes were there?"

Good question, Gomez. I wasn't sure myself, but I could give it a try. I started counting on my fingers. "I don't remember the name of the first couple, because I was only there for a couple of months. But I seem to remember, vaguely, that they were nice enough. Then I was sent to...."

She broke in. "Why were you taken away from the first couple?"

I shrugged. "Why does CPS do anything? The next place I don't remember much about, either, which is probably good, but I stayed there until I was around six. They went back East, so I moved again." I continued on, counting off the five foster homes I'd lived in before I reached the age of nine.

Then I stopped. Another desperate look out the window. Still no geese. No herons. Where the hell were they when I needed them?

"Go on, Lena," Gomez said, her voice now a purr. "You're doing very well."

"Well, uh, after the sixth home, I, uh, wound up at the Giblins. He was a minister, his wife taught Sunday school. They had a lot of foster kids and took us camping all the time. But then Mrs. Giblin had a stroke and died, so I was sent to the Johnsons, foster home number eight. They took in foster kids for the money. God knows they didn't care anything about us. And then came the artist, she was home number nine. She and…."

The smell of turpentine, linseed oil, White Lilac cologne. "You're my own sweet girl, Lena, my own sweet little girl."

I took care that my voice didn't waver. "…and her husband were going to adopt me, but then she developed breast cancer, so CPS moved me again. Let's see, foster home number ten, that was…."

Gomez broke in. "Go back to foster home number six."

"Uh, why?"

"Because it's the only home you haven't described at all."

I looked up at the ceiling. Recessed fluorescent lighting. I hate that stuff. Makes everyone look green. "That's because, uh, there wasn't much to tell."

The monster in the closet.

No. I refused to revisit that nightmare.

Gomez' voice was firm. "Humor me."

Oh, hell. "They had a nice house. Big. And a dog. His name was Sandy, which I now realize was pretty funny because of that play about Little Orphan Annie. Annie's dog was named Sandy, too."

"What happened to Sandy?"

I looked at Gomez in surprise. "Little Orphan Annie's dog?"

"No, Lena."

"Oh. Well, nothing happened to my, uh, foster home number six' Sandy. Why do you ask?"

"Because your voice shook when you mentioned him."

Impossible. If I could control myself when talking about the artist who had almost adopted me, why would I waver when talking about some damned dog? Maybe I'd been hanging around Megan and her strays too long.

Jesus. That three-legged dog.

"Oh, you're right. I forgot. Sandy disappeared one day. Didn't come back. Which made me sad. Then I went to the next foster home, the Rev, and...."

"No, Lena, we're not through with foster home number six. Tell me about the people. What were they like?"

The monster in the closet.

"The people? Oh, they were ordinary people. Nothing special." I had to give Gomez something, though. Otherwise, she would never ease up. "Listen, Gomez. I started having problems at home number nine, the home of the artist I was telling you about. That's when I began stealing."

No lie there. I still had the satin pillow I'd stolen from the artist's husband. *Welcome to the Philippines* was embroidered on it.

Gomez' eyes flickered. "We can talk about the artist during your next visit, but right now, I want to hear more about home number six. What were the people's names?"

I drew in a deep breath. "Uh, Wycoff. Norma and Brian Wycoff."

"Tell me what they were like."

The air in the room closed in on me like a living thing, like the air in Patriot's Blood while it burned. Suddenly, I could not catch my breath or see through the red film that edged my vision. Even the roaring that had plagued my ears after the explosion was back.

From a distance I could hear Gomez shouting. "Lena! Put your head between your knees!"

For once I did what I was told. In a few minutes, the breathing eased and the darkness slid away. But I couldn't lift up my head. It was too heavy.

"Lena, are you all right now?"

I wondered where the geese were, the heron. Fishing, probably, in Eldorado Park. I hoped the water wasn't too polluted. We can't have three-legged herons, can we? Just three-legged dogs no one loved.

But that was wrong. I loved him.

No, *Megan* loved him. Not me. I didn't have a dog. Never did. Foster children weren't allowed to have pets. Too much baggage.

No dogs.

Never.

Ever.

Gomez' voice, as if from miles away. "I'm getting you some water."

I heard Gomez' small refrigerator open, the clink of ice against glass, water pouring.

"Drink this." Cool glass in my hand.

I drank. The roaring in my ears faded, the remaining blackness vanished.

"I pushed you too hard too soon." Her voice sounded oddly tender. I wasn't used to that. From anybody.

"Too…too soon?" My voice had returned. "What, are you nuts? I'm still, um, having some physical problems from the fire. Look, it has to be around time for me to go, right? I'm obviously not feeling well and I need to lie down."

"You need help, Lena, that's what you need."

I managed a laugh and grabbed my crutches. "These are all the help I need." I lurched to my feet. "I'm outta here."

She opened her appointment book. Now her voice held no inflection at all. "Same time next week, Lena. You still have five appointments left before you fulfill the Court's requirements."

The monster in the closet.

Ignoring that old nightmare, I limped to the door. “I can’t. I just can’t.”

“If you want to keep your private investigator’s license you will.”

I stood in the doorway for a second, trying not to scream. I couldn’t take this. But I had to. Like I had taken so much for so many years. And lived through it all. “Okay, Gomez. See you next week.”

“I’m looking forward to it, Lena.”

The only thing I was looking forward to was getting back to my apartment and falling into bed.

I prayed I wouldn’t dream.

Chapter 30

When I hobbled sans crutches down the stairs to Desert Investigations the next morning, I discovered Jimmy already at his computer. Was it my imagination, or was he looking older these days? Maybe he missed my delightful presence at the trailer. Not.

"Hey, look at you," he said, smiling. "On your own again."

"Call me Speedo." I limped over to my desk and sat down a little too quickly. Now my ass hurt, too.

My sour mood must have communicated itself to him, because he said nothing more, just went back to work on his computer. While he did his finger dance, I looked through the big plate glass window onto Main Street. Deserted. At nine o'clock it was too early for tourists, but they'd be along as soon as the art galleries opened. Especially since the weather was mild. The sky had clouded over again, but perhaps the sun would soon emerge. We Arizonans were so spoiled. We averaged, what, three hundred and twenty-five days of sunshine a year, yet we belly-ached all the way through those other forty.

The telephone calls hardly lightened my gloom. People wanted this, they wanted that. Husbands wanted to find out if their wives were cheating, wives wanted to find out ditto about their husbands. When I explained that Desert Investigations did not take marital cases, they cursed me.

People don't like each other any more, do they?

Toward the end of the day, when the phone rang again, I prepared myself to repeat the usual speech, but the voice on the other end of the phone had me smiling instead. Dusty.

"Hey, I got back from the trail ride last night, so let's get together."

My first instinct was to tell him I was busy, but he would know better. Besides, after my treatment of Jimmy, I needed all the friends I could get.

"A movie?" I suggested.

"Sounds good to me. What's playing?"

Leaning over, I plucked the *Scottsdale Journal* out of the trash can and found the Arts & Entertainment section. Scanning through the movie listings, I found a Meg Ryan romance, the latest Quentin Tarantino gore-fest, another Eddie Murphy comedy....

And *Cold Sky*, written and directed by Sappho, a.k.a. Victoria Alden-Taylor.

"I'm in the mood for a Western," I told Dusty. "How about you?"

At the sound of his laugh, I realized my mistake. The man had spent several days out on the trail with a passel of dudes, trying to recreate an Old West that had never existed in the first place. "Oops," I said. "Well, there's a horror flick at the mall, one of those guy-in-a-ski-mask-type things."

The laughter died down. "Lena, you know I hate malls. The Western sounds fine. Who knows, maybe it'll even be accurate."

"So what did you think of the movie?" I asked, as we left the Camelview, Scottsdale's only remaining venue for art films. Not wanting to deal with my crutches in a crowded theater, I had left them back in the apartment, so now I limped badly. No problem, though. Dusty had his arm around me.

"Well, I'm not sure you can call it a Western." He chuckled as he hoisted me into the front seat of his pickup truck. "Even though it had cowboys, Indians, and horses."

"And lesbians."

"I really liked that part."

I gave him a look. "I'll bet you did, cowboy."

Another chuckle. "You've got to admit, babe, it was a pretty good flick."

For all my carping, I thought so, too. And the movie had delivered a surprise. Regardless of its artsy-fartsy trappings, the movie had a strong love story. The fact that the love element had been between two women—a school teacher and a saloon gal—was immaterial. Sappho's film revealed her warm heart.

The question was, where did she get it?

I had my own heart troubles. Or lack thereof. That night, as we lay together in my bed, I found that I could not respond to Dusty's caresses. After almost an hour trying to light my fire, he finally gave up and rolled over on his back.

"I'm sorry," I said, trying to keep my voice from shaking. "You can, well, you know. Anyway, I don't have to respond for you to enjoy yourself. I hear married people do it like that all the time."

He leaned over and stroked my hair. "But we're not married, are we?"

It was a measure of my distress that I had even pronounced the M-word, and now I regretted it. "You sure you don't want to, um…?"

"No, Lena, I don't want to um. I want to lie here beside you." His arms tightened around me.

I sniffled, then tried to hide it with a sneeze. "I think I'm getting a cold."

"You're such a terrible liar. That's one of the things I love about you." He buried his nose in my neck, then followed it up with kisses designed more for comfort than arousal.

Blinking my tears away, I said, "I'm such a mess."

"Yes, honey, you are. But so am I. So are half the people in this world. They simply put on a better front than we do."

I started to argue about that, then stopped. Maybe it was true. Maybe I was no more troubled than anyone else. I had almost convinced myself of that when I finally fell into a dreamless sleep.

Chapter 31

Time for the dirty work.

A quick call to the Hacienda the next morning revealed that Zach was back from Iowa but was too busy meeting with editors to see me. No problem. I didn't want to talk to him quite yet, either. Next, I dialed Captain Kryzinski's number to tell him to prepare for an arrest in the Gloriana Alden-Taylor case. I struck out there, too, only getting his answering machine. Loath to leave the details on the tape, I said that I'd figured out who had really killed Gloria Alden-Taylor, and that it wasn't Owen.

Then I hung up and told Jimmy.

"But...but Zach seemed like such a nice guy, Lena!"

Jimmy had always been too trusting. "That's what he wanted everyone to think. But after he inherited Patriot's Blood, he revealed his true colors. Believe me, Mr. Nice Guy he ain't."

The real Zach would kill his grandmother to inherit. The real Zach would ignore his pregnant wife and, in true Alden-Taylor fashion, follow his own obsessions. Not for money. Not for power. Just for the sake of a literary imprint. Obsession didn't have to be carried in the genes, after all. It was a virus, infecting everyone it touched.

You didn't have to be a true Alden-Taylor to be a sad excuse for a human being.

I should know.

I'm the expert on sad excuses.

When I went out to the Neon, I noticed that the early morning clouds had scuttled away, revealing a sky so blue it looked phoney. I stopped for a second to enjoy it. To the north, Mummy Mountain rose green and purple against the far-off McDowells. A gentle breeze whispered in from the south. These days of grace were why we Arizonans put up with our 120-plus-degree Julys and August monsoons.

I closed my eyes and smelled sage, damp earth.

Then I opened them again, aware that all I was doing was killing time.

I didn't want to do what I had to do, which was to ask Zach my final questions, then tell him what I already knew. There was no danger because Zach would hardly try to kill me in front of Rosa, Megan, and a pack of editors. But the visit would give me a chance to advise him to call his lawyer and arrange a deal. If he turned himself in voluntarily, he would be able to plead down, maybe even to Manslaughter Two. What would he get then? Fifteen years? Ten? With good behavior, he could be out in seven. It was all ridiculous, of course, for murderers to serve so little time, but that's the way the court system worked, and not only in Arizona, either. Selling a little weed could get you thirty years, but stone cold killers had their hands slapped if they bought the right attorneys.

As I drove up the dirt road to the Hacienda, I realized that Megan would not look upon a seven-year absence from Zach as a mere hand slap. Yet there was nothing I could do. I could only hope that when I got to the Hacienda, she would be out rescuing another stray. I didn't want to see her eyes when I confronted her husband with my knowledge.

Part of my wish came true. By the time I arrived at the Hacienda, Megan was gone. But so were Zach and the Patriot's Blood editors.

"No more business today," Rosa told me. "Mr. Zach and Miss Megan, they went to visit at the hospital. Miss Sandra, she gonna get released tomorrow. I think they gonna hire a nurse to take care of her until she can do for herself, then they say they gonna help her move."

"Move?" For one wild moment, I had a picture of Sandra, Caroline, and John-John moving into John Brookings' trailer at Wigwam Court. But then I remembered that under the terms of Gloriana's will, Sandra had inherited enough to buy a house. How nice for Brookings.

I thought about the will again. Would it be declared null and void once Zach was convicted of murder? Probably. Then again, Arizona did not have an automatic Son of Sam law, the law New York state had once enacted to keep killers from profiting in any way from their crimes. As usual, legal matters were more complicated out here in the Wild West. There was a remote chance Zach could be found guilty of murder and, with some fancy-footed legal maneuvering, still claim part of the inheritance through a blind trust. It had been done before. The greatest likelihood, though, was that once his guilt had been confirmed through trial, Sandra would successfully challenge the will. That would make her mother and aunt happy.

But where would it leave Megan?

I looked around the Hacienda's courtyard at Megan's menagerie—the dogs, the cats, the rabbits, the pig, and the llama—and decided not to think about it. I couldn't bear to.

"Thanks, Rosa," I said. "I'll go to the hospital and see them there." Still safety in numbers. I started to turn away from the door, when Rosa's voice stopped me.

"They been gone two hours already, Miss Lena. They probably already up at the parcel by now."

"Parcel?" My confusion must have shown on my face, because Rosa explained.

"The land Miss Gloriana own near Pinnacle Peak. Mr. Zach, he said they were meeting some real estate guy up there after he and Miss Megan leave the hospital."

The land Megan and Zach had such different plans for.

I asked Rosa for directions and limped back to the Neon. With the new freeway completion, the trip should take no more than a half hour. Which was exactly why the Pinnacle Peak area, at one time so remote, had skyrocketed in value. A small building lot now could cost as much a completed home in other areas of Scottsdale or even Paradise Valley. How many acres had Zach inherited? I searched my memory and came up with forty. Then I did some quick math, whistled. The sale would buy a lot of decaf mocha lattes at Starbucks.

Or a stack of really dull experimental manuscripts for Patriot's Blood Press.

The drive to Pinnacle Peak took longer than I'd planned, due to a nasty wreck south of the Frank Lloyd Wright Boulevard exit. As the EMTs scraped bleeding suburbanites out of a Lexus and a Beemer, I sat in the Neon, wondering why people wanted to live so far away from their jobs. My own situation was perfect; business below, apartment above. No dangerous commute to work, only a walk downstairs. Thinking about the stairs set my feet a-tingling, so I turned the engine off and flexed them. Still sore, but better than yesterday. There was a good chance I would be back to normal in another week. Well, normal for me, anyway.

By the time the police redirected traffic around the carnage, I'd been massaging my feet for almost half an hour. I hoped that by the time I reached Gloriana's acreage, everyone would still be there. The fact that a real estate agent had been thrown into the mix complicated things, but I could work around that. I'd ask Zach a couple of pointed questions, then tell him I needed to have a private meeting with him and his attorney this afternoon at my office. There was no reason to involve Megan.

Following Rosa's instructions, I left the blacktop and its surrounding subdivisions behind and drove east along a primitive dirt road for almost a mile. Then I cut north again at an almost invisible fork and headed toward the McDowell Mountains. After bumping along the road for ten minutes, I finally saw a familiar pickup truck parked along the shoulder. But I did not see a realtor's car. He was probably long gone.

Megan would be there, though, enough protection. Besides, I was packing. I put a reassuring hand on my carry-all and felt the comforting weight of my .38 and the rattle of handcuffs.

I pulled the Neon alongside the pickup and got out.

"Zach? Megan?" I called.

To my consternation, I could not see anyone, merely miles and miles of sand and cactus. Overhead, two hawks circled, their shrill cries competing with the sighing wind.

"Zach?"

"Over here, Lena!" Megan's voice.

I finally found her walking along a shallow gully that had probably been a raging torrent the day before, carrying the runoff from the rains in the McDowells.

"Better get out of there," I called down to her. "It might start raining again up north." Getting caught in a flash flood was a leading cause of accidental death in the Southwest.

She smiled up at me, the shadows gone from under her eyes. "You're right. I'm being stupid."

I would have helped her all the way up, but my feet were still so sore that I didn't trust them. When she neared me, I put down my carry-all and held out my hand. With some difficulty—Lord, she was *so* pregnant—I hauled her up the rest of the way.

When she was up on safer ground, I asked, "Where's Zach?" I looked around, expecting to see him emerge from behind one of the many saguaros behind me.

"He stayed at the hospital. I've been dealing with the real estate broker myself." Her eyes were not only lighter, but they positively gleamed. She looked rested, too, as if she had finally managed a full night's sleep.

"So where's the broker?"

Her smile grew. "Gone. He already has a buyer, a developer from Tucson. Poor Gloriana, she loved this place and had even talked about turning it over to the Nature Conservancy. But Zach and I will put it to better use."

Money for manuscripts? Money for the Hacienda? Why should that have made Megan look so happy?

Perhaps seeing the puzzlement on my face, she answered my unasked question. "Zach changed his mind. I told you he would."

"Changed his mind?"

She nodded in satisfaction. "Yes. When he got back from Iowa last night, we had a long talk. The manuscripts hadn't been as good as he'd been led to believe, just pages and pages of self-involved angst. You know. 'Life is cruel but I'm the only one who's sensitive enough to care.' Just the usual Creative Writing 101 drivel."

Since I knew life would soon turn cruel for Megan, I didn't smile. "So you're getting your mystery imprint after all?"

"Oh, yes! Not only that, since I know more about that kind of thing than he does, he's going to let me help choose the manuscripts. I know I can make it work. The imprint will more than pay for itself; it'll make enough money to let Zach buy all the experimental stuff he wants."

I looked off across the desert, at the gently rolling land leading up to the spectacular mountains. Forty acres. Forty very expensive acres. "So now the money from the land sale goes for…?"

Her smile was blinding. "For my no-kill shelter, of course! Zach told me to go ahead and find some land and have an architect start drawing up plans. Oh, Lena! It's what I intended all along."

What I intended all along.

Her face changed. "I meant, what I *wanted* all along."

With a sick feeling, I realized her first statement had been the most accurate. What she'd *intended* all along. What she'd *intended* when she put the water hemlock in Gloriana's salad.

"Uh, that's wonderful news, Megan," I told her, inching toward my carry-all, which was now closer to her than me. "But, well, I drove up here to talk to Zach, and since he's back at the hospital, I'd better…."

With astonishing agility for someone in her condition, Megan bent down and plucked my .38 out of the carry-all.

She'd obviously used a gun before, because when she aimed the barrel at my chest, her hand didn't waver.

"I screwed up, didn't I, Lena? I talked too much, like I always do." She didn't look so beautiful any more, just deadly.

Maybe there was a way out of this. "I don't know what you're talking about, Megan, but you'd better give me that gun. It could go off."

Her laughter held little of its former joy. "Well, I hope to God it can go off. Now that you know what I did, I'm going to have to kill you, too."

She stood with her back to the edge of the gully. With rising optimism, I realized I might be able to rush her and tip her backward into it. I shifted my weight forward.

But she saw the plan in my eyes and drew the hammer back on the .38 with a practiced movement. "You'll be dead before you're halfway here. You're still limping pretty bad."

I raised my hands. "Megan, you don't want to kill me."

The laugh again, the half-crazy laugh of the obsessed. "You're right, I don't want to. But it's you or...." Tears welled in her eyes, but her jaw remained firm. "It's you or me. Why couldn't you leave things the way they were? Owen would never have gone to prison, not with that expensive attorney I made Zach hire for him. If you hadn't become involved, Gloriana's death would only have been another unsolved Arizona mystery."

"Not *death*, Megan. Murder. You murdered her."

"Gloriana was a terrible person. Those books, those games, they were pure evil."

I did not think this was the right time to discuss the pros and cons of the First Amendment, so I kept quiet.

She tossed her head, and in that moment, I saw an echo of Gloriana's blind self-righteousness. "What kind of person would publish books that ruin lives, that only add to the world's misery? Just so she could save a house? Gloriana had no love in her, none at all. Maybe what I did was wrong, but what I did, I did for love. Gloriana never cared anything for anyone, just the Hacienda and her stupid pedigree. She didn't even care for

Zach after she got the DNA results back. Oh, you don't know what she was like, Lena! That day she came screeching up to the house, kicking those poor animals out of the way, yelling that Zach…that our baby…that they'd never get a dime, that she'd rather leave his share to the Nature Conservancy! Thank God he wasn't there to hear it."

She jabbed the gun toward me for emphasis. "She…she called him a *bastard.* And she called our baby a bastard's bastard!"

"Where was Zach when all this happened?"

"Up at WestWorld, helping set up the SOBOP display. It would…it would have killed him if he'd heard the way the old bitch talked about him!"

As Megan howled with grief and outrage, I saw her finger tighten on the .38's trigger. I had to keep her talking.

"Tell me how you did it." Murderers liked to share, especially those who killed for love. They wanted you to *understand.*

She calmed, and a note of pride entered her voice. "It was easy. Everybody thinks pregnant women can't do anything but sit around and knit, but we can hike as well as anyone else. When Zach came back that morning and told me about everyone picking that water hemlock, I realized he'd given me the solution to our problems. So I got on the Internet and found out what it looked like. Then I drove up to Oak Creek Canyon and hiked in. Zach was so busy at WestWorld that he didn't even notice I'd disappeared for half the day.

"Once I got back to Desert Shadows, everything went just like clockwork. The publishers were in the last seminar, so all I had to do was slip into the banquet hall and put the hemlock into her salad."

"What if someone had seen you?"

She shrugged, and the nose of the gun went up. "All they would have seen was a pregnant woman leaning over a table. And anyway, if that had happened, I would have removed the hemlock and tried something else. But nobody did see. I just…I just…." The pride drained from her face, leaving it forlorn.

"What, Megan?"

"I just wish it hadn't hurt her so much. If I'd known, I'd have found another way."

Of course. This was a woman who couldn't bear to see an animal hurt. And a human being was a kind of animal, even cold old Gloriana. Given Megan's druthers, she would probably have preferred disposing of Gloriana via a nice clean shot of potassium cyanide. Or a decompression chamber, the kind they used at the dog pound.

"Now I have to kill you, too." Tears threatened her eyes again, but the nose of the .38 came back down, pointing toward my heart.

I held my hands higher. "Megan, did you ever see a person get shot?"

She looked at me in surprise. "Of course not."

"Well, I have. It's not like you see on television. Not at all. Gunshot victims usually don't die right away. They linger for a while. They gasp. They convulse. Oh, Megan, if you think Gloriana died hard, wait until you see what a .38 does to the human body."

The gun wavered. This tender-hearted murderer didn't really want to hurt me.

Just kill me.

"Megan, you haven't told me everything yet. What about the office? Once Gloriana was dead, why did you need to bomb Patriot's Blood? You knew that Zach had already canceled production of those awful books and games, so there wasn't really any need to destroy the place. And how did you know how to build a bomb, in the first place?"

Never had I seen a face so miserable. "Oh, God! That was wrong of me, so wrong. I…I didn't know that Sandra would be there. Zach had already brought Casey home, so I took it for granted that Sandra was home with her kids. But I guess Rosa was still taking care of them. I certainly never thought for a minute that anyone else would drop by the office, either. When I heard…when I heard that I'd almost killed two people, I wanted to kill myself."

I remembered her visit to me in the hospital, her haunted face. How could I not have realized, then, that I was looking at guilt?

I shifted my weight on my sore feet, making sure she saw me. No matter how she'd hardened herself in the past weeks, she remained acutely attuned to suffering.

I was right. Her face crumpled even further, and tears began trickling down her flushed cheeks. "Oh, Lena, I'm so, so sorry for what I did to you and Sandra."

Not sorry enough to put the gun down, though. I had to keep her talking.

"You still didn't explain why you bombed the office. Or how."

"Because I'd been wrong about Zach. Instead of selling the land out here and using it for the no-kill shelter like we'd talked about, he decided to put everything back into Patriot's Blood. So I thought…I thought that if I bombed the damned place, he'd give up in disgust and go back to our original plan. But I was wrong. He was almost like Gloriana, hell-bent on getting his way no matter how it affected anyone. As for knowing how to make a bomb, well, Gloriana had published this horrible book called *Recreational Explosives and How to Build Them.* All I had to do was follow the diagrams."

Poetic justice, then. Patriot's Blood had been reduced to rubble by one of its own products.

"Lena, I'm sorry." The voice firmed, the finger tightened. The time for talk was over.

I threw myself to the side a split second before the gun went off. Rolled. Toward Megan.

The noise of gunshot. A thud of impact as the bullet hit a saguaro behind me. Before Megan could adjust her aim, I grabbed her around the knees. Brought her down.

But even as she fell, she maintained a death grip on the .38.

I lunged at her again, and we fought for the gun. Ordinarily, I am very strong, but since my injuries, I'd allowed myself to go to seed. No visits to the gym, no jogs in the park, no weight-lifting. All I had done was sit around nursing my sore feet, and now a pregnant woman proved stronger than me. I couldn't bring myself to do the one thing that would probably have worked—kick her in the stomach. When I tried pinning her to the ground with my knees on her shoulders, she easily rolled me off. I scrambled to regain my footing, but she sat up, straightened the .38, and pointed it at me again.

But something in her eyes had changed.

"Back up," she ordered, her voice flat, devoid of all inflection.

Trying to read her and failing, I scrambled backward over the sand, feeling behind me for a stick, a rock, any weapon.

Then I saw. Understood.

She turned the .38 toward herself.

Toward her mouth.

She was done with killing, couldn't take it anymore.

Now only one victim remained.

"No, Megan!" I cried, as I scrambled toward her, reaching for the gun. I could smell her sweat. "No!"

For a second, I touched cold steel, but then her foot came up and kicked me in the stomach. The air left my lungs in a wheeze, and I fell away from her, coming to rest against a barrel cactus. The spines poked into my skin but I hardly felt it, so desperate was I to catch my breath.

"I have to end this," she said, the gun almost at her mouth now, hammer still cocked. Then she closed her eyes tightly, as if she couldn't bear to see herself die.

I finally managed to take in some air. In desperation, I blurted out the only thing I could think of.

"Megan. Remember the baby."

Her eyes flew open.

"You can't kill the baby, Megan."

"The baby." A mere whisper. But she halted the gun's progress toward her mouth.

I rose to my feet.

Ran toward her.

Bent down.

Took the gun away.

This time, she didn't resist.

She didn't resist when I pulled my cell phone out of my carry-all and called Kryzinski. Didn't resist when I told him what had happened and where to find us. Didn't resist when I took the handcuffs out of my carry-all and snapped them around her slender wrists.

"I'm sorry, Megan," I told her.

She still didn't resist when I sat down next to her and waited for the law to arrive.

"I'm sorry, Megan," I said again, as I put my arm around her trembling shoulders.

She didn't resist my touch.

And there we were. Two sad, sorry women, sitting together in the desert.

Chapter 32

A week later I drove back to the Hacienda, this time in the Jeep. My feet had healed, if not my soul.

Rosa let me in, but with no smile this time. "Why you do that to my sweet girl?" she asked.

I shook my head. "I had to." It did not escape my notice that I sounded like Megan.

Megan, who remained under suicide watch at Maricopa County Medical Center.

But I had saved Owen. Exchanged one life for another.

As I walked into the Hacienda's spacious hall, cats and dogs swarmed around me. Now that their savior was gone, what would happen to them? Maybe I....

No. I couldn't.

"Mr. Zach, he in the library waiting for you." She gave me a not-too-gentle shove in that direction, almost knocking me off my feet. Her sweet girl. Had Gloriana ever been someone's sweet girl? Probably not. Maybe that had been her problem. A woman can only go so far on strength alone; at some point, she needed tenderness.

Zach was standing in front of the desk when I entered the library. He motioned to the chair across from the basinet where Marcello Alden-Taylor slept, milky drool covering his chin.

I had been at the hospital the night he was born, four hours after his mother had been charged with murder.

"Satisfied, Miss Jones?" Zach asked, his glare as hostile as Rosa's. "Thanks to you, my son has lost his mother."

I shook my head. "I'm sorry." It seemed like I couldn't stop sounding like Megan.

No surprise there. What Megan didn't know, what Zach didn't know, what none of them knew, was how much she and I had in common. They also did not know that as I first stood over Megan in the desert, watching her weep, that I almost—almost—didn't call Kryzinski. That I almost walked away from the whole thing. Almost pretended that I didn't know what I knew.

Almost.

Until I remembered Owen and the wife and children who needed him.

"You said you had something to show me, Mr. Alden-Taylor." I recognized that the time for first names was over.

He leaned down and opened a drawer in the desk. Took out a sheaf of papers, most of them singed at the edges. "The ATF returned these to me. They belonged to my stepmother."

Stepmother? Then I realized he meant Gloriana.

"Sit. Read." He thrust the pages at me.

I moved two cats out of the chair, sat down, and looked at the pages in my hand. The stationery and handwriting were familiar, but they reflected an entirely different tone than those I had read before. There was no self-satisfaction here.

> *Yesterday my life changed.*
>
> *Yesterday I learned that Zach is not my grandson, not my son's son. The boy I raised with such great hopes isn't an Alden-Taylor at all, although he bears our name.*
>
> *He was Michael's son. My husband, who couldn't keep his hands off the help, had impregnated my own sister's maid.*
>
> *Did my son know?*
>
> *I think back, remember my son's face when he held that baby in his arms, and I must believe he couldn't possibly have known. There was too much love in his eyes.*

But perhaps I am wrong. Perhaps he always knew he was raising his brother, not his son.

Last night, when Zach came by the Hacienda, I confronted him with the DNA test results. As I watched him read the report, I steeled myself to tell him that he wasn't an Alden-Taylor, that he didn't belong to us, that he had to resign from Patriot's Blood, that he had to give his house back to me, that he was disinherited, that when I died, my money would go to the Nature Conservancy.

Not to a bastard with none of my blood.

But before I could say any of this, he put his arms around me and said that it didn't matter, he still loved me. That blood made no difference.

When I pushed him away and looked at him—really looked at him—I saw no proud Alden-Taylors there. No Plymouth Brethren. No presidents. No generals.

Just my husband's eyes.

And oh, God, I loved Michael so.

There was no way I could disown his son.

Shaken, I handed the papers back to Zach. "She says that she thought about leaving your share to the Nature Conservatory. Why not switch heirs and leave everything to Sandra?"

I had never seen such a sad smile. "Because the DNA tests revealed something else. Sandra isn't my cousin—she's my half-sister."

My mouth dropped. "Sandra was Michael's child, too?"

He nodded. "After Gloriana pulled herself together and left, I drove over to my aunts' house and demanded the truth, all of it. They told me that my grandfa…that my father had an affair not only with their maid, but with both of them, too! Lavelle got pregnant. When Gloriana went over there waving the DNA results around, they told her the entire truth. That only Sandra—through Lavelle—had real Alden-Taylor blood. They told Gloriana that if she didn't rewrite her will and leave it all to my cous…my half-sister, that the entire estate would go to someone with no Alden-Taylor genes. Me. A maid's worthless bastard."

I digested this for a moment, thought about the damage one selfish, promiscuous man could do to a family. And then I considered Zach's own culpability.

"But Zach, if you knew Gloriana had a change of heart about the will, that she decided not to disinherit either you *or* Sandra, why didn't you tell Megan?"

His eyes welled. "My grandmo...my stepmother didn't tell me she'd gone by our house, so I didn't know Megan knew anything. I...I probably would have told her, because everything had changed for me, too. But I needed some time to work it out, to come to terms with who I really was. To think about my real father. And my...my brother. And sister. In the end, I waited too long. I was too caught up in my own dreams."

A single tear ran down his face. "I waited so long I turned my wife into a murderer."

That made two of us, then, mired in guilt. Zach, because his own Fever had blinded him. Me, because....

Well, because.

Chapter 33

The greeting Dr. Gomez gave me was warmer than Rosa's, but not by much. I knew I had already failed at my anger management sessions, and unless I was wrong, she'd tell the Court that, too. They would probably lift my license, but at least Jimmy would be able to keep Desert Investigations open.

As for me…

I didn't know and I didn't care.

"Let's see," Gomez mumbled, flipping through my file. "Where did we leave off last week?"

I looked out the window. Who knew that blue could look so unforgiving?

"We were talking about the foster homes," I told her. As if she didn't know. "And why I started stealing."

Nothing about her smile looked genuine. Her eyes were too calculating. "That's right, Lena. You started stealing when you lived in foster home number six, I believe."

"No. Foster home number nine. The artist. The one who got breast cancer."

The smile vanished. "Her getting cancer was certainly unfortunate for the both of you, but I still want to hear about home number six."

"*Foster* home number six," I reminded her. "And I've already told you. It was nothing special."

The monster in the closet.

"Why don't I believe you, Lena?"

"Because...because...." Because I was lying.

I got up from the sofa, but instead of leaving Gomez' office, I merely walked to the window. On the west lay the faux adobes of Scottsdale, on the northeast, the cotton fields of the Pima reservation. Where Jimmy had been born. Where his parents died. Where he had been found and adopted by a loving Mormon couple.

So lucky. Oh, so lucky.

"You want to know about foster home number six?" I asked, turning back toward Gomez.

She said nothing, merely nodded.

I walked back to the sofa and sat down. My feet didn't hurt at all, anymore. In fact, I didn't feel anything anywhere.

"Let's see. Foster home number six. That was Norma and Brian Wycoff. He was an engineer, she was what we call today a stay-at-home mom. She was perfect, everyone said. Handmade quilts, home-baked pies. Tidy print house dresses, never too much makeup. Never talked back to her husband. A meek, agreeable mouse, but a pretty mouse. And Mr. Wycoff, he was so understanding. Every Thursday he'd come home early from work to watch me so that she could volunteer at church."

"What was he like, Lena. Mr. Wycoff?"

I hoped that my laugh would loosen the tightness in my chest. It didn't. "Mr. Wycoff liked little girls."

I told Gomez, then, how it began. There had been touchings. Innocent, at first. Later, not so innocent. I had tried to tell Mrs. Wycoff that the way he touched me made me uncomfortable, but she ignored me. And why not? Who was I, really? Nobody at all. Just a foster kid in a state where there were too many foster kids. Everyone knew that foster kids made stuff up, that they weren't to be trusted.

"I have a memory..." I began.

It was Thursday. I came home from school to a house that seemed empty at first. Sandy greeted me at the door with his little yips, his pink tongue kissing my ankles. I petted him for a while, then let him into the backyard where we both danced among the dandelions. Me, gracefully. He, the best he could. The day was one of those Arizona miracles, a sky-dome of pure blue broken only by the silver flash of two planes leaving Sky Harbor Airport. As the jets continued their path, the contrails crossed, forming a crucifix.

"Sandy!"

He ran toward me with his endearing hobble. I hugged him, his yellow fur giving rise to the most beautiful perfume in the world.

"Sandy, do you love me?"

He woofed his answer.

"You're my family, Sandy. My only family."

I left my dog in the dandelions and went back inside, where I picked up my schoolbooks and climbed the stairs to my room. I shut the door behind me, locking it carefully, as foster kids always do. We know what the world is like.

But then I discovered that all I had done was lock the danger in. When I went to my closet to hang up my sweater, he was there.

Waiting for me.

Mr. Wycoff.

The monster in the closet.

"He raped me."

Silence from Gomez, as if she had been expecting this. Who knows? Maybe she had.

I took a deep breath. "Mr. Wycoff raped me. And he continued to rape me every Thursday for the next year."

See? Telling isn't so hard when you don't feel anything.

Gomez finally spoke. "Why did it go on so long, Lena? Why didn't you tell anyone? Any doctor..."

Exasperated, I snapped, "Well. I didn't know that, did I? I was only nine."

But there was another reason.

I didn't tell because of Sandy.

I brought myself under control again. After all, it didn't matter anymore. Nothing did.

"Before the rapes began…this dog I had, Sandy. A little yellow dog that reminded me of a dog I'd owned years before. Sandy was a butt-ugly cross between some kind of terrier and a pug, but he was my own dog, not the Wykoffs'. I'd rescued him from the middle of Camelback Road right after he'd been hit by a car. I ran out into the street, picked him up and carried him to a veterinarian's office I'd passed on my way home from school. I told the vet I'd pay for his treatment out of my allowance. She didn't say anything to that, merely gave me a strange look, but she kept him from dying. She couldn't save his leg, though, and she told me she wasn't sure she could find a home for a three-legged dog."

A three-legged dog, like Megan's Stumpy. And we all knew what happens to ugly, three-legged dogs, don't we?

Gomez frowned. "How did you manage to keep Sandy? You told me foster children weren't allowed to keep pets."

No, they weren't. Not unless the pet could be used as a bargaining chip for a nine-year-old girl's silence.

I looked up at the ceiling. White. Textured. One black fly walking across it.

"Mr. Wykoff followed me one day and found out what I was doing with my allowance. To my surprise, he paid the entire bill, brought Sandy home, and said I could keep him. Oh, I was so happy! I finally had something of my own to love! The rapes began about a month later. That first time Mr. Wycoff said if I told, he'd hurt Sandy."

I felt nothing now, of course. Feeling nothing makes life so easy.

Silence again. A silence so complete I could hear a car's horn on the street below. I could even have heard my heart beat….

If I'd had a heart.

"When it got really bad, I'd beg Mr. Wykoff to stop. Then he'd whisper one word, *Sandy,* and I'd shut up."

Sandy. With his wet, brown eyes and snaggly smile.

Sandy. My only family.

Sandy. Mr. Wykoff's only weapon.

"What finally stopped it, Lena?"

I went back to the window. Looked out. Nothing. Only traffic. No birds, no three-legged dogs. I closed my eyes against the afternoon glare, and for a moment remembered my cheek against soft fur, my voice assuring Sandy that I'd never let Mr. Wycoff do anything bad to him. Not ever.

Or at least as for long as I could stand…

It.

I turned back to Gomez. "What stopped it?"

I walked back to the sofa, sat down again.

"I have a memory…."

Thursday, a winter day, rape day. The taunting sky as blue as ever. Like I usually did in the pre-dawn hours of Thursday, I'd thrown up, but still I forced myself to pretend nothing had happened and got ready for school. If I stayed home Mr. Wykoff would…

It would last all day.

As I dressed, I realized I couldn't take *it* any more, that if Mr. Wykoff did…*it*…to me again, I would die. Just die. Nothing, not even Sandy, was worth the pain anymore.

Before I left for school, I went into the kitchen, and when neither Mr. nor Mrs. Wycoff was looking, I slipped a butcher knife out of the drawer. I ate my bacon and eggs quietly, ignoring Mrs. Wycoff's vacant chatter, Mr. Wycoff's deep looks. After he left for work and his wife began baking muffins for the church bake sale (apple cinnamon—on bad days I could still smell them), I went out in the backyard and did what I had to do to Sandy.

Because it was Thursday.

After the business with Sandy was finished, I hitched up my backpack again and continued on to school. By then, I felt nothing, not even the nausea that had plagued me during the night.

That nothingness was to follow me for the rest of my life, but I had no way of knowing it, then. If I had, would I have changed any of my actions? Probably not.

Because it was Thursday.

I must have looked and behaved the same as before, because none of the teachers noticed, none of the students. But surely there had to have been something in my face....

But perhaps my face was as cold then as they say it is now.

The morning passed and the teachers talked about plants, the glorious American Constitution, the misery children suffered in the rest of the world....

"We must think kindly of those poor children in China," the social studies teacher told us.

We all nodded our heads. Those poor children in China.

When afternoon arrived, I skipped my last class and walked home quickly, determined to finish what I had begun.

Mr. Wycoff arrived a few minutes later, but this time, I was the monster in the closet.

He opened the closet door to play his peekaboo game, but I was there waiting for him, holding the butcher knife in my shaking hands. With Sandy gone, there was nothing else Mr. Wycoff could take from me.

He opened the closet door...

He opened the closet door...

Saw me.

"Why, little Lena..." he began, that horrible smile on his face.

His smile disappeared when the blood began.

"He didn't die," I continued, to erase that look on Gomez' face. "I was only a nine-year-old kid, not strong enough to get the knife in very deep. But looking back and knowing what I know about anatomy now, I think I nicked an artery."

Gomez' voice, usually so controlled, trembled when she asked, "What did you do next?"

What did I do next? The short answer would be, I walked out of the house and never looked back. But there was more, the most important part of the memory, really. I understood that now.

"The police found me a few hours later at the edge of the park near my school," I told Gomez. "My hands and clothes were still stained with Mr. Wycoff's blood. I was just standing there, looking into the yard of a house across the street, watching the little girl and her parents play with their new dog. An ugly yellow dog with only three legs."

Not my Sandy anymore. Theirs.

Before I'd gone to school that morning, I'd given away Mr. Wycoff's only weapon.

Given away my only family.

Given away my Sandy.

Sandy must have smelled me, because for a moment he stopped chasing the little girl, stood unmoving on his three spindly legs and pointed his nose toward the park. Whined. Tried to clamber over the fence. Then the girl grabbed him around the neck, gave him a big hug, and he turned away from me for the last time.

I felt numb.

"You can probably guess the rest of it," I told Gomez. "The police took me to Juvenile Hall, and you know how it goes there. They examined me. Mentally. Physically. I remained true to the Foster Child's Code. I didn't tell the police a thing."

I didn't have to.

The "incident," as CPS called it, had been hushed up. Why remind the public that little girls seldom fare well in foster homes? But when the state's doctor handed over his report, the police swooped down on Mr. Wycoff in his hospital bed and charged him with child rape. As it turned out, there had been other "incidents" with little girls.

When last I checked—last week, as a matter of fact—Mr. Wycoff was still in prison. If he ever gets out, well, I'll be waiting.

I didn't tell Gomez that, though. It wouldn't look good on my anger management report.

"That was the end of it," I told Gomez, finishing the story. "After a brief stay in Phoenix Children's Hospital, CPS released me to foster home number seven. Reverend Giblin and his wife. I guess CPS was learning to be more careful. Life got better."

But I never saw my Sandy again.

When the session finally ended and I headed for the exit, Gomez did something she had never done before. She rose from her desk and crossed the room, stopping only inches from me. I turned to her in surprise.

"You have so much courage, Lena Jones," she said. "Don't you ever wonder where you got it?"

I didn't answer her right away. Instead, I remembered my dream of the young man and woman standing in that long-ago meadow, saying goodbye to one another, the man looking at me with the knowledge of death in his eyes, telling me to remember him.

I made my escape from Gomez' office. But before I closed the door behind me, shutting away the sorrow in her face, I told her something that should have made no sense, yet made all the sense in the world.

"Where did I get my courage, Dr. Gomez? I haven't the faintest idea."

But I was lying again. I knew where my courage came from.

I'd inherited it.

Gloriana Alden-Taylor would have approved.

Epilogue—One year later

From the *Scottsdale Journal:*

PERRYVILLE, AZ—Inmates at the Perryville Correctional Facility for Women have a lot to smile about these days. Thanks to the efforts of inmate Megan Alden-Taylor, they are enrolled in a program which trains service dogs for the disabled.

Alden-Taylor, who is currently serving a six-year sentence for negligent homicide, oversees the training of dogs rescued from Maricopa County animal shelters. At the present time, ten dogs and ten inmates are involved in the program. However, Alden-Taylor says she hopes that the program spreads to other correctional facilities in the state.

"This is a way for inmates to contribute to the community," Alden-Taylor said, hugging a Golden Retriever mix. "Giving these animals another chance at life helps us make amends for the crimes we've committed."

Rescuing animals runs in the Alden-Taylor family. Her sister-in-law, Sandra Alden-Taylor-Brookings, who with her husband, John, runs the popular Hacienda Guest House, contributes a portion of the profits to the animal rescue program.

Megan's husband, Scottsdale publisher Zachary Alden-Taylor, recently purchased a sprawling ranch near the prison, where he and more than fifty volunteers rescue and treat abandoned and abused animals.

Much of Zachary Alden-Taylor's own animal rescue program is paid for by his company, Patriot's Blood Press, one of the most successful independent mystery publishers in the United States.